cocoa beans

cocoa beans

a novel

MICHAEL J. HUGHES

ISBN #: Softcover 0-7388-2717-7
Library of Congress #: 00-191401

To order additional copies of this book, contact:
Xlibris Corporation
1-888-7-XLIBRIS
www.Xlibris.com
Orders@Xlibris.com

Contents

*Dedicated to all those
who went to Milton Hershey School,
and to those who worked there and tried to
make life better for us.*

A thousand paths wander through these woods
past trees, rocks, clouds and earth, the same
yet different for each wanderer.
A thousand-thousand paths
crossing, overlapping, each trail unique
to the wanderer, and to the woods.

Let us have wine and women, mirth and laughter,
Sermons and soda water the day after.

Lord Byron, "*Don Juan*"

ONE

1

I looked at my hair in the mirror. As usual, it looked as though it had been cut by someone who couldn't care less how it looked. Which was exactly the case. As long as it didn't touch your ears, your eyebrows, or your shirt collar, the barber didn't care what it looked like—he was being paid by the hour.

"I said, 'What do you say?'" the barber said, standing in the rec room entrance. When I didn't respond, he started toward me down the basement hallway.

I shook my head and returned my gaze to the mirror. How was I ever going to meet girls looking like this? Chances were bad enough already—everyone knew we were from Milton Hershey and since Milton Hershey didn't have any girls there was only one thing we were after. And what kind of girl would take a chance with a guy that wanted her for only one thing? Especially that one thing. It wasn't true, but it made sense. Take a guy on a desert island who's been eating nothing but coconuts and bugs for three years. What's he after, conversation?

The barber grabbed my arm and turned me from the mirror. "What do you say?"

I pulled free of his grasp. "I said I'd say thank you after I looked at it and if I liked it." I looked at Huey toweling off in the shower stall behind us. "What do you think, Huey?"

"Depends on what you like, bro."

"It's a butcher job!" shouted one of the guys waiting their turn and watching from the rec room.

"Like all of them!" another added.

"Who said that?" the barber said. "Who's the wise guy?"

"Humphrey Bogart."

"You guys just better watch it. You're next." He turned to me. "Are you going to say thank you?"

"Why should I? I don't like it."

His eyes narrowed beneath his bushy black eyebrows. "What's your name again? You're going to be sorry. Next time you're really going to get it."

"It can't get any worse!" someone hollered.

"Quiet!"

He started for the rec room. "I don't have to take this. Not from you guys, not from anybody." He stopped at the now empty doorway and glared inside. "Where's that Bogart kid? He's next."

I'm sure if the Home had allowed us to wear our hair longer—like most other teenagers—our problems, which mushroomed into their problems, would have been greatly reduced. It would have been one less thing to annoy us and could have made meeting girls easier, providing an outlet to offset the pressures of living with the school's antiquated rules and regulations during a time of sit-ins, love-ins, rock fests and anti-war demonstrations that were always occurring without our participation.

The school had its reasons, however. By keeping our hair short, they hoped also to keep at bay what they saw happening at other schools and what their continued opposition to longer hair was helping to foster at ours: misbehavior and disrespect for authority. Had we been rich kids at a private school things would have been different; our hair wouldn't have mattered as much because our money and time spent at home would have made our lives, and meeting girls, easier.

But we weren't rich kids. We were boys with one or both parents deceased, whose surviving parent or guardian, out of necessity, enrolled us in a school that cost nothing, used its majority holding of Hershey Foods for backing, the founder's will for guidance, gave us the basics—food, clothing, shelter, education—and in return, expected us to live like monks and look like clowns.

Besides our hair, our clothes proved an equally difficult obstacle in meeting girls. They bought quality clothing with Milton's endowment and then fitted us as though appearance didn't matter. One waist size fit all heights which produced zippers a foot long and crotches that inseamed just above the knees. This was 1970, flares and bell-bottoms were in style, but they weren't supposed to flap in the wind inches above the ground, exposing our ankles and the solid, kick-the-cow-once-and-kill-it black or brown wingtipped Weinberg shoes we wore at church, school, in the barn, and playing ball at the student home because sneakers were to be kept at school. We cornered the market on colors so brilliant and effervescent they were perfect for ceremonial feasts. We would "pick" which pants we wanted from a choice of three or four, out of a bin of waist sizes two or three inches greater than what a normal teenager would choose for himself, and then the ladies who altered them not to our liking sent out striped, checked, paaisleyed and polka-doted shirts that didn't match. Spotting a group of us, a stranger would say, "Look, junior scientists."

Dressed like that with haircuts to match, how could we meet girls and get them to do what we wanted when they could tell instantly we were Homeguys and knew what we wanted, which was what any boy wanted but we could never get because everyone thought that's all we ever wanted? It drove some of us to lying to get what we wanted. "I'm not from Milton Hershey. I'm retarded."

Huey stepped out of the shower. "Who was that you took to the prom last night, Crazy?"

I winced. My luck at the junior prom, coupled with my haircut, made me think I might never find a girl to fondle and call my own. "She was just some jerk I got off the list."

"She looked all right."

"Yeah, but she had her hair up in a bun, and I like it down. And she kept saying, 'Oh, who's that? Where's so and so?' She and her friends were all over the place."

Originally I wasn't going to go to the prom because I had to take a blind date.

I hated blind dates; they made me nervous. Most girls did, actually, which was why I always had blind dates–I was a social imbecile. But this was our junior prom, the only one I'd ever have, so I figured why not? Maybe I'd get lucky and get one I liked.

So I took my date's name from a book listing the name, address, phone number, and height of girls who had gone on blind dates to one of our dances before and hadn't refused two dates in a row since. Because I preferred girls close to my own height of 5'9", I picked the first one I saw over 5'5".

The girl I really wanted to take was the girl of my dreams who had just started working at the drugstore in town: tall and slender, long beautiful dark-brown hair, blue eyes, great legs, two breasts, and a smile so sweet it made me smile every time I saw her. But I was too shy to ask her out. I could barely look at her when ordering a soda, let alone try to talk to her.

So I wound up with a girl named Stephanie, who looked nice enough but whose mouth rarely stopped moving. She and her friends talked continuously and kept leaving the table to approach guys they knew from previous dances, or whose names they knew, to talk to them.

Halfway through the dance, after one fifteen-minute stretch of sitting at the table with just the other guys, I went with Rich, a teammate of mine on the swim team, to the food table. We were there for ten minutes, eating and joking with other guys when Stephanie suddenly appeared. She planted herself in front of me, set her hands on her hips, tilted her head, chin forward, and said, "What are you doing over here?"

Ten seconds earlier Rich had chomped down on a piece of frosted cake to demonstrate how big a bite he would have taken out of this good-looking girl's backside who had walked by us and said "Hi." Not to be outdone, I rammed a whole piece into my mouth just as Stephanie arrived.

I held up my finger and mumbled a polite, "Wait a minute."

Someone leaned over my shoulder. "Well, Rich, what do you think?"

It was Brownie, a friend of ours who was in the same homeroom as me. He'd been talking to us before the pretty girl walked by. He now grinned his big, toothy grin and said, "With his mouth full like that, it's hard to tell what he's doing here at the food table."

"I know," Rich said. He looked me up and down. "I'm not sure, Brownie, but I'd say he's doing the hundred yard dash."

Brownie nodded. "Could be," he said.

"Shut up, you jerks," Stephanie said.

Brownie and Rich gaped at each other. "Jerrrks," Rich said.

I chuckled, and Stephanie's face hardened. "Did you hear me?" she said.

"M-yeah," I mumbled, my mouth still full.

"If you guys don't come back to the table, right this minute, we're leaving."

"Ewwwwwww," Brownie said, "that would be terrible."

Stephanie glared at him, then turned her gaze on Rich and me. "Well . . . ?"

"We'll be there," Rich said.

"Right now!"

All around us, heads turned.

"Excuse me," Brownie said, "but what unit are you a housemother at again?" Rich and I smiled.

"I think we're going to leave," Stephanie said.

"Why don't you?" Rich said. "It won't make any difference. You've been gone most of the night anyway."

She glared at him a moment, then swiveled her piercing brown eyes expectantly at me.

"He's right," I said. "You have been."

In seconds Stephanie was at the table telling Rich's date and the other girls what happened. When they looked at us, Brownie gave them a big shrug with arms outspread and Rich waved. The girls pushed back their chairs, grabbed their purses and headed for the door. Outside, they marched past the plate-glass windows, their mouths and hands in constant motion. Stephanie peered inside. We waved. She threw us the finger and mouthed "Assholes!!" with such hatred we burst into laughter.

The rest of the night we stuffed our faces and had a good time.

Huey stepped up to the sink next to the one I was sitting on. "Didn't she leave early with a bunch of girls?"

I told him what happened. He said, "We don't need that crap from them. We get enough of it from the houseparents and officials."

"Damn!" I said and sprang to my feet. "Where's a clock?"

"In the rec room. Why?"

"We're supposed to be back by three to unload some straw before milking."

I hurried to the rec room. The clock above the door leading outside read five of three. "Come on, barn guys, let's go. We're late." I held the screen door as several guys went out.

The barber came around the chair. "Is your name Purenut? Is that it?"

"Crazy, I didn't get my hair cut yet," Martin said.

"Too bad. You better go next. You knew you were supposed to get it cut before the house guys."

The barber grabbed my arm. "I'm talking to you. Is your name Dave Purenut?"

I pulled free. "It's Bogart. Humphrey."

He grabbed at me again but I jerked back and his finger caught my shirt pocket, ripping it. I inspected the tear, then pointed at him. "You're in trouble," I said.

I stepped outside and hurried up the driveway. Behind me the screen door swung open. "*You're* the one that's in trouble. Wait till next time, *Purenut.*"

I waved my arm. I had bigger things to worry about. Like what was I going to tell Suds was the reason we were late? It'd be another twenty-five minutes before we got back and out to the barn. He'd want a reason and expect me to give it.

2

Milton Hershey was divided into three divisions: junior, intermediate, and senior. The junior division housed the kindergarten through fifth grades, the intermediate the sixth through eighth, and the senior division ninth through twelfth. We lived sixteen guys to a unit, and were governed by a live-in married couple called houseparents, who were relieved every other weekend by the second helps. Each unit had a name. My unit was Brookfields, and our houseparents and second helps were the Sawyers and Muncees, respectfully. Disrespectfully, we called Mr. Sawyer, Suds, Mrs. Sawyer, Bones, Mr. Muncee, Sherlock, and Mrs. Muncee, Big M.

Beside each senior division unit was a dairy farm, and every day, twice a day, we milked cows, once at six a.m. and then again at four p.m. Most units had large, spacious barns that lofted to four or five floors above ground level within which a year's supply of hay and straw would be loaded every summer. Our unit, however, could store no more than five or six loads of hay and straw in the storage area located above our calf pens. This meant we had to reload continually throughout the year, usually getting supplied by Longmeadows–Huey's unit–which we "volunteered" to help fill to the rafters each summer.

That's why we were supposed to get back by three o'clock–to unload two wagonloads of straw before milking time. Why we were getting our hair cut on a weekend was another matter.

We had a week left of school after the seniors graduated, and the normal procedure would have been to be called up to the barbershop by homerooms and butchered during school hours. During the summer, they would pick one student home that the guys in nearby units would walk to, unit by unit, to get their hair cut. Why they were starting a week early, no one knew; we just did what we were told.

The guys had crossed the highway which ran by Huey's unit, and farther down, intersected with the road that led back past our unit. I crossed over and was about to follow them through the enormous field they were shortcutting when I noticed the rows of lumpy, dark earth.

"Hey, you guys," I called, "this stuff looks plowed. It might be planted."

They stopped and gazed at the ground. "So?" Kingston, a sophomore, said.

"So, you might kill whatever it is you're stomping all over."

"So?" said Peters, a freshman and Kingston's roommate.

"Hey, I don't care," I said. "But if you get caught, don't blame me."

"We're not going to get caught," Kingston said. He, Peters, and the others turned and stomped their way toward our unit, leaving Gary standing alone.

Gary was a freshman, had been in the unit beside mine in the junior and intermediate divisions, and knew as well as I did that a place where you could get in trouble for not wearing an undershirt under your school shirt, house shirt, barn shirt, play shirt, or church shirt was no place to take chances. "Come on, Gar," I said. "We'll run and beat them anyway."

We ran along the highway then up the road and reached the unit thirty seconds behind the others. All of us changed into our barn clothes, put on our boots, and were outside behind the barn by three thirty.

"You're late," Suds said.

He stood atop the wagonload of bundled straw, dropping bales onto the conveyor belt that extended up and through the double doors on the upper level of the barn. "Dave, you and Gary load the belt. The rest of you get up top. I got things to do."

Gary and I began sending up the bales that had bounced off the conveyor belt and lay scattered about the ground and against the wooden fence that enclosed the feeding lot and adjoining pasture. Suds climbed down from the wagon and wiped his forehead, neck, and mouth with a red bandanna. "You guys should have been back here at three o'clock, not three thirty," he said. "We've got cows to milk."

I didn't answer; neither did Gary. It was possible Suds might let it pass.

"Gary, I'll throw them down," I said, and climbed to the top of the wagon. Starting from the back, I lifted each bale by the two pieces of twine that wrapped it, swung it forwards and backwards then used the momentum to toss it over the front end of the wagon. Of all the tasks we had to do, this was one of the ones I minded least—as long as we were only doing a couple of loads. It was clean, physically exerting, fresh air work, and I liked tossing the crisp, dry bundles over the edge and watching them sail to the ground, sometimes breaking apart, sometimes landing where I aimed them, and sometimes hitting close enough to Gary to make us both smile.

"Where's Martin?" Suds asked after I had thrown my first four bales.

"He didn't get his hair cut yet," I said.

"Why not?"

"I don't know. He was–"

"Any house guys go before him?"

"I know there was at least one."

"I told you guys the barn guys were to go first."

"I know," I said, and tossed another bale. "I don't know why he didn't go first."

"Where were you?"

"I was talking to one of my friends in their bathroom."

"You should have been making sure he got on the chair first, not in the bathroom talking to your friend."

Suds had his faded US ARMY baseball cap tipped back on his downy-white crew cut, his head tilted back, his eyes squinting. He was serious.

"Martin knew he was supposed to go first," I said. "Why should I have to make sure he does what he knows he's supposed to do?"

"Because you're going to be the only senior. Mrs. Sawyer and I expect you to set an example."

"I went before the house guys," I said.

"That's not good enough. You know what's right and you know what's wrong. Things will go a lot smoother around here if everything goes right."

He watched me throw the next bale. "You read me, Dave?"

"Yeah, I read you, and I don't think it's right. I'm not the houseparent."

"But you're the only senior. So get used to it."

He was wrong. Sure, I'd be the only senior and elected president of the unit, but no way should I be made deputy warden.

"Hey, Mr. Sawyer . . . " I said, catching him before he turned the corner of the barn. "If you're going to make me act like a houseparent, can I start telling these guys what to do?"

"If they're supposed to be doing it, go ahead."

I grinned and looked at Gary, hoisting a bale onto the conveyor belt. "Okay, pea brain," I said, "let's move it! Come on, tote those bales. Faster! Faster!"

I tossed three bales quickly over the side while Gary stood and watched. "Hey, deaf and dumb," I said. "Let's go. I'm a houseparent. Move it."

He looked to make sure Suds was gone. "Stick it up your ass, mule breath."

I pointed. "You're gonna be sorry, fella. When I get down from here, I'm gonna teach you a lesson."

Gary bent to lift another bale and extended a trembling hand. "Look, I'm shaking," he said.

Seconds later, the next bale I threw slammed into the conveyor belt within a foot of his head. Mr. "I'm shaking" jumped about five feet.

"Mrs. Sawyer?"

I waited until Bones turned from the counter where she was cutting three apple pies sent in on the meal truck into eighteen pieces—one for each guy and one for her and Suds. "My shirt got ripped." I showed her the tear and told her how it happened.

"Why wouldn't you say thank you?" she said. "Your hair looks fine to me."

"It doesn't to anybody my age. It's way too short. I might as well be in the Marines or eighty years old."

"That's better than having it long and looking like a sissy, like at other schools."

"Not to girls, it isn't. We'd have a better chance of meeting them if it was longer."

Eddie—soon to be my roommate once the seniors left and the current dining room guy responsible for setting the table before meals—picked up two dessert plates. "Yeah, Mrs. Sawyer," he said. "Don't you realize Crazy's so ugly he needs every break he can get?"

"Ha, ha, ha." I whacked him in the shoulder.

Finished with the pies, Bones turned to me. "That looks like an old shirt. After it comes out of the laundry, give it to me and we'll send it to the clothing room. Either they'll fix it or send you a new one."

I thanked her and went into the living room to watch TV. Just as I laid down on the floor, Suds walked in. "Did you guys walk through the field out there today?" He was asking everyone, but his eyes settled on me.

I waited for Kingston or one of the others to speak up. Some of the house guys might have walked through it, too. Besides Eddie, and the cook, and the seniors who were getting ready for their prom, everyone else was in the living room.

"Well?"

"I didn't," I said.

"Somebody did, because the dairyman over at Longmeadows saw them. There will be no Catherine Hall privilege tonight."

Catherine Hall was the intermediate division's school building, one end of which contained athletic facilities consisting of lap and diving pools, a gym with several basketball courts, an outdoor hockey rink, a weight room, a large rec room, and outside tennis courts. During the summer a rotating system was used allowing each unit, in conjunction with many others, access to the facilities twice a week. This was the first night it was going to be open and I had planned to meet my buddy, Jim, there.

After Suds left I looked at Kingston. He sat in the corner armchair next to the bookshelf and intercom system, watching TV and ignoring me.

"Kingston. Why didn't you say something?"

He grimaced. "I didn't know what he knew."

"Now you do. Why should Gary and I and anyone else who didn't cut through the field get punished because you did?"

"I wasn't the only guy."

"You're one of them. You're the one who said, 'Oh, we're not going to get caught.'"

He clicked his tongue, said, "All right," then pushed out of the chair. A minute later he trudged back into the room. "He said you still can't go. You had you're chance to speak up and didn't."

I shook my head. If not for the illegal party we had planned that night, I would have been more than simply disappointed. I raised my arms toward the ceiling. "They just don't listen to me. They know I'm right. I'm always right. Yet they still don't listen. I don't get it."

"That's because you're stupid," Gary said.

"Stupid . . . ? Stupid? My ears must be deceiving me. I just thought I heard something squeaky call me stupid."

"You're ugly, too."

Between Gary and me, lay Peters. I laughed out loud, twice, then struck. Gary rolled, Peters cowered, and I barely grabbed the back of Gary's pants.

I dragged him over Peters' body. "I really don't want to have to do this, Gar, but you forced me into it." I cradled his left leg in my right arm and his head in my left, then brought them together. "When you called me stupid, and ugly, that was like saying, 'Crazy, bend me into a pretzel, please.' Now wasn't it? Isn't that what–"

"Chow time!" Suds said, coming around the corner.

As Gary and I walked by him, Suds said, as though for the thousandth time, "No wrestling in the living room."

After supper I asked to use the phone. I wanted to call Jim and let him know I wouldn't make it.

"Who you calling?" Suds asked, not bothering to lower the newspaper he was reading.

What business was it of his? I didn't have to tell him. I had my one phone call I could make a week. As long as it wasn't longer than five minutes or long distance, I could call anybody I wanted.

Too bad I couldn't say so without getting in trouble.

"I'm calling my friend, Jim. I was going to meet him at Catherine Hall, but since you won't let us go, I have to let him know."

"You had your chance to speak up."

"I did. I told you I didn't walk through the field."

He turned a page. "That's not what I wanted to know. I wanted to know who did walk through it."

"No you didn't. You wanted to know if any of us did. Not who exactly."

He lowered the paper. "And you knew someone did."

"That's right. But I told you I didn't. I'm not going to squeal on someone else. If they did it, they should admit it. And if they're wrong, then they should get punished, not everybody."

He lifted the paper, once again obstructing his face. "You do things your way, I do things mine."

"But I don't think your way is right."

He turned a page. "That's too bad, isn't it?"

I stared at the paper. Right at the middle. Right where an ax would go slashing through and split his big, blubbery, bucket-shaped head into two pieces, as equally useless as the original.

"Yeah, it is," I said.

I headed for the telephone. You want an example? You keep acting like that, and I'll give you an example.

3

Doing things illegal at Milton Hershey was like being asked to walk in any direction. The minor infractions, such as not shutting your window or incorrectly making your bed, cost you a demerit or two on the merit system used for ranking students. Unless you were shooting for membership in an organization that required you to be in the top five of your unit, you didn't mind getting demerits. Which the houseparents realized, compelling them to use their next level of retribution: they'd not allow you to go on privileges or to events that were every student's right and the only way we had, other than school, to get out from under the houseparents' domain.

"No town privilege for you, Mr. Wise Guy," or "I know somebody who won't be going to the game tonight," were expressions they used to some degree of effectiveness–next time we had to be more careful. If we weren't and got caught, we could be thrown on restrictions for a week or two, which meant you could do nothing beyond the mundane. No privileges, no events, no games, not even going outside after supper or on weekends to play ball.

Worse still were detentions, leveled at those who committed the most vile and heinous of crimes such as smoking cigarettes or hooking out. Detentions were restrictions plus so many hours of work to work off. Instead of being bored to suicide on restrictions, detentions had you working around the unit doing things that the houseparents had trouble finding for you to do because they already had the house guys spending an hour every day cleaning, vacuuming, dusting, mopping; and on Saturdays doing an additional two hours or so of work after breakfast, performing chores regularly that most people wouldn't do but once a year.

Beyond detentions for life, the Home could threaten you with expulsion, which, although every one of us would have preferred living at home, we knew our parents or guardians couldn't afford, either financially or time wise–that's why we were in Milton Hershey. Thus, being kicked out was about the only thing that truly kept us from doing certain things, or at least made us very cautious when doing them.

Like drinking and having the illegal party we were having for the seniors that night. Just the party would have been detention territory; the alcohol put it into the realm of detentions till death, or even expulsion.

The fact that Sherlock had gone away for the weekend considerably reduced our chances of detection. His main responsibility as dairyman was managing the barn. An additional requirement, as was the case with all dairymen at Milton Hershey, was that he and his wife would serve as our second helps. In partial compensation, they were furnished living quarters in our unit. The Muncees lived upstairs on part of the third floor opposite from the end where my room was located on the second floor. The Sawyers lived in the same layout as the Muncees, but on the first floor. We rarely worried about the Sawyers at night, though, or even Big M. They slept after sending us to bed. It was Sherlock, who loved sneaking around and catching guys doing things illegal, who kept us watchful.

In fact, the party hadn't been conceived until after we saw Sherlock and Big M get into their car with their suitcases Friday night. If they didn't return before Saturday night, we'd have the party. Carl, one of the seniors, snuck in two bottles of Strawberry Hill Wine just in case.

At midnight, half an hour after the seniors returned from their prom, the guys started sneaking into my room—Mike's and mine. Across the hall was Carl's and Eddie's room. Around the corner to the left were the steps leading downstairs to the dining room. Everyone else's bedrooms were around the corner to the right and along the hallway leading past the bathroom to the stairs at the other end—the Muncee's and Sawyer's end.

Amidst low-volume rock and roll from Eddie's radio and occasional forays downstairs to raid the pantry of goodies that wouldn't be missed, we sat playing cards by flashlight, quietly telling jokes and reminiscing of times past. Carl did most of the drinking. The rest of us didn't like the taste or were too worried what might happen if we got drunk or caught. But we did take a sip now and then, and this, coupled with the fact that what we were doing was a mortal sin in the school's eyes, added a thrilling edge to our hushed festivities.

By two thirty all but five of us had gone to bed. We were five and a half hours past our normal bedtime; in three hours and fifteen minutes we'd be getting up to do chores. I was so tired I could fall asleep instantly. Even so, I wasn't going to bed until Mike did.

Mike was my roommate for the last two years, and one of my best friends. As long as he stayed up, I'd stay up. He would be graduating in two days and I might not see him again for a long time, possibly ever. His draft number was thirty-seven. Already they were on number fifteen. There was no way he would not be drafted and probably sent to Vietnam. To avoid the inevitable, he was joining the Air Force as soon as they reached number twenty-five. In all likelihood he'd still go to Vietnam, but at least it wouldn't be as a front line target in the Army or Marines.

We had talked about his avoiding the draft by moving to Canada, but that wasn't in Mike's nature. He'd do what he was supposed to. As would I. Which is why I was hoping the war, and the draft, would end before I graduated the following year. Better still, I wanted it to end before Mike had to go over.

Carl grabbed the wine bottle and held it out. "Who wants some?" When no one replied he shook it. "Well . . . ?"

"Here, give it to me," Mike said. "And lower your voice."

"Why should I? I'm graduating."

Mike took a swig. "Because if you get caught drunk and they don't give you your diploma, you won't be going to college." He handed the bottle to Carl.

"Ahhh. They won't catch me. Besides, I don't get drunk."

Outside, a car pulled into our driveway and basketball court. Eddie shut off his flashlight. "Is that Sherlock?"

Mike went to the window as Carl heaved forward, went too far, and fell to his knees. "Shit." Eddie and Gary helped him stand. Everyone was set to run if it proved to be Sherlock.

Mike let the curtain fall back. "It's just somebody turning around."

Carl plopped to the floor. "Whew! I need a drink." He took one, then said, "A toast. I want to toast you poor slobs who have to stay after I graduate." He aimed the bottle at each of us in turn. "To Crazy. You only got one year left. Give 'em hell, boy."

He took a swig.

"To Eddie, my roommate. Two years ain't too bad. Shit, it was only two years ago that I had two years left." He laughed and took another swig.

He put one of his massive arms around Gary's shoulders and held him in a one-armed bear hug. Outweighed two hundred and twenty to one hundred and twenty, Gary had long ago given up trying to squirm free of Carl's grasp. They were eye to eye as Carl spoke.

"My big buddy, Big Gar. You put up with a lot of crap from me, huh? You know why? Cause you're all right, Gar. No shit. If you hadn't of been, I wouldn't have messed with you like I did. You know what I mean?" He flexed his arm and squeezed Gary's shoulders two inches closer together. "Huh, buddy?"

"Oh, yeah," Gary said. "I consider myself *real* lucky that you've been beating the crap out of me all this time. Now I'm just glad I know it was because you were my *friend* that you did it."

Carl laughed. "That's what I mean. You're all right, Gar." He held the bottle aloft. "To you, Big Gar. If anyone ever messes with you, let me know and I'll come back and beat the shit out of them. Okay?" When Gary didn't answer, Carl squeezed him. "Huh?"

"Yeah, yeah, okay. Just get off me."

Carl relaxed his grip and Gary squirmed free.

After Carl drank a toast to Gary, he drank one to Mike, who drank one to Carl. I was next. "Here's to you two jerks. I hope we get some good dirt to replace you." I took a swig. "And good luck in the Air Force. Hope you get so far away from the action you don't even know there's action."

"Me, too," Mike said.

Eddie took the bottle. "Except for women action. You want lots of that. Here's to women."

"Hear, hear," Carl said. "Come see me at college before you go, Mike, and we'll take care of that. And when you get back, too." He grabbed the bottle and took another drink. "Gonna drink one in our honor, Big Gar?"

"Sure," Gary said, accepting the bottle. "Why not? Now that I'll soon be a sophomore and not some lowly dirt. Have fun whatever you do."

After Gary took a swig, Mike stood up. "That's it for me. I'm beat."

"Ah, come on, Mike," Carl pleaded. "Stay up."

"Nope. You guys can stay, I don't care."

"Good."

I started to rise. "Not you, too, Crazy," Carl said. "Just one more hand of five-hundred Rummy, okay? For old times sake. We'll finish the bottle."

I sat back down.

By now we were two thirds of the way through the second bottle and Carl had drunk nearly a bottle and a quarter himself. That's why his speech slurred, his eyelids drooped, and the final quarter wasn't finished when the card game was. "I'll be right back," he said and left for the bathroom.

In his absence we decided the quickest way to end the festivities was to get someone to chug the final bit of wine. Our choice was unanimous, and we devised a plan to make it seem as though it were chance.

When Carl returned, he sat down and grabbed the bottle. "Anybody interested?"

"Why don't we just chug it, Carl?" I said. "We're tired."

"Just who's going to chug it?"

"Not you," I said. "Well, maybe you. It just depends on who picks the wrong number."

"Who wants to chug it?" he said, and looked around. When no one replied, he said, "I do."

"Go ahead," Eddie said. "Bottoms up."

Carl grinned and swayed to his feet. He raised the bottle. "Here's to you poor slobs. Stick it to 'em."

The three of us began a whispered chant: "Chug . . . Chug . . . Chug . . . Chug . . . " Carl brought the bottle to his lips, mumbled something, and tilted the bottom toward the ceiling. His Adam's apple rose then plunged with each swallow. The last few swigs of strawberry essence descended into the neck of the bottle. Two more gulps and–

Mike screamed. A scream so loud and terrifying, we knew instantly of the hideous creature crashing through the window to tear off our heads and inhale our innards. And we reacted as one–we froze, into instant, spitless paralysis.

Mike began a second death cry, and Eddie made the first move. From a cross-legged sitting position, he sprang like a jack-in-the-box for the door and grabbed the knob by extending his short body its full length, leaving him stretched like a plank between the door and floor. His toes clawed through the carpet until his knees touched the floor, then he pulled on the doorknob. Only the door wouldn't open because Carl had fallen against it.

Eddie arched his body and yanked backwards, forcing Carl forwards just enough so that Gary, who was in the process of standing, caught him in the groin with his head. Carl groaned, instinctively brought his hands–and bottle– to his groin, where Gary's head was not out of danger. A hollow, heavy thud preceded Gary's howl. With Carl off the door, Eddie had gotten it partway open, put his leg through and was about to stand when Carl was sacked by Gary and collapsed, all two hundred and twenty drunken pounds, back against the door. Eddie's outcry matched Gary's.

Above this commotion Mike's shrieks of terror continued, gradually changing into cries for assistance. "My glasses!! My glasses!! Where are my glasses!?!"

The adrenaline now surged not to save us from a horrendous death, but from detection by Suds. As Gary, Carl, and Eddie scurried to their rooms and the deepest sleep of their lives, I ransacked Mike's desktop for his glasses, groping in darkness because the electricity was shut off by a master switch at night, and wondering why he needed them, why he didn't get them himself, but most of all, why was he screaming so fucking loud?

Finally I found them. "Mike. Mike," I said, shaking his shoulder. "Your glasses. Here. Look." I held them to his face.

"Huh?" He moved his head back.

"It's your glasses. You wanted them."

"What do I want them for? I'm in bed."

"How should I know?" I said. "You're the one who was screaming for them. Those guys flew out of here so fast they–"

The hall lights snapped on. Mike lay back in bed, and I hurried over and slipped into mine.

4

Sud's footsteps thumped down the hallway, around the corner, and stopped a few feet from our door. He could say something, or he could return to his apartment, knowing we knew, he knew, something was up and therefore we'd not do it again.

"All right," he said, his voice loud and resonant within the hollow silence, "I want to know who the noisemakers are. If I don't find out, we're all going to get up a couple hours early and start chores and keep right on working until bedtime. No town privileges, no TV, no snacks, no going outside." He let us fill the silence with canceled plans and visions of working all day.

I looked at Mike, who raised then lowered his eyebrows. The noise had started with his yells. Though I was partly to blame, I wasn't about to admit it to Suds. He'd want to know who else was in on it and then make me do all the work when I didn't tell him. No thanks. If anyone had to speak up, it was Mike.

Half a minute past, then Suds banged on our door. "Okay, get up! If nobody wants to own up to it, we'll all just get up and start working. Come on, get up. Eeeeeeeverybody up!" His voice trailed around the corner.

"Mike, Carl's drunk," I said. "If Suds sees him, he's nabbed."

Mike hurried to the door and opened it. "Mr. Sawyer!" he called and waited for Suds to come back around the corner.

I checked and cleared the floor of debris–the radio and bottle of wine were gone–then stood beside Mike. Across from us, Carl's door remained closed.

Several guys trailed after Suds, who planted himself in front of us, hands on hips, looking just as he must have looked at his new recruits for twenty years. Only now, his six-foot frame had acquired a layer of flab and ballooned in front to include the forty pounds he had gained since retiring from the army as a drill sergeant and joining Milton Hershey fifteen years before. He weighed a fat and flabby two thirty-five.

"That was me, Mr. Sawyer," Mike said. "I was dreaming and started yelling for my glasses."

Suds looked at both of us. Our conditioned blank stares revealed nothing. "Why were you yelling?" he said.

"I don't know, I was dreaming."

"What was all that racket? Screaming don't make the house shake."

"That was me," I said. "I fell over the chair trying to find his glasses. I couldn't see in the dark."

"Why didn't you just wake him?"

"I heard you're not supposed to wake up people who are talking or walking in their sleep. They go bozo on you. Might kill you or something."

"That's a bunch of horse crap," Suds said. "Just slap them across the face and they come right out of it. I've done it plenty of times."

"You mean next time I can punch him in the face and he'll stop?"

"I didn't say punch."

Mike said, "You punch me, numbnuts, and you'll be the one dreaming—in the hospital."

"And who's going to put me there?"

Mike pushed my shoulder. "I will."

I pushed him back. "I doubt it."

"Okay, cut the crap and get back to bed," Suds said. "Everybody back to bed." He turned and herded the rest of the guys toward their rooms.

Mike and I waited until we were sure Suds was gone, then snuck across the hall. Carl was dry-heaving into a waste bucket between his knees, the room reeked of putrid wine, and Eddie stood at an opened window, leaning as far out as possible. "If Carl doesn't stop it," Eddie said, "I'm going to throw up. I swear."

Less than forty-eight hours later, the seniors were gone.

There can't be very many other places where graduation is felt as keenly as at Milton Hershey. After years of being told what to do, how to do it, where to do it, when to do it, and how long to do it, you're finally free to do whatever you please. No more hassles with houseparents or officials. No more keeping quiet when you'd rather speak your mind. No more being told to do something and having to accept "Because I said so" as the reason why. No more impossible situations where, when you're right and know it and you refuse to do something a houseparent tells you to, you're sent into Homelife where officials tell you you were right in the first place but since you didn't listen to your houseparents you were wrong and you're punished for disobedience. In short, the only people you have to answer to after graduation are yourself and the law. It's quite a change and the feeling of freedom is exhilarating.

Unfortunately, all those reasons why seniors feel so great after graduation produce a mammoth load for those left behind. You know you have so many more years of the same old crap before you graduate. From first grade on, whenever I went to a graduation service, I would come back feeling cheated, dealt an unfair hand in life. Why did my mother have to die? Why did I have to spend so many years in this place? Why couldn't I live a normal life like everyone else? Why me?

But my junior year was different. After Mike and Carl and the others graduated I felt elated. For the first time in eleven years I could see light at the end of the tunnel, without obstructions, curves, or bends. The next class to graduate was going to be mine. I couldn't wait. Every day brought me one day closer to liberation.

I was enjoying this sense of near freedom on the Tuesday after graduation when I was reminded that I was still in the Home and shackled to its trials and tribulations. The cause of that reminder was Brubaker, our principal.

Mr. Clarence P. Brubaker, the third, was a tall, angular, stiff-backed, red-haired, impeccably dressed, Yale-educated nimrod with deep-set eyes and the nose of a platypus. The way he walked and talked and acted so scholarly, you'd have thought he was an ambassador to the royal court of France during the sixteen hundreds. Just that didn't bother me, though. It was his holier than thou attitude, and the way he expected everyone to listen to his every word that annoyed me. He was no better than us. But he acted it, and that's what bothered me.

A junior class meeting to nominate class officers had been scheduled for after lunch. Everyone was in the auditorium, talking and waiting for the meeting to start when Brubaker walked on stage. He came from behind the curtain, walked to the lectern and stood there, waiting for silence. He could have said something and everyone would have quieted, but he didn't. He simply stood tall, erect, and waiting.

I was sitting by myself, off to the right, and saw him appear. As the talking continued, his thin lips pressed together and his eyes seemed to set even deeper in their sockets. The more he seethed, the more I smiled. I enjoyed it so much I turned away from the stage, put my left arm over the back of the seat, and started mumbling loud enough to equal the rumbling, rolling hubbub of the others. The longer the noise level stayed at one frequency, the longer it would take for the others to notice Brubaker and quiet down. The longer Brubaker was ignored, the more beneficial his lesson and the greater my enjoyment.

My mumbling diminished in direct proportion with the conversations of my classmates. Within a minute there was silence and Brubaker was giving everybody his "I don't like to be kept waiting" look. Only I didn't see it. I was still facing backwards, completely engrossed in nothing in particular. How was I to know someone was up there? Had there been an announcement? A "May I have your attention, please?" that one would expect from an intelligent human being who wanted to speak to a gathering unaware of his presence?

Only when the guys seated several rows behind me looked my way and smiled did I know there must be someone there. I turned and settled in my seat, took a deep breath and exhaled as my eyes met Brubaker's. "Go ahead, bore me," my expression said.

"Get out," Brubaker said, his lips barely moving.

Was he talking to me? He couldn't be. What did I do? He must be talking to someone behind me who did something I didn't see. I looked over my left shoulder, then my right. I looked at Brubaker. Are you talking to me?

He took one giant goose-step, flung his arm out, and pointed. "You in the red shirt, GET OUT!"

I checked my shirt. He did mean me. I looked at him as though he had a serious mental problem, then exited, stage left. All the way back to my locker I smiled. I had finally bothered him as much as he bothered me.

I was still smiling on the way to my next class when I past the first guys coming back from the auditorium. "Hey, Crazy," Rich said, stopping me. Rich was smiling too. "Brubaker wants to see you in the auditorium."

My smile vanished. "What for?"

"You were nominated for class president."

"What?!"

"He wants everyone who's been nominated to stay after the meeting."

I was dumbfounded. I couldn't believe somebody had nominated me for a class officer–president no less–without asking me first. Now I would have to get out of it, no doubt embarrassing myself in doing so. Whoever was responsible, was a moron.

"Who nominated me?"

"Huey did. I was sitting beside him. He said he liked the leadership qualities you showed at the start of the meeting. I thought so, too. I seconded it."

"You jerks," I said.

Rich's laughter trailed after me as I headed toward the auditorium.

5

Brubaker stopped talking and waited as I started down the long center aisle to where he stood in front of the fifteen to twenty guys seated in the first few rows. They turned to see who was coming and their faces lit with merriment. Huey's grin outshone them all.

"What are you doing here?" Brubaker said, when I reached the pack of hyenas.

"Aren't you having a meeting for guys nominated for class officers?"

"Yes."

"I was nominated."

"Oh, really?" he said. "For which office?"

"President."

"Fine example you've set."

"That's what I was told. That's why they nominated me."

"Sit down."

"But I don't–"

"I said sit down!"

His nose flushed sudden red, like a creature entering attack mode; so I sat down.

"As I was saying . . . ," Brubaker said, "Mr. Stevens asked me to explain the limitations on your campaigns. He will return tomorrow, but he felt that since the elections are Friday some of you might like to post your mimeographed sheets today. Each of you will be allowed three different carbon sheets, twenty copies per carbon, for a total of sixty sheets. It is up to you to place them where you think they will be most advantageous. However, you may not place them on display cases, windows, . . . "

As soon as he said, "the limitations placed on your campaigns," I raised my hand. Our eyes met several times, and each time he ignored me. I lowered my hand.

"Are there any questions?" he asked when finished. His gaze stopped on me. I stared silently back.

After the meeting, Huey put an arm around my shoulder as we walked up the aisle. "I didn't know you wanted to run, buddy. You got my vote."

"I didn't, and I don't."

"What are you going to do?"

"You'll see. And thanks for nominating me, jerk."

"Any time, pal. Any time."

There were three of us nominated for class president: Pete Bacus, Al Rose, and myself. One of Pete's five signs read, "Vote for PETE" and each letter of his name began a new word: Positive, Enterprising, Trustworthy, Enthusiastic. Al had one that read "ROSE is for you" and his self-proclaiming attributes were Respected, Open-minded, Sincere, Experienced. I had one carbon made for twenty signs which read, "You got to be crazy to vote for PURENUT." Under the letters of my name I put Psychotic, Unfit, Repulsive, Expendable, Nuts, Unbearable, and Two-faced.

I placed the signs that afternoon and the next morning I was sent to Brubaker's office before first period. His secretary announced my presence then asked me to be seated. A minute past. He was either busy or trying to make me wait and worry. I began reviewing my answers for a chemistry final that afternoon. Minutes later his door opened. I didn't look up. With peripheral vision I saw his secretary look from me, to him, to me. I bit my tongue so I wouldn't smile. I turned a page.

"Mr. Purenut, would you mind stepping into my office?" Brubaker said.

On his large, uncluttered desk, with its felt-green protector and gold-plated pen set, sat papers atop a manila folder beside which lay several of my signs. He motioned me to one of the chairs in front of his desk, then sat in his, a massive leather throne with thick arms and a back high and curved.

He lifted one of the pieces of paper. "I've been studying your record, Mr. Purenut, and to be quite candid, I found it puzzling. On the one hand, you've made the honor roll or distinguished honor roll every marking period since sixth grade. On the other, you've yet to be accepted into the National Honor Society. Teacher evaluations reveal a majority of your teachers feel you are a good student: hard working, attentive, intelligent. Some grade you above average. However, there are a few who feel you have an attitude problem: that you're a troublemaker, disruptive, uncooperative, and so forth."

He'd been looking down his oversized nose, through half-glasses, quoting from the paper. He set down the paper and glasses, lifted his head and continued looking down his nose. "How would you explain that?"

What was there to explain? I was a good student, most teachers liked me, some didn't. So what? I shrugged and said, "I don't know."

Brubaker waited, then made an empty handed expression and mimicked my shrug.

I returned his hand flip and shrug as if to say, "That's right, I don't know and I still don't know after you did this."

His responding shrug was so exaggerated his shoulders nearly touched his ears.

I could do that, and I did.

"Stop that incessant shrugging," he said. "You look ridiculous; like some tropical bird in a mating dance."

Talk about ridiculous and tropical—tell me he didn't look like one of those monkeys with a banana for a nose.

"You find this situation humorous?" he said.

I shrugged without thinking.

"If you do that once more, you'll find yourself on detentions for a very long time. Do you understand me?"

This time I knew what I was doing: I nodded.

He raised a finger. "Verbal answers, Mr. Purenut. I've had enough. From now on, you either respond with verbal answers or you'll be on detentions until the day you graduate. If you graduate."

I stared at him.

"Do you understand me?"

"Yeah."

"Yes," he corrected me.

"Yes," I said.

DING! End of round one. I felt good, too—unscathed and confident I wasn't overmatched.

He took a deep breath. "Well . . . , I can certainly see why some of your teachers completed their evaluations the way they did. However, I am still interested in hearing how you might explain it."

"Explain what?" I said. "I don't know what you want to know."

"The fact that you have been eligible for the National Honor Society three times and have failed to be accepted. The fact that some teachers give you high marks and rate you an above average student while others consider you a troublemaker with an attitude problem. I'd like your opinion on all this."

"Simple. Some teachers like me and some don't."

He shook his head. "Teachers do not base their evaluations and recommendations upon their compatibility with students."

"Then I don't know what it is because I'm sure only the teachers that don't like me give me bad evaluations and say I'm a troublemaker."

"Are you a troublemaker?"

"Nope."

"Why would they say you are?"

"Maybe they can't take being shown when they're wrong?"

"And you know when your teachers are wrong, Mr. Purenut?"

"Sometimes."

"And you always say something?"

"Sometimes. Not always, though."

"Oh, that's right, sometimes you do this . . . " and he shrugged with an expression of such helpless, head-wobbling stupidity, that I grinned. " . . . Correct?"

"Sometimes. Shrugging's an answer."

"But don't you think discussing matters is much better than several rounds of . . . " and he shrugged again, tilting his head this way then that, one idiot shrug for me, the next for him.

"It's a little better, I guess."

"Good," he said. "So . . . , what you're saying is, these teachers that are wrong–in your opinion–hold it against you when you correct them, correct?"

"No. Only the ones that can't take constructive criticism hold it against me."

"Oh, I see. It's the teacher's character flaw that results in your poor evaluation, is that it?"

"That's one way of putting it."

"Perhaps you could give me an example?"

"Sure." I had the perfect example–Mr. Asp, our history teacher. He was boring, taught by going over just what was in the book, and was continually criticizing our appearance, behavior, vocabulary, posture and other things that had little to do with history class. He and the ever-correct Brubaker, as teacher and student, would have brown-nosed each other into a circle.

"I won't name him," I said, "but he doesn't like us getting out of our chairs before the bell rings, which is fine, and we usually don't. But last week he gave us a study period, and when it was time to go a couple of the guys were already at the door because we had a test the next class and the teacher puts the tests on the desk so you can start right away. So just before the bell rings, he makes us all sit down and starts lecturing us about not being in our seats.

"Now he knows we have that test because one of the guys told him, but he keeps us there anyway. After two minutes we're still there and guys for the next class are waiting outside. So I looked over my shoulder at the clock. Maybe he didn't see it, or maybe he'd take a hint or something. But no, he says, 'That's right, Mr. Purenut, it's getting late, but *you'll* stay here until I tell you to leave.' Then he got on me for a while, and then on the class again. Eventually we were five minutes late for the test."

I sat back, my example unassailable.

"And . . . ?" Brubaker said.

"And? And what?"

"Where's the character flaw?"

I almost stood up. "Are you kidding me—where's the character flaw? He kept us there when he knew we had a test. He kept us *all* there when only a couple of guys had been wrong. And then he got all upset when I looked at the clock."

"I see nothing wrong with any of that."

"Nothing wrong? All of it's wrong."

"On the contrary. Misbehavior is best corrected immediately. I know of no student who is harmed by being reminded of the rules. And I doubt your glance at the clock was as innocent as you portray it."

"What do you mean?"

"I mean, you could have done this . . . " and he glanced at his wall clock and returned his eyes to mine, " . . . or you could have done something like this . . . " and his eyes rolled, his mouth gaped and his shoulders slumped as complete boredom escorted his look to and from the clock. He finished with a sigh and the stare of the dead. "And I'll bet your look was more like my second example," he said.

"It was a little closer to the second than the first."

"Then I can't blame your teacher for reacting the way he did. I reacted the same way yesterday to a very similar expression of yours."

Good one!

He smiled.

I shook my head. "No, no. He didn't have to get bent out of shape like that."

"He had every reason to. You were being disrespectful."

"No, I wasn't. Besides, I could have done it to some of my other teachers and they wouldn't have had a fit like he did."

"You wouldn't have acted the same way with other teachers, because you like them."

"No, he reacted different because of his character flaw."

"Which is?"

"I don't know," I said. "Whatever it is that made him get upset when I looked at the clock."

"You mean the same flaw I have?"

I smiled then shrugged for lack of an answer.

"Are we going to start this again?" he said.

"No. I just don't know what to say anymore."

"Because you're wrong."

"No. Because I just think we're not going to agree no matter what."

"I agree with that," he said.

"So do I."

He regarded me a moment, then said, "Well." He lifted my signs. "Perhaps we can discuss your campaign now. I assume you're not interested in running for office?"

"Nope."

"That's fine. Though I would have preferred you told me yesterday."

"I had my hand up."

"As I remember, I was talking at the time."

"Yes, you were."

"I think I see where this is headed," he said, "and since we obviously won't agree, perhaps I can accelerate matters. If you collect the remainder of your signs, we'll officially end your campaign. Fair enough?"

"Sounds good to me."

Halfway done with retrieving my signs I felt someone behind me. I turned to find the assistant football coach inches away, glaring at me. "What are you doing?"

I told him. He grunted and left. A feeling of frustration and disappointment came over me. I had always wanted to play football, but ever since quitting in ninth grade because the coach kept wanting to use me as a lineman and not at wide receiver where I wanted to play, I had never tried out again. I came up with an excuse not to tryout each year knowing it was just that, an excuse. It was the same with the girl of my dreams who worked at the drugstore—I was too chicken to give it a try but had never given up the hope of eventually trying. Why was I like that? It bothered me a lot sometimes and sometimes not much at all. This time it bothered me.

I returned to Brubaker's office with sixteen signs. "If you have four of them," I said, "I've got the rest." He handed me the ones on his desk. "What should I do with them? Throw them out?"

"Unless you'd like to frame one?"

"No thanks."

"I guess we're finished. I hope I haven't kept you from a test?"

"No. We have one this afternoon in chemistry."

"Will you be making the honor roll this period? Or distinguished?"

"If I get a 'B' in chemistry I'll probably make distinguished."

"I hope you do. Either way, you'll be eligible for the National Honor Society again. Perhaps you'll make it?"

Thinking of Asp, I said, "I doubt it."

"You never know."

"Yeah, but–"

"Yes, but." He raised his eyebrows.

"Yes," I said.

"It's for your own good, Dave."

I nodded.

"Good luck," he said. "Have a nice summer."

I left his office in a quandary. For three years I had detested Brubaker from a distance. Now, after our first encounter of any substance, he seemed almost human. His "good luck" and smile had been sincere. Could I actually end up liking the pelican-nosed snob? Other guys did. Even some of my friends.

"See 'ya, Crazy," somebody said.

Almost abreast of me, going the opposite way, was Artie Crenshaw, a guy in my homeroom. He should have been in English class, not walking the hallways with grim-faced Horrible Hatch, a Homelife official.

"See 'ya, Artie," I said. "Where're you going?"

"I'm getting kicked out."

They past me. I stopped and turned. "Why?"

"Get to class," Horrible said.

I watched them walk the empty corridor. "Good luck, Artie," I called before they got too far. "We'll see you around, maybe."

Horrible looked over his shoulder, and I started the other way.

6

Getting out of the Home wasn't that rare. I'd known several friends that had done it over the years. Sometimes it happened after a guy ran away. Instead of being brought back as usually happened, their parent would decide to keep them out. More often, however, either their mother or father had remarried and they could go home to a "family," or their guardian had a change of mind about keeping them in.

When younger, we considered them lucky for getting out and ourselves unlucky for having to stay. It wasn't fair–being there in the first place because our parent had died, and then being left behind. As we grew older, we could better understand our circumstances and why we remained; but guys were still lucky for getting out.

What was unlucky, and rare, was getting kicked out. Especially at the end of your junior year. One more year and the Home would pay three-fourths of the tuition of any college we attended. That benefit was gone for Artie.

When I entered class, the guys were studying as Mr. Hart stood beside the door, removing notices from the bulletin board. He smiled. "Saw your poster, Dave. Very original."

"That's the last one you'll see because I quit."

"Chicken," Brownie said, sitting nearby.

I looked at Artie's place–his books were gone. "What time did Artie get called out of class?"

"Ten minutes or so after it started," Mr. Hart said.

"Why?" Brownie said. "What's it to you?"

"I just past him in the hallway. He was with Horrible. He said he's getting kicked out."

"What?" Mr. Hart said.

"What for?" Brownie said.

"I don't know. I asked, but Horrible wouldn't let him talk."

No one said anything. Artie had been in the Home since fifth grade. Most of us had been in the same homeroom with him since ninth grade, which meant we had attended every class together, every school day, for the past three years.

"Will he get credit for this year?" Jim asked from across the room.

"Absolutely," Mr. Hart said. "He'll get a final grade based on his work to date."

Someone said, "The seniors had a party after graduation last night. Maybe he went and got caught? His brother was there."

You wouldn't get expelled just for hooking out, and we all knew it.

"Maybe Rose will know?" Jim said.

Al Rose was in Artie's unit and also in section 11-2. They were taking the chemistry final the next period. The period after that we had math class, which was down the hall. We could catch him then.

Al didn't come out of the chemistry final when the bell rang, nor did anyone else. Our section and the section due in next were waiting when the door finally opened and the guys trudged out. We pulled Al aside and told him what happened. He said Artie had gone to the party, but had gotten back without getting caught. "I'll bet that's where Horrible and Kramer were going this morning," Al said. "They past us on the way in. That also explains the essay test we just got."

"Essay?!" Brownie said.

Al nodded. "When we got into class, Mullins started handing the tests out, saying, 'Some of you are going to be in for a big surprise.' Artie had one of the tests back at the unit. They must have found it. And something else."

"Essay?" Brownie said again.

"Yeah, and don't ask me the questions, because he's curving our grades with yours. Man, are they tough."

Al left us there, still wondering about Artie and now worried about the test.

I didn't know if it was us, Mr. Mullins, or the subject, but chemistry was the first subject we ever had that demonstrated our stupidity as a group. Anyone who could fathom chemistry beyond the facts had to be blessed. The chemical chart, we could handle. Protons and neutrons, okay. From there it accelerated into the realm of the unknown.

Which is why we cheated; there was no other way of passing the course with the high marks expected of college preparatory students. The graduating classes before us cheated, and the ones behind us would cheat. Why should we be different?

We also cheated in English, but not because of its difficulty, but because there was too much to study. Every unit had study period from seven thirty to eight thirty at night, Sunday through Thursday. One hour. How could we study numerous writers and poets and their volumes of work when we also had four other subjects to study in that one hour? We could study on weekends, but our lives were regimented enough; the little free time we did have wasn't going to be spent studying.

So we cheated. We got copies of the tests any way we could. Sometimes they were tests from the year before. Other times they were stolen from the teacher's unlocked cabinets, the questions copied, and the tests returned. Whether our section pilfered them or another section did, we always shared; we were in this together.

There was, however, one guy who never cheated. Jim. No matter how we justified it, Jim considered it dishonest, and he was too honest to cheat. He therefore suffered the clicking tongues and disappointed looks of teachers who felt he was not living up to his potential.

"Ehn," Jim would grunt, when the teacher asked if anything was wrong and suggest he expend the necessary effort to equal his classmates' performances.

"See, Jim?" we'd say. "Even *he* wants you to cheat."

"Ehn," Jim would grunt again.

Grunting was Jim's trademark. He had a grunt for every occasion. He had pleasure grunts, like when we'd get something good to eat—which was rare—he'd let slide with an occasional grunt to let you know how tasty it was. He even had a grunt to let you know he thought the next bite would be even better. He had frustration grunts, aggravation grunts, embarrassed grunts. Grunts for every occasion.

His dismayed and anguished "Ehnn!" after we were given a few minutes to look over the chemistry tests that afternoon said it all. We were goners.

Instead of the standard multiple guess, true/false, and fill in the blank questions that we had all the answers for, Mr. Mullins hit us with essay questions taken from material found at the bottom of the page under 'footnotes and asterisks;' from facts and data at the end of chapters where you were sent for further details; or from information at the end of the book under 'supplements to the chapters.' It was material no one read unless specifically told to, and no one ever studied unless warned to. In the game of education, this stuff was out of bounds. I could make just enough sense out of each question to realize I hadn't any idea how to answer them.

Mr. Mullins fixed us each with a disappointed, bushy-eyebrowed stare as he walked from desk to desk handing out the tests. When finished, he stood looking as forlorn as a bloodhound. "You know why you're getting these essay questions," he said. "What else is there to say?" He waved for us to begin. "I'm very disappointed."

So were we. On the last day of classes we found out everyone had failed.

But we didn't care. Everyone's grades dropped an equal distance, classes were over for the summer, and rumor had it Artie was going to be in town for Friday night town privilege. We'd finally find out what happened.

7

We got up in the mornings at five forty-five. If we didn't start our morning chores on time, do them right, or finish them fast enough, the houseparents let us know. In the dining room, one houseparent headed one table, the other houseparent headed the second, and both kept watch on the third. One of them dropped us off at school in time for homeroom period where our homeroom teacher made sure everyone was present. We had five minutes to get from one class to the next. Each teacher knew he should have a full class or could ask and get the reason for the absentee.

Lunch began with grace at twelve o'clock with everyone seated by homerooms and the homeroom teacher heading the table. After lunch we had to stay on school grounds and had to be in class before the bell rang for the next period. At three forty-five our last class ended and we headed for homerooms and any last announcements. The final bell rang at three fifty-five and we had five minutes to get to our long, limo-type "wagons" where our houseparents waited to take us back to our evening chores and dinner, after which we had till seven thirty to do what we wanted but without leaving the property, and with the knowledge that the intercom system which connected with every major room and hallway of the unit, for speaking as well as listening, could be turned on by the houseparents and our activities monitored–a fact we countered whenever necessary by lowering the volume at our end, closing doors, or stepping into the stairwell or outside.

Study period was between seven thirty and eight thirty. No talking. Eight thirty was snacks in the kitchen, over by eight forty-five because the guy cleaning them had to be done by nine o'clock: bed time. Lights out, no talking. At five forty-five, it started all over again.

This was our life from Monday through Friday throughout the school year. Even if you were on a team or in a club that met after school, your whereabouts were known and your behavior supervised. Like rats in a lab, we suffered constant surveillance, which caused claustrophobia, paranoia, and suffocation. There was no escape.

Until, that is, Friday night, and Friday night town privilege.

Between six thirty and nine o'clock on Friday nights the school released the senior division–four to five hundred deprived, restless, and horny Homeguys–unto the streets of Hershey. Never mind that this small, bucolic town had only a bowling alley, a drugstore, and a department store to amuse us–it didn't matter. Just being out from under someone's watchful eye soothed us. Besides, there were girls out there. Not many, of course, because most listened to their parents and stayed away from downtown on Friday nights. But girls who were rebellious, teases, adventuresome, ugly, or forgetful, sometimes strayed into town. And that one girl gave hope to all five hundred of us.

Depending on the season, we had alternatives to simply roaming the streets of Hershey. In the fall, the football stadium which sat below the hill our high school occupied overlooking the environs of Hershey, and in which we, Hershey High, and Lower Dauphin used as home field, usually had a football game we could attend on Friday nights; and in the winter there were wrestling matches or basketball games at the high school. Through late spring and early fall, however, it was Hershey Park that provided us with our greatest diversion. We had free passes to every ride, but more importantly, girls from Hershey and neighboring towns did not avoid the park like they did downtown Friday nights. So it was there, drawn like rutting moose, that most of us spent a majority of our town privileges when the park opened for business, which it did Friday nights through Sunday only, beginning in late spring until school let out for the summer, when it would open full time.

The Friday we got out of school was the third weekend it was open. Of all the rides in the park, the only ones I liked were the roller coaster, bumping cars, jungle safari, and turnpike. Jim and I rode each of these a few times, but spent most of the evening looking for Artie and checking out girls.

Around eight thirty we headed for the upper section of the park where we had come in. We planned to shoot pinball before heading back to the community center parking lot, where the houseparents had let us off and would be picking us up.

As we walked the uphill path from near the turnpike entrance toward the penny arcade, I thought about the drugstore girl. I didn't even know her name. She had to have a boyfriend, though, because she'd been asked out by a couple of our guys and always refused. Whoever the lucky, poor slob was, I envied and pitied him. His cute, adorable girlfriend was living in a town around which lived almost twelve hundred boys in an all-boys school. Boys she had to serve every Friday night. It must have caused him to worry, all those guys and not one of them able to turn her head with him not there to turn it back? There were also the guys in her own high school, who probably thought the same thing we did: "Too bad for him."

That's why I felt a sense of urgency. With my shyness, inexperience, and habit of taking forever to do certain things, someone could become her boyfriend before I got the nerve to take my turn at bat.

"You want to check out the drugstore on our way back?" I asked Jim as we neared the top of the hill.

"Sure."

Jim didn't know of my love/lust for the drugstore girl, and my request wouldn't give me away. "Checking something out," was what Homeguys did lots of Friday nights, and included people, places, or things. With limited funds—we received a weekly allowance ranging from a dollar for seniors to a nickel for the kindergarten through second grades—we couldn't afford to do much more than observe.

Inside the store, I hoped the sight of my girlfriend being ogled by the other guys would firm my resolve to speak to her before the next ice age.

Jim grunted. "Look at that."

We'd just come in sight of the penny arcade. Outside its doors milled seventy to eighty Homeguys. Maybe Artie was there?

As we hurried over I looked for one of the Homelife officials who cruised or walked the streets Friday nights. Any time a crowd gathered, they usually appeared shortly afterwards to break up or stop any fun about to occur. None were in sight.

I spotted Huey among the crowd, his arm around an underclassman's neck. "Hey, class treasurer. What's going on?"

"Hi, guys," Huey said. "Kramer's out back sitting beneath the balcony. If he stays out there long enough we're going to drop an egg on him."

"Ehn," Jim said, registering a sympathetic grunt for Kramer, one of the Homelife officials.

"Who's dropping it?" I said.

Huey squeezed the head sticking between his arm. "Tell my buddies who's going to drop the egg."

"I don't know, Huey. I have no idea."

"Did you see anybody?"

"Nope. Nobody,"he said, shaking his head. Then suddenly his arms shot out and up. "I wasn't even there!" he said.

Huey laughed and released his captive, who came up smiling. "He's learning," Huey said. "Pretty soon he's not even going to be a dirt anymore."

"Have you seen Artie tonight, Huey?" I asked.

"Yeah, he just left. Poor bastard. Some dirt and some other guys from another unit got caught hooking out Monday night. Horrible grilled the dirt first and he squealed on Artie, said he saw him with a beer and cigarettes at the party. So they searched his room for cigarettes and found a pack, only inside they also found two joints. And that was that. Gone."

I had never asked, but I thought Artie and a couple other guys might have smoked marijuana. I'd been thinking about asking, though, because I'd been considering trying it. Now I wasn't so sure. Artie was the third guy in two years to be kicked out because of pot. I didn't want to be the fourth.

A kid rushed up, holding two eggs. "Huey, I got 'em."

"Good job," Huey said.

"Where'd he get those?" I asked.

"From one of the food places his cousin works at."

It had gotten louder around us. "Shhhhh!" Huey hissed. "Quiet." Others shushed others, and the noise subsided. "Where's Brownie?" Huey said. He stepped onto the top step of the center archway of the arcade. "Brownie!?"

"Yo!" Brownie moved through the crowd like a heron through water, head and neck bobbing atop his tall, bony body.

"You doing it?" Huey asked.

"Are you?" Brownie said.

Huey handed him an egg. Guys started inside. Huey thrust his hand against an underclassman talking excitedly. "Hey." The rush halted. Huey lifted a finger. "Nobody saw nothing, heard nothing, or seen anyone. Got that?"

"Yeah," Brownie said, "or we'll rip your freak'en heads off."

"And keep quiet," Huey said.

The penny arcade was a long, ground level building with a slick wooden floor, filled with games, picture booths, ski-ball alleys, pinball machines and anything else with an appetite for change. The backside of the arcade had a balcony overlooking benches that belonged to the basement snack bar. The benches faced out over the wooded hill on which the arcade was built. To get to the arcade from the benches and snack shop, you had to walk along a path around the building. It was a secluded spot. Nice and peaceful. A place where no one, not even an official like Kramer, would suspect a reenactment of Pearl Harbor.

Kramer was one of three Homelife officials for the senior division. They were the school's henchmen and were supposed to dispense justice fairly and equitably. If you thought something wasn't right in your unit, or that a houseparent had done you wrong, you went into Homelife. Right or wrong, we were usually shown the error of our ways and dismissed with Homelife fresh atop our lists of dislikes. The most that would happen–if anything–was an official would talk to the houseparents about the problem, thereby giving the houseparents another reason to make your life miserable. Despite this fact, guys continued to go in.

Of the three officials, Kramer was the one I always signed up to see. He was bald, roly-poly, closer to fifty than forty, had a smile plastered on his face, and called everyone "buddy." He reminded me of chip-creamed beef: tolerable, not liked especially much, and only good when compared to something worse, like his fellow Homelife officials Horrible Hatch and Old Man Hatch, a nephew and uncle link that somewhere in its genealogy included the missing link. Old Man Hatch had been called Old Man Hatch for so long he should have been dead. Most of the time he wasn't in because of illness, and when he was, you thought he should be out recuperating from whatever was causing him to cough, wheeze, dribble, have that whitish-gray color, or walk so slow you thought he might soon slow right down and die. I figured DEATH was lurking in his waiting room and I didn't want to be around when the final disease hit for fear it was contagious.

Horrible Hatch instilled a different kind of fear in us and for a different reason. He was a mental case with substance. About forty, built like a large, wide stump with thick limbs, he had the alarming habit of turning homicidal whenever you mentioned a certain word. Problem was, we had no clue what words ignited him. You could say "Brillo pad" and suddenly find a maniac crawling across his desk with destruction in his eyes. No one ever signed up for Horrible. You were always sent to his office.

If it had been either of the Hatches sitting on that bench, the egg droppings might have been considered, but not dropped. Old Man Hatch might have died from a heart attack, crushed skull, or some rare allergy to eggs, and Horrible's killing spree would have been legendary. But Kramer was open season. Even though he harmlessly enforced the school's rules against us, he was there, we were Homeguys, he had been involved with Artie's expulsion, and how many times did opportunity knock with such a tempting idea?

With a hundred or so of us following in attempted nonchalance, Huey and Brownie led the way to the balcony. We shuffled quietly onto its wooden floor, nearly forty feet long and several feet deep, and jammed together shoulder to shoulder.

Huey and Brownie extended the eggs beyond the balcony, then Huey silently counted, his fingers popping into the air one at a time. One . . . Two . . . Three!

The eggs dropped; or rather, one did. Huey didn't release his. He smiled as Brownie spun on him with a look of shock and betrayal–then he dropped his.

Everyone leaned forward.

Brownie's egg hit Kramer on the right shoulder and crumpled backwards onto the ground. Kramer jumped, his ice cream cone nearly slipping from his hand. He said, "What the. . . ." just as Huey's egg splattered dead center into his leathery bald head. Kramer hunched forward, then leapt off the bench and looked up.

The guys in the back had been leaning forward on their tiptoes, with their weight on the backs of the guys in front of them. Despite these efforts, they never saw the near-perfect bombardment, nor Kramer leaping into the air, spinning, and looking up. That's why they were still leaning forward when those of us in front jerked our heads back—right into the noses, chins, eyes, foreheads and cheekbones of those behind.

A unified outburst of moans and cries preceded then merged with the heavy shuffling and panicked murmurs of the fleeing mob. As I pushed forward, I touched the puncture wound where what felt like a beaver had bit my skull. Would I need a tetanus shot? Or worse, get rabies?

In the back aisles of the arcade I felt confident of escape as I past other, less mobile cowards. Just before exiting I spotted Jim playing pinball. He hadn't gone to watch because it wasn't a nice thing to do. I had gone to watch for the same reason.

I ran over. "Jim, let's go."

"I didn't do anything." He sent a ball into play.

"Neither did I, but I don't want to have to tell Kramer I didn't see *no*-body coming through here, do you?"

Within a span of two seconds, Jim responded by saying, "Ehn," because I had a point, "Ehn!" as he pushed the corners to make the ball bounce farther, and "Ehhnn!!" to register TILT and release anger at having to abandon the game. Then he grabbed me and shoved backwards, catapulting himself forward with a grunt of excitement and escape.

Outside, once you past the souvenir shop, you could either head left toward a side gate with one full-body turnstile and be out of the park sooner but farther from the community center parking lot where it was almost time to go, or you could go straight and cut around or through the rows of green benches used for the outdoor stage and attack a gate with three hip-high turnstiles and a fence that could be scaled, leaving you much closer to the road over the railroad bridge into town. Jim and I chose the benches.

I ran between them, racing Jim. The three people on stage stopped their performance and stared along with the twenty or so audience members scattered about. Because the turnstiles were logjammed, I jumped on the fence and scaled up and over the eight-foot barrier. When I landed, I bumped into someone. Rich. We punched each other. Someone yelled, "He's coming!"

Kramer hesitated at the corner of the souvenir shop. Left or straight? He wiped his head with a napkin then started toward the left, stopped, and turned around. Another official, one from the intermediate division, hustled around the corner. They talked briefly, then hurried left.

I had a sudden inspiration. "Horrible's with him!" I yelled.

Immediately efforts intensified at the turnstiles as though guys had already started dying. Some yelled, while others, rather than wait, crawled or dove over the three-foot high casings separating the turnstiles.

At the bridge we converged with the guys who had escaped through the side gate, and dashed over it like gremlins on the run. The townsfolk stood with backs against walls or in doorways out of harm's way. We past the department store, took a left at the light onto Chocolate Avenue, and ran the short block to the next light and a right onto Cocoa Avenue.

The guys who had been hanging out at the corners and along the wide, stone balustrade and sidewalk behind the community center, or across the street in front of the drugstore, stretched and strained to see what was causing the stampede. When the pack reached them and they still didn't know, they joined the exodus, knowing safety was in numbers.

We ignored the two streetlights, causing cars to stop as we streamed by. I ran to the window of the drugstore and saw my sweetheart's lovely back. I waited, then waited some more until she turned from scooping up ice cream. She saw the guys at the counter looking outside and followed their gaze, which gave me a perfect view of her beautiful face.

It was several seconds before I realized she could see me looking in like a dumbstruck dummy. I grinned, and for some reason, she grinned, too. That made me smile, then yelp. I dashed across the street. What a girl!

Though I was fairly certain no one would identify to Kramer any one of the one to one hundred and fifty guys now stampeding into the parking lot, I decided to circle around and come up from behind. After the first parked car, I turned in, then ran commando style toward the back, using every available vehicle for cover. The closer I got to the back, the more guys I encountered hidden in dark spaces either smoking with their buddies or making out with their dates. The sound of my blitzkrieging footsteps propelled their brains into survival mode–the guys with cigarettes flicked them into the air and assumed a posture of innocence, while the guys wrapped around their dates, preoccupied and unwary, didn't notice me until they instinctively ducked to avoid the fists of the enraged father there to pummel them for molesting their daughter. Both groups cursed me as I stayed my course to the rear.

I made a left near the back of the lot, ran twenty yards, then headed back toward the middle. I slowed as I neared the first few guys, all of whom were watching the last of the others coming in the front.

"What's going on?" I asked the guy closest to me.

He jumped at the sound of my voice. "I don't know," he said. He was an underclassman I didn't recognize. The guy in front of him turned. "Crazy," Brownie said. "Where'd you come from?"

"I've been here. Where'd you come from?"

"I've been here."

A sudden quiet fell upon the parking lot as a car rolled toward the center and stopped. Out of it stepped the other official and Kramer. As they asked questions, the guys responded with shrugs and shaken heads. Kramer pointed to a kid with a yellow shirt with large black squares on it. I'd seen the same shirt as we crossed the bridge. As they questioned him, the kid shook his head, then pointed at another kid.

"He's not squealing, is he?" I said.

"He better not be," Brownie said.

The second kid stepped forward. He wore the same shirt as the first kid–who now pointed to another kid with the identical shirt. A fourth guy stepped forward wearing the same distinctive black on yellow. I counted seven guys with that color and style of shirt. Brownie and I smiled at each other. For once, looking like junior scientists had paid off.

Kramer and the official conferred for a moment, then got in their car and drove away. I joined in the spontaneous celebration that followed, whooping and hollering with my fellow inmates. This had to be an omen for the year to follow. My last.

TWO

1

Monday, June 16, 1970

*O*kay, Teach, though I don't see how this
has anything to do with speed-reading, I'll
go along with your request. There's just one thing. Due to the fact that this'll be
a diary, I'm hereby stating that all that follows may or may not be true, and the
people you encounter might or might not be real. Why? Because in this democratic society in which we don't live here at the Home, we both know anything
you say, write, or do can and most likely will be used against you if you're caught
and can't escape or plead insanity. This being the gospel according to Saint
Experience, I'm not taking any chances.

You got that, PUS SUCKER!

Oh, not you, Teach. That was for any mealy-mouthed, low-life, snake in
the manure who happens to go any further in this diary and isn't named Mr.
Hart or Danny Numbnuts (the fictional author of this fictional diary). You hear
me, CRAP-FOR-BRAINS? If you're not one of us, this is personal, private, and
reading any further really casts doubts on your mother's character and bedtime
habits and makes one wonder if the male contributor to your DNA had a tail.
So put the diary down, wipe the drool from your lips, the sweat from your hairy
palms, and act like you're human.

You don't think I'm paranoid, do you, Teach? I just like to play it safe.
Besides, any reference that depicts a member of this school's administration,

faculty, or houseparent staff as anything other than angelic, just couldn't be true. Right? Right.

Hey, I like that. New rule, Teach. Any time I ask a question and receive no immediate response from you, that means you're in agreement with whatever I say. Okay? Well, okay! Let's test it. First, don't you think I'm doing the right thing by changing names and stuff? I thought so. And you'd do the same, wouldn't you? Mm-hm. Come to think of it, wasn't it you who said this place reeks with filthy, immoral, degenerative, blood-sucking eggheads? I thought that was you. I admire you're outspoken honesty and hope it helps in your job search for next year.

Now can you see the value in why everything written in here may not necessarily be true? I thought you would.

Now that that's done, I might as well start this exciting diary with the only thing of interest that happened to me today—I made a fool of myself.

I was walking down the hall after class to catch the bus back to the unit when I spotted a dirt we got last week. His name was Harry I. Fooledya. At least I thought it was him.

Being Joe Niceguy, I thought I'd say something to him and make him feel a little more at home. So I got beside him and said, "How'd your testing go today?"

Harry I. Fooledya looked at me with a look of confusion. "What?" he said.

I figured I caught him off guard, he wasn't expecting a senior to be such a nice guy, and so I repeated the question. "You talking to me?" he said.

Teach, there was nobody between him and me, the wall was on his other side, and I'm looking him straight in the eye. Who else would I be talking to?

But I'm a nice guy. And patient. So I said, "Didn't you come today to take those interest tests that all the dirt take?" I knew he did. He was coming this week, two other dirt in our unit were coming next week, and the other two were coming the week after that. He even walked down to the highway with me and the other summer school guys this morning to catch the bus. How dense could he be?

Harry's head inched back a couple inches and a look of insult appeared. If I had been the dirt and he the senior, I swear he would have lumped me. "NO," he said.

Now I was confused. No dirt in our unit was going to summer school, so if they went at all, it had to be for the tests. That had to be the reason he came, unless he was a liar of proportions that I thought would only be seen in this diary. Unless . . .

I looked at him looking at me as though I should die, and I noticed that his glasses weren't at the end of his nose looking like they were about to drop off like they usually were, and that was because his face wasn't as oily as it usually was. Then I noticed his hair. That wasn't oily, either, which really threw me because I remembered watching him get on the bus and wondering if his dirty blond hair would be only blond if he'd wash it regularly. And that's when it hit me–this wasn't the kid I thought it was. It just looked like him from the back at a glance in a crowded hallway.

So here I was, thinking I was being Joe Niceguy to a dirt, when actually I was being Joe Moron to someone who wouldn't care if I exploded.

To cover up, I asked him what he did come for. He said, "typing," and I nodded and said, "Oh," like it all made sense and the world was safer. Then I spotted an imaginary friend ahead of us, yelled, "Hey, Charlie!" and vanished down the hallway.

We were probably thinking the same thing as I disappeared. "What an asshole."

(PS–You don't mind if I swear now and then, do you, Teach? Good. I didn't think you would.)

Tuesday, June 17, 1970

I might as well spill my guts right up front, Teach–I don't sleep like a baby like I wish I could. Once I get to sleep I'm okay, but getting there's the hard part. My problem is I'm always thinking. Thoughts just keep zipping through my head. And if I try pulling a fast one and start dozing off in less than an hour or two, my mind jerks me awake, tells me I should get to sleep, and when I don't, it starts chanting, "You've got a problem . . . you've got a problem . . . you're an idiot . . . you've got a problem . . . "

I think my problem can be narrowed down to three things: this place; the fact that this place doesn't have any girls; and most of all, the fact that they send us to bed at nine o'clock, when I'm not even close to being tired.

Anyway, last night was one of those nights. I was still awake at 4:30, and when Suds, our housefather, came around at 5:45, boy, was I tired.

I'm a milker this week. My first cow's fast and I was off her in five minutes and on to my next. Each cow has its own numbered stall and a chain around its neck with a tag with the same number, which is how we keep track of them and how we refer to them. Not as Bessy, or Mabel, or Mrs. Sawyer, but as Two-ninety, One-fifty-five, or Two thirty-three.

The second cow of my rotation is One-eighty, and of all the cows I've ever had, she's the worse. If someone gave me a gun and said, "Go ahead, shoot her," I'd pull the trigger so fast they'd think there was something wrong with me. I'm not alone, though. Everyone in the unit would blow her away.

Picture this. I'm a dirt, first time in the barn. These big black and white creatures, some of them higher than me at their shoulders, got me scared but I sort of like them. They're docile. And quiet. You can pet them and they seem to like it. They're like great big no-barking, chained-down, harmless dogs that give us milk so that we don't turn them into hamburgers.

My first job is to curry and brush them. Starting at the neck and shoulders and working my way back to the rear-end, I take the curry comb, a kind of circular wire brush, and run it across their fur, pulling out all the dead and loose hairs. Then I use a regular brush and smooth it down until it's nice and shiny.

I'm told to be careful around One-eighty. I am. First day, nothing. Second day, nothing. Third day, I'm talking to her in whispers. "You're not so bad, are 'ya? Huh, girl? Yeah, good cow." By the fifth day, to me, she's just a misunderstood cow, and secretly, she's my favorite. Then the brush slips from my hand and falls into the gutter. "Whoops. I'll have to wipe that off," I say as I bend down to get it. "Don't want to get crap on my favorite—"

WHACK!

All I saw was a blur, and that's it until one of the guys was standing over me asking me if I'm all right, and I'm thinking he's the one with the problem because I see all these tiny specks flying around his head. What's he got, fleas?

They were stars, Teach. She hoofed me to the head. I had to have five stitches and two shots. That's why I'd gladly start her on her way to Hamburger U. if they'd let me.

But they won't because she's a great milker. She puts out forty pounds, twice a day, without a problem. All four sections drain equally fast. No massaging to help along a bad section. No small front section and large back, or vice-versa, and the inevitable holding up of the milker at the smaller end until she's done milking.

She's just a perfect milking machine—with a torturer's brain. She'll be harmless for days or weeks at a time and you'll forget not to forget to stay alert and that's when she gets you. She'll kick you; hit you with her tail then kick you; shove into you while you're milking her to knock you over then stomp on you; kick off the milker; try kicking you while you're putting it on or while you're milking the cow beside her.

She deserves to be hung, but they won't because she's a milker's milker. Got the picture? "It's your own fault," they tell us. "You know you have to watch her."

Anyway, today I washed her, dried her, checked for mastitis, threw on the milker and then squatted there. She milks for about ten minutes, and then is done almost at once. There's nothing to do but wait. So, being tired, I closed my eyes, and being tired, I fell asleep. Pretty soon I was dreaming, and boy, what a dream!

Do you ever go into Hershey on Friday nights to the drugstore? If you do, check out the girl dishing out ice cream and sodas. The tall, slender one with long brown hair, blue eyes and a smile so cute you'll probably want to beat on your chest and give the old Tarzan cry when you see it.

Anyway, there I was, walking down the midway of the Chemung County Fair (That's where I'm from; Elmira, New York, Chemung County) and all of a sudden this goddess stops me and asks where the ice cream stand is. I couldn't believe it, it was her, my true love, right there in Chemung County, asking me, me(!) a question.

I said, "It's right down this way. I'll show you."

Those words right there, Teach, were a definite clue I wasn't in the land of reality. Because normally, when a girl, especially a good-looking one, talks to me, I become incoherent and appear mentally deficient. And seeing as how it was her, I should have stuttered something like, "Ahhhm, buhla tazar abuka . . . " And then she'd of walked off.

But she didn't, and there we were, walking side by side. Outside, I was calm and cool, carrying on a conversation with this beautiful girl. Inside, a maniac was screaming nonstop while doing double back triple spin flips with two tucks. The only bad part was that when we got to the ice cream stand I'd have to say goodbye. But when we got there, for being such a nice guy, she asked me to join her.

That was it, Teach. Proof beyond all proof that she was in love, too. Get the ring, grab the license, let's tie the knot!

About halfway through our ice cream sundaes I started hearing this sucking sound. I was looking down when it started, and I didn't look up right away because I didn't want to embarrass her for slurping her Sunday. So I kept my head down. But the slurping got louder and louder. No wonder she didn't go out with any of our guys yet—she ate like a pig. The noise was so loud I figured she just had her lips to the bowl and was sucking away. Finally, it got so unbearable I had to ask her to keep it down for fear we'd get arrested.

When I looked up, her beautiful face turned into a collapsed utter, with all four teats stretched to their full length by a milker sucking for dear life. The next instant, One-eighty kicked the milker off and the four suckers started vacuuming the floor of straw and cowshit. I leaned over to grab it, but my foot had fallen asleep, and I fell forward.

Sure enough, One-eighty went into a song and dance routine with me as the stage. She walked from side to side and back and forth depending upon where she could step on me the most. Every couple of steps she would stop and whip a vicious kick with whatever leg could do the most harm to yours truly.

I would have been able to get out faster than I eventually did, but my whole left leg had fallen asleep. So all at once I was trying not to damage the milker, worrying about the disappearing straw ruining the milk in the holding tank, wondering why my left leg felt dead, and dodging vicious kicks—or trying to.

After five or six direct hits, I just started crawling and kept crawling until the kicks stopped—screw everything else. Luckily most cows aren't like One-eighty. They're so fear stricken that at the slightest sound or touch they immediately move as far from the source as possible, which gave me room to escape.

I walked around to the other side of One-eighty, picked up the milker, then pulled out the straw clogging two of the cups. I was going to start beating her but Suds walked up then and demanded to know what was going on.

"One-eighty kicked off the milker, and when I bent over to pick it up, I fell and she started kicking and walking all over me."

"You should've had hold of the milker and it wouldn't have fallen off."

"I was fixing the lines. They were dragging on the floor."

"They shouldn't have been on the floor."

"They weren't. They must have slipped or something."

"Yeah. Or something."

He didn't believe me, but what could he do? He pointed at the milk line. "Look at all that crap that got into the line."

Mixed in with the pure, white, foamy milk were bits of straw and crap. "Hey, I didn't kick the milker on the floor," I said. "If you want, I'll beat her so she doesn't do it again?"

"Don't get smart," he said.

He watched me pull the hoses of the milker off the main line. "You're getting too big for your britches," he said, and walked away.

"Yeah, right," I said to myself. "And your brains are too small for your head."

After he disappeared into the milkroom I looked at One-eighty. She was chomping on some hay, head up, watching me with those big fat cow eyes. If cows can smile, she was grinning.

Fortunately, I got the last laugh. A few punches here, a couple kicks there, and her smirk was gone. Now she'll behave herself until her next opportunity to maim and mutilate.

Wednesday, June 18, 1970

We've got to nip this in the butt, Teach. It's only been three days and already he's driving us all crazy.

You know who I'm talking about. Let's call him Timmy Technical, the Pork Chop with the big mouth and all the wrong answers who sits up front and acts like you're the bestus teacher in the world because he really thinks you're so stupid you won't know what he's doing. (Maybe he's not so . . . well, let's skip that for now). Anyway, he's the same guy who asks all those idiotic questions after every speed-reading story. Really, Teach, we wouldn't mind at all if you walked up to him, smacked him up side the head a couple thousand *times and then told him to shut up or else you'd slit his throat. We'd be screaming, "Do it! Do it!"*

The person who said, "The only dumb question is the one that isn't asked," never knew Timmy.

Friday, June 20, 1970

Since nothing happened yesterday, I skipped the entry, figuring I'm entitled because my average is beyond a page a day. But nothing much happened today, either, so I thought I'd describe one of our new dirt for you.

When they first came in last week I figured Jonathan was going to have the hardest time fitting in. He's just under six feet tall and maybe weighs one-twenty. He's real skinny, and he's constantly hunching over like he doesn't want to be noticed. I've started trying to get him to stand taller by pushing in on his hunched back and shoving back on his curved in shoulders and saying, "Come on, Jonathan, stand up!" I do it good-naturedly so I don't think he minds–especially since he smiles whenever I do it. He also has a healthy case of acne and his feet are size 12. Guys have started calling him "Shoes" as a nickname, and he hardly talks.

I knew he was in trouble the first time I heard him speak. We were all outside picking up sides for touch football when Eddie, my roommate, asked, "What's your name?"

"Jonathan."

"What?"

"Jonathan."

"No, I mean, what name do you go by?"

"Jonathan."

Thinking this would do it, Eddie said, "What do your friends call you?"

"Jonathan."

That's when I knew he was in trouble–the poor kid didn't have any friends except his mother.

"What about Jack?" Gary asked.

Jonathan shook his head.

"How about John?" I suggested.

"My name's Jonathan," he said, kind of embarrassed, but sticking to it.

"Johnny?"

"Jackie?"

He shook his head. "Jonathan."

"What size feet you got?" Kingston asked. Everyone looked at his feet, including Jonathan. "Size twelve," he said.

"They're almost as big as my dick," Eddie said.

(Teach, that's what he said. Honest. Besides, it's my diary. I can write what I want, right? I thought so. And that's what he said only if we remember I'm lying about just about everything, okay? Good.)

"That's what we can call him," Kingston said after Eddie's comment.

"You can't call him dick," I said.

"No, not dick. Shoes."

"Okay, Shoes, you're on my side," Eddie said, immediately liking the name.

Jonathan stood there a second, reluctant to move, as though by doing so he was accepting the name. But what else could he do? Throw a tantrum? He moved.

During the game Jonathan proved he was no budding athlete, but he tried and I liked that. That's why at snacks later on, I got beside him and said, "Don't worry about the name Shoes. It's not your fault your name's Jonathan. At least it's not Gary." I said "Gary" like I was throwing up, right into Gary's ear, who was standing near Jonathan. "Only Rhino turds are named Gary."

Gary just graduated from Dirtdum, Teach, where he was a good one.

"Yeah, well at least it's not Dave," he said, and faked upchucking into the sink. "Only sissies and cow puke are named that."

I pinched him in the arm. "Yeah?"

"Yeah," he said, then whacked me and darted out of reach.

I'm top dog, Teach, the only senior in our unit, and look what kind of respect I get. The masses better start being servile and fawning or heads will role.

Sunday, June 21, 1970

Did you ever go to the Sunday Morning Worship Service, Teach? Boy, are they boring. It's the same thing every week: prayer, song, bible reading, glee club, song, bible reading, sermon, song, prayer, and finally, a prayer thanking God it's over. It's the right idea, I guess, but jeez. It's just like when I go to the Catholic church afterwards, the same stuff over and over again. But at least there I get to look at girls. (Hope I'm not struck blind for that comment.)

Anyway, the reason I brought it up was because today somebody finally got a point across to me. After eleven years, something sinks in. Hallelujah, brother!

When it came time for the sermon, the guy got halfway to the podium and stopped, stared at the ceiling for awhile, then bent down and leaped into the air like you do when you have a jump ball in basketball. He did this a couple of times, looking like a fool because the closest thing to him–the ceiling–was forty feet in the air.

After a while he shrugged and continued to the podium. Then he looked at the junior division guys, who had been laughing at him, and said, "What are you laughing at? Huh? You think I looked funny? Is that it? Well, I had a reason for doing what I did." Then he started talking to everybody.

"When I was sitting over there earlier I noticed those lights up there, and I thought, 'I wonder if I can jump up and touch them?' I knew they were pretty high up, but still, if I really had a good jump, and really tried, maybe I could? But then I thought how much of a fool I'd look like if I didn't do it, especially in front of all you people. So I thought, 'Nah, I won't do it.' But I still couldn't get it out of my mind. So as I was walking up here, I looked at them one more time, and I thought, 'Why not?' So I tried. And I really gave it my best shot." He shrugged. "I didn't do it.

"But you know what? At least I tried. I'll always feel better knowing that."

He went on from there, but the main thing was to give it a shot. Knowing you gave it a shot, even if you don't get it, beats the B'Jesus out of the torment you go through wanting and wishing you'd give it a try. And if you never do, you'll always wish you had.

Sort of like with me and my dream girl at the drugstore. I'm too chicken to ask her out because I don't want her standing on the counter, belly laughing, and broadcasting to the world, "He just asked me out. Can you believe it! Ha, ha, ha, ha . . . "

So what if she does, right? The point is, at least I'd feel better knowing I tried—especially after I gunned down every one of the bastards laughing with her.

But he did talk about preparing for what you're after to make it your best shot possible. So I'll start rehearsing being swauvaa and de-boner. And I'm also going to start running and working out every day. There's something athletic I always wanted to do but was too chicken to try. Now, if I get in good enough shape, I'll try it. If I ever make it, I'll let you know what it was. And if you ever see me with a smile glued to my face, you'll know the drugstore girl has found her destiny.

Saturday, June 28, 1970

Good news, Teach. I found out last night that Miss Wonderful's first name is Lisa.

"How do you know that?" I asked Gary. We were standing at the candy counter acting like we were deciding what to get, but actually were checking her out.

"It says so on her tag."

"What tag?"

"Her nametag, dummy. Right there below her left shoulder, above the flower."

Imagine that? I've been so stunned by her beauty I never noticed it.

Lisa. It even sounds Italian and Italian-looking girls tickle my fancy more than any others—as long as they're not growing mustaches and beards. And besides being beautiful with that gorgeous smile, Lisa looks one hundred per-cent Italian.

"Lisa," I said, so only Gary could hear. "Lisa and Dave Purenut. Sounds just right, don't it?"

"Yeah. About as good as Dave and Raquel Welch Purenut."

"I'm sorry, but you're just going to have to tell Raquel that I've found my final love. And while you're at it, you might as well tell Sophie Loren, Ann Margaret, Jennifer . . . "

"You got any girls in Pennsylvania you want me to tell?"

See what the world's coming to, Teach? Nobody respects their elders anymore.

The Twig's right, though. As hard as this is to believe about such a wonderful and modest guy like myself, there isn't anyone I'd have to tell that I found another. Of course, as soon as I finish my double-oh-seven training I'll be asking out Miss Wonderful and changing all that.

Sunday, June 29, 1970

My housefather's really starting to get hard with me. Just before the seniors graduated he told me he and Bones (his unlucky wife) expect me to set an example because I'm the only senior. I didn't like it, but I figured I usually don't get in trouble so I'll just act normal and that should be enough. Makes sense, right? Wrong. He's starting to act like a jerk and I can't act normal because I have to speak up which is something I usually don't do. (I only speak up frequently in your class, Teach. You lucky dog, you.)

Like I've started my last year, so it makes sense that I'm a senior, right? Well seniors get to go on park privilege Saturday and Sunday during the summer, not like everyone else who has to pick one or the other of the afternoons.

So today, I got my bathing suit and towel and headed for the door, all psyched to meet Jim at the pool where we'd ogle all the girls. Suds was in the kitchen with two kitchen guys checking their work when I walked through.

"Where do you think you're going?" he said.

"On park privilege." I raised my towel in case he was blind. "To the pool."

"No, you're not. You had your park privilege yesterday."

"Yeah, but I'm a senior. Seniors get to go both days."

"Did you start classes yet?"

"No."

"Then you're not a senior."

The bastard. He was giving me a hard time for nothing. The seniors last year were going both days during the summer, and he knew it. But I had him, Teach.

"*I am too a senior,*" *I said. "It came out in the bulletin a couple weeks ago.*"
"*I didn't see it.*"
"*It was still there. Ask these guys. Or call another housefather or Homelife, and ask them.*"

He stormed over and stuck one of his fat porky fingers in my face. "*You don't give orders around here. I do. What I say goes. And until I see it with my own eyes, you'll get one park privilege, not two. You're no better than anybody else.*"

"*But that's—*"

"*The discussion's over. One more word and you're on detentions. Now get upstairs and change your clothes.*"

See what we have to go through? I know I'm right, but when I prove it, will I get that lost privilege made up to me? No. Will anyone say anything to him? No. Of course, I could have just gone into town, but then Homelife would have said I was right in the first place but wrong for disobeying a houseparent and thrown me on detentions. So either way, we get screwed. Nice, isn't it?

Because we only get one call a week (another real intelligent mindless stupid rule we have to follow), I had Jonathan call Jim to let him know I wasn't coming, and then tonight I called Brownie and found out his unit saves the weekly bulletins, so he'll bring me the one I need tomorrow in class so I can ram it down Jerkface's throat.

I should sleep like a log tonight, huh?

Monday, June 30, 1970

Right after lunch I showed Barfbrains the bulletin Brownie gave me. He read it, then said, "*Huh. I guess I was wrong. Sorry.*" Then he smiled and shrugged, like he really was sorry and we all make mistakes and what can you do? Then he left, leaving me there feeling like I had a pile of crap in my hands with no where to fling it.

He got out of it awfully easy, didn't he?

Jonathan got nailed by One-Eighty tonight. (He's milking her now; I'm the hay and straw guy.) I came in from putting out silage and he was walking around, rubbing his leg and saying, "Ow! Ow! Ow!"

To make him feel better, I told him about when she kicked me in the head. Hey! Maybe that's my problem?

Tuesday, July 1, 1970

I just found out I missed my sister Lynn's birthday. It's not until tomorrow, but there's no way I can get a card to her in time. I even had it marked on the calendar. Too bad it's one of those monthly calendars and her birthday's the second of the month.

She's a year older than me, and I have another sister, Maura, three years older, and that's it, except my father. No brothers. So it's not like I got too many to remember, you know?

Maybe I'll call her. But then I'd have to reverse the charges, and I don't like doing that because if we were loaded with money, I wouldn't be here.

Oh, well, she'll understand. I'm a jerk and we both know it.

Pray for me, Teach. They put Timmy Technical in our car today. Now I have to listen to him yapping for three hours non-stop while trying to learn to drive. And just like in class, he already knows everything there is to know about driving. This could turn homicidal.

Wednesday, July 2, 1970

The sophomores are starting to pick on the dirt for no reason. I don't mind if there's a reason for making a guy do something or giving him lumps, but if there isn't, then it's time to put a stop to it. Tonight at snacks I told no one in particular that if guys keep getting beat for no reason, then I'm going to start picking on people for a very good reason.

I hope the silence that followed was an indication the KING had spoken and his subjects would obey.

Never mind that the twig, Gary, sauntered up to me and said, "If you touch one hair on anybody's head around here, I'll beat the living crap out of you." Of course I had to bear hug him into submission. And of course Suds had to walk in and catch me.

"Quit picking on everyone," he said, "or I'll start picking on you."

Start? He's halfway round the track.

Friday, July 4, 1970

"This piece is for me," I said, after examining the cake on the table, and picking the largest piece. This was even before we sat down to eat. Since I'm the only senior, and the head of my table, I feel entitled to a few just desserts every now and then. I think choice selections (occasionally) are within reason and don't do much harm to group morale. When those guys are seniors they'll probably do the same thing. Seniors before me did it. Rank has its privileges, just so long as you don't abuse them. Right? Right.

At the end of supper, everyone at my table was enjoying their dessert except me. I was finishing off the last of my macaroni and cheese, and gazing at my piece of cake. There it was, the biggest piece; deep, dark, chocolate cake, moist and firm, topped by a creamy wave of white icing. And the best part was, it was all mine.

I was still staring at it when Suds came walking by, picked up the plate on which it sat, and disappeared down the hallway and into his apartment with it.

Everybody thought that was pretty funny. Except me. I had to settle for the piece left at Suds' table, a little cube about the size of his brain.

Should I hook out tonight or not? My roommate wants to. Says there's bound to be fireworks, but I don't know. Says there'll be tons of girls, which would be nice. Says we won't get caught, either. How's he know all this stuff, you know?

I probably will, though. You only go round once, right?

Saturday, July 5, 1970

I past my driver's test today. I didn't go through the serpentine as fast as I should have, and I thought I messed up a couple other places, too, but she past me and that's all that counts. Thank God, too. Now I only have to see Timmy once a day.

We did hook out. Zilch. No fireworks anywhere. Can you believe it? Maybe this is a commie community? What would you say to that, Comrade?

Tuesday, July 8, 1970

Jonathan got nailed by One-eighty again tonight. I didn't see it because I was out in the lot putting out silage. When I came back in, Suds was yelling at him. "I don't want to hear it. I told you to be careful around her. If it happens again, you're in trouble." Then he turned and saw me. "What are you staring at? Get to work!"

I made it look good until he walked away, then I started back toward Jonathan just in time to see one of the sophomores who've been picking on the dirt, sneak up behind Jonathan and lump him on the back of the head, then run off.

He couldn't run far enough, though. I got to him and asked him why he did it. "I don't know," he said. "Because."

"Because" didn't make it, especially since he was in the kitchen when I made my "don't beat the dirt for no reason," announcement. So I gave him a lump, a good one, so that he was feeling as bad as Jonathan.

"Now I had a reason for doing that, and if you got a good reason, then I don't mind. But if I catch you doing it again, or even hear about it, you're really going to get it."

He got off easy, and he knew it. I usually go for the leniency approach, Teach. Mostly because I don't like administering lumps or whatever else is called for. This way I don't feel as bad and maybe the guy will lighten up himself when it's his turn to be the dispenser of justice.

After that I went over and talked to Jonathan. I told him I never saw One-eighty kick a guy twice so soon and I thought it was because he hadn't beat her the first time. He didn't beat her this time, either. I volunteered to do it, but he declined.

Oh, well, eventually I bet he does it.

Thursday, July 10, 1970

Did I ever get butchered today. It's going to take at least three months before my hair grows back to where it was yesterday, and that ain't saying much. This new barber really thinks he's Buster Badass or Danny Do-What-He-Wants.

"I don't have to take this from you punks. I don't have to take this from anybody." Keep rearranging those words and you'll have his half of almost any conversation we had with him. He combs the hair on top of our heads oppo-site the way we comb it and then cuts it off. No wonder we look like Helen Keller cut our hair.

I guess I was lucky, though, because last time he promised to "get me" because I didn't say thank you. He must not have remembered, but when you look at me now, he couldn't have "gotten me" much worse than he did, you know?

Friday July 11, 1970

We were late for the barn this afternoon. Dickie-boy, which is the nickname of Harry I. Fooledya from my first entry and the laziest, smelliest, dirt I've ever seen, was sleeping when Suds announced it was barn time over the intercom. He was still sleeping when we sent Jonathan up to get him. Then, when he's about to put on his boots, he remembers his shoes are outside drying off. He runs and gets them, but then won't unlace them and put them on the easy way. He has to stomp around the room trying to jam his heels into the back of his shoes, which were already smashed down from always putting them on that way.

"Unlace them and put them on right," I told him.

"But I almost–"

"What are you, deaf? Unlace 'em!"

He finally got them on, then his boots. As we were walking out the door we met Suds coming our way.

"You guys aren't going to Catherine Hall tonight," he said to me. "Maybe that will teach you to get out to the barn on time."

I didn't say anything. I wasn't going to go anyhow, but some of the other guys were. That's why I paid no attention later when they gave Dickie-boy lumps and warned him to quit screwing up. He'd better, too, or else he's going to have a mighty sore dome.

Monday, July 13, 1970

Our wardens left on their vacation today, and I'm happier than they are. They've been getting on my back so much it's pissing me off. They couldn't even leave without harassing me one last time.

At breakfast my table ran out of milk before I had had enough. Since Dickie-boy took the last full glass, I told him to get some more. (The guy who takes the last of anything has to get more, partial helpings excluded.)

Dickie-boy was rising to the occasion when Bones told him to sit down.

"Why can't he go get some more?" I asked.

"Because you finished it. If you want some more, you go get it."

If she was watching me that close, then she saw how little I got, too.

"Yeah, I finished it," I said, "but there was so little there it dehydrated before it hit bottom. Anyway, it was Dickie-boy's turn."

So I lied. You can see the reason for little white lies, can't you, Teach? Being out-gunned, we've got to be sly and crafty.

She then did the unexpected and asked Dickie-boy if it really was his turn. I guess my lying is becoming more believable with age. I turned to Dickie-boy, victory at hand.

"Yeah, I guess so," he said.

I couldn't believe it. Yeah, he guesses so?! Victory was ours, and he blew it. What a jerk.

I was bracing myself for Bone's attack when, from my left, came a voice from heaven. "It's not his turn, it's mine."

An out and out lie, of course, but who cares? I turned to see my savior, Joe, one of the new dirt who's been having no trouble fitting in, pushing back his chair.

I smiled. "Well, I knew it was one of you two guys' turn, but I thought it was Dickie-boy's."

Joe grabbed the pitcher.

"Sit down, Joe," Suds said. "Whoever wants the milk can get it themselves."

So they're ganging up on me, huh? The bas–

"But I want some," Joe said, and went and got some. After he poured himself a glass, he handed me the pitcher. "Thanks, buddy," I said, grinning from here to Rome.

See the difference between a good dirt and a Dickie-boy, Teach? Takes all kinds I guess.

Bones gave Joe a dirty look, but I think she thinks he was really telling the truth, so she won't harass him too much. It's me she's after. And Suds too. Why? Who knows? Thank God they're on vacation, though. We'll all get a good break.

Wednesday, July 15, 1970

What a night I had last night, Teach. Thrills and chills, excitement left and right. The best night I've ever had. You could torture me to death right now and I'd still die happy.

What started it was Eddie and I decided to hook out. His girlfriend, Ann, works at Hershey Park and the park had a pool party in Hershey Pool for employees and their guests. I was hemming and hawing about going until Eddie said, "You don't have to stay with us. Roam around. There's going to be hundreds of girls there. In bathing suits. All those tits and asses and–"

He had a point, you know?

Not only was hooking out exciting, but we had to do it with our dairy-man, Sherlock, on duty. His real name's Mr. Muncie. We call him Sherlock because he loves catching guys doing things they're not supposed to. He doesn't squeal on you when he does catch you, just makes you do extra work around the unit and take all his stupid comments about trying to pull a fast one on "Old Sherlock." (He gave himself the name and likes when we use it.)

So with this in mind, and being an idiot, I listened to Eddie and followed him out our window and onto the kitchen porch roof. This was supposed to be less noisy than the creaking floorboards and squeaky doors inside the unit. What a mistake. The roof's made of some crinkly kind of metal that kept "popping" with every step or when just shifting our weight. Not only that, to get to the ground we had to swing over the edge, hold onto the rain gutter, then drop down. All I could think of was slipping, snapping my neck and becoming a vegetable for the rest of my life.

Once down, we became Joe Commandos, running bent over across the basketball court, behind the garage, along the barnyard fence and then onto the 17th fairway of the golf course that borders our unit. From there it was an easy mile jog to the pool.

I've met Ann's friends before, and since none of them excite me, I took off early to go swimming. First I swam across the big U-shaped part, then did laps in the lap pool, then went off the boards and sliding board for awhile, all the time thinking I was probably the only Milton Hershey guy besides Eddie on this hot summer night, cooling off in the refreshing water—all illegally. Quite the thrill, Teach. (And we must remember, all in my imagination, too.) He-he-he.

After about forty-five minutes, I went back to Eddie and discovered some Hershey guys had joined the group. I'd been returning so as not to leave Eddie alone with the girls. But now, with the enemy there, I felt no such obligation. So I picked up my glasses and went on a girl-watching expedition. I walked the entire perimeter of the pool, then sat on a bench near the diving boards and watched the people going off.

And then, all of a sudden, I was sitting forward like a hunting dog trained on its quarry. Because right there, waiting to go off the high dive, was what looked like my dream girl, Lisa. I couldn't believe it. I waited until she did this cute little jump, holding her nose, and swam to under the lights at the ladder before I was absolutely sure. It was her. *AAAAHHHHH!!*

I turned into an immediate schizoid. Part of me was doing those back flip triple spins for having hooked out and found her; part of me was keeping me glued to my seat, making up excuses why I couldn't talk to her; and the loudest part was screaming, "Get up and go talk to her! Or at least get near her! Do something! Come on!!

It took about two minutes of self-abuse before I finally got up. I dashed back to Eddie, dropped off my glasses and hurried back. I couldn't do the intelligent thing, though, and get in the same line as her. I had to do the moron, chicken-shit thing and stay at least a board away. And being blind, I couldn't even check her out very well. My irate side started yelling again. Then I went off the slide, and she the board, and I got to the ladder just before her. Instead of going up first, I swung to the side and waved her up.

She smiled that beautiful smile of hers and said, "Thanks."

I said, "You're welcome," then watched her go up while trying to make it look like I wasn't. Then I stuck my head underwater and screamed. Boy is she ever healthy, Teach.

Two dives later, I did my "back drop" off the high when I knew she'd probably be looking. All it is, is standing with your back to the water and just falling backwards. There's no skill involved–you land right on your head every time–but it looks suicidal and most people won't even think about doing it. Ten minutes later, after a few more back drops with a couple other dives and cannonballs thrown in so as to make it look like I wasn't showing off, I finally got in line behind her. I wanted to say something but what was I supposed to say?–"Hi, I'm a blubbering idiot who's put you above all beings, real or imaginary; will you marry me?"

But it was nice anyway just standing behind her and seeing her curves up close.

Then, all of a sudden, she turned around to look for a friend or something, and like the jerk I am, I looked up and to the side like there was something of interest up there in the pitch black night. What an idiot, huh?

My irate side was ripping into me, when I heard, "Are you the guy who's falling off the board backwards, not using your arms?"

All my sides fainted dead away, Teach. Nobody knew what to do.

I looked into her blue eyes–real pretty, kind of a deep, tropical ocean blue– and thought, "Look at those eyes. Ho-lee shit." I gave her a kind of half-assed nod and shrug, and said, "Yeah."

"Doesn't that hurt?"

A conversation, Teach! Can you believe it? I could have run full force into a brick wall and it wouldn't of hurt.

"Nah," I said. "If you don't have any brains, you don't feel it."

She sort of chuckled and smiled her gorgeous smile. "Well, it looks like it hurts."

"It doesn't really," I said, thinking it would be great if I could get her to do one and see that it doesn't. "All you do is keep real stiff and fall backwards. It's easy. Try it."

Her eyes widened and she shook her head. "No thanks." It was her turn and she started up the ladder.

"No, really," I said. "It doesn't hurt at all. Honest." I was staring straight up, watching her hips move from side to side and thanking God for this moment.

She laughed. "That's okay. I like my back the way it is."

I liked everything of hers the way it was.

That was the extent of our conversation for the evening, except when she was leaving the diving area with her friends she looked up, saw me gawking, and said, "Bye." "Bye," I said, then did my dive and hustled out of the water so I could follow at a distance. She sat down with a bunch of her friends, including some guys who hadn't got wet yet and who started falling all over themselves trying to make intelligent conversation with her. The lucky stupid bastards.

Not bad for a shy guy, huh, Teach? And that wasn't even the end of the night's excitement. Because when we got back to the unit, the basement door we'd asked Gary to unlock after lights out was locked. So were the kitchen and living room windows that Eddie and I had unlocked after supper as back up. That meant we either had to go back the way we came in–which I nixed right away–or wake up Gary.

So we started hitting his window with pebbles and clumps of dirt. I'd just stood up with a nice sizable piece of terra firma when I spotted a blur, inside the unit, passing from the dining room into the kitchen.

SHERLOCK!!!

"Eddie, it's Sherlock!" I said, and sprinted by him toward the other end of the unit. "He's coming out the kitchen!"

Our unit's shaped in a snub-nosed 'L', with the kitchen and dining rooms being at the short end. Eddie and I got to the other side of the long end of the unit just as the kitchen door eased open. Sherlock didn't even shut the door; he just made sure it stopped moving. Then he slunk off the porch and headed around the corner.

We sprinted on tiptoes to the porch. Just as we went through the door we could hear Sherlock scurrying back our way. We ducked going through the kitchen so he wouldn't see us then bolted upstairs and hopped into bed, sweating like pigs. Thirty seconds later Sherlock crept up to our door and stood there. For twenty minutes. One sound and he would have come in. Even after he walked away and the stairway door opened and shut, we didn't move. Good thing, too, because ten minutes later it opened and shut again and we heard his footsteps creaking down the stairs.

Sherlock's the only person I know who's like that. He has to catch you red-handed or he hasn't caught you. Unless he can leap out of nowhere and scream, "Ah-ha!" and watch your eyes pop out of their sockets, it's no fun for him and he lets you go.

Anyway, that was it. What a night, huh? Probably the most exciting night of my life. So far, anyway. Because we got to remember, I've now talked with my dream girl. E-e-e-Y-Y-A-A-H-H-H!

Friday night, here I come!

Saturday, July 18, 1970

Right now I'm heading in for our last day of summer school, my final in advanced math, our last speed reading class, then on to vacation. I liked doing this diary and I'll probably keep at it—sort of, maybe—for the rest of the summer as you suggested. I might sign up for the SPARTAN and yearbook staff next year, seeing as how you're the top dog. If I don't, we'll still have each other's wonderful company for homeroom and then for English Comp, right? (Yeah, I'm excited, too.)

Anyway, thanks for letting me swear and write about whatever I wanted in here. It felt good. And I had fun. See 'ya.

PS: I thought I'd leave you hanging, but then I'm a nice guy so here's what happened last night at town privilege. Nothing. I psyched myself up to go in there and say "Hi," and make sure she remembers the idiot doing the "no brains" dive off the high board, and she wasn't there. Bummer. I hope she's there when I get back.

PPS: If you're real nice to me next year and give me good grades whether I earn them or not, I'll keep you informed of our red-hot love affair. Okay? Okay.

PPPS: Have a nice rest of the summer.

2

That summer I did two things during my thirty days vacation I had never done before. First, every day but seven, I exercised as though the reward was sex. In the mornings I ran three miles, did push-ups, sit-ups, pull-ups, chin-ups, and used my father's bowling ball and bag as a weight to work my shoulders, arms and chest. In the evenings I did sprints, lots of them. This was a continuation of the workouts I started after the Sunday sermon of "giving it a shot." My plan was to be in such superb physical condition that when school started, I could ask to tryout for football and be confident of handling anything asked of me. As far as making the team at the position I wanted to play—wide receiver—I knew I could. I'd always had the hands to do it; I just never had the nerve to try. Now I did.

The only days I didn't workout were the seven days I spent with Eddie at his cousin's place in the mountains of Pennsylvania, forty miles southwest of Elmira. His cousin had just graduated from high school, had a summer job, and Eddie wanted someone to hang out with during the day—a reasonable request considering the accommodations: a lonely cabin beside a man-made pond in the middle of a thousand acres of land his cousin's family owned and partially farmed. Outhouse-equipped, fireplace for heat, radio for entertainment, the pond for baths, guns for shooting, and not one adult to dampen our spirits with rules or restrictions.

It was life on the frontier, made more memorable one afternoon by the rattlesnake that couldn't slither off the dirt road before Eddie ran it into a sloppy pile of coiled snake, flickering tongue, and raspy, threatening rattle.

Eddie suggested catching it, but when I refused to be the decoy, we settled on a solution only the snake disliked: we stoned it to death.

That night, Eddie's cousin told us it was a yellow timberback rattler, male. It measured forty-four inches and had twelve rattles on its tail. I kept the rattle and Eddie the battle-scared skin. The first night back from vacation, Eddie hung the skin from the center of our bedroom ceiling light. Through the bottom most hole in the skin, I looped a string and attached the rattle so it dangled an inch below the tail. Entering the room, you couldn't miss it; obvious, yet cool, a monument to our manhood.

Monday morning, Suds, who had been off the weekend, pounded on our door, opened it, and announced, "Time to get up," like he did every morning. He started to leave, stopped, leaned back. "What's that?"

"That's our rattlesnake skin and rattler," Eddie boasted. "Crazy and I killed it at my cousin's place this summer."

"Take it down," Suds said, and left.

Eddie and I looked at each other. "Jerk," I said. "Asshole," Eddie said.

Eddie thumbtacked the skin onto the two-inch wide corkboard that ran around the room a foot below the ceiling. I hung my rattler over the nose of Snoopy, lying atop his doghouse piggy bank. The rest of the day the thought of how Suds had ordered our trophy taken down gnawed at me. No explanation, not a request, an order. I remembered him taking my piece of cake. No explanations then, either. An attitude I could rely on through graduation?

I took out the sign I'd bought at the Chemung County Fair my last week of vacation. It read, "USE OTHER DOOR." When I bought it, I wasn't sure I'd be allowed to hang it where it would be its funniest–on our door. I tacked it up. Guys would think it funny because there wasn't another door to use. "USE OTHER DOOR." That means *you* Suds. Stay away.

Next morning, after he woke us, Suds swung the door open and jerked his thumb at the sign. "Take it down."

I jumped to the doorway. "How come?"

"Because I said so," he said, and continued around the corner.

I followed. "Why can't we have it up?"

He turned and made a sweeping gesture. "Do you see anyone else with stuff on their doors? It's not allowed."

"I didn't know that."

"Now you do. So take it down."

I tacked the sign to the corkboard above my bed.

"Dickie-boy!" I said, as he walked into the dining room.

Dickie-boy hadn't returned from vacation on Saturday, and no one had told us why. It was Tuesday evening. I was headed outside to do my workout. "A bit late, huh?" I said.

"I don't care. I'm getting out."

"Really?" I immediately thought of his vacant spot being filled by a senior and my troubles with Suds ending.

"My mom's getting re-married."

"Richard?" a woman said from the kitchen.

"In here, Mom."

A small, roundish, middle-aged woman walked into the dining room. She smiled and said, "Hello."

"Hi. Taking your son out of the school, huh?"

"Yes, I am." She looked around, then whispered, "He never liked it here."

I laughed. "Who does?"

I looked at Dickie-boy, thinking it might be better for him if he hadn't gotten the chance to get out. "Well, Dickie-boy, take it easy. Good luck."

"Yeah. Right."

I did my sprints in a happier mood. With a senior hopefully on the way, one of my problems was solved. Maybe it wouldn't be long before football and Lisa would also be positive sides to my life?

"Huey, how you doing?" I said, and slapped him on the shoulder. He was leaning against the railing of the bumper car ride. It was Friday night, a week before school started.

"Hey, bro. Doing fine. Just checking out the girls."

"Any good ones?"

He nodded toward a car zipping by. "That blonde's pretty cute."

"Too bad she's with a guy."

"But she keeps smiling at me. Maybe it's her brother, or maybe she just wants me?"

"Maybe."

Huey was on the football team, and he and the other members had spent the past week and would spend the following week at Camp Milton, the wooded campgrounds with bunkhouse located a few miles from the high school. They slept and ate there but spent the day at the high school in football practice. I knew if I wanted to make the team I should find a way to get out there and talk to the coach. I had spent town privilege looking for team members, passing up one after the other for reasons not justifiable.

"How's football practice?" I asked.

"Hot."

I wanted to ask him to ask the coach if I could tryout, but I didn't. Instead, I compromised. I told myself I would exercise even harder and the first day of class I would walk into the coach's office and ask him myself. It was an excuse, but I couldn't force myself to do what I wanted.

Why? Why couldn't I? Why didn't I have the guts to do what others did without eve thinking about it? What was wrong with me?

I walked into town knowing that if Lisa were working my life would brighten. She hadn't been there the previous Sunday when I checked during park privilege, and she wasn't there now. How could I discover the girl of my dreams, actually talk to her, and now not have the chance to follow up on it?

3

The following Tuesday we had the annual school picnic, what we called the Farmer Olympics, with every student, houseparent, teacher, and official in attendance. At ten o'clock we gathered at Hershey Stadium and had contests of little skill and no daring: three-legged race, backwards race, pie eating contest, and others. Afterwards we walked to the park's picnic area for lunch, then spent the afternoon on the rides.

The teachers and officials were parceled out one or two to a unit. We got a new teacher happy to sit beside Suds and Bones at the head of the table. The picnic tables were long, able to seat two units to a table, and I took the seat in the middle, farthest from the ends. The empty seat on my left belonged to the other unit and didn't have a place setting.

"Gary, pass the mustard," I said, after I had gotten my two ham sandwiches. He was seated to my right.

"What's the magic word?" he said.

"I think it's this," I said, and thumped him on the shoulder.

"Just what I like to see," someone said on my left. "Student harmony."

Brubaker, with a plate, napkin and silverware, was settling in at the space beside me. "I hope there was a reason for that?" he said good-naturedly.

"There wasn't," Gary said. "He just likes beating on guys littler than him."

"He didn't pass the mustard when I asked for it."

"He didn't say please."

"I don't have to; we're on a picnic."

"I'll have to add that one to my list," Brubaker said.

I'd been eyeball to eyeball with Gary. Brubaker said, "Dave, isn't it?"

"Yeah."

"Yes."

I raised my eyes to the ceiling. "Yes. And this is Gary. The squealer."

"I'm sure Gary was merely assisting you in maintaining proper table manners. Isn't that correct, Gary?"

"Yes-s-s-s," Gary hissed into my ear, making me grin.

"So, gentlemen," Brubaker said, "how were your vacations? Anyone do anything exciting? Dave . . . ?"

By the time lunch ended, Brubaker acted as though we had expanded upon a friendship he assumed had started with my aborted run for office. I wasn't so sure. It still felt unnatural talking to him.

Friday, the first day of class, I was the first one in homeroom and found Mr. Hart emptying boxes of books and supplies. While I placed pencils and tablets at each desk, he informed me that we would be doing our diaries for composition class and asked if I had anything interesting to use for the first entry. I told him about the snake.

"Maybe you could submit it to the *SPARTAN* later this year?" he said.

"Maybe." I handed him the remaining pencils and tablets. "Thanks," he said, and smiled in a peculiar manner.

"What's so funny?"

"I was just picturing you and your Miss Wonderful together."

Eureka! "Did you see her?" I said.

He nodded. "She is pretty."

"Of course she is. When did you see her?"

"Just before summer school ended. Has anything further happened?"

"No. I haven't seen her since the pool. I don't even know if she's working there anymore."

"You'd better get moving. A girl like that isn't going to be available for long."

"Tell me about it."

Brownie strutted into the room, grinning and tanned beneath his blond hair. He stopped abruptly. "Look at him, brown-nosing the teacher already. Purenut, you make me sick. If anyone's going to suck up for a better grade around here, it's going to be me. Right, Mr. Hart?"

"No doubt you'll be needing to," Mr. Hart said.

I lay in bed thinking. Why am I such a goddamn chicken shit? Such a spineless, worthless, cowardly worm?

I had walked past the football coach's homeroom eight times during lunch that Friday. The first two without looking in to see if he was there. Then I heard his voice, and the next six times I past at various speeds but never went in. Bolstering myself for the ninth time, the *final* time—as were the last five—I saw him walk out of his room, turn, and head in my direction.

"Stop him! Ask him!" I had told myself as he approached, came abreast of me, then past by.

What a jerk. A gutless wonder. I wasn't worth shit. I *had* to ask him. I *had* to!

B-R-R-A-A-N-N-NG! . . . B-R-R-A-A-N-N-NG! . . . B-R-R-A-A-N-N-NG! . . . B-R-R-A-A-N-N-NG!. . . .

I jumped at the fire alarm sounding; had I been sleeping it would have been much worse. Eddie, a deep sleeper, struggled with the intrusion. I got up and stood over him. "Oh my God, Eddie. Run! Run, Eddie!"

He thrashed about, then sprang to a sitting position. "What? What?" His head jerked from side to side. He spotted me laughing. "Asshole."

We joined the procession headed to the living room, where everyone slouched into chairs or lay on the floor. After the last of us arrived, Suds stopped the alarm.

"Two minutes and ten seconds," he said. "You could all be dead in that time."

At the moment, nobody cared. It was one thirty in the morning.

"We're going to be doing this again real soon. If you guys don't get down here in less than a minute, we'll just keep doing it until you get it right. Got that? Now get to bed."

I stopped on my way out. "Mr. Sawyer, have you heard if we're getting a replacement for Dickie-boy?"

"Not yet."

"Boy, I hope it's a senior."

"That makes two of us," he said.

He said it like the new guy would make all the difference; like life would suddenly be roses for him and Bones; like I wasn't doing whatever the hell he thought I was supposed to be doing.

Up yours, too. You're no bargain, either, asshole.

4

The intercom clicked on. "Dave . . . telephone."

Telephone? Me? It was Saturday evening, seven o'clock. There was no reason for anyone to call me. Unless it was my sisters or father. But they rarely called because long distance cost money and a stamp cost only ten cents. If it was them, something was wrong.

I got up from the mat where I'd been doing pushups, put on my shirt, and headed upstairs. Was it Dad? An accident? Or Maura? Or Lynn?

I past through the kitchen, into the dining room, headed for the office. From the living room where he sat watching TV, Suds said, "Five minutes."

Fuck you. I know we have only five stupid minutes to talk, asshole.

"Dave?" a girl's voice asked, once I said hello.

"Yeah?"

"Just a second. It's him," she said to someone with her.

"Crazy!" somebody shouted into the receiver. "It's me, Carl."

"Hey, Carl. How's college?" Carl was attending Franklin and Marshall College in Lancaster, about forty-five minutes from Hershey.

"Great, buddy, great. That's why I called. Did you know Mike's going into the Air Force next week?"

"No. I knew it'd be soon, though."

"Well, it's now, the poor bastard. Anyway, he's here."

"Yeah?" Mike lived in Philadelphia, not that far from Lancaster.

"Yeah!" Carl shouted back. "He decided to spend his last free weekend with his pal, drinking and chasing women, and we're coming down there tonight around ten thirty to pick you and Eddie up and bring you over to one of the frat parties."

"I don't know, Carl," I said.

"Come on, Crazy, show some balls. This is Mike's last weekend. You're not going to see him again for another two freak'en years."

He was right. If they got drunk, I could always drive back myself. "All right," I said.

"Great. We'll pick you up where the service road cuts through the fairway."

I found Eddie in the upstairs bathroom, kneeling in front of a toilet, puking. Nothing we ate, just a bug of some kind. I told him of our plans and he said he'd join us if he was feeling better. I left to finish my workout.

Our shower was an open, four-by-six foot stall with large showerheads at each end. The water hissed from tiny holes, creating a massage-like, soothing spray. After showering, I liked to close my eyes, drop my head, and let the water beat against my neck, thinking of nothing. Which is what I was doing when the water shut off with a thump.

I didn't move nor open my eyes, only smiled. It had to be Gary. "Whoever turned that off, better turn it back on and they better not burn me when they do."

"You'd better stop using so much water when you shower," Suds said.

I smiled at my blunder and was about to apologize when Suds pointed at the shower floor. "Look at all that water. You must have been in there an hour."

Whenever the drain clogged, the water backed up, and with sixteen guys using the same shower every day, it clogged often.

"The drain's clogged," I said, and stepped out of the shower.

"Or else you're taking too long to shower."

"I didn't take any longer than usual."

"Which is too long. If you had to pay for the water, things would be different. Stop using so much water."

As he walked out of the room, I gave his back the finger. The drain *was* clogged. Besides, he wasn't paying for it either.

At bedtime, Eddie still felt ill. I went to Gary's room. He was the basement bathroom guy that week. I told him about my encounter with Suds and asked him to use a declogger the next morning. "What's in it for me?" he said.

I snared him in a headlock. "What's in it for you? Let me see. How about . . ." and I lowered my voice, " . . . sometime after ten thirty you sneak downstairs and unlock the basement door?"

"You hooking out again?"

"There's no fooling you, Gar," I said, and released him. "So you'll do it?"

"Yeah."

"What a pal. And tomorrow, the drain?"

"Up yours, Purenut."

When the Volkswagen bug pulled into the service road and stopped at the chain link fence, I didn't move. The only person I could see was a girl in the passenger seat. Then the driver leaned forward to peer into the darkness and I recognized Mike.

I walked to his side of the car. He stepped out and shook my hand. "Where's Eddie?"

"He didn't come. He's sick."

Mike held the seat for me. "Come on, get in. This is Beth."

"Hi," she said cheerily. "Here, have a beer." She smiled as she gave it to me, then stayed seated with her arm along the back of the front seat.

"Where's Carl?" I asked.

"Past out," Beth said.

Mike pulled out, headed toward Hershey Park Pool. "We were drinking last night, got pretty drunk, so the first thing Carl does when he wakes up is have a beer to get rid of the hangover. It worked, only he kept drinking and now he's out."

"He had encouragement from some fraternity brothers," Beth said.

"He's in a frat already?"

"Not yet, but he's found one he likes. Drinkers."

"Is that whose party we're going to?"

"Nah," Mike said. "I drank too much last night, and I don't feel like drinking tonight. I thought we'd just drive around and give Beth a tour of Hershey and the Home." He looked into the mirror. "That's all right with you, right?"

"Sure."

"You don't like partying?" Beth asked.

"Beer doesn't taste that great to me. And then I was worried about you guys, especially Carl, getting drunk or getting me drunk and never making it back."

"He's lying, Beth," Mike said. "He knows the women will be attacking him and he might not come out alive."

"I can see that. I know a few sorority sisters that would go after him."

"Yeah, right," I said.

She winked.

I liked Beth. She had a quick smile and a happy spirit. "Where'd you guys meet?" I asked.

Beth looked at Mike. "At the party last night. Carl introduced us. My dad went to Milton Hershey too, and we got to talking, one thing led to another, and here we are." She raised her can of beer. "To Milton Hershey boys. Some of the nicest in the world."

I raised my can. "Choice."

"Exactly," Mike said.

We sat for over an hour on the small white stones that formed the large white letters "WELCOME TO HERSHEY" on the hillside in front of the high school. Then we drove around showing Beth where we grew up, contrasting the clean, manicured, orderliness of the divisions with stories from our past. She'd visited before as a little girl, and we found her father's units as well as ours. It was a relaxed, enjoyable time.

"We should do this again, sometime," Beth said, once we'd parked at the service road and gotten out of the car.

"How about when you get out of basic training?" I said.

"Nope," Beth said, and shook her head. "We're already going to Florida for some fun in the sun."

I knew, and Mike knew I knew, that that would be the first time he ever traveled with a girl. It also meant he probably spent the night before with her—another first we both knew each other knew about. I smiled, he grinned.

Beth wrapped an arm around Mike and squeezed close. "Love at first sight, don't you know."

"That's good," I said.

"We'll do it when I get back from Nam," Mike said.

"All right. Unless I get drafted, then maybe we'll do it there. Otherwise, whatever college I'm in, we'll get together here."

"Deal," Beth said, including herself in the reunion, which made us laugh.

"Well," I said, and stuck out my hand. "Good luck in Nam. Stay out of trouble, and I'll see you when you get back."

"Thanks," Mike said, shaking my hand.

Two years as roommates in the intermediates, and two in the senior division. There was more to say, but what? And how? We knew what the other felt and wished for without saying it. Still . . .

"Oh, come on," Beth said. "Give each other a hug. You're like brothers, for crying out loud. Go on. It ain't going to kill you."

She pushed on Mike's back and my shoulder, until we embraced, then patted both our backs. "There. That's better."

Mike and I grinned.

"Now give me one." She hugged me, then kissed my cheek. "And don't be so shy. You're a nice guy. If you ever come to F & M I'll introduce you to some of my sorority sisters. They'll like you." She winked again and got in the car, which Mike had already put into gear. "Take it easy, Crazy."

"You too, Mike. Good luck. I'll see you when you get out."

"Let's hope so," he said.

Beth smiled reassuringly. "Bye."

"Bye, Beth." I smacked the top of the car and Mike pulled away. As they puttered down the road, Beth leaned over and honked the horn. Mike waved out the window. I waved back.

5

I could do fifty-five push-ups, seventeen pull-ups, one hundred and fifty sit-ups, ten forty yard dashes one after the other and beat any guy in the unit on any one of them, and I still couldn't ask the football coach for a tryout. Time was running out, Suds was getting on my back for the stupidest reasons, Lisa had probably joined a convent, and acne was blossoming on my face like flowers in spring time. What was next, insanity?

My worries created a stop and go sleeping pattern that didn't start till after one or two in the morning. By mid-week, I was so tired I went to bed early hoping the extra half-hour might provide ten minutes of additional sleep. It did, maybe more. Then:

B-R-R-A-A-N-N-NG! B-R-R-A-A-N-N-NG! B-R-R-A-A-N-N-NG! . . .

I jolted up in bed, my heart pounding. What was it? What was wrong? Which way should I run?...

B-R-R-A-A-N-N-NG! B-R-R-A-A-N-N-NG! . . . A fire alarm. A stinking fire alarm!

I plopped back in bed. What an asshole! Would he be like this forever? Was there no stopping him?

A minute! That's all. Get down there in time and he'll lay off.

I sprang out of bed and shook Eddie's shoulder. "Eddie, get up. Fire alarm. Let's get downstairs in time and fartface won't pull any more drills. Come on."

I rushed down the hall, hurrying everyone up and down the stairs. Jonathan past by the stairwell. I grabbed him. "Jonathan, where're you going?"

"I got to go to the bathroom, Crazy. Real bad."

"One or two?"

"Two."

I started him into the stairway. "Not up here, buddy. Suds will give us a hard time, say you didn't make it, you would have burned. Go downstairs in the basement."

"Oh-h-h-h," he moaned.

"Make way for Jonathan," I said, leaning over the railing. "Emergency number two. Make way."

The guys let him scurry past. I ran back checking the rooms, then hustled down the front stairs and into the dining room. I knew I was doing just what Suds wanted, but if it would stop him from pulling the fire alarms, it was worth it.

"That's everybody," I said, as I walked into the living room. I sat beside Eddie. Close, but I was sure we had beaten a minute.

Suds remained at the doorway, facing the stairway, arms akimbo. "That's everybody, Mr. Sawyer," I said again.

"No it's not," he said.

"Jonathan's in the basement going to the bathroom."

"What's he doing down there?"

"I told him to go there instead of upstairs so we'd all be down in time."

"He's supposed to be *here*," Suds said. "Not downstairs."

"He had to go to the bathroom. What did you want him to do?"

"I want him down here first. Then he can go to the bathroom."

"But he had to go," I said. "Sometimes that can't wait."

"Horseshit."

I slouched against the couch. There was no reasoning with Suds. He was always right.

A minute past before Jonathan hurried into the living room. Suds shut off the alarm. "Jonathan, whenever there's a fire alarm, you come down here first, no matter what. You got that?"

"Yes, but I—"

"I know other people think they're the boss and tell you what to do, but don't listen to them. Okay?"

"Okay."

Jonathan sat down, eyes downcast.

"Over two minutes," Suds said. "Half that is what I want."

"What if you counted when Crazy came in?" Gary said. "When Jonathan was downstairs? Was that good enough?"

"Doesn't matter. You've got to be *here*, all of you. What if Jonathan had gone back upstairs? Who'd have known?"

Then it would have been suicide, and we still made it down in time.

"Okay, back to bed."

Upstairs, Jonathan knocked on our door. "Crazy, I didn't–"

"Forget it, Jonathan. It wasn't your fault. If I didn't make you go downstairs you might have been down in time anyway. It's Suds. He's being a jerk."

It took me another three hours to get to sleep, and in the morning, tiredness turned to anger, anger at Suds and anger at myself. I was sick of being bossed around, told what to do and all the rest of it. But most of all, I was sick of being a chicken about asking the coach for a tryout. Today I *was* going to do it.

After lunch I approached his office abusing myself with every vile, disgusting name I could think of. I slowed near his door, went past, then abruptly spun around and charged in. No one was there.

Why me? I meet the girl of my dreams and she disappears. I workout like a madman, suffer psychological damage trying to work up the courage to talk to the coach, and he's not here. Was I going to miss out on my whole life?

I stepped out the door.

"Hey, you!" the football coach bellowed from halfway down the hallway.

I froze. What would I say? A kid he doesn't know, alone in his room? This wasn't how it was supposed to happen.

"Get in here and shut the door," he said, and walked into his room. He began erasing the blackboard. "What were you doing in here?"

"I was coming in to ask if I could tryout for the team."

He stopped erasing. "The football team?" I nodded. "What grade are you in?"

"I'm a senior."

"Why didn't you tryout at the end of last year like everyone else?"

Freud would have trouble with that one. "I don't know," I said. "It's a long story."

He resumed erasing the board. "I'm sorry, son, but that just wouldn't be fair to the other guys. They've worked out all summer, sweated through two weeks of double practices at Camp Milton. They're a team. Bringing someone in now just wouldn't be right."

I thought of telling him how I worked out all summer, too, how I would have loved to have been at Camp Milton, that I'd do anything he wanted to be accepted by the team. But I didn't. He'd still say no, so why bother?

"Okay," I said. "Thanks anyway."

Outside his door my disappointment hit bottom, but only a glancing blow because I squelched it with psychotic, eternal optimism. At least I had finally asked him, right? And I knew all along the longer I waited the worse my chances would be. But what would happen if during the first game our wide receiver revealed the hands of a fish? What if it almost cost us the game? Would the coach then consider giving me a tryout for the better of the team?

I thought so. I hoped so.

We won our first game 24-0, and our wide receiver played well. My disappointment at never being able to play football and in myself for letting it happen, now smacked bottom like a watersoaked blanket. Why had I waited so long?

Because I was a spineless, useless, idiot, that's why.

6

"You're using too much electricity."

"You take too many showers."

"Watch your mouth, Mr. Smartmouth, or you'll be on detentions."

"You don't need that much suds when you do the dishes."

"I'm sick of you not listening to me. If you don't start listening to what I say, you're going to find yourself in a lot of trouble."

I found out from Sherlock, not Suds—he never mentioned it, that we were getting a new guy. A junior, not a senior. From then on Suds never let up. Any annoying comment he could make, he made. If something wasn't my doing, it was my fault for letting it happen. More and more I said nothing in his presence and ignored whatever he said. I didn't look at him. He didn't exist.

I was thankful on Thursday when the weekly bulletin came out announcing swimming practice to start the next day—less time I'd have to spend around jerkface.

After study period Gary caught me heading downstairs for snacks and told me his name wasn't on the list for the swim team. "There's even freshmen on it," he said.

"I guess Coach just missed it."

We were walking through the dining room. Gary whispered, "Do you think Suds will let me go?"

Suds' disposition toward the other guys had been steadily souring as my failure to be the perfect senior continued. He still had moments of normalcy though.

"I don't know," I said. "All you can do is ask."

Jonathan was the only one in the kitchen, a glass of milk in one hand, a cookie in the other.

"Jonathan, you hog, you," I said. "How's it hanging, limp and ready?"

Jonathan jerked his head toward the pantry. Suds emerged carrying a can of cookies to put with the one already on the counter. "Watch your language, Guttermouth," he said.

Suds returned to the pantry, and Gary looked at me. I motioned for him to go ahead and ask.

As other guys entered the room, I filled a glass with milk, took some cookies, and sat on the radiator in the corner.

"Mr. Sawyer," Gary said, once Suds returned with a plate of the previous night's dessert, blueberry pie. "Did you see the weekly bulletin tonight?"

"I put it up, didn't I?"

"Did you see my name's not on the list for the swim team?"

"So?"

"I'm on the team. I guess the coach just forgot to put my name down."

"Then it will be there next week, won't it."

"Definitely," Gary said. "So I can go to practice this week?"

"Not until it appears in the bulletin. That's the rules."

I shook my head. Figures he'd do something stupid like that.

"You got a problem with that, Purenut?" Suds said.

Other guys had been blocking his view of me while getting their snacks; they'd moved and I hadn't noticed.

"Sort of," I said.

"And what's that, Mr. Know-it-all?"

I said, "He was on the team last year, you know he'll be on it this year, it says 'swim team' practice starts tomorrow, he's a member of the 'swim team,' and if you'd call Homelife and ask them they probably wouldn't even care."

"And what if I don't want to call Homelife? What if I just want to go by the rules like every other unit?"

"It's your unit."

"That's right, it is. And until you learn that, life around here is going to be miserable for everybody."

Suds pulled another fire alarm that night. Though I hadn't been sleeping, the jolt of fear I experienced ignited an immediate response.

"Fire!" I popped up in bed and screamed as loud as I could. "Fiiii–yerrr! A freak'en fire!"

I jumped out of bed and bounced Eddie's shoulders into his mattress. "Fire, fire, fire!" I whipped open the door. "Fire! Get out. It's a real fire!"

I slammed open the door across from ours and screamed fire, then ran around the corner and down the hallway, yelling as loud as I could. "Fire! Fire! Get up! Get out! Fire!!" Forget calm and orderly, this was a raging inferno and I was insane with panic. I burst into rooms screaming and brandishing the fire extinguisher I had grabbed from the bathroom wall.

"Come on, get out of here!" I yelled at Joe and Martin, both fumbling with their pajama tops. I stuck my head out in the hallway. "Fire! Get out!" I looked back in. "Fuck your pajamas, Joe, take 'em with you. Just get out of here!"

Martin and Joe swept by me, joining the others scrambling for the stairs, half-dressed and stumbling into each other. I pushed them forward. "Jesus Christ, come on–Eddie's freak'en dead!!!"

I threw back my head and released a county-wide bulletin: "FIIIIIIII–YYYEEERRRRRRRRRR!" Then I replaced the extinguisher and hustled downstairs. It had to be less than a minute from the first clang of the bell. I felt great.

"What the hell was all that about?" Suds said as I entered the dining room.

"What?"

"All that screaming and hollering 'Fire!' horseshit, that's what."

"You wanted us down here in a minute didn't you? Here we are."

Sherlock and Big M, clad in robes and slippers, rushed through the laundry room and into the dining room. "What's going on?" Sherlock said. "Is there a fire?"

"It's this smartass here," Suds said.

"You wanted us down here in a hurry, this is what it takes."

Suds stuck a finger inches from my face. "You do this again, and you'll be on detentions for a month."

"What if there's a real fire? Would you rather the guys burn, or do you want me to mouth off?"

"That's your problem—you're doing too much mouthing off. It better stop."

"I'll do whatever it takes if there's a fire."

"You'll do what I tell you. Now get to bed!" He turned to the others. "All of you, get to bed!

7

The next day, after a sleepless night, I signed up at Homelife to see Kramer. I had to try something, anything, to stop the fire drills. Kramer called me in at two o'clock. "How's it going, buddy?" he said, when I appeared in his doorway.

I'd been in to see him before, but we weren't buddies. "It's going okay," I said, and sat down. "I came in to talk about fire drills."

"Necessary things, fire drills. Lifesavers. I'm a member of the volunteers, and I've seen what happens if you don't get out. Fire drills are very important."

"Yeah, but—"

He held up his hand. "I know they're a pain in the rear, but you have to have them. You just have to."

I shook my head. How was I going to convince this junior fire chief that three fire alarms in two weeks was too much?.

"Did you have one recently?" he asked.

"Last night."

"How long did it take for everyone to get downstairs?"

"About forty-five seconds."

He hitched forward in his seat. "Great. That's excellent time. Really. Mr. Sawyer must have been pleased."

"Sort of. But he's still going to have more. I know he is. We've already had three in two weeks."

Kramer settled back in his seat. "That's his prerogative, Dave. Practice makes perfect, you know. It's not going to kill you."

"But it won't kill him not to have so many, either. We can do it fast enough now. Can't you get him to stop?"

"Dave, it's his unit. I'm sure he has a reason for doing so many."

"Yeah–to bug us."

"No, no. Mr. Sawyer's a reasonable guy. He must have other reasons. Just wait, it'll end before you know it."

I knew going in that no matter how reasonably I asked, Kramer would find a way of doing nothing. That's why I had formulated a second plan.

"Well, I hope so," I said, as though reluctantly giving in. "I guess you really can't have enough of them. Can't hurt, anyway."

His round face beamed. "There you go, Dave. That's the way to think."

"You probably should have so many of them you could do them in your sleep."

"That's right. I wish everyone saw it that way."

"They should. In fact, that's the other reason I came in today. As president, I'd like to pull a fire alarm for our unit."

His smile shortened. "What do you mean?"

"I want to pull a fire alarm without telling the houseparents or second helps."

"Oh . . . ," he said, his smile vanishing into his puffy cheeks.

"I was thinking about it the other night. There's more guys in the unit than there are houseparents, right?" He didn't answer. "Right?"

"Yes, but–"

"And who's more likely to discover a fire if there's sixteen of us and only two of them? Us, right?" I nodded, drawing a nod in response. "And the houseparents have never gone through a fire alarm without knowing about it first. How are they going to react to a real one? We don't know, right?"

"No, but–"

"So if I pulled one and we didn't tell them, it'd be for their own good. For their own safety. Right?"

"Well . . . "

"And I would tell you first. That way you can tell the fire department it's only a drill, and you can be there when the Sawyers come out of their apartment. They'd understand. Like you said, they're reasonable people."

I waited, suppressing a grin at the thought of how reasonable Suds would be after bolting for his life from a raging inferno–just for practice.

Kramer sat forward and cleared his throat. "Well, Dave, you have the right idea. It's important that the houseparents be able to react to the fire alarm. But I . . . " He shook his head. " . . . I just don't think it's the right thing to do."

"Why not?"

"Well . . . it hasn't been done before, and it's . . . It just wouldn't work."

"Yes it will. Just pull the alarm. They'll hear it. It rings all over the unit."

"That's not what I mean. I–"

"And you know what you said, 'Got to have them. They're lifesavers.'"

"That's true. I just don't think the houseparents will appreciate it."

"But once you explained it to them, they would. It's for their own good."

"No," he said, "I don't think so."

"Then why don't you just do it? They do it to us."

"Because it's their job, and it's a safety issue."

"And it would be a safety issue for them. So why not just do it?"

He didn't answer and wasn't going to.

"You said they wouldn't appreciate it. Do you think we do? We don't. But they keep doing it. So why not do it to them? Fair is fair. Or don't you care if they die in a fire?"

He lifted a forefinger. "Let's not lose our temper and say something that'll get us in trouble. You know we care, just like you know why we wouldn't let you pull an alarm. That's the way it is."

"Yeah, it is. And it stinks. We've had three fire alarms in two weeks. I'm sick of them. We're all sick of them."

Kramer didn't say anything, he simply sat there staring at me. We both knew I was right, and that he didn't have the guts to do something about it. None of them did.

I stood up. "Yeah, well, see around, buddy. Thanks for all your help."

Friday night Lower Dauphin had a football game in the stadium. Normally Suds would let us off in town, then we could either walk back to the unit or meet him in the community center's parking lot for a ride back. But that night, as he dropped us off, he told us to meet him in the parking lot. When someone asked about walking back, he said, "Can't any of you understand orders? I said be in the parking lot!"

Not until I looked to see how much time remained in the game and saw the scoreboard's clock did I remember his orders. It was twelve of nine. "Oh, shit!" I said, and jumped up.

"What's the matter?" Huey asked.

Huey's unit was also close enough to Hershey so that they could walk back from town privilege. They could also stay till the end of the game, like we could the previous years. I told him why I had to leave, then hurried down the bleachers.

I ran through the kiddie section of the park, across the bridge spanning the turnpike ride, then past the arcade and outside stage. Running into town, I saw the rotating clock on the side of the bank. Eight fifty-four. The stadium clock must have been fast. I turned the corner at the department store and saw the drugstore–Lisa. I hadn't seen her since before vacation. A quick look wouldn't hurt.

I ran to the window and found my view blocked by a group of elderly people milling through the racks of knickknacks. The clock read five of. Still time. I moved to the door and opened it, hoping to zip in and out. A frail, white-haired lady using a walker and about to leave, looked at me questioningly. I stepped back and opened the door wider. She smiled. "Thank you so much."

Move the walker, pull yourself up, brace yourself, then move the walker a few inches farther. Four complete cycles and the back leg of her walker hit against the second door. She was with the group that had been blocking my view at the window–the group which now stood waiting behind her. One of them pushed open the other door. As she struggled through, I looked at the clock. Four of. I thought of the wagons, some probably already full and leaving the parking lot, causing other houseparents to get impatient. Come on!

The woman stopped just past the door and patted my arm. "You're a very nice young man. Thank you."

"You're welcome."

I glanced toward the counter and still couldn't see. Forget it. I had to get to the parking lot.

Once she cleared the door, I started to release it, then held on because the ladies behind her began filing through without bothering to take it. First man through, I eased the door closed until he grabbed it. "Got to go," I said.

I couldn't cross because of traffic. On the other side I saw the first of the wagons coming down the tree-lined side street of the community center, and I couldn't tell if our wagon was among them. I reached the island halfway across when the light changed. I concentrated on spotting our wagon or the guys in it.

After it past, I saw them. Gary sat in the back seat, which faced opposite the others, window down. "Gary!" I yelled, and waved. "Gary!!"

He saw me, then turned in his seat to tell Suds. I darted back across the street between cars. When I looked up, the wagon was accelerating out of the second turn, headed for the bridge. Gary hung out the back and lifted his outstretched arms.

"Bastard! Fucking jerk."

I walked to the drugstore. Lisa wasn't there. I got back to the unit around twenty of ten and rapped on Suds' apartment door. "It's me, Dave. I'm back."

I started down the hallway. Seconds later their door jerked open. "Where do you think you're going?" Suds said.

Where do you think, asshole? "To bed."

"You missed the wagon."

"Yeah, I know. I yelled as you went by. Didn't Gary tell you?"

"He told me," Suds said, "but you were supposed to be in the parking lot by nine, not at the lights at two after."

I didn't say anything.

He said, "Last year I would have stopped."

"Last year you would have let us walk back."

"That's right."

I gestured in agreement. So things were better last year. So what?

"Why were you late?"

"I was at the football game. I forgot we had to meet in the parking lot."

"Maybe you'll remember if I take your relaxed time away this weekend?"

Relaxed time started the first weekend after school began. It rotated from bedroom to bedroom, one room a weekend, and allowed the two guys whose turn it was to sleep in and skip all chores from Saturday morning through Sunday night. This was Eddie's and my first time that year, and Suds was holding it over my head.

"Yeah, maybe," I said. "And maybe not."

"Why don't we find out then? You'll do Eddie's chores in the barn tomorrow."

In our room Eddie informed me he was milking One-eighty and that she had a ripped teat.

"Figures," I said.

The only thing that could make me feel better right then was using my sister's record player that I had brought back from summer vacation. Just before the seniors graduated, a notice had appeared in the bulletin stating that students could own and use one of the following: a radio, record player, or cassette player. Prior to that only radios were allowed. Shortly after the bulletin came out, during a unit meeting, Suds said we could only have radios. When I asked why, he said, "Because it's my unit, I do what I want." I didn't say anything, but I didn't forget. Rules were rules.

That's why I brought back the record player: to prove him wrong. I didn't have any records of my own so I had to borrow some. I played them every day. Now I couldn't find it. "Eddie, did you take my record player?"

"Nope."

"No kidding around. I mean it. You're not hiding it, are you?"

He got up from his desk. "No. I'll bet Suds took it while we were at town privilege."

"That bastard. Come on, help me check."

We searched our room, then went to everyone else's to make sure no one had borrowed it. By bedtime we knew—Suds had taken it.

8

That night, instead of sleeping fitfully after taking several hours to nod off as I had been doing the past few weeks, I did exactly what I did the night before—I didn't sleep at all. When it was time to get up, my eyes felt like they were swiveling in sockets encrusted with sand. Whenever I blinked I could hear a clicking noise. I was exhausted, strung out, and pissed. Pissed at Suds, pissed at Milton, pissed at life.

Suds was in the milkroom when I went in. "Eddie's milking the left side, middle," he said. "Start with Two-sixty, then One-eight–"

"I already know what cows I'm doing," I said, and picked up two metal buckets, one filled with washing solution, the other holding the strainer cup and paper towels.

"Make sure you clean One-eighty good. She's got a torn teat."

I lifted the milker off the hanging rack. "Did you hear me?" he said.

"Yeah, I heard you. I'm not deaf."

"The way you listen to rules, you'd think you were."

He stood at the sink with his back to me. The bastard. I thought for a moment, then figured, why not? As calmly as I could, I said, "Mr. Sawyer, did you take my record player from my room?"

"I sure did."

"How come?"

"I told you guys we weren't going to have them in our unit."

"But they said in the bulletin we were allowed to have them."

He swung around. "I don't care what they said in the bulletin. This is *my* unit."

"You cared about it last week when you wouldn't let Gary go to swim practice."

He smirked. "That was different." He turned back to the sink.

God I hated that bastard and the power he had over me. And for what? Because my mother had died? Bullshit.

"That's not right," I said.

"Isn't that too bad."

"Yeah, it is. It's so bad I think I'll have to go into Homelife and see what they have to say about it."

"You do that, and while you're there, you might as well ask for a transfer."

Transfers to another unit happened occasionally and occurred at the houseparent's or student's request. I had never considered one until the problems with Suds had started. "Maybe I will," I said.

One-eighty's teat had a two-inch scab, cracked in three places and pink around the edges. I worked carefully, but couldn't avoid being kicked in the hand while I washed her, then in the leg when I checked for mastitis. Each time I retaliated with uppercuts to her belly. I detached the milker, and barely avoided another kick.

"Did you milk her dry?" Suds asked, as I flipped the milker to the other side of the railing, preparing to milk the next cow.

I made my reply seem unconvincing. "Ye-ah."

Suds bent down and probed One-eighty's utter. Her left hoof flashed up and kicked his hand.

"Feels good, don't it?" I said.

"Watch it," Suds said. "You're getting yourself in deeper and deeper, Mr. Wiseguy."

I turned back to the milker. Chalk one up for Mr. Wiseguy.

As my Saturday morning after-breakfast chore, Suds told me to clean all the pitchforks, shovels, and scrapers in the barn. The other barn guys scrubbed the inside walls and washed the windows, inside and out. They finished around ten o'clock. I saw them headed into the unit, and since we always made sure everyone was done before any of us quit, I stuck my head out the door. "Gary, what's going on?"

He shrugged. "I told him you weren't done yet. He said, 'Don't worry about it. Leave.'"

I returned to my work. This shit couldn't keep up. No way.

Two hours later I was on my last shovel, scrapping years of crud off the bent-in and damaged corners with a wire brush. The pitchforks, scrapers, and other shovels leaned against the wall behind me, their metal gleaming. The barn door opened. I watched through the cows' legs until I saw the knee-high green boots. Suds. I dropped my head to my work and didn't look up when he approached. He turned a scraper around to inspect the other side.

"You almost finished?"

"This is the last one."

"You can leave that go. The meal truck will be here soon. Don't be late."

If he didn't want me to be late, why didn't he come out sooner? Asshole.

I dumped the bucket of water, wrapped an arm around three pitchforks, and left.

After lunch I went to our second football game. Because it was an away game, only seniors and band members could go. We won 40-0, and that's when I knew my dreams of playing football were over. The team didn't need another wide receiver; ours were good enough. What depressed me the most was that I think I could have been just as good, only now I'd never know.

The bus dropped me off at the intersection below our unit. I walked back feeling like I never left. A light rain had started. Suds was watching TV with his door open when I reported in.

"I need somebody to scrape the lot. Take Gary and go do it before milking."

The barnyard lot around the feeding bins was made of slabs of cement which we scraped clean with the scrapers, then shoveled into the manure spreader. It wasn't that bad of work, nor was it something that had to be done on schedule. Especially if it was raining and the solid piles of manure would turn to sludge.

"It's raining out," I said, thinking Suds didn't know.

Mimicking a whining child, Suds said, "A little *rain's* not going to hurt you."

In the same voice, I said, "Well if you would of had the guys *doing it* while I was *working* all morning, then it wouldn't have to be *done* now, *would* it?"

"Just for that, Mister, you can do it yourself."

"Just for what?"

"Using that tone of voice."

"It's the same voice you used on me."

He pointed. "Get outside . . . start scraping the lot . . . or you're on detentions. Not another word."

I stared at him with absolute hatred, then left.

I scrapped the lot; milked my cows; got knocked down by One-eighty while Suds watched, my hand landing in cow shit; ate supper; watched TV until bedtime; all the while barely speaking. Anytime Suds came near me, my eyes locked straight ahead. I wanted him purged from my life. I wanted him hurt. I wanted him dead.

Another sleepless night—the third in a row. When I picked up my milker and buckets, Suds said, "Make sure you check your cows; there was mastitis on the filter yesterday," implying somebody let it go instead of hand-milking the section containing mastitis. Did he think it was me? Up yours, asshole.

After second church I found an uncleaned kitchen floor and garbage to be taken out. Only if you were a house guy and went to second church did they make you do the floor and take out the garbage for missing your normal after-dinner chores. My house chores were on relaxed time; I was a barn guy. All I was doing was my dishes.

Before I finished them, Bones strode through the kitchen toward the pantry. "Make sure you clean the floor when you're done. And take out the garbage."

She reappeared carrying two pieces of pie. "Does that mean I don't have to work in the barn tonight?" I asked.

"What do you think?" she said, and continued out the door.

I think you and your fucking asshole husband should have your eyes ripped out, shit-for-brains.

While wiping the floor, having already taken out the garbage, cleaned my dishes, and swept the floor, someone came to the doorway. I looked. It was the biggest asshole in the world, who I looked right through. Fuck you.

Afterwards I laid down on my bedroom floor between the beds—out of sight, out of mind—my arms folded across my chest, one ankle atop the other. I needed sleep. It felt like I'd been up for a week. My eyes fluttered when I closed them. I squeezed them tight, then relaxed. Sleep, goddamn it!

Someone nudged my shoulder. My eyes burned, then fluttered as I focused. It was Jonathan. "Sorry, Crazy. We got to load some hay."

"Okay, Jonathan. I'm coming." He left and I laid back down for just a second.

"Hey . . . Hey!" Someone kicked the sole of my shoe. "Get up." I jerked awake. It was the asshole of the universe. "I called for the barn guys to load hay fifteen minutes ago. What are you, a privileged character?"

I stood up, our eyes met. FUCK YOU. He trailed me out the door, complaining about shit I didn't listen to.

After we loaded the hay, Suds told me to scrape the lot again. "It wasn't done right yesterday."

It was done as good as it always is, asshole, and you know it.

It was three thirty. By four o'clock, milking time, I was still scraping the lot. So what? He wanted it done, I'd take my time and get every piece of his relatives there was to get.

Suds charged outside, bent over and pointed to the space deep under the feed bins that was never cleaned unless specifically mentioned. "Get that crap under there."

Because the scraper wouldn't slide under the bins, I had to walk inside for a pitchfork—a shinny clean pitchfork I spent hours cleaning the day before. "Let's go!" Suds said. "We don't have all day."

I looked at him. Why not, asshole? and continued my steady pace.

When I picked up my milker and buckets it was quarter after four. Suds followed me out of the milkroom, telling me how sick he was of me not listening, not doing my job right, causing trouble, making it rough on everybody.

"Hi, Jonathan," I said, walking by Jonathan, the blubbering Asshole not really there.

I got to the first cow and began washing her, steady and sure. Suds' face was red. "If you're not done when all the other milkers are, you're doing all the supper dishes by yourself." I looked at him. "That's right, *all* of them. *And* clean the dining room." He leered. "How do you like that?" He walked away.

The fat, sickening, putrid bastard. He knew I couldn't finish with the other guys. They were already two cows ahead.

I popped on the milker. Here I was, taking all this shit from the biggest asshole in the world, day after day, and for what? For what?! I didn't even goddamn know.

Right then, I could have killed him. All I needed was permission. No gun, no knife—just my fucking bare hands. I wouldn't give a shit, either.

I imagined his fat, fleshy skin spilling over my hands as I dug my thumbs into his throat. His air would cut off, his eyes bulge, he'd thrash about. I'd squeeze harder. Fuck you, you fucking asshole. Die!

I envisioned doing it twenty, thirty times, and each time it wasn't enough.

"Hey, Crazy!"

Joe was directly opposite me, squatting at his cow. "Hurry up. We're going slow."

If they didn't get done ahead of me, they'd get in trouble. And it wasn't their fight, it was mine. I waved the offer off. "Forget it. Screw him."

"What did you say?" Suds said, walking toward me from a few cows down.

I didn't answer.

"I said, 'what did you say?'"

"I was talking to the cow."

"You just better start hurrying or you'll be doing the dishes by yourself."

"Why should I hurry? You know I can't make it."

"That's not my fault."

"Yes, it is," I said, and stood up with the milker, having finished the cow. "You're the one who made me scrape the lot a second time."

"You should have done it right the first time."

"I did," I said to his face as I stepped by him to One-eighty's stall. "We never do under those bins unless we're told to."

"Horseshit. You're to do under there every time the lot's scraped."

"Then how come we don't?"

"You're supposed to."

"Maybe you just planned it that way so you could give me more work to do."

"Just never you mind. You'll have all the work you need after supper tonight."

As I started washing One-eighty, she kicked my wrist. I leaped up and drove my boot into her stomach.

"Hey! No kicking the cows."

"I'm sick of her kicking me and everybody else. Maybe if we do something about it instead of letting her kick the shit out of us, she'd stop."

He pointed. "No kicking. And watch your mouth. That'll cost you demerits."

"Yeah? Yeah?" I could have killed him. "Okay. All right . . . " I smacked One-eighty on the rump. "Get over there." I shoved her against the railing, squatted and rammed my head into the hollow spot between her thigh and stomach, then jammed my shoulder against her upper leg and ran my arm down along the rest of it to her knee. I pushed up hard with my legs, forcing myself into her, trapping her against the railing. With my head, shoulder, and arm wedging her leg back, and my squat-thrust position holding her still, she couldn't kick me, only try. It was an uncomfortable position and would have been easier to just dodge her kicks. But I had a point to make. I wanted to punish her and show Asshole I didn't have to take shit from everybody and everything.

I washed her utter and teats vigorously, fighting to keep her against the railing. "Watch what you're doing," Suds said.

"I am." I grabbed dry towels, then rammed back into position while drying her off, checking for mastitis, putting on the milker, and while she milked, with Suds watching the entire time. When finished, I yanked the milker off, smiling at how she jumped.

"Watch it." Suds said.

"What? I'm in a hurry, remember? You don't want me to do the dishes all by myself, do you?"

"Just watch what you're doing and don't get smart."

He left for the milkroom. Once he got inside, I jumped up and shouted, "Okay, keep it slow. I'll move it."

I could make it, too. If I rushed like a wild man and they took their time, I could finish same time as them and prove Suds an asshole. Maybe.

I washed and dried the cow beside One-eighty, then pulled a quick stream of milk from each teat into the strainer cup. A yellowish lump appeared on the wire mesh. Straw or mastitis? I rechecked them and yellowish lumps shot out the third teat: mastitis.

Shit! Shit, shit, shit!

Now I had to milk that section by hand. Which meant I lost. It would take longer, and I'd be doing the dishes by myself. Son of a bitch!

For a moment I thought of letting it go, not milking that section by hand, just letting the contaminated milk flow into the milkhouse with all the rest. Who would know? Who would care?

But I couldn't. Just like everything else, I couldn't do what I fucking wanted. Son of a bitch, bastards!

I hooked the milker onto the cow, took the tube for the teat I had to hand-milk, bent it beneath the milker, and lodged it into place to cut off the suction. I started milking the infected section by hand, catching the milk in the strainer cup and tossing it into the gutter whenever it filled.

I stared at the cup and squeezed streams of milk into it, my mind vacant. All I felt was pressure, like I was jammed against an immense wall with nowhere to go. Not up, or around, or anywhere–just a solid mass that smothered everything but the act of squeezing the teat and the rasping sound of milk squirting against the metal cup.

Then I heard, "Well . . . Looks like I know who will be doing the dishes all by his smart-alecky self tonight, don't I?" Suds chuckled as he walked away.

I started trembling. What the fuck was I going to do? I couldn't take this asshole anymore. Not one fucking second more. I wouldn't kiss his ass, and I couldn't take any more of his shit. That was it. I didn't give a shit what happened, I just couldn't take it.

My eyes started watering. Was I crying?! I blinked to clear them and they started to spasm, clicking madly. I squeezed them harder. God was I tired. I opened my eyes and the spasms returned. "What the fuck?" I started to fall, caught myself and stood, my eyes blinking uncontrollably. Was I going nuts? I felt the weight of the strainer. I flicked it downward to empty the milk and lost my grip. It landed in the gutter, in manure. "Shit!" Wouldn't anything go right? I straddled the gutter, trying to stop the blinking with one hand and reaching for the cup with the other. Only then did I remember I was behind One-eighty–only after the blur.

She kicked me just above the left ankle, knocking my foot off the edge and into the gutter. I fell face forward and my left knee slammed into the edge of the gutter then slipped in. My left elbow hit the stall floor, my forearm tearing against the edge. I stopped myself from going completely into the gutter by stiff-arming the floor on the other side with my right hand.

A second kick slammed into my left shoulder. Pain then fear shot through me. I pitched right, away from One-eighty just as her hoof snapped the air beside my head. My back jammed onto the metal loop securing the handle of the bucket. The bucket spilled inwards, drenching me in water.

I staggered up. My knee hurt, my shoulder hurt, my back, my forearm. My clothes stuck to my body–my back soaked with water, my left side covered with shit and urine. My eyes burned. A whimper wheezed through my clenched teeth.

I stumbled against the bucket, reached down and grabbed its handle. I swung it in a wide arc and smashed it down on One-eighty's backside, grunting with contact.

I hit her again, and again, and again. I used every fiber of muscle I had worked so hard on all summer to keep swinging and smashing the bucket down. I wanted to pound it clean through her body. I wanted to smash that fucking wall into a million pieces.

I hit her back, along her spine, against her shoulders. Aiming for her head, I swung the bucket into the pipeline above, breaking it. Milk poured out. She pulled back and tucked her head under the railing. I continued down her back, hitting her with the bucket, kicking her, punching her.

That fucking wall would never bother me again.

With my chest heaving and One-eighty cowering in front of me, I stopped. I stood there a moment, then stepped over the gutter to the main floor. First person I saw was Suds, ten yards away, watching.

The wall returned. I glared at him, my grasp strangling the bucket handle. You want some of this, asshole? Huh?! Come on!! Say something, you big fat ugly prick!

I couldn't stand looking at him, so I looked away and saw Jonathan, then Gary, then all the others, staring. I chuckled, then half-laughed. Those guys probably thought I was nuts. Thought I–

Suds moved, and my head snapped back, my eyes daggers. Ready, Fat Boy? Huh?! Say something so I can bash your fat fucking ugly face in. Come on! Right now! Come on!!

"I think you better go inside now," is all he said.

Two breaths and my rage subsided. I dropped the bucket and walked out.

THREE

1

Monday, September 15, 1971

*W*hew! Talk about lucky, Teach. Here I was, thinking my only chance of getting off easy for going berserk was if they thought punishment might trigger another explosion, and they send me in to Horrible, a guy they could do studies on for abnormal behavior. How was he going to think what I did was crazy? I was worried my little skit would trigger one of his big ones. "Berserk? You want to see berserk? I'll show you berserk . . . " and then he'd rip me to shreds.

But all he did was ask me my side of what happened, nodded a lot, and then said what happened was unfortunate but understandable, and best handled by putting it behind us.

There is one thing they want me to do, however. From their standpoint, it makes sense; from mine, it's no longer necessary. It might prove interesting, though, and maybe even helpful in some way. You'd probably agree with that, huh?

What is it? I've got to go see one of the school's psychologists.

I had never met Dr. Davis, but I always liked him. He was a short, thin, mostly bald, middle-aged guy always wearing suspenders and a smile. He had one of those quick, happy walks that made you think he was moments away from whistling. Once, when I was a sophomore and on my way to the barbershop, I past him in the hallway. We were the only ones in the corridor. He wore bright blue suspenders with yellow flowers and as we past, he smiled and said, "Hi, how 'ya doing?" and it felt like I was being wished a great day, a wonderful past and a bright future. All in that cheerful little, "Hi, how 'ya doing?"

"Hi, Dave. Come on in. Have a seat," he said, the Tuesday after my dance with insanity. "How 'ya doing?"

This time his "How 'ya doing?" had concern in it. Concern stemming from what Horrible had told him, which was probably based on the lies Suds had told. He wouldn't have been informed of Suds' "We expect you to set an example" speech at the start of summer, or of the numerous times since then that I'd been pushed and shoved into a position I couldn't get out of until One-eighty kicked the way clear. That caused me anger and disgust, which produced an attitude of indifference and only brief responses until his good-natured persistence prompted an extended reply.

"All right," I said, sitting up in my chair. "You want to know why it's useless? Because you already know everything that happened. My houseparents told Homelife and Homelife told you. So why should I bother with my side of it? Everything I say is going to be a lie, so what's the use? I'm okay now, why not just leave me go? Okay?"

He smiled. "Feel better, Dave?"

"No."

"You will. Believe me."

He hooked his thumbs into his dark-green suspenders and rocked back into his swivel chair with a look of someone about to enjoy what followed. "First of all, Dave, I don't think everything you're going to tell me is going to be a lie. . . . Most of it will be." He eyed me with arched eyebrows until I grinned, then nodded and resumed. "Secondly, Homelife and houseparents aren't always right. . . . Usually they are."

"Yeah, right."

"And finally, this is my job. They pay me to listen to you guys to see if I can help. Half the time you just need to get something off your chest. You can't do it in Homelife because they know you're lying. And your houseparents . . . That's where most of your troubles stem from. Who's that leave? The teachers and me, and the teachers have jobs to do.

"So why not tell me your version? I'm a reasonable guy; I was a teenager once. What do you have to lose? Besides, we have to talk about something–Homelife's making us."

I shook my head. "It'll take too long to tell my side of it. And half the things I'll forget, then I'll remember them later and it'll look like I'm making it up."

Dr. Davis looked to his left, his right, examined his watch, then turned his hands palms up. "Do I look in a hurry? I'm not going anywhere. Besides, I already know most of what you tell me will be lies, so what's a few more? Come on, Dave, talk to me."

I had a better idea. "I know what I can do. I have a diary I've been keeping since summer school. That has everything in it. How about reading that?"

"I'd rather you told me yourself."

"But this has everything just as it happened. It's easier. I'll talk to you about anything you want, just read that first. Come on, I'm the one with the problem."

He thought a moment then snapped his suspenders against his chest. "All right. I'll do it. But any questions I have you have to answer. Deal?"

I read a magazine while he read my diary. He asked about Lisa and some of the guys. Later he said, "What's the other thing you were going to do as far as 'giving it a shot' is concerned? Besides Lisa?" I told him about football. "How'd that make you feel?"

"I was disappointed, but . . . I can always tryout in college if I want."

"Good attitude. You tried and that's the important thing."

When finished he placed the diary on his desk. "I liked it, Dave. Well written and informative. How are things now between you and Mr. Sawyer?"

"Okay."

"Why the smile?"

Since my attack on One-eighty I hadn't spoken to Suds, or in his presence. Nor had he seen me express any mood other than suppressed anger, bordering the psychotic. I wanted him to fear a relapse. If he didn't want me kicking in his door at midnight carrying a pitchfork and screaming for a pig to slaughter, then he'd better leave me alone. The plan was working, which was why I was smiling.

"I can see its potential, Dave," Dr. Davis said, "but how will it work in the long run?" We discussed alternative ways of dealing with the situation until it was time for his next appointment, then scheduled another meeting for the following week. "By that time," he said, "everything will probably have blown over and things will be back to normal. If not, and you feel like you might blow your top again, come in and see me. Deal?"

Dr. Davis should have struck a deal with Paul, the guy who replaced Dickie-boy. But then who could have guessed that level-headed, just do what you're supposed to and I'll leave you alone, Bones, would declare a vendetta against someone she didn't know and carry it out with the intensity of a piranha? "I'll tell you one thing," she said at supper the night before Paul arrived, "he's got another thing coming if he thinks he can get away with what he did at his old unit. He won't. And he'll be sorry if he tries."

Bones followed this declaration of war with an act of aggravation: she made Paul cook, which placed him in her vicinity morning and night, and she watched him like we watched good-looking girls. "Is this how you did things at your old unit—only half right?" she'd say when she found him doing something she didn't like. "You better straighten up fast or you'll be sorry. I'm not going to take . . . " Yap, yap, yap, yap. Day and night. Every day.

Paul did the smartest thing he could: took her constant harping, said nothing, and did as he was told. It worked. After three days she seemed to let up on him, and even complimented his Saturday morning breakfast of fried eggs. But then he got caught with cigarettes at the football game and was given four weeks of detentions with twenty hours to work off, and Bones started riding him as though he'd been trying to make a fool of her. She promised him he *would* straighten out or he *would* be sorry.

He worked three hours Saturday night cleaning walls, and all afternoon Sunday cutting grass, washing the wagon, washing the outside windows and scrubbing the rec room floor.

"You think you had it tough before. I haven't even started!" Bones told him Sunday afternoon while some of us stood nearby.

When she left the room, Paul said, "Fuck you, Bitch."

As happens with many an explosion, the spark that triggered Paul's was a simple one: he asked Bones where she'd like him to put the butter. I was drying dishes and moments before saw him standing with the butter dish in hand and knew what he was thinking: should he leave it out now to make sure it would be soft in the morning for buttering toast, or put it in the fridge and take it out later? Then he saw Bones watching him and asked the question.

"Where do you *think* I want it?" Bones said.

Paul stared for a moment, then dropped his gaze and let out a deep breath. "Well . . . ?"

"How should I know? Why do you think I'm asking?!"

"Don't you raise your voice to me. You hear me? You ever do that again and–"

Paul screamed, head back, eyes clamped shut, right hand squeezing into a fist. A three-second cry of aggravation and frustration that anyone could see was the result of going as far as you could.

Anyone, that is, except the person shoving him. Bones snatched up a serving ladle lying on the counter. "Don't you *ever* make a fist at me again, do you understand? Do you! Because if you do, I'll hit you so hard you'll–"

Paul leaped to a drawer and yanked out a carving knife. "Go ahead and hit me! Go on! I'll run you through so fast! Bitch!"

Nobody in the kitchen moved.

"As a matter of fact," Paul said, his eyes widening with manic delight as he moved to within inches of Bones, " . . . I think I'll run you through anyway!"

Suddenly Suds was at the door. "What the hell's the–" He raised his hands. "Paul, take it easy. Just take it easy."

The ladle Bones held clattered to the floor.

"Paul, do you hear me?" Suds said. "You hear what I'm saying? Take it easy."

"I'll take it easy when *she* leaves me alone. You hear me? Leave me *ALONE!*"

Bones started trembling. Suds inched forward. "She hears you, Paul. She'll leave you alone."

"She'd better!" He moved back then darted forward, "'cause I can do this any time I want! You got that!?"

Bones' lips quivered in a soundless reply, and Suds stepped a foot closer.

"She hears you, Paul. Now just calm down. You'll be left alone."

"I'd better. She's been on my back since the day I got here, and I didn't do noth'en!"

"I know. I know. You'll be left alone."

Paul looked from Bones, to Suds, then back to Bones. "Okay, then." He lowered the knife.

Suds wrapped Bones in his arms and turned her toward the door.

After they'd gone, Paul picked up the ladle and put it in the wash water. "Whew!" he said, with a nervous smile. He held out his hand–it was shaking. "Holy shit."

"I think she'll get off your back now, Paul," I said.

"I think so too."

We all started laughing.

2

My second meeting with Dr. Davis occurred the week before Paul's snap. His theory of what happened between Suds and me revolved around my being the only senior. Had there been other seniors, they would have spoken up now and then while I remained silent, and the resistance Suds felt would have seemed normal–spread out–and things would not have gotten out of hand.

Two days after Paul gave Bones flashbacks of childhood, I met with Dr. Davis again. Like me, Paul had received no additional punishment and a trip to Dr. Davis, who explained during our session that Bones' unusual behavior toward Paul was a 'taking up of the torch' from Suds. Just like another senior would have relieved me, she was relieving Suds.

"So when you going to call them in to explain the situation like you did to Paul and me?" I asked jokingly.

"Thursday morning. I talked with Homelife and they agreed it was a good idea. I also recommended another senior be transferred to your unit."

"Are they going to do it?"

"I believe so."

"All right, Dr. Davis. Thanks a lot."

Dr. Davis' recommendation was aided by the fact that Bones could not function normally with Paul around. His "I can do this any time!" threat made her treat him like a leper she didn't dare offend, which weakened her role as an all-powerful houseparent and threatened to cause long term instability and rebellion in the unit.

Paul was transferred within a week.

Knowing they'd replace him with a senior, I plunged into a search for someone I liked and who wanted a transfer. Brownie's housemother had been going through menopause for the previous two years and had assumed an extremely ugly disposition; one she seemed to be settling into for life. Noting this, Brownie figured my unit was a better choice and immediately went in, asked for, and was granted a transfer.

Monday, September 22, 1971

Teach, we had a class meeting today that wouldn't even bear mentioning except I know it's going to prove fatal to my health. Our advisor, Mr. Stevens, is certifiable and here's the proof: he wants 100% attendance at our Halloween dance. Did you hear that? 100% at one of our dances. That's like expecting us not to complain when you give us those wonderful poems to analyze. It won't happen.

Why? First of all, some guys are liable to be sick or on detentions and won't be able to go. Second, not everyone will be able to get a date. And most important of all, number three, not everyone will want to go. Like me.

Why? you ask again. Because other than Lisa, who's no longer around, there's no other girl I know of that I'd want to take. And I don't, repeat DON'T, want another blind date. The last one was a jerk of jerks, and I ended up wishing I hadn't gone. Blind dates make me sweat weeks before I have them. In fact, a drop just rolled down my side because I've been writing about them.

God, I hope he doesn't get 100% attendance. Pray for me, will you?

"Pay attention please," Mr. Hart said. "Mr. Stevens asked me to pass this around and return it today. It's self-explanatory. Mark the appropriate box and pass it on."

This was the day after our class meeting, and it was a sign-up sheet he was circulating. We had two choices: "getting own date" or "would like a date provided." I past it on without marking either. Moments later, Brownie said, "Hey . . . , Purenut didn't check a box." He waved the form in the air and grinned at me; I scratched my head with my middle finger.

Once the sheet reached his desk, Mr. Hart said, "Dave, you didn't make a selection."

"Hey, that's news," Brownie said.

"I don't want to go."

Jeers and chicken-squawks filled the room.

"Then why don't you return the sheet to Mr. Stevens. He'll want to talk to you."

On my way to deliver it I ran into Huey, who was in Mr. Stevens' homeroom. He took the sheet without asking questions. The next day Mr. Hart told me Mr. Stevens requested I drop by when I get a chance. Two days later, that chance still not having arrived, Mr. Stevens walked into our class during study period and asked for me.

"There's the chicken right there," Brownie said.

"Dave, could I talk to you outside a minute?"

Once in the hallway, Mr. Stevens said, "How's it going?" We'd never met before–he was a math teacher for shop guys–and his statement was more of a greeting.

"All right," I said. "How about with you?"

"Fine." He waited, an expectant look in his eyes.

After ten years in the Home I had learned not to answer unasked questions; in a situation like this, I had the patience of quicksand.

Five seconds past before he held up the form. "You didn't sign the paper I sent around to all the seniors."

"I know."

He waited some more. Ten seconds past. "Why didn't you sign it?"

"I don't want to go."

"Why, Dave? We're trying to get one hundred percent attendance. You don't want to spoil that, do you?"

"No. But I also don't know any girls, and I don't want to take a blind date and end up with a jerk like I did last time."

"You don't know one girl you could ask?"

Lisa. My lovely Lisa. But where had she gone? "There was one, but she moved or died or something. So that means there's nobody."

"Then how about a blind date?"

"I don't like blind dates," I said. "They make me sweat. They make me want to throw up. Okay?"

"Come on, Dave, I'm being serious."

"You don't think I am? Look at this . . . " I raised my right arm, exposing a sweat ring the size of Alaska. "And this . . . " Texas lay under my left. "Before you showed up, it was the Mojave Desert under there."

"But what if you get a cute girl? One you like?"

"I've heard that before. It never happens."

He ran his fingers through his black curly hair. "You're going to be the only senior not signed up, you know that, don't you?"

"You mean there's not one other guy who said, 'Thanks, but no thanks?'"

"By the time I'm done, there won't be."

"Sure, Mr. Stevens. How many didn't sign up? Ten? Twenty?"

"Eighteen. But I've already reduced that to fifteen. Soon it'll be zero."

"Soon it may be one, but not zero."

"Okay," he said. "When I get this down to one, I'm coming back to change your mind."

"Maybe and maybe not."

On Friday night Hershey High played Palmyra in Hershey Stadium. When Jim, Brownie, and I reached the stadium, Brownie suggested we sneak in over the fence. I seconded it. Jim grunted his disapproval.

"Okay," Brownie said, "you pay, and meet Crazy and me on Palmyra's side."

Hershey Stadium sat twelve thousand and was built during the Depression, as were the high school, the Hershey Park Pool, the community center, the Hershey Bears Hockey Arena, and other buildings with the same solid, sturdy construction. Beneath the stadium's seats stood the wooden concession stands. An eight-foot fence encircled the stadium and football field.

Brownie and I found a secluded spot to scurry over the fence, then met Jim near the concession stands. We walked up the ramp and out to the railing that bordered the cinder track surrounding the football field. This was our favorite spot during two other school's football games—as close as we could get to the cheerleaders. We rarely ventured into the stands unless it promised to be a good game. Since both teams had losing records there was no need to abandon our girl-watching positions. Except for one: there were more cheerleaders on the other side, and they could be prettier cheerleaders, or hornier cheerleaders, girls willing to make eye contact or talk to us or make any move that boys like us dreamed of.

Front and center on Hershey's side proved no better except for the tall, slender, dark-haired cheerleader standing near the twenty yard line. From a distance she looked just my type, and an awful lot like Lisa. Could it be?

I told Brownie and Jim I was going to the bathroom, then walked beneath the stands to the third to last ramp leading out to the track. Shrill voices floated toward me: "First and ten, do it again! First and ten, do it again! . . . " A blond cheerleader hopped sideways into view. She'd been next to last. The cheer ended. I moved to the opening of the tunnel and looked left.

Lisa.

Face flushed, her chest rising in deep breaths beneath her woolly cheerleader top, she hung her head then flipped her thick chestnut hair back and gave it a shake. She swooped down, picked up her pompons and trotted over to join two other cheerleaders, her slender legs moving as gracefully as a deer, her calf muscles slightly accentuated. Boy, was she pretty.

And then she smiled. A sincere, full of delight smile. "Man!" I said aloud.

After their cheer, she walked back to her station and stood, back to me, watching the game. Even from behind she looked gorgeous.

What should I do? Show myself, hoping she might recognize me from the pool? . . . Nah—she wouldn't recognize me. Should I go to the railing and gawk at her like some love-struck idiot to show my interest? . . . Nah—she'd just think I was some horny jerk staring at her and would rather I didn't.

Then what the hell should I do? How were you supposed to meet a girl if—

"Hey!" Brownie said, making me jump. He and Jim had been cruising along the railing. "You said you were going to the bathroom. Who you looking at?" He eyed the cheerleaders.

"I'm not looking at anybody. I went to the bathroom, came up here and was just checking out the cheerleaders."

"Sure, Crazy," Brownie said, watching Lisa. "Isn't that the chick that works in the drugstore? Damn she's nice. I'd like to grab her pompons."

Jim motioned toward Lisa with his head and raised his eyebrows. I shook my head, then stopped as Brownie turned. "Got the hots for her, huh, Crazy?"

"No, I don't have the hots for her. I was just—"

"You don't have the hots for her?"

"No, I—"

"He's queer, Jim," Brownie said and threw out his arm to draw Jim back. "Anybody doesn't have the hots for her is queer."

I started to admit to the 'hots' for her, changed my mind and decided I didn't have to admit to anything. "Up yours," I said.

"See? I told you he was queer."

The crowd roared and the P.A. announcer's voice echoed across the stadium, "TOUCHDOWN!" Jim and Brownie looked toward the far end of the field. I stared at Lisa. She jumped into the air several times with her pompons above her head, did a cartwheel, went down into a split, zinged right back up to leap into the air again, high-kicked one leg, then held both pompons aloft, shook them and smiled her gorgeous smile.

Now there was a girl I could take to the Halloween dance. If only I had the balls to ask her.

3

Friday, September 26, 1971

Just so you know, the bluish-red lump on the side of my head isn't another pimple emerging. It's where some chicken-shit bastard from Cumberland Valley punched me after the game last night. I wish I could say, "Yeah, but you ought to see the other guy," but I can't. I never saw him.

It's all my angel Lisa's fault. She was at our game last night, in tight jeans and fuzzy sweater, and after watching her for four quarters, I was hooked and just kept following her like a zombie until somebody yelled, "Hey, cow, eat shit!" and I found myself on their side of the parking lot. Being a chicken-shit bastard myself—though a smarter one—I yelled "up yours" and did a U-turn and made it almost to our side when I crossed paths with a bunch of their guys trailing after Jonathan, harassing him and making him go the wrong way. I stopped him, they got to harassing me, some of our guys showed up, some of theirs, more of ours, and then a snub-nosed, squatty, Elmer Fudd look-a-like referred to Jonathan with a racial term, which caused me to call him an asshole, to which he pushed me and said, "Yeah?" to which I said, "Glad you agree," and pushed back, and when he return pushed I grabbed his arm and yanked him into the mob behind me where he disappeared like a bug in a swarm of ants. That's when the invisible man's fist smashed my head and I ducked and got knocked over by the charging mob.

The brawl ended shortly thereafter when Horrible showed up pulling guys apart and screaming if anybody wanted to fight they could fight him and he'd rip their limbs off. Being all chicken-shit bastards, nobody took him up on the offer.

When I was knocked down my glasses got knocked off and trampled. I was sent to the eye doctor's on Tuesday for a new pair and on Thursday to pick them up. I was surprised with their color and design—they actually looked stylish. This bolstered my confidence, and that night, I deliberately missed the after-practice bus at Catherine Hall, declined the coach's offer for a ride, and set off on the five mile walk to the unit, through Hershey, via the drugstore. Maybe Lisa worked during the week? If so, there would be no better time to meet her.

When I looked in the drugstore window, I froze. The ponytailed girl behind the counter turned around, tore the receipt off her pad and placed it in front of the two women sitting there. It was Lisa, in all her glory. And me, all alone.

I took the last seat on the right. The two women waddled to the register at the other end where Lisa stood tidying up. I watched her run a dish cloth between silver canisters, align them, then wipe each top making sure it was securely shut, all as the ladies approached. She turned, smiled, and had a laugh with them while she took their money and made change. She wore a white blouse and a brown skirt that reached to just below mid-thigh, with a small blue apron in front. On her feet were white moccasin shoes with blue beads along the front edges.

I was still staring at her when she wished the ladies good night, reached into her apron and started toward me. I ducked my head down.

What should I say? What do I want to order? Should I say "Hi?" Should I mention the pool? Should I stand up and pledge undying devotion? Here she comes! How's my hair look? Are there zits all over my face? *Should* I say "Hi?" Should I look up surprised in a funny kind of way? . . . or casual? . . . or maybe even suave? . . . Yeah, right, that's a laugh. Here she comes! AHHHHHH!

"Hi," she said.

"Hi," I answered. Her beautiful blue eyes and sparkling smile beamed just for me. I couldn't take it; I dropped my gaze to the counter.

"Can I get you something?" she asked.

"Ahm, yeah . . . ahh, I'll have a ah..ahmmm . . . " I didn't know what I wanted, or even how much money I had. I'd only counted it five times on my way from Catherine Hall, but now I couldn't remember. " . . . What do you have?"

She pulled a menu from the stand in front of me. "Here, call me when you're ready."

"Ehn," I said, Jim-like, embarrassed that I didn't know what I wanted, that she had to give me the menu instead of me taking it myself, that I didn't know how much money I had, that I had a speech impediment, that I hadn't a brain.

"Take your time." She smiled and returned to cleaning.

God, what a girl! I was being an idiot and she was being nice to me. If only I had the guts to ask her out and she'd say yes. Damn would that be something.

I felt the change in my pocket and remembered I had four quarters and two dimes. Let's see . . . a dollar for a tip wouldn't leave much . . . so I'd order just a scoop of vanilla. I saw the Showboat Delight on the menu and suddenly had my opening. The dessert read "your choice of dry or wet nuts." I had always wondered what 'wet nuts' were. Now I could ask my darling Lisa. What a conversation starter! What a genius!!

Lisa was standing on her toes, reaching over the canisters and scrubbing a spot on the ledge above which held bottles of nuts, sprinkles, cherries and whatever. I waited and watched. One foot lifted off the floor, then began jerking in small circles as she rubbed. Her ponytail swayed between her slender shoulders and against the white of her blouse. Her back angled down to a small waist, and her firm, round backside shook beneath her skirt as she rubbed and rubbed that wonderfully dirty spot.

"You ready?" she asked.

She was looking at me, looking right at her butt.

I nodded, then moaned. What a jerk! Now she was going to think I was some hornball just sitting there looking at her butt.

"What would you like?" she asked, pad ready.

"I was waiting till you got done," I said. "I wasn't in a hurry, so I didn't want to bother you."

She shrugged. "I can clean anytime."

"Yeah, I know, but . . . it wasn't like I was holding off just so I could stare at you, cause I wasn't. It probably looked like I was, but I wasn't. I mean I was looking at you, but I was just waiting till you got done. And I wasn't looking just at what it looked like I was looking at. I just happened to be looking there when you looked over and–"

She chuckled and patted my arm. "That's okay. I believe you."

"Really?"

"Yes. Now, what would you like?" I glanced at the menu, raised my eyes to ask about the nuts, and she added, " . . . to eat."

My face flushed. She laughed. "Sorry," she said. "I couldn't help it. Go ahead, what do you want?"

A sense of humor and everything–she was getting even better!

I said, "I know what I want, but first I wanted to ask about something I saw on the menu. It says 'your choice of wet or dry nuts.' What's the difference?"

"Dry nuts are chopped up walnuts. Wet nuts are in a kind of sauce. I don't know the ingredients, but you can taste them if you want. Would you like some?"

She seemed eager to give me a sample. "Sure," I said.

She dipped a wooden spoon into one of the smaller canisters and brought it back with one hand beneath it. "Open up," she said. I did what I was told. "There," she announced happily, and withdrew the spoon.

One exploratory taste and I gagged and grabbed for the napkins. It tasted like bitter, green, pulverized wood.

Lisa started laughing.

I spit the mix into the napkin and wiped my tongue with another. "That's disgusting," I said. "It's sickening."

Lisa held her stomach as she laughed. She stopped long enough to say, "You like it?" then burst into more laughter.

It took her half a minute to stop. I didn't mind because now it was okay to watch her. Finally she took a deep breath and smiled. "I don't like that stuff either, but I like letting other people taste it."

"I can see that."

She readied her pad. "So what would you like?"

Back to reality. "I'll just have a scoop of vanilla ice cream. In a dish."

"You don't get nuts with that," she said.

"I know. I don't have enough for something that does. I was just wondering."

When she returned, the dish contained an enormous mound of ice cream covered with dry nuts. "What's that?" I asked, worried I might not have enough money.

"That's a scoop of vanilla ice cream."

"One scoop?"

"Yeah. A big one, but just one."

"But the nuts, I–"

"You're allowed to sample the dry nuts, too. I just put yours in there."

I didn't know what to say.

"Okay?" she said.

"Yeah, sure. Thanks."

"You're welcome. I had a good laugh."

She moved to the other end where a man had just sat down. While she got him coffee, I pondered the idea of asking her to the Halloween dance. For a minute I was psyched for it and confident I could. But by the time she had finished and began wiping the counter, I knew I wouldn't. Not right then. I was too chicken. And I didn't want to ruin any chance I had of gradually getting to know her and then asking. If I asked her then and she said no, that would be it. I'd be branded 'reject' forever.

But I had spoken with her. If I could just talk with her more, what a start that would be.

I watched her wiping the counter, leaving large, gleaming circles in her wake, and thought about what to say. Being at work, would she have time to chat? I should get to the pool party as fast as possible. At least I wouldn't be stuttering and stumbling over that. But how to start without sounding like an idiot?

She was almost on top of me when I spotted my opening. "Do you know what time it is?" I asked.

She looked behind her, at the clock above the register. "Six thirty."

"Thanks. Didn't know it was there."

She brushed hair from her forehead, exhaled, and sat on a stool on her side of the counter.

"Tired, huh?" I said.

"Yes."

"From what?" This was perfect!

"School . . . practice . . . now this, and when I get home, I still have to study for a test."

"Wow, busy little devil," I said.

"Too busy."

"What kind of practice?"

"Cheerleading. We're learning new routines and it's kind of tiring doing it over and over."

"Doing lots of kicking?"

"Some."

"That's good," I said. "I like watching cheerleaders kicking."

"You do, do you?" she said.

Billy Bold became Bob Ball-less, and I lowered my eyes. "Well, not just kicking. I like watching them do anything. They can stand there and not even move. It beats watching our cheerleaders, anyway."

"You're from Milton Hershey, right?"

"Yeah. Which is why I like watching cheerleaders."

"Or waitresses," she said.

I smiled, embarrassed. "Yeah."

Maybe she liked that I had been ogling her? Yeow!

"How come you're here now? I thought you guys were always locked up."

"We are. I missed the bus after practice tonight so I walked back."

"Football practice?"

"No. Swimming."

A lady sat down beside the man at the counter. While Lisa waited on her,

I gave myself a pep talk and as soon as she returned, I jumped in. "You know, I don't know if you remember, but we kind of met before."

"We did? When?"

"This summer. At the Park's employees' pool party. We even talked a little bit."

"Really?" She tried to remember. Even with a furrowed brow she looked cute.

She saw me grinning. "We did not," she said.

"Yes we did. Just because you don't remember doesn't mean we didn't. It was something special for me. I'll always remember it."

She smiled. "You're making this up."

"No, I'm not. I'm the guy who was falling off the dive backwards."

She studied my face. "Really?"

"Yep. I can tell you what we talked about. I told you how easy it was and how to do it–by just relaxing and falling backwards. I tried to get you to do it, too, but you wouldn't. You said you liked you're back just the way it was. And I said I liked everything of yours the way it was."

"You did not," she said quickly.

"Well, I was thinking it."

We grinned at each other a moment, then I had to look away. She was just too gorgeous, especially when she was smiling. Her blue eyes radiated joy that seemed to touch her soul.

"You finished?" she said.

My dish was empty. I wished it wasn't. "Yeah."

She pulled it to her side but stayed seated. "Will you get in trouble for missing your bus?"

"Nah. My houseparents are pretty good ones. I had to walk back. That's punishment enough."

"That's nice."

I laughed.

"What?" she said.

"You think it's nice that I had to walk back and got my punishment."

"That's not what I meant. I meant it was nice your houseparents wouldn't punish you."

"I know. I laugh at a lot of things like that. I got a weird sense of humor."

"That's nice," she said.

Two women approached the counter. I said, "Could I have a glass of water, please?"

"Since you said please, I guess so."

The faucet was near the register. As she got it, I slipped a quarter and two dimes beside the plate, then walked over and drank the water while she rang up my bill. Her fingers touched mine as she gave me change. "How was the ice cream?"

"The best I ever had," I said. "And thanks for the nuts. Both kinds."

She smiled. "You're welcome."

I floated back to the unit. Nothing could have bothered me then. Not even Bones blaming me for something another guy did. I simply informed her it wasn't me and how I knew it wasn't. She said she was sorry. "That's all right," I said. I'd met the girl of my dreams. Life was beautiful.

4

The third Monday in October was an Indian Summer day, warm and gentle. As we rode up the high school hill, the countryside unraveled below us in bright autumn colors. Leaves blew across the road and trailed behind us. Though I hadn't seen Lisa since the drugstore episode–nearly a week and two Fridays before–I knew I eventually would. Other things were going well, too. With Brownie in our unit, Suds and Bones were returning to normal. I hadn't heard from Mr. Stevens about the dance, which I took as an indication he was having trouble getting the other holdouts to go. In football we were still undefeated, and I knew I could always tryout in college. My classes were going well.

I scrambled out of the back seat whistling. I was still whistling when I past the glass case outside Brubaker's office where they posted a copy of the daily bulletin. A guy I knew only as being another senior, walked away from the case, saw me and said, "Hey, you going to the dance?"

I stopped whistling. "Huh?"

"You should," he said, and headed down the hallway I'd just come up.

I continued toward my locker. How did he know I wasn't going to the dance? Was he in Mr. Stevens' homeroom? Why would he even bring it up?– we hardly knew each other. Why would he care?

"Crazy, old buddy," Huey said, and plopped an arm across my shoulders. "How come you're not signed up for the dance yet? You going?"

"What's going on?" I said. "You're the second guy who asked me that already."

"You're in the bulletin," Huey said. "You and twelve other guys. It says we're supposed to encourage you to go so we get one hundred percent attendance."

"You're shitting me. I don't believe it."

"Nope. Why don't you just walk up to some girl you like at a game or on town privilege and ask her?"

"Because you need elephant balls to do that."

"Mine are big, but they're not that big."

"You're doing that?" I said.

"You know that new drugstore girl?"

"The tall, thin one with brown hair and blue eyes who's cuter than shit?"

"That's the one. Next time I see her, I'm asking."

I was amazed and worried at once. Huey would definitely ask her, so I'd better next chance I got.

We'd reach the steps that led down to the cafeteria and up to the second floor. Huey started up. "If she goes with me, I'll let you have a dance with her."

"Okay. And if I ask her first, vice versa."

"Okay, bro," Huey said, and smiled. "One of us handsome dogs ought to be able to snag her."

In homeroom, I stared at the last item in the bulletin, back page. "Below are the names of those students who have not yet signed up for the senior's Halloween Dance. We ask that everyone encourage them to participate so that the senior class can continue its unblemished record of 100% attendance at all functions." Signed: "Thanks for your help. Mr. Stevens, class advisor."

What bullshit. This was our first function as seniors, so how could we be continuing anything? The sneaky bastard.

Dr. Davis leaned back and hooked his fingers into his red suspenders. "So, David, things back to normal at the hacienda now that Mr. Brown's arrived?"

"Almost."

"That's good. What else is new? Anything?" He didn't smile, but nearly did.

"Here we go," I said. "One more person who wants to know why I haven't signed up for the dance yet."

"Well, now that you've brought it up, why aren't you going to the dance?"

I knew there was no use resisting. "I didn't sign up because I don't know any girls to take and I don't want to take a blind date because every time I do I get nervous and sweaty weeks before it happens and it's not worth it."

"Did you ever have a girlfriend?"

"Nope."

"How many blind dates have you had?"

"I don't know; six or seven, maybe."

"Did you like any of them?"

I nodded, remembering back to ninth grade and my first blind date–Joan, at a unit party. "Yeah, the first one."

"Why did you like her?"

"Because she was kind of cute, and thin, and she had a pretty good sense of humor. Stuff like that."

"And . . . ? What happened?"

Joan was a mistake I worried I'd be paying for until Death stepped in. "I was a jerk," I said. "She was a year older than me and I didn't have her address– though I knew I could get it–but I didn't, and I never followed up on her. She just broke up with another Homeguy that was a junior and I figured they'd get back together or something stupid like that. I was a jerk, I admit it."

"I wouldn't say you were a jerk necessarily, but it couldn't have hurt to try."

"I know. If I ever get the chance again I will."

The thought of missing out on Lisa like I missed out on football struck me then. I *had* to ask her out.

"What about the other dates?" he asked. "None of them appealed to you?"

"Nope."

"How come?"

"Well, the last one was a jerk but the others . . . I don't know. They either didn't look cute to me, didn't have a sense of humor, or we just sat there all night not talking, and that's no fun."

"That's true. But none of that's so bad. Why do you get nervous and sweaty thinking about blind dates?"

"Come on, Dr. Davis, let's not do this. Who cares?"

"I do. Examining your feelings is good therapy, Dave. Trust me. These symptoms, why do you think you get them?"

I answered in one breath. "Because I don't know what the girl's going to be like and I'll probably end up sitting there like a jerk all night and not talking and feeling uncomfortable."

"So?"

"So, I don't like it. I'd rather not do it. I'd just rather not go."

"But you might meet a girl you like, Dave, like your first blind date."

"But I'll probably get one that I don't, like all the rest. So why bother?"

"Because it can't hurt to try, that's why. What's the worst that can happen—you sit there and don't talk. So what? Just think if you meet a girl you really like?" He raised his eyebrows, widened his eyes, and grinned. "They can be a lot of fun."

"I know. I'd rather just wait till college when I can meet the girl in class or something and act normal."

"You have to live for today, Dave, not tomorrow."

"I know, it's just . . . I just don't like that blind date crap, that's all."

"The more you do it the more you'll get use to it."

"Okay, you made your point. But I still don't want a blind date. I had one last time. I'll take a break this time and try again next time."

"Deal," he said. "But what about a girl you know, then? One that . . . wait a second. What about that girl in your diary? The one in the drugstore? What's her name? Lynn or . . . "

"Lisa."

"That's the one! What about her? She'd be one heck of a date, huh?"

"Yeah, but—"

"No buts, Dave. You like her, don't you? You'd like to go out with her, wouldn't you? Why not ask her to the dance?"

It took me a few seconds to admit the truth. "Because she's just too good-looking. I don't have a chance with her."

"How do you know that? She's a girl, you're a guy, what else does it take?"

"Half the guys in school like her, and in her school too, probably. I'm a moron; what chance do I have? Even on a good day I don't look that good. And–"

"Hold it right there. I'm going to set you straight on something." Dr. Davis came around the desk and sat on the edge. He grabbed a gold-framed picture near the corner and flipped it around. "See that? That's my wife and kids. What do you think?"

It was a backyard picture. Summertime. His wife, seated, was smiling at a baby she held under the arms with its toes touching her lap. The baby was turned to face the camera and giggling. Beside them stood a son and daughter, six and three maybe, also smiling. "Nice picture," I said.

"What about my wife. Do you think she's attractive?"

There was no doubt about that. "Yeah, she's good-looking," I said.

He struck a pose. "And what about me? Tall . . . well-built . . . fashionably dressed . . . dashingly handsome . . . " He ran his hand over his balding head " . . . thick, golden locks. Just the type you'd expect to be with a woman like that, right? What did I have to offer her? Huh?"

"I don't know. You married her, didn't you?"

"Exactly! That's my point. Girls don't care as much about looks as guys do. They're more intelligent than we are. It's what's inside that counts. Your personality, whether you're a nice guy or not, funny, considerate, kind–stuff like that. Sure, looks matter, but if you got all the other stuff, as long as you're not Frankenstein, you can win them over." He gestured. "Even a jerk like you has a chance with a girl like Lisa." I laughed. "It's true. You're maybe a bit odd but you're a nice guy, right? You're sort of funny; and you don't look too, too bad– you're not Frankenstein. What else do you need? And you've talked to her already, right?"

"Yeah."

"That's half the battle, getting to meet them." He returned to his seat. "Now all you have to do is talk to her some more and show her what a nice guy you are. Have you tried?"

"I already seen her actually. About two weeks ago I missed the bus after practice, walked back, and stopped in to see if she was there. She was."

"Did she remember you?"

"No."

"But you talked to her, right?"

"Yeah."

"For any length of time?"

"About . . . " I began to grin. " . . . ten, fifteen minutes, maybe."

"Fifteen minutes! She's in love with you, Dave."

"She is not."

"I'm telling you, she is. Holy Moses. Why didn't you ask her then?"

"I was going to, but I chickened out. I figured I'd get to know her better first."

"But that's a perfect way to do that, and a reason to ask her out."

"I know. It's just . . . I don't know."

"Dave—fifteen minutes. A girl won't spend fifteen minutes talking to you if she doesn't find the experience pleasant. Especially if she can say, 'I got things to do,' and leave. Right?"

"I guess so."

"Which means she enjoyed herself, don't you think?"

"Probably."

"Which means there's a good chance she probably likes you. Did you get that impression?"

"Sort of. She was smiling a lot and laughing, anyway."

Dr. Davis stared, open-mouthed. "Dave!" he said, and bounced his palm off his forehead. " . . . Join the people who can add: two and two equals she likes you. Fifteen minutes, smiling a lot, laughing? What does she have to do, wear a sign that says, 'I like Dave, I hope he asks me out?'"

I laughed.

"This girl likes you, Dave. My suggestion is, you ask her out, the sooner, the better. If she's as attractive as you say, you're not the only guy after her."

"That's for sure."

"So, you'll ask her out then, right?"

"Yep."

"And soon?"

"Yep."

"And since she likes you, there's a good chance she'll say yes, right?"

"Right."

"So you feel good, right?"

"Yep."

"Wait'll you go out with her, and hold her hand, and get a good night kiss.

You think you're smiling now."

I laughed, and Dr. Davis grinned.

5

Friday, October 18, 1971

Two weeks to go and seven names left. Coming down to the puking wire.

Guess what, though—I have a sure-fire, guaranteed-not-to-fail way of not going besides not going and being the only one who doesn't go. My buddy, pal, friend, and swim team teammate, Rich Weiss, is on the list and he told me he's not going because his girlfriend that he just met can't go and she told him not to go either, and he said okay because she's kind of active hormonally if you know what I mean and that means a lot to guys like us, and Rich wouldn't want to chance loosing out on that just to go to some stupid dance with a blind date that'll probably be uglier than I am.

Through tears of joy, I agreed wholeheartedly. And I also have our summer school buddy, Timmy Technical's assurance that he's not going. He says he doesn't want a dog for a date. But what about the poor girl that gets him? I'm no bargain, but at least I'm halfway normal. He'd have trouble being taken at a giveaway to cannibals.

But who am I to judge? I just hope he sticks to his word and doesn't go. He'll buckle, though. Which'll leave Rich.

Doesn't this suck?

The following Wednesday my breathing stopped when I saw *no* names listed, one under the other, where they should have been occupying the last item in the daily bulletin. Had Mr. Stevens gotten everyone else to go and simply signed me up because he knew I'd go if that were the case? But then I saw my name, and Rich's, and Timmy's, *beginning* the sentence they usually ended. We were down to three.

Friday I asked Sherlock for a late, which was staying out on town privilege an extra two hours and walking back to the unit. You were allowed one a month, and I wanted to ask Lisa to the dance after town privilege ended for everyone else–if she was working. She hadn't been the Friday before, and the following Friday would be the night before the dance, too late to ask then. Not only because it wouldn't give her enough time, but because Mr. Stevens questioned me daily. I knew he was doing the same with Rich and Timmy, and my overriding feeling was one of doom–I'd be going once they gave in.

After bowling with the other guys from the unit, I headed for the drugstore at quarter of nine. As I neared the department store, I saw Jim leaning into a car and kissing a girl as she slowly pulled away. When she broke free, she beeped, and Jim waved.

"Hey, lover boy," I said in a high-pitched, Gary-like voice. "That's somebody's daughter. No molesting her."

He trotted stiff-legged toward me, his mouth opened like a chimpanzee straining with excitement. Ehnn!" he said, and jabbed my shoulder. "I asked her. She can still get you a date."

Jim had offered to ask his on-again, off-again, now on-again girlfriend, Tracy, to get me a date several weeks before. I declined. Besides not wanting a blind date, if it didn't work out, Tracy would pester Jim all night to find out what I thought, then I'd have to lie to Jim, or Jim to Tracy, or we could all tell the truth and end up sitting around having a great time not talking. That happened once with me and Eddie and his girlfriend, and I didn't want it to happen again, especially since it could trigger another off again episode between Jim and Tracy.

"No, thanks," I said. "I'll stick it out. Maybe Rich won't go."

We were at the light. "Where're you going?" Jim asked.

"The drugstore. I want to get some candy."

"Yeah?" He grinned. "Why don't you ask her to go?"

"I might. If she's there. And nobody else is around–like you."

"I got a late, but I'll leave early."

Jim grunted with delight as we past the drugstore window. "She's here."

Inside we moved toward Lisa's end, the right side. Another girl, almost as pretty, worked the left side. Despite it being nearly nine o'clock, a few Homeguys still sat along the crowded counter. Two of them jumped up and hurried out. The guy they had been sitting beside was Huey.

"How can you say no to such a nice guy like me?" Huey said, his arms out, his voice loud and playful.

Lisa smiled at her counterpart as they past each other. She breezed by Huey. "Huh?" he said.

"Easy," she said. "Like this: no."

Huey clasped his hands to his chest. "Dagger to my heart."

Jim and I sat beside Huey, me between them. "Asking her to the dance, huh, Huey?" I said.

"Yeah, but she's not biting."

That was good. And bad. If she wouldn't go with Huey, why would she go with me?

Keeping her head down to ignore Huey—who was staring at her as though love struck, Lisa stepped up to the counter and began clearing it of dishes and crumbs. "Gosh, you're pretty!" Huey said. "Won't you go to the big dance with me?"

"No," she said, and smiled despite herself.

"But you don't even know when it is."

"It's next Saturday. Somebody else already asked me, and I told him no, too. I'm busy."

That was that. Being busy might have been an excuse, but saying no to two guys was a definite statement—she didn't want to go.

I'd have given anything to have disappeared then. My chance at the dance was gone, and I didn't want Huey and Jim being there if she recognized me. I don't know why, I just didn't.

She fished out her pad and pen, looked at me, stopped for a second, then smiled. "Hi," she said, glad to see me.

Jim and Huey stared at me. "Hi," I said, glad she was glad.

"You want something with nuts on it this time?"

"No, thanks. I'll just have a medium coke."

"Coming right up." She left to get it.

Huey shoved my shoulder with his forearm. "You didn't tell me you knew her, bro. You dog!"

Jim shoved me the other way. "She didn't even take my order!"

"Yeah," Huey said, and shoved me back.

"Ehn," Jim grunted, with a return shove.

I shook them off. "Cut it out. I just talked to her once. Well, twice, but . . . "

"Ehnn!" Jim punched my shoulder.

"She likes you," Huey said.

"Huey, she—"

Lisa approached with my coke, a large one. "I made a mistake," she said. "You'll only be charged for a medium."

"I told you she likes you," Huey said. "You like him, don't you?"

"Sure I do. He's a nice guy. We went swimming together."

Huey's and Jim's necks nearly snapped, they turned so quickly. Jim tried to pinch me.

I shoved his hand away. "We were in the same *pool* at the same *time*," I said.

"Going off the boards right behind each other," Lisa said. "And talking."

"I'll bet that was nice," Huey said.

"*I* enjoyed it," Lisa said. "What would you like?" she asked Jim.

"I'll have a medium cherry coke."

As she was getting Jim's order, Huey whispered, "Now's your chance, bro. Ask her to the dance.

"Huey, she just said no to you and another guy. She doesn't want to go. She's busy."

"How do you know she just wasn't saying that? She doesn't know me; she knows you, *and* she likes you. Ask her."

"Yeah," Jim said.

"I can't take rejection as easy as you can."

"Then I'll ask her for you."

"No, Huey, don't. I'll feel like a jerk. She'll think I can't ask for myself."

"Then ask her yourself."

"I don't want to. She won't go."

He patted my shoulder. "I'll get her to go with you. Watch."

Lisa arrived with Jim's order. Huey said, "Hey, what if—"

"Huey!" I put my hand over his mouth.

He pulled it away and kept me at arm's length. "If you go with me, I'll let you dance with my pal here." He released me. "Now that wasn't too bad, was it?"

"He's a jerk," I told Lisa.

"What about it?" Huey asked. "Will you go?"

Lisa glanced at me, then nudged a crumb off the counter. Her nails were painted a pretty pink. "I can't," she said, shrugging one shoulder. "I'm busy."

"Well, if you change your mind, let me know, and you can still dance with this bum."

Lisa left.

What was she thinking? Had she been lying to Huey and then caught in her lie when I arrived? *Did* she want me to ask her? It kind of looked that way. If not the dance, maybe just for a date?

"Hey, what about you?" Huey said to the other waitress. "You want to go to our Halloween dance with the handsomest and most modest guy in Milton Hershey?"

"And be your second choice?" she said.

"I was just saving the best for last," Huey said. "What do you say? Is this my lucky night?"

The girl looked at Lisa, who shrugged. "Maybe," she said.

Before we left, Huey had her name and number and a promise to go if she could. And I had a feeling, that if I asked Lisa on a date, she just might go. Yeah!!!!

In the lobby of Founders Hall before Sunday service, somebody tapped my shoulder. As soon as I saw Rich's face, I knew he was going to the dance. "Ahh, man, Rich!" I said.

"I couldn't help it, Crazy. Honest."

"Sure, pal."

"Listen, you know how I told Mr. Stevens I wasn't going to chance losing my girlfriend over some doggy blind date? Well yesterday at the game, he found me, took me over to their side where a buddy of his from college was standing with this girl, a good-looking girl, and introduced us. She was in his buddy's homeroom at their school. I hardly had to say anything–Mr. Stevens did most of the talking. And now I got a date."

"What about your girlfriend?"

"Who cares?" Rich said. "She's kind of a bitch. This girl's nicer."

I moaned.

"Sorry, Crazy. Really. If he hadn't done that, I wouldn't be going."

I couldn't blame him for taking a date with a pretty girl. "At least Timmy's still out there," I said.

"I don't think so," Rich said. "Mr. Stevens told me he had him almost convinced to go. He used a picture of the girl. He had one lined up for you, too."

That was it. I'd lost the battle.

6

Tuesday, October 28, 1971

I called Hilda tonight, Teach, and let me tell you, I'm in trouble. Big trouble. Hilda was expecting my call, I could tell, and it still seemed like she wet herself with excitement. She, and her mother, and her grandmother have been waiting a long time for this call. Their little brontosaurus is growing up.

She said she's 'above average' in height and will be wearing a blue dress and glasses. She didn't even ask me what I looked like. What's that tell you? Must mean she's so nice, like Mr. Stevens promised, she doesn't even care if I look like Godzilla.

God I hate this. I think I'd rather have my name back in the bulletin again, all by itself, than go through this crap.

I was amazed when I first saw Hilda. My mouth dropped straight open. "Holy shit," I said.

"You got first prize there, buddy," Huey said, standing beside me outside Founder's Hall.

We had run into each other in the bathroom. He came in to comb his hair. I was stuffing a wad of toilet paper under each armpit.

"What's that for?" Huey asked.

"To keep me dry until I meet Hilda, then I can come back in here and throw up if she's worth it."

"Positive, Crazy. Think positive. She may be the babe of the ball."

"Not with my luck."

We walked to the rotunda. The tables were arranged in a semicircle with a space in front for dancing and the deejay's table. Marble shown shinny and creamy white in every direction: on the floor; on the broad steps that curved up to the balcony entrance of the auditorium; on the walls rising thirty feet to the flags rimming the interior of the domed ceiling; on the three long steps on both sides of the rotunda bordering the spacious sitting areas arranged with lounge chairs, love seats, end tables, lamps, and couches.

A quarter of the guys were already seated at the tables with their dates. The rest stood around talking and checking out girls. Now and then someone would come in from outside looking for a particular guy. The message was always the same: "Your date's outside." If it was his girlfriend or a promised good-looking date, the guy left immediately. If not, questions were asked and answered, and you knew what the guy's date looked like by the way he went to get her: slumped shouldered indicated one end of the spectrum, cartwheels the other.

"When's your date getting here, Huey?" I asked.

"She's not. She couldn't get off work."

"You mean you don't have a date?"

"Nope. I'm just going to find my own little–"

"The bastard! I got a date and he knew we didn't have one hundred percent attendance? The son of a bitch. The–"

"Whoa there, partner," Huey said. "I haven't told Mr. Stevens yet. He still thinks I got one."

"Oh." I half-laughed and shook my head. "I hate this crap."

We walked outside to the top of the steps. Below us, cars continually pulled into the curb and girls of all shapes and sizes emerged. Most waited until someone approached who was either their date for the evening or willing to run inside to find them.

"What's your date look like?" Huey asked.

"I don't know. Blind, tall and wearing blue."

Two minutes later Huey smacked me. "Hey!" he said. "Maybe that's her there, without glasses on." A pretty blond wearing a blue dress had just stepped out of a car.

"That'd be great," I said.

She walked to the bottom of the steps and stopped. Huey gave me a nudge. "Well go on down there and find out."

"Wait a second, Huey."

He shoved harder, sending me down two steps. "Go on. She ain't gonna hurt you."

"I know. I just want to see if somebody else talks to her first."

"That'll be me," he said, and started down. "I don't mind meeting a pretty girl."

He talked to her for a minute before bounding up the steps. "Not for you," he said. "You seen Woods around?"

"Timmy?"

"Yeah. Imagine that?"

We found Timmy at the food table. When nervous and alone, he ate. When nervous and with somebody, he talked and talked and talked.

"What a shame," Huey said as Timmy duck-walked to his date. "At least I got a dance with her."

"You do?"

He stuck out his chest. "They can't resist my big, burly charms."

"Hey, Crazy," someone said. I turned, saw the guy's grin, and depression swept over me. "Where is she?" I said.

"At the bottom of the steps." His grin broadened to a smile.

"Bad, huh?" Huey asked.

The guy shook his head and laughed. "She's different, all right."

I felt like throwing up.

"Come on, there, partner," Huey said. He grabbed me by my shoulders and led me outside.

"I knew it," I said. "I knew this would happen. All because Stevens had to have one hundred percent attendance. And he even promised me she was going to be nice, *real* nice. Son of a bitch."

"Easy, bro, you ain't even seen her yet."

We stopped where we had stood before. Though there were several girls below, Hilda was easy to spot. She was the real nice big one, dressed in blue.

Huey gave a long, low whistle. I couldn't have agreed more. "Holy shit," I said.

"You got first prize there, buddy," Huey said.

She was one of the biggest girls I had ever seen. She stood over six feet tall, weighed more than one hundred and eighty pounds, and had big, broad shoulders like a farm hand you'd never let go. She also had reddish-orange, wavy hair, glasses too big for her face, and a nose that zoologists would classify with the Brubaker species.

"Jesus Christ," I said. "She could make our football team."

"May . . . be," Huey said.

And I was going to have to be her escort for three hours, looking like David and Goliath. One hundred percent attendance wasn't worth that.

"I knew it, I knew it, I fucking knew it."

I felt ill, and it was all Mr. Stevens' fault. He had wheeled and dealed everyone into going to the dance, even when they didn't want to. Through embarrassment and peer pressure and the stupid bulletin announcements, he got the last holdouts to go, promising good-looking dates, and here I was, with the daughter of Joe Nose and the sixty-foot woman.

Huey said something, but it was so unbelievable, I couldn't have heard him right. "What?"

"I said, 'I'll take her for you.'"

"Really?!"

He nodded, and my relief skyrocketed. My savior! My hero! My–

"For fifty cents," he said.

I didn't have fifty cents. Not on me. "Wait here." I ran inside. The third guy I asked loaned me the money. I ran outside and gave it to Huey.

"Now you got to dance with her once or twice during the night," Huey said, "so I can dance with Wood's date."

"What?" That wasn't part of the deal. That was–

Huey held out the fifty cents.

–That was a bargain. "Okay," I said. "Anytime you want, I'll dance with her."

"And let everyone know I'm you, not Huey."

I followed them inside and closed in as they reached their table. Talking loudly I said, "Crazy, are you sure I don't owe you more than fifty cents?"

"Absolutely, Huey. Absolutely." He pulled Hilda's chair out and winked at me.

"Okay, Crazy, just checking." I nodded in greetings to each guy there to make sure they had caught on. Four grins told me they had.

Within fifteen minutes I had been to all the tables. I told them just enough so they knew not to call Huey, Huey. Nobody did, and I spent the rest of the night exulting in my freedom.

Only my talk with Mr. Stevens impinged on my mood. He apologized for Hilda being so big and offered to repay the fifty cents I had given Huey. I refused his money, saying it couldn't make up for the weeks of worrying and crap I had taken for being one of the holdouts, especially on Monday, when my name had been the only one listed.

"Oh, come on," he said. "It wasn't that bad."

"How would you know? It wasn't your name in the bulletin every day. You weren't the guy the teachers, houseparents, and everybody else kidded every day, every hour. I hate blind dates–hate them. And you say it wasn't that bad? You come on."

"What's the big deal, Dave? It's only a dance."

"The big deal is, they're always making us do stuff around here: get up, go to bed, milk the cows, clean the unit, do this, do that; and you come along and make us do something else we don't want to. What's the sense in that? Don't we have enough crap to do already?"

"I never thought about it like that," Mr. Stevens said.

"Well, I have. What's the big deal before if we didn't go? Nothing. Nobody would know about it, and nobody would care. But you put it in the bulletin, and I end up with a giant redwood for a date."

He laughed. "Okay, I apologize. I'm sorry. What can I do to make amends? Here, take the fifty cents. It's not half a week's wages to me like it is to you."

I deflected his hand away from my jacket pocket. "I don't want it. You can't make it up to me. It's impossible."

"But do you forgive me?" He put his arm around my shoulders. "Let me buy you some goodies and punch." As we headed toward the food table, he said, "I wanted everyone to go for class unity, Dave. I figured if we all . . . "

By the time my plate was filled, my annoyance had past. I was a death row inmate strapped into the electric chair when the order came down to set me free. I was too happy to be angry.

Even my three dances with Hilda proved enjoyable. What I thought was desperation on the phone, had been genuine enthusiasm. She had a natural, uninhibited, almost wild rhythm for fast dancing, and when we slow danced, her height and closeness had her breasts nearly surrounding my neck, giving me ideas I had never considered on such a grand scale–but would from then on. She and her friends had a great time, and I realized as the night past, that had I taken her as my date, I could have been part of that fun.

After the dance, on the bus back to the units, the guys, especially Brownie, who's blind date had turned out to his liking in every way except she had a boyfriend, kidded Huey and me about Hilda, her size, and our switching positions. I didn't mind and joked along with them. Nor did it bother me when Brownie brought it up in front of Suds and Bones once we got back to the unit, after I had explained how Huey had taken Hilda because he was dateless and more her height.

"She was more than tall," Brownie said. "She was gigantic. She was the biggest guy there."

"What did you do all night?" Bones asked me.

"Stuff my face, drink punch, goof off."

"Sounds like a good night," Suds said.

"It was."

Brownie and I turned from their doorway, headed for our bedrooms. "Hold on a second, fellas," Suds said. "We got a call from Carl tonight. The other guys know, and we didn't know if your roommates would be awake, so we thought we should tell you. You may not be as concerned with this, Alan; you might not have known him."

"Did something happen to Carl?" I asked.

"No, Carl's fine. He called about Mike." Suds wagged his head. "I'm afraid he died yesterday, Dave. He was killed in a helicopter crash, transferring bases."

7

How could Mike be dead? The guy who was my roommate for two years in the intermediates, for two years in the senior division, and my swim team teammate for seven years? The guy who told me what "sixty-nine" meant. The guy whose mother had taken me home for Easter vacation in sixth grade when my father couldn't because of illness. The guy I first tried beer with. The guy I first hooked out with. How could he be gone?

He had called me three weeks before to tell me he had had a fantastic time in Florida with Beth, was leaving the next day for Vietnam, and would write once he got settled. He was going over as an Air Force supply clerk, coming back in two years, then going to college where we had a reunion planned to get pie-eyed together. We were going to come back to Homecomings and laugh at each other as we got old, fat, and bald. We'd sneak out to the unit and let the cows out of the barn, or maybe carry a calf into the kitchen. We would dump soap powder into the fish sculpture outside Founder's Hall before the home-coming Saturday night dinner. We'd be at each other's weddings, maybe in them. We'd send each other pictures of our kids, ourselves. We'd get together for vacations, talk on the phone, do all the stuff we never talked about doing but simply knew we would. How could he be gone?

It didn't make sense. It wasn't fair. His father had died when he was young, just like my mother. Now he died, even younger. What kind of bullshit was that?

The letter I'd been expecting arrived Monday night. For an instant, when I saw his name and address, I thought of him as being alive. Then I remembered he wasn't. I went to my room to read it.

> *Hi Crazy,*
>
> *Got to make this fast, buddy.*
>
> *Nam's okay so far. I'm as far away from the action as you can get and still be here. So that's good. More on that next time.*
>
> *I really like Beth. She's something else. She may be it for me. And she has some real nice sorority sisters. I'll set you up. No dogs, promise.*
>
> *Now my real reason for writing. I got a cousin that's in the Home or soon will be. His dad died last year. He's in the sixth grade and his name's Bobby Spangler. Would you look him up and go see him before church sometime? He's a nice kid. His brother's here in Nam somewhere. Green Berets. I'm going to look him up. But my mom said Bobby's really scared so would you just check on him? You know what I mean.*
>
> *Thanks, pal.*
>
> *Got to go for this to get in the mail. I'll write more next time.*
>
> *Take care,*
>
> *Mike*
>
> *PS: Got a girl yet? Get one. They're fun!*

I smiled. Mike was like that. Always enthusiastic, always having fun. And now he was dead.

I sat there a long, long time thinking about him.

Going to lunch the next day, my homeroom section ran into Mr. Stevens and his homeroom section. Huey was there, Brownie was there, and the joking about Hilda commenced with a flurry–joking that had become more and more tiresome as it continued through Sunday church service, all day Monday, and into Tuesday. Now it was aggravating.

Mr. Stevens looked at me and shook his head. I said, "Not that bad, huh? This is what it was like as soon as you put my name up. And now I'm still getting it."

"It'll pass," Mr. Stevens said.

"When?"

"When we say so," Brownie said.

"You wanted to know how to make it up to me?" I said. "Put it in the bulletin how it turned out. You let everyone know I didn't want to go, I think they should know what happened."

"Oh, no," Mr. Stevens said. "No more bulletins for me."

"Everybody knows how it turned out anyway," Brownie said. He "woofed" like a dog, and a chorus of barking erupted around us.

"See what I've been taking?" I said. "For what? Because I got just what I thought I was gonna get? That ain't right."

"Ahhhh, poor baby," Brownie said.

"Dave, forget about it," Mr. Stevens said. "It's over."

"Then why are they still kidding me about it?"

He shook his head as our sections parted ways.

The jokes and ribbing continued throughout the day. Quick, harmless comments made as we past in the hallways. Or guys would smile when they saw me, which had the same affect. By the last period their sum total drove me to see Brubaker.

Without the bulletin lists broadcasting our reluctance to go, most of the before and all of the after kidding I was taking wouldn't have happened. Since Brubaker let Mr. Stevens use the bulletin, I thought he should let me use it. It could be a lesson for other students, showing them how allowing peer pressure could cause them to do things they normally wouldn't and how badly those things might turn out.

Brubaker's pleasant disposition vanished when he heard my request, and I found myself the object of a highbrow, big-nosed, stare. I hadn't been forced to go. I chose to go. "The only one who can benefit from a lesson in this, is you, David. Now, if you have nothing of importance to discuss . . . "

I tried Homelife next. Mr. Kramer proved as useful as when I had asked to pull the fire alarm. He could see my point, but not clear enough to help me in any way.

That left it to me. Wednesday morning I taped a note to the bulletin case outside Brubaker's office as soon as I arrived.

Fellow Students:

I just thought it only fair that you should know what my date (that I foolishly let myself be pressured into) for the Halloween dance turned out like. The facts are, she was over six feet tall, weighed 180 pounds or more, had orange hair, freckles, enormous glasses, and a nose bigger than most. Call her what you like, but she wasn't what I was led to believe I would end up with, although she was what I had feared deep down in my gut I would eventually get.

There's a lesson to be learned here and I hope you've learned it. I have.

PS: I asked this to be put in the bulletin but was refused. Why is that, do you think? After all, is not fair, fair?

The note was up at lunch time, but gone when I reported to Brubaker's office at two forty-five.

8

Brubaker tossed my note onto his desk. "What is the meaning of this?"

I watched it spin to a stop. "It's what I think is fair. I told you I was—"

"I'm not concerned with what you told me, nor think, for that matter. I told you yesterday this would not be placed in the bulletin and that—"

"It wasn't in the bulletin. It was—"

"Do not interrupt! Sit there and listen to what I have to say, without speaking, for as long as I continue to speak. Do you understand?"

I stared at him. He said, "Answer me. Do you understand?"

"You told me to sit here and listen without speaking. If I answer you, I'll be doing just what you told me not to."

His lips tightened. "This is the type of disrespectful, immature behavior that is at the root of your problems. You have a history of . . . "

Brubaker cited my repeated failures to make the National Honor Society, my aborted run for office, and my negative teacher evaluations as proof of my delinquency. My attitude was indicative of "students today," whose morals, discipline, and quest for knowledge were slipping precipitously to a point where there would be no point in attending school. Pot smoking, draft dodging, peace rallies, long hair; where would it end? If no one was held accountable for their actions, what kind of society would we have? Responsibility and respect were words that the younger generation did not want to hear, to accept, or to deal with. They'd rather . . . " Blah, blah, blah, blah.

I sat expressionless and stared at his high-backed leather chair as he paced the room. Why didn't he just tell me my punishment and let me go? I knew I'd get in trouble when I posted the note, but I never figured on a daylong sermon that included communist aggression, pollution, and space exploration. Where the hell was he going with this? Was there no evil in the world I couldn't be blamed for?

I glanced at him as he past behind his chair. His intense, unseeing stare reminded me of someone pleading for a great cause, possibly in front of thousands at the United Nations, or in the subway beneath New York City.

He turned and caught my eye. "*Dis!* respect. *Ir!* responsibility. Those are words you understand and embrace. If all students . . . "

I looked at his chair and suppressed my first grin since Mike's death. Was he going berserk? It looked like it—wild eyes, spit popping out, rambling about something only he could follow. Pretty soon the guys in white would burst in, strap him into a straight jacket, and haul him off, still blabbering, to the funny farm where his favorite spot would no doubt be the jungle gym, swinging from bar to bar and yodeling like one of those banana-nosed monkeys.

Brubaker stopped in mid sentence. "Would you care to tell me what is so humorous? What could possibly be causing that imbecilic smirk, given your situation? This is the type of behavior that is responsible for your presence here in the first place. Behavior that only a—"

"I was thinking of you in an insane asylum," I said, not wanting to hear it any longer. " . . . hanging from monkey bars and screeching like a chimpanzee."

He stared without speaking for several seconds, then stepped to his desk and sat down. "If you weren't receiving therapy, I'd insist you get it. You are on two weeks detentions. After lunch report to my office for work detail every day. Dismissed."

He made the work details somewhere heavily populated so the guys would know I was being punished. I didn't care. At least if they joked or smiled now, it was because of something I did, not for something that was done to me.

That Friday, Huey found me outside the math wing picking up litter. He told me he had called the drugstore girl who couldn't make it to our dance. She told him Lisa liked me, liked me enough to go out with me probably. "I told you, you should have asked her," Huey said. "Now it's too late."

"For the dance, it's too late," I said and smiled. Lisa and me on a date. Wow!

"No, for everything," Huey said. "Some Hershey guy's taking her out for the third time in a week tonight. He'll be in and you'll be out, by the time you're off detentions and can talk to her."

"Can't you say something to her for me?"

"When? She's on a date tonight."

"Then what about the girl you know? Can't you ask her to say something?"

"I already told her you like her. She said the same thing I did, 'you should of asked when you had the chance.'"

I couldn't believe it. I'd done the same thing with Lisa that I'd done in football: waited too damn long. I couldn't even call her because no calls, in or out, unless emergencies, was part of detentions, as was no swim practice, which meant I couldn't miss the bus after practice to see her, either.

Damn! Son of a bitch!

It was a lousy two weeks. I thought constantly about Lisa and how she was slipping from my grasp. I wrote Mike's mother a letter, telling her what a great guy he was and how much I'd miss him. Huey talked to the drugstore girl again, who said she thought it was probably too late. Somebody brought in an obituary from the *Philadelphia Inquirer* about Mike. My father had the second Friday, Saturday, and Sunday of my detentions off from work, something his schedule as a postman allowed once every two months, and he'd planned on coming down with my sisters to take me out for the day on Saturday and Sunday–something the Home allowed a student to do one weekend a month and which I hadn't done since summer vacation and would not be allowed to do now because I was on detentions. And Brubaker set a limit on how much I had to do during my noontime work details, which prevented me from doing what I had done the first day–as little as possible.

The day my detentions ended, in our parting talk, I told Brubaker the lesson I learned was that if somebody has the power, and you don't, then it doesn't matter if you're right because they're going to get you no matter what. He said that wasn't the lesson I should have learned, then proceeded to tell me what it was until I yawned like a bloodhound and he said, "Get out, get out, get out!"

Though my detentions had ended, I couldn't get interested enough in Lisa to ask her out. Why bother? She was already taken. The first town privilege I went on, I saw her but refused to go into the store with Brownie and Gary. Seeing her smile at me would only remind me of what I could have had, had I had the nerve.

What did anything matter, really? If Mike had died, any of us could die. The war was ending, but would it end before I graduated and got drafted? I could be just as dead as he was, a year from now, so why bother?

Dr. Davis called me in for another chat. I barely talked. I agreed or disagreed with whatever he said but refused to discuss my reasons. He tried kidding me into answering further, then began a mild lecture, thinking I was sulking over the punishment I had received. At first I didn't care, but then his tone changed. "Life's like a game, Dave, whether you like it or not. If you want to accomplish something, if you want to get somewhere, it will be a lot easier if you learn the rules and start playing by them."

"What's it matter what game we're playing and the stinking, rotten rules we're using?" I said. "We're just going to die, aren't we? So what's it matter?"

"Where'd that come from, Dave–'we're just going to die anyway?' What brought that up?"

"What's it matter where it came from? It's true isn't it? Why don't we just all kill ourselves and get it over with?"

He leaned forward. "Dave, what's going on? Tell me. It might help."

"How will telling you help anything? Will it bring my buddy back to life? Will it change anything that's happened the last couple of weeks? Huh? No!"

"Is your buddy the alumnus just killed in Vietnam?"

"Yeah. He was my roommate last year. For the last two years, in fact. And for two years in the intermediates. And now he's dead. So now I've told you, and it still hasn't helped. How's that?"

I wiped my eyes–they had started to water. Dr. Davis held out a box of tissues. I took one.

"Dealing with the death of someone close to you takes time, Dave, as every boy in this institution knows. It's not easy. There's no 'how to' rules or guidelines. Everyone's got to deal with it in their own way, at their own pace."

I was staring at the middle of his desk and could see him looking at me. I half-nodded.

"I sort of know how you feel. My father past away just last year; we were very close. I can tell you this, though: you will start feeling better. It'll take a while, of course, but you will. Did you share a lot of good times?"

"Yeah. A lot of them."

"That's good. In time, instead of feeling sad when you think of him, you'll start remembering those times and laughing about them; enjoying those moments. You'll know your life was richer for having known him. Your memories will make you smile. That's what I've been finding with my father, and I think the same will happen to you. So keep that in mind as you deal with his passing, okay?"

I nodded, grateful for his concern.

"There is one other thing I'd like you to keep in mind, Dave. I won't belabor the point, but now may be the best time to bring it up. You touched on it earlier.

We all do have to die. It's a fact of life. But instead of not caring about how we live our lives, we owe it to ourselves to make the most of every moment. None of us knows if we'll be here next year, or next week, or even tomorrow. There's no guarantees. So plan for your future but live today as best you can. Enjoy every possible moment. If there's something you want to do or try, then do it. That Lisa girl, ask her out. Anything else, do it, Dave. Take the chance. Time waits for no one. And when it's over, if you haven't made the most of it, there will only be one person who will have lost out. So get out there and do those things you want to do."

The more I thought about it, the more I knew Dr. Davis was right. Mike had always done what he wanted. If I died right then would I have had as much fun as he had? No. It would take me three lifetimes to equal the enjoyment he had gotten out of life. I rarely did anything I wanted. I was too worried about what other people might think, of embarrassing myself, of not succeeding. If I died tomorrow would any of it matter? If I died two thousand years from now would it matter? No and no, so what the hell, I was going for it.

FOUR

1

Lisa came out of the kitchen undoing her apron. While she talked to the lady working with her, I chugged the rest of my cherry coke and walked to the register. "Finished?" she said.

"Yeah." She began ringing up my bill. "Are you done?" I asked.

"Finally."

She'd been too busy to talk other than her cheerful greeting and taking of my order, and I'd been too chicken to request she interrupt her efforts at leaving early. Now was the time, however. I'd taken the late specifically to ask her out.

I looked outside. Nobody—no parents, no boyfriend. "You getting a ride home?"

"No. I walk." She gave me my change and shut the register. We stood for a moment.

NOW, Idiot!

"I was wondering, Lisa," I said quickly, awkwardly, "if maybe you'd like an escort home? You know, protect you from all the fiends in Hershey?"

"I don't live that far away. I always walk home."

That could be taken as a no, but then I wasn't being completely honest, either. "Actually, I'd kind of like to walk you home. You know, talk some more and whatever? I won't bother you. Honest."

She laughed. "Okay. Let me grab my coat."

I shouted an exuberant, inner yelp, then began preparing for round two.

Outside, she led me along the Community Center. "How long's it take to walk home?" I asked.

"About fifteen minutes. When it's real cold, ten."

For a while we talked about her school, cheerleading, and work, then came around to why she hadn't seen me in awhile. I told her about my two weeks detentions, the note, and the Halloween dance.

"What kind of girl were you expecting?" she said.

"Not someone ten feet tall. And my class advisor promised me she'd be real nice, and he meant more than just her personality."

"What kind of girl did you want?"

"Same as every Homeguy, one who . . . " The obvious answer of beauty and hormones suddenly vanished before a more glorious one. "Well, actually, if I had my choice, I'd kind of like somebody like you."

As the words left my mouth, I smiled, reflecting what a bold, direct and honest statement I'd made. But then Lisa's return look–her beautiful blue eyes and prolonged, appreciative smile–made me look away and begin babbling. "I mean, you know, somebody who's nice looking and . . . I mean you're more than just nice looking, you're good looking, real good looking, but we can't expect to get goddesses as dates. And then somebody who's kind of healthy like, you know, not fat–slim and trim. And somebody with a sense of humor that you can talk to, like you, and not feel nervous with and have to ramble on and on like an idiot, like I'm doing right now."

"You're doing all right," she said. "This way." We turned up a wide, tree-lined street.

"How much farther?"

"Three blocks. If you're running late you don't have to walk with me."

"No, it's not that. It's . . . I have plenty of time."

But I didn't. We walked half a block in silence, my mind racing for the best way to ask her out without looking like a fool, being embarrassed, or becoming tongue tied again.

"What's your name, anyway?" she asked suddenly.

"That's right, you don't know it? It's Dave . . . Purenut. Or Crazy, because of the Purenut. Most guys call me Crazy."

"I like Dave. Mine's Lisa."

"I know. I saw it on your . . . " I looked at the bulge in her jacket, underneath which lay her breast. "..your ahm . . . "

"Blouse," she said and smiled.

"Yeah, blouse."

Jeez, what an idiot! I looked skyward in anguish and saw hundreds of stars. "Wow, look at all the stars."

"There are a lot," Lisa said. "Come on, I know a great spot to see them."

We ran down the block, took a right, went thirty yards and cut into a driveway beside a funeral home. "You sure you want to go back here?" I said.

"Yes. There's a back parking lot. It's my dad's place."

The parking lot measured thirty by forty yards and was bordered by the funeral home behind us, garages to our left, tall shrubbery on the right, and a large, stone church across the way.

"Look at them now," Lisa said. "There must be millions." The sky glimmered like a seabed filled with diamonds. "Isn't it beautiful?"

I looked at her staring into the sky. Her smooth neck curving upwards; her soft, dark-brown hair falling back—and it wasn't the stars that had me awestruck, it was her and my closeness to her. "Yeah, they're amazing," I said.

"Look, there's the Big Dipper."

"Where?"

"There." She pulled me beside her so I could sight along her arm. Strands of her hair touched my ear, her grip gently held my arm, her scent smelled soft and feminine. "Do you see it?" she said.

"No," I lied. "Where?"

She pulled closer so that our cheeks were a breath apart. All my senses locked into her presence. "Right there," she said.

My mind raced for a course of action. If I was experienced and knew what I was doing, was I supposed to make a move now? Take her in my arms, stare deep into her eyes, then plant one on her that she wanted as much as I did? Was that what I should do?

I looked for anyone watching us. All I could see was the church. Which meant GOD. GOD would be watching. And behind us loomed the funeral home. Who knew how many sets of dead people's eyes were watching from there, their souls floating above in silent disapproval? Heaven and hell, there to watch me try and make out.

"Do you see it?" she asked, and looked at me, causing her hair to brush across my cheek and obliterate any concerns I had of who might be watching or the punishment I might suffer.

"I think so," I said. "I don't know. I'm probably blind."

She laughed, lightly smacked my shoulder and stepped away. "I love looking at stars on a night like this. It reminds me of summer camp." She turned in a slow, arms-out circle, head up, and I could picture her doing it as a little girl surrounded by her friends. I wish I had been at that camp.

"Well . . . better get home," she said, and led us out to the street.

I had less than two blocks to ask her. When I couldn't think of an easy way to ask her, I thought of Mike and began a countdown from five . . . four . . . three . . . two . . . "Lisa," I said, palms sweaty, eyes downcast. "I was wondering if you'd like to do something sometime? Go to a movie or something?"

There. It was out. I pulled on my jacket. It felt like a sauna inside.

"I can't. I work or cheerlead Friday nights."

Was that a polite way of saying no? Or did she mean just not on Fridays? She had to know I meant more than just Friday nights, right? Maybe she wanted me to be more aggressive? Be bold. Was that it? I unzipped my jacket. I thought this dating crap was supposed to be fun?

I was going to ask her anyway if things worked out, so why not now? "What about on a Saturday night then? Our Christmas dance is coming up and if you want you could–"

She put a hand on my arm. "Dave, listen. I like you a lot. You're a nice guy and you're funny. But I just started dating a guy and we said we'd only date each other."

Maybe she was just being nice, maybe not, but the message was clear. "Okay," I said.

"Really, I do like you. If you had asked me out after we first met in the drugstore I'd have gone out with you."

"Really?" She nodded. "Wow. What about the Halloween dance? Would you have gone with me?"

"Maybe. If you'd have asked first."

"I can't believe it. What a jerk! The chance of a lifetime and I blew it."

She tugged me to a stop. "I'm home." It was a two-story brick house with shrubs and shutters.

"Nice house."

"Thanks. And listen, you're not a jerk. You're a nice guy. A real nice guy."

"Well, then, if I'm such a nice guy, if things don't work out with you and Mr. Lucky, would you go out with me?"

"Sure."

"Will you let me know?"

"Sure."

"Great. Thanks."

"You're welcome." She leaned forward and kissed me on the cheek. "And thanks for walking me home."

I beamed brighter than the stars. She laughed. "Bye."

"See 'ya."

She walked to her door, waved, and went inside.

Wow! The girl of my dreams actually liked me, liked me enough to go out with me. And all this time I thought she never would. How many other girls could I have gone out with? How many other girls would I go out with? And the girl of my dreams, if things didn't work out, could still go out with me. Yeow!

2

Tuesday, December 2, 1970

I showed up for my first day at rehearsals today, Teach. Do you know Mr. Hayes, the Catherine Hall English teacher who's also the drama coach and who I'm glad I never had? He's a bit excitable, ain't he? I got to Founder's Hall after swimming practice and he was telling everybody to "pay attention." I reached the front of the stage and waited. After a while he saw me, put his hand on his hip, and demanded to know, "What are you doing there?"

It was obvious I was waiting for him to finish talking so I could say something. But I didn't point that out. I said, "I'm Dave Purenut. I'm here to help with the play, remember?"

"Of course I remember. Do I look like an idiot?" The guys behind him started nodding their heads.

"I mean what are you doing there!" He pointed to where I was standing. "Nobody stands down there or back there!" I think he meant the auditorium

seats behind me or maybe the rest of the world. "It's distracting. If you're here to help, get backstage and start helping. You're useless there."

I felt like telling him his brain was useless. Instead I went backstage and found someone with intelligence who showed me how to change the lights according to a diagram of what they wanted where. It was kind of interesting.

Because all the parts, including extras, had been cast when I spoke with Mr. Hayes about signing up for the Christmas play, he refused my request. Because Mike's death had imbued me with psychotic determination, my persistence and persuasiveness overcame all his objections and he brought me on as the only non-acting stagehand.

I liked the various functions I was assigned, did well what I was asked, and became a valuable asset to the production. There was a large workroom with a radio, where I painted sets, made small props, and did a half-assed job putting together half-assed cavalry uniforms. Sometimes I'd be up in the control room helping with the lights or on stage rearranging pieces between scenes. If I had nothing to do I'd wander around backstage, up on the cat-walks, or sit around and watch the guys acting. The play, written by Mr. Hayes, was about a cavalry troop preparing to retaliate against Indians in-volved in Custer's Last Stand. None of the men were looking forward to their task, many were scared, and all took comfort from their colonel, who they didn't know was just as worried as they were. Timmy Technical played the colonel, and his talkative, know everything attitude served him well. One scene, after they receive news of the massacre, involved everybody listening to the colonel tell them of their orders. I was sitting between two curtains in the back when someone whispered, "Hi."

A girl, about my age, wearing a winter coat and baggy sweat pants, stood watching behind me. "Hi," I whispered, and turned back to the scene.

What was a girl doing in our building, backstage, watching rehearsals? And a cute one at that?

"Do you think they'll be much longer?" she asked.

"I don't know," I said, and took a longer look. Thick, auburn hair pulled into a ponytail, full red lips, light green eyes. Yep, cute all right.

She said, "Bye," I said the same, and she walked behind the curtains to reappear on the other side where there was more open space. She took off her coat and began stretching. She wore a pink top with an open collar.

From where I was sitting, I could watch either her or the play without moving my head. Though I was careful to divert my eyes, she caught me looking several times. It wasn't until the fourth time that my mind registered what my hormones had already realized: she didn't care that I was ogling her. In fact, it looked like she knew I was watching and liked it. In fact, she was stretching this way and that, her clothes tight against her lean, supple body for my benefit. She was trying to get me excited!

I couldn't believe it. Why would some cute, strange girl–who had to know somebody of importance to be doing what she was doing in our building–be trying to get me hot? I looked around to see if someone else might be the object of her intentions. No one. Maybe it was wishful thinking? She was stretching but unaware of my presence? That could be it. Maybe she needed glasses and couldn't see me watching her? Or maybe she figured I was a typical male chauvinist pig best handled by ignoring me?

Whatever the circumstances, she had my complete attention. She had her legs out to the sides, body stretched forward, head down, hands over her head, arms lying flat on the floor. Slowly she drew her torso upright, arms spreading above and out like a blossoming flower. She continued back until her palms touched the floor behind her. She held this pose for five seconds, then dropped her head farther back and arched her spine, pushing her chest out. And there they were, two little peaks jutting gloriously above her breasts and making me feel like a bull at a heifers-in-heat show. Her goddamn nipples!

She brought her head forward, eyes closed, then opened them and glanced admiringly at each of her breasts. Then she turned those light green, almost transparent eyes right on me, and smiled. She brought her left arm up, twisted, and her gaze left mine as she stretched both hands to her right foot.

I left. I couldn't stay. Parts of me were ready to engage in mortal combat, wrestle whales, or backpack the arctic.

I went to the workroom and sat down. Holy shit. Was she giving me hints or just trying to drive me crazy? Or both?

In ten minutes my curiosity made me return. She stood on stage, in a scene with two of the leads.

"Who's that?" I asked a guy standing nearby.

"Mr. Hayes' daughter, Nancy. She's playing the colonel's wife."

"I thought it was just the cavalry and some Indians?"

"It was. Hayes re-added some scenes. He was trying to get her to agree to play them. I guess she did."

"She do any nude scenes?" I said.

"I wish."

"Me, too. I'd bet she'd be good at it."

Nancy stayed on my mind for the next few days. I couldn't figure it out, so I told Eddie about her.

"She wants it," he said. "And I'd give it to her. Nancy the nymph!"

"How do you know she wants it? You weren't there."

"I know, all right. When she had her legs spread out like that, she was saying, 'Put it right here, baby.'"

"Maybe she was just stretching."

"I'd give her something to stretch," he said. "She wants it, Crazy, and you got to give it to her. It's your duty."

Maybe she did want it? She might. If Lisa liked me, why couldn't she? The thought was both exciting and scary. I wouldn't know what to do exactly, but I had the necessary parts that were eager to participate. Would she laugh at me for being inexperienced? Would she not want to do it, then? Maybe she'd like to help me learn? Yeow! Should I make a move, ask her out? Why not? What could I lose?

In the next few days I discovered Nancy was a college freshman, had a boyfriend–maybe; joked with everyone; was the best actor in our play; spoke to her father when he needed spoken to; and was constantly surrounded by guys. She'd say "Hi," in passing, but showed no further signs of wanton lust. Had I had imagined it all?

Gradually I stopped watching her during rehearsals and hovering nearby. She was cute, but all the guys were hanging around her. Why be one more?

The workroom was windowless and stuffy. The night I painted the "stockade" the temperature was over seventy-five degrees. I took my shirt off and left the door open. On my knees I could reach two-thirds the way up the ten by five foot sections of Styrofoam. I finished one section, leaned it against the wall and pulled the next section to the center of the room.

"Want some help?" Nancy said, as I laid the section on the floor.

She stood just inside the doorway, leaning against the handrail, arms close in, chest out. Three steps down and she'd be in the room.

"I only have one brush," I said.

She skipped down the steps. "That's okay. You do one side and I'll do the other. Then you won't have to get up." She knelt in front of me on the other side. "Your name's Dave, right? Mine's Nancy."

"I know."

I started painting. What should I say? I wasn't prepared for this; I'd given up thinking about her as a date. I also felt self-conscious with my shirt off. And nervous. Why did girls do this to me? Why couldn't I act like any normal, sex-starved boy?

"You don't talk much, do you?" she said.

"It depends. Sometimes I don't have much to say."

"Which from what I've seen, is most of the time."

I straightened up to move to my left with the bucket, and responded with a shrug. I dipped the brush.

"You've got a nice body," she said.

Yeeooww! I could only half suppress my grin before I resumed painting.

"You do. Do you exercise a lot?"

"I'm on the swim team. I also got a half-barrel chest that gives me pecs without really trying."

"What do you mean? Show me."

I put down the brush and sat back. I indicated the half-barrel shape of my chest. "See how this is kind of round? Most guys' chests aren't like this, they're wider. See this?" I rapped my fingertips against the center of my chest, producing a sound like hollow wood. "Most guys have muscle here. But because my chest is more round, it pulls the muscles away from the center leaving only skin and bone, and it bunches it up over here on the sides, giving me pec muscles. It looks good but I really didn't do anything to get it."

"Can I feel that, where you hit yourself?"

"I guess so."

She leaned across and rubbed her fingertips in the center of my chest, up and down, feeling the breastbone. She rapped lightly against it. "That's neat," she said, and lifted her eyes to mine and smiled. I looked away. "And this is all muscle?" Her fingers caressed the outside of my left pectoral muscle and across the nipple.

I jerked back. "Yeah," I said.

She grinned.

Yeeoowww!

"My turn," she said, and wiggled her fingers. I handed her the bucket. She dipped the brush, flipped her hair back, and started painting. "I've never seen you around here before," she said.

"This is my first time doing anything with the plays."

"You don't want to act?"

"I wouldn't mind, I guess. I just asked too late."

"I wasn't going to, either, but I just broke up with my boyfriend and have lots of time."

Was I supposed to comment on that? With what? Was it a hint or just a fact? But more importantly, if she leaned over any farther, I'd be able to examine her chest almost as easily as she hand mine.

She said, "You're a senior, right?"

"Yeah."

"I'm a freshman at Lebanon Valley College. I commute, but next semester I want to live on campus. Get away from my parents. They're all right, but . . . "

While she talked, I concentrated on the V-shaped opening of her pullover top with its collar and four buttons below the neck. I couldn't see anything, but I could if she'd lean over more and if her hair, which she kept tossing back, would stop falling down to block the view, and if the fourth button, the bottom most one, were unbuttoned instead of buttoned. If all that happened, then I think I'd have a nice view of her breasts, something I'd never really seen much of before other than in magazines or the occasional glimpse of a sales lady's which were usually too wrinkly to look at or so big they looked like somebody's ass. But Nancy's would be within touching distance, and they'd be young and firm and smooth and soft. If only she'd bend over more!

She finished doing the top half of what I had done and sat back. "There." She leaned over to give me the brush, then stopped. "Wait a minute. I should finish my side first, then you can finish yours. That's fair."

A women's lib jab, which I generally ignored. But fair was fair. "You're right," I said. "Go ahead."

She smiled, dipped the brush and started painting. This time she did lean way over, bracing herself with her right hand on the Styrofoam. Only now her hair fell straight down and blocked my view completely.

She finished, handed me the brush, and stood up. "Are there any rubber bands around? This hair's driving me crazy."

"Over on that desk."

"How's it look?" she asked when she returned.

It was pulled back in a ponytail and stuffed inside her top. She stood in profile, head high, chin out, shoulders square, chest erect.

"Okay," I said.

"'Okay?' You're supposed to say, 'Beautiful. Marvelous. It accentuates your exquisite facial structure. Divine.'" She knelt on the floor. "Not just 'okay.'"

"That's what my okay means."

"Sure it does. I hope you don't just say, 'You look okay,' to your girlfriend when she asks how she looks."

"I don't have a girlfriend."

"Why not?"

I sat back, finished. "This is Milton Hershey. We don't have any girls."

"That's no excuse. They're around."

"Yeah, well . . . " Was that a hint?

"Don't be so shy. Just ask. All they can say is yes or no."

"That's true." That was a hint, right? Right?

She helped me carry the finished section over beside the other and drag the next one to the bucket. "Whew! it's hot in here," she said.

"Yeah, it is." I knelt down to paint.

"I wish I could take my shirt off like you did yours."

There was something in her voice, an undertone, hinting at nudity, whipped cream, and perhaps Jell-O. "It's all right with me," I said.

"It is, is it? I'd bet you'd like that."

"Fair is fair."

"You're right. But my father would have a rhino." She knelt down. "It's not like I'd be naked. I have a bra on"—that tone again—"a small one, kind of lacy, but still it's something. It's not like you'd see all of my boobs.

My nipples would be covered." She grinned. "Just barely. It'd be like I had on a real small bikini top. I'd do it in the summer, why not now?"

I could only nod—my brain was starting to coagulate. A cute girl like this, right in front of me, talking about her tits and nipples and lacy bra? It was hot in there.

"Nah, I better not," she said.

Nancy had no trouble doing most of the talking, and what she talked about made sense and was interesting. That's why I had calmed down by the time I finished painting two-thirds of half the board. I gave her the brush and bucket. She dipped her brush and I noticed the loose folds of cloth from her top lying against her jeans. She had pulled it from beneath her belt. My eyes darted to the V-shaped opening—the fourth and final button was open.

It was hard not to get caught looking down her top, and harder still not to go up on my knees so I could see all the way down instead of just the top half of her left breast—even though that was wonderful to see, all soft and white and curving out like it did. While she talked of her classes, I contemplated the different vantage points from which to stargaze. If I moved to my right I'd be directly across from her and could see both breasts at once if she lifted her head. Farther right, past her, I could see more of her right breast. Wasn't one supposed to be bigger than the other, or hang down lower or something? Maybe I'd see more of one than the other? But which one? And if I stayed where I was, it would be right where she would start doing her two-thirds of the board, leaning so far over I'd probably see her goddamn belly button! Should I . . .

She caught me staring. "What are you looking at?" she asked, and looked down at her top. When she looked up, I pointed. "I think you got some paint on your top."

She inspected the material. "It doesn't matter. This is old." She ruffled her top and smiled. "It's cooler this way."

I nodded. "It is hot in here."

"It is. I wish I could take it off." That voice again, and that look, now with a pouting lower lip.

She continued painting, her movements slower and her voice like honey. When she finished her third of the first half, she moved to her right and placed the bucket on the Styrofoam. She leaned over and braced herself with one hand, now three feet away and directly in front of me. She turned her head toward the bucket, dipped the brush, and watched motionless while the excess paint dripped off.

And there they were. The two loveliest breasts I'd ever had the pleasure of seeing so close. Hanging down, smooth and round and soft, and seeming ready to burst from the small lacy white of her bra. Just barely out of sight because of the way the cloth of her top angled down, were her nipples. Goddamn!

She started painting, head down, blocking my view. I exhaled. What the hell was I supposed to do? I knew what I wanted to do, but just because she was showing me what she had did that mean she wanted me diving head first down her top?

She dipped her brush sooner than she had to and each time used the same picture-perfect, all encompassing, immobilizing poise. A few inches more and I'd see everything!

"Are you looking for a girlfriend?" she asked.

The question had something to do with whatever she had been saying, but it wasn't B follows A, and right then I couldn't follow anything. "Ahhmmmm," I said, my mouth dry, her breasts confusing things.

She lifted her head and our eyes met. "Are you?"

"I don't know. I . . . " She looked back at the paint, I looked down her top– Damn! " . . . I'm too retarded. I don't know."

She laughed. "Well, you know, if you–"

Someone was at the door. "Nancy, you're wanted on stage for a scene."

She placed both hands on the board, shoulders forwards, and turned her head. "Now?"

"Yeah."

"Okay. I'll be right there."

While she was talking, I was staring. I could see everything, including the smooth, translucent bottom lace of her bra, with her nipples, erect and jutting against the material.

She turned to me. "Got to go."

I nodded.

"Aren't you going to say you had fun?" She was still leaning forward. "That you hope we see each other again?"

I nodded. "Yeah."

She laughed. "Is there a clock in here?"

"Over there."

She turned her head and I watched her breasts sway with the motion and settle still. "Six thirty," she said. "I'll have to leave soon. I hope this won't take long." She continued staring in that direction. "That's a pretty neat clock, isn't it?"

I was viewing the eighth and ninth wonders of the world. I didn't look at the clock. Who cared what it looked like? Fuck the clock. "Yeah," I said.

"I like how the ship's ends touch the nine and three, and how the mast and rudder hit the twelve and six. They could do that without the numbers even."

"Yeah."

She took a deep breath, her chest swelling toward me. "Oh well." She sat back and smiled at me. "Thanks for letting me help. I had fun. If I get a chance, is it okay if I do it again?"

"Sure."

"Great, it's a date. Well . . . " She stood up. "See 'ya."

I watched her leave, then exhaled. Whew! Talk about hot. She did want me to make a move, right? Right?

3

Because I didn't have to work any of the Saturday morning after-breakfast chores, it gave me a bright side to look at no matter how boring the "Youth for the Future" seminar at Lebanon Valley College might be. I signed up for it the day after I talked with Dr. Davis about Mike's death. I figured at the very least, I would get out of the unit and there would be girls there. Maybe I'd meet one? And now that I knew Nancy went there, I'd be looking for her.

I was the only guy from my unit going. At the next stop Huey got on the bus. He had gone the previous year and told me his plans of attending the conferences with the most girls. "What about the ones you signed up for?" I asked.

"Doesn't matter. All they do is check us in, give us name tags and lunch tickets. They don't care which conferences we go to. So girls, here I come."

"That's a good plan," I said.

"You with me?"

"Sure. I don't remember which ones I signed up for anyway. Except the first one, on Vietnam."

"I signed up for that one, too. That one we'll go to. The others, it's sex city."

After finding the right building and getting our lunch tickets and nametags–the "Hello, my name is . . . " kind that Huey filled in with "Don Juan,"–we went to the auditorium where the "Vietnam, Right or Wrong?" conference was being held. Though the place was packed, Huey found seats beside two cute girls. Moments after he greeted them the lights dimmed and a documentary began about the history of Vietnam. When it finished, the screen lifted, revealing two long tables with several microphones on each. From both sides, guys in uniforms climbed the steps and took seats behind the tables. On the right sat mostly longhaired guys, vets from Vietnam. One guy had only one arm. On the left were guys still in the service, shorthaired and mostly older. They were there to answer questions, and after the first one–"Do you think we should be there?"–a guy on the right said, "Hell no!" and people clapped. That question took fifteen minutes.

The answers were heated and emotional. Both sides believed they were right, the one saying we had to do what our country asked, the other saying we had no business being there. Ten minutes before the session ended, they showed a film about our guys fighting there. Most of them accepted their fate, and all but one wished they didn't have to be there. Then a voice came on saying in one battle twenty-four of our guys had been killed winning a hill that we abandoned two weeks later. With the music from the Battle Hymn of the Republic playing in the background, they showed the high school graduation pictures of each soldier and gave his age and hometown. The oldest was twenty-three.

As the music came to an end, a photograph appeared of two guys carrying another on a stretcher. The guy lifting in back was crying, the guy in front wore an expression of hatred and disgust. On his helmet was a peace sign painted in white. The guy on the stretcher looked like he wasn't going to make it, or was already dead.

When the lights came on nobody spoke. A lot of sniffling and muffled crying could be heard. I wiped my eyes. Mike's picture could have been up there. Just like those guys, no one would ever see him again. We weren't winning the war, it looked like Tricky Dick was trying to pull out before the next election, so why were our guys still being sent over? It sucked. If you didn't go, you were a traitor, draft dodger, and coward. If you did, you could get killed, captured or maimed, or end up killing people you didn't know, all for a cause that was ending. What kind of choice was that?

Someone on stage said, "I'd like to thank everyone here for coming, participating, and giving us an experience we shall long remember. May peace come soon." He started clapping, and everyone joined in, rising to a standing ovation.

As people began to leave, Huey said to the girls beside us, "Which conference are you going to next?"

"The women's rights one."

"They won't attack me for being a guy if I go, will they?"

"I don't think so," the one said.

As they moved up the aisle, Huey whispered, "We're on the move, partner. Let's go reel these babies in."

"I'll pass, Huey. I don't get into that women's lib stuff. All they'll be doing is bitching about guys."

"All right. I'll hook up with you at lunch."

He followed the girls and I went the other way. Of the three conferences I past, none seemed interesting so I walked back and spotted Huey in the auditorium doorway. "Hey, Don Juan, what are you doing?"

He said, "I walked in the room and was the only guy there. This woman says, 'Can I help you?' like she had a list of who was supposed to be there. So I said, 'I doubt it,' and left." He looked inside the auditorium. "You want to do this one again?"

"Nah. Nothing's good down that way. I was going to check up here."

"We better hustle."

The first sign read, "Understanding, the Key to the Future." The room was large and had less than thirty people inside. A projector was set up. We went in.

"One of you gentlemen want to close the door?" a small, older man wearing blue jeans and plaid shirt said from the front.

His name was Professor Karrington, but said we could call him Bob. He was a psychology/sociology professor who ran informal classes. He had us form a large oval in the center of the room, then introduce ourselves, telling our school, year, and anything else we'd like people to know.

I was sitting to Huey's right, near the end of the oval. Huey said his name was "Don" and coughed when he said, "Juan." I gave my name, school, and year. Most everyone did the same or added one thing more until the girl across from me. Small and petite, she looked attractive except for her rigid posture and stern face. Beside her sat a much larger girl with the same prison guard expression. They smiled frequently, but not genuine, joy-filled smiles like Lisa's; more like reflexive grimaces. As one talked, the other would nod in agreement.

"Hi, I'm Betty Auger, a junior, from Anville-Cleona. I'm vice president of our debate team, and I'm in the chemistry and physics clubs. I've been in our school band since ninth grade. And Hillary . . . " she nodded to her right and received a grimace in return " . . . and I are hoping to establish a women's rights association in our school, which will be the first in this area."

Before speaking, Hillary waited for the hosannas resounding within our heads to subside. "Hi, I'm Hillary Seton, also a junior at Anville-Cleona. I too am . . . "

God, they made me sick. Who cared about that crap? They had probably been in the women's rights conference the period before and had brought up the "we're establishing" bullshit which no one but them cared about. On their gravestones it would read, "Helped Found the . . . " Jerks.

After everyone had spoken, Bob explained that this was a freewheeling class where he hoped everyone would participate. "This is a discussion of understanding—ourselves, each other, other countries, other cultures. Through the understanding of different peoples and countries, their needs and desires, I believe we can move toward a better world."

I listened but didn't participate as the discussion moved to what we thought other countries wanted for themselves, and what our country wanted. People gave their opinions here and there, but Betty or Hillary had something to say on every subject and would nod or shake their heads to whatever else was said. In fifteen minutes I couldn't stand them. Given the slightest pause after Bob asked a question, one or the other would jump in. "Well, I think . . . "

I started getting restless. Bob was at the other end. I moved back and hid behind Huey. I'd sit up, slouch, lean forward with elbows on my knees. Every time Hillary or Betty opened their mouths, I shifted into another position. Once Hillary caught me and glared. I looked away in boredom.

"What do you think needs to change for better understanding throughout the world?" Bob asked.

Betty didn't hesitate. "I think there needs to be more women in government," she said, "in every country. Men have ruled supreme for far too long, and look where it's gotten us? The women's liberation movement will . . . "

As soon as she started talking I sat up. When she mentioned "women in government" my head dropped back. The words "women's liberation movement" made me grimace. When I opened my eyes, Hillary was glaring at me. I returned her gaze for a moment, then looked away. Why didn't they both just up and die?

" . . . Once we learn to give equal rights to everyone within our own country, and other countries do the same, then perhaps all countries can treat each other equally."

"Anyone else want to–"

"Bob," Hillary said, then pointed at me. "This . . . person right here, made a face of disgust while Betty was speaking. I'd like to know why."

"Who's that?" Bob asked.

Grinning, Huey grabbed his seat and hopped back so everyone could see me.

"Did you do that?" Bob asked.

"Yes," Hillary said.

"Yeah," I said.

"Would you like to tell us why?"

"Not really."

"Why not?" Hillary said.

"I know I'd like to know," Betty said.

"Everyone would," Hillary said.

Under his breath, Huey whispered, "Tell 'em to fuck off."

"What's so funny?" Hillary said. "We have as much right to speak as you do. Just because we're women doesn't mean we don't. Our rights are the same as yours. You're no better than we are."

I blew out my breath. Mike died so this asshole could be an asshole like this?

"See?" Hillary said. "There it is again. That same disgusted look."

Huey turned his head so they couldn't see him. "Tell 'em to fuck off!"

"It's ignorant males like you who are making it so difficult for women to gain equality," Betty said. "It'd do you good to attend the women's rights seminar today. You might learn something."

"Now ladies," Bob said.

"I'll bet he won't," Hillary said. "He doesn't have the courage."

I sat forward; that was it. "You want to know why I made those faces and won't attend that stupid meeting?"

"Yes," Hillary said.

"It's not stupid," Betty said.

" . . . Because I'm sick and tired of hearing about women's rights. It's all bullshit. It's all one way."

"It is not."

"You want this, you want that, but I never heard you screaming for the right to get drafted, did I? Did I?!"

Their righteous, hostile faces froze. I was at the edge of my seat, wishing I could leap across and ram my fist down their throats to bring Mike back to life.

"No, I never heard you yelling for that. You know what it's like to sit and worry what your number's going to be on draft day? Huh? No! You know what it's like not to be able to plan your future because you may be drafted? No! You don't know that, do you?"

"I have a brother who—"

"Yeah, your brother! Not you! Or you! No, your brother. I didn't go to that stupid women's lib crap meeting because I was in the Vietnam meeting, where you should go, and you. You'll see guys blown away, with bloody faces, no arms, no legs, guys dead, and know how many are women? None! Zip! Zero! No women! Why not? Don't they have the right to get their faces blown off like guys do? Huh? Don't they have the right to come back with no legs and no arms, or come back and be put in mental hospitals because they saw their buddy's head blown off? Huh? All those white crosses from graves from World War II, World War I, the Civil War, on both sides, thousands and thousands of them, how many of those are women's graves? Huh? Not too goddamn many. Twenty-four guys were killed in one battle in Vietnam. Know how many were women? None! If we really had equality, half of them would be women, and maybe my buddy would still be alive, and you'd be in Vietnam, dead, or maybe even a prisoner. I know I'd be for that kind of equality. How about you? Huh?!"

I was on my feet, screaming and leaning into Bob, who had been trying to calm me down but now asked me to leave. Huey stood up to help him. As they moved me toward the door, I was still yelling.

" . . . Would you like to be dead or a prisoner in Vietnam? Huh? Talk about courage. You ain't got shit for courage. I wouldn't want you beside me anyway. You'd be worthless. All you can do is shoot off your big fat mouths. So why don't you just eat shit and fuck off!!"

Bob hurried me into the hallway. "Take him for a walk," he said, and shut the door.

Huey gave me a jubilant one-armed squeeze. "All right! Mr. Silent speaks his mind. Way to go, Crazy."

"Those fucking assholes," I said. "Mike died for them? Bullshit!"

Huey and I walked around campus, into and through various buildings, and by the time we sat eating lunch with the two girls who sat beside us in the Vietnam meeting, my mood was a pleasant one. Then I spotted Hillary and Betty walking through the cafeteria, methodically searching every face at every table, followed by a heavyset, bald man wearing a bow tie.

"Oh, jeez," I said. "Here come the assholes."

We sat in the far back corner. Huey spotted them, then motioned behind us. "There's an exit. Want to take it?"

"No. I don't care. They can't do anything."

Hillary suddenly stopped. "Over here! He's over here."

Hillary and Betty marched to our table and stood across from Huey and me. "That's him, Mr. Carey," Hillary said. "He's the one who was yelling and cursing at us. Professor Karrington can confirm it."

I said, "And he can also confirm you started it by calling me a coward."

"That's not true," Betty said.

"It isn't," Hillary said. "I said–"

"It doesn't matter," Mr. Carey said. "I'll ask Professor Karrington." He peered at my nametag. "Dave Purenut." He wrote it down. "What school are you from, Dave?"

"Milton Hershey."

"And she did call him a coward," Huey said. "And that one called him ignorant."

As both girls denied it, Mr. Carey put up his hand. "All right, ladies. Not now." He looked at me. "I expect you to behave yourself the rest of the day. And don't be surprised if someone from your school gets back to you on this."

4

Old Man Hatch agreed in principle with what I had told Hillary, but not with my choice of words, and gave me ten days restrictions for swearing, name-calling, and disrupting the conference. I was allowed to continue swimming practice, but not helping with the play. Though it was a fair and lenient punishment, it caused me much more aggravation than Old Man Hatch intended. I'd been smiling all weekend about the peep show Nancy had given me and fantasizing about an encore. Was she trying to excite me for a reason or just having fun? Or were those looks and sultry voice just my imagination twisted by spermatozoa multiplying out of control? Either way, I wanted to be there in case there was another showing, and to ask her out.

My restrictions ended the night of the full dress rehearsal. Thinking I wasn't going to make it, Mr. Hayes had delegated all production night responsibilities. "Stick around," he told me. "We'll find you something."

I didn't spot Nancy until I was helping to carry railing on to the stage. She walked by us, said "Hi, guys," kept going, then stopped and watched us put it in place.

"I thought you were on detentions and wouldn't be here anymore?" she said on my way back.

"It was only restrictions—for ten days. They ended yesterday."

"What happened?"

"It's a long story. I'll tell you some other time."

"Okay."

She smiled then, her green eyes twinkling, and I knew it hadn't been my imagination. She had been trying to excite me and was eager to do it again. "See you later," she said.

I followed the other guys back to the workroom. What do I do now? What would she do now? Show me as much as last time? More than last time? What if she showed up buck raving naked in her goddamn birthday suit with nothing on? Yeow!! I guess it'd be my move then, right? Yeeeowwwwww!!

It felt like a zillion hormones were playing bumping cars inside my body. I carried heavy props by myself, rushed when my hands were empty, hurried when they were full, and joked with everyone. When everything was set, Mr. Hayes sat in the middle of the auditorium and gave the order. The lights dimmed for the opening night scene inside the fort. When the curtain rose, one guy was walking sentry. He stopped, looked hard to the right, and called, "Sound the alarm! Someone's approaching!"

This was when news of Custer's defeat reaches the fort. The guys stood behind the curtain, ready to file out as if being roused from their bunks. I walked up to the last guy. "Where's Nancy? She's not going to miss her part, is she?"

"She doesn't come on for about fifteen minutes. I don't know where she is."

I walked to the other side. More guys and the colonel. I still couldn't believe it was Timmy, or how good a job he was doing. On cue, he led the others on stage. I started back to the other side and ran into Nancy rounding the curtain.

"There you are," she said. "Come here." She grabbed my hand to lead me away.

I resisted. "What? What do you want?"

She grinned. "I'm not going to hurt you. Come on. I need your opinion about my wardrobe. Hurry. I've got to get ready."

She led me to a small room with stool-like seats in front of mirrors with lights around the edges. There were six seats, three on each side, and an open area in the back with a wall-length mirror and a wooden bar across its front.

"Now my father wants me to wear this for my opening scene." She removed the heavy cloak she'd been wearing to reveal a full-length, grayish flannel robe, with sleeves and a high neck. She pulled her hair into a ponytail and held it behind her head. "Like this. What do you think?"

"It looks good," I said.

"Yeah, but I want to wear this." She undid the string at her neck and pulled the robe over her head. Underneath she wore a pair of powder blue panties with white trim and a bra to match, both barely covering their objectives.

What the hell was I going to do now?

She laid the robe over one of the stools. "I don't know," I said, my eyes roaming up and down her body. "I mean I think it looks good, but man, those guys aren't going to remember their lines. I wouldn't. And the guys in the audience! They'll–"

"No, dummy," she said, "I don't mean these. These are my own clothes.

Do these look like clothes from back then?" She spread her arms, then turned her backside toward me.

"I don't know," I said, and sat down to hide my excitement. "I never get to see girls clothes like that—now or then."

"Well, they're not. But I saw this picture of women in a brothel and some of them wore something like this. Wait'll I show you. I got it from Lebanon Valley's wardrobe room."

She grabbed a flimsy thing on the stool beside the robe and brought it over her head. It was a light blue, translucent nightgown, that reached to mid upper-thigh. She put on a different robe that wrapped around and tied in front. She left it open and studied herself in the mirror. She pulled on the material just below the bra. "That doesn't look right, does it?"

She was asking the wrong person. She had great legs that the nightie let you see most of, and it's sheerness let you see her bra and panties. What didn't look right? It was mesmerizing. "It looks good to me," I said.

"Nah. The bra isn't right." She reached up, undid the bra, and pulled it off. She adjusted the material so it fell nicely over her breasts. She smiled. "There, that's better." She turned to me. "Don't you think?"

I could hardly believe it—she was *asking* me to stare at her breasts. It was like gazing at them through light-blue tinted glass. I could see everything. If she walked on stage like that, with the robe open, legs bare, panties showing, breasts as plain as pie, it would cause instant erections clear to the balcony.

"Well, what do you think?" she said.

I looked at her eyes, those mischievous, playful green eyes, and shook my head. "If you go out there like that, . . . I don't know."

"It *does* look good, doesn't it. I want it to seem like we were just making love. Imagine all those boys and how excited they'd get?"

I laughed. "And the guys on stage will be speechless. The play will be over."

"No it won't. They know their lines. They'll do it."

"What'll your father say?"

"Oh, he knows my way is better; more realistic. If they'd just been making love she'd come out and want to get him back, not caring what the men thought, maybe even liking them looking at her. If they weren't, why would she even bother coming out? She wouldn't. She'd stay in bed. I would."

"So do it your way then," I said.

"He won't let me."

"Well . . . you're stuck then, right?"

"Not really." She looked at herself in the mirror. "I can still do it my way. All he'd do is yell and be mad for awhile."

"Then do it your father's way tonight, and your way tomorrow. That'd work."

"That's what I was thinking. Should I?"

"Why not?"

She turned to me. "Stand up."

"What?"

She walked over and tugged on my arm. "Come on, stand up. I want to try one of my scenes out a different way."

"But–"

"Just stand up, 'ya scaredy-cat. Come on." She tugged with both hands.

"Okay, okay." I started up then faked a cramp in my calf that allowed enough body gyrations and arm movement to rearrange and camouflage things.

"Okay, what?" I said.

She placed one foot, then the other, in front of me, toe to toe. "Now this is the going away scene before the Colonel goes off to find Sitting Bull. He may not come back. This may be the last time we ever see each other. Your hands are here."

She placed my hands on her hips, the nightie slick beneath them. I could feel the warmth of her skin and the curves of her body. Her breasts loomed firm and erect a foot away. A fragrance of fields and flowers reached me. She placed her forearms on my shoulders. "My father thinks it should be a brief hug, like it's difficult to part, and then a quick kiss and you turn and hurry away to the men, who are watching. But I think it should be more like this." She eased forward and melted her body against mine, slid her fingers into my hair and gently guided my head down until our lips met. From my knees up, her body pressed against mine. Yeow!!

She stepped back after two seconds. "Loosen up. You're stiff as a board." She twirled the hair at the back of my neck, a pleased look on her face. "You may never see me again. Put your arms around me . . . Squeeze me . . . Feel me. My hips, my breasts, my lips. Wanting you . . . Needing you. This is our last moment together. You've got to feel it." She rocked my shoulders back and forth.

"Come on, loosen up. Let yourself go. You may never have this chance again. Make the most of it." She smiled, put her hands around my neck, and moved in like a dog to dinner.

I did what I was told as best I could, and damn did it feel good. I'd never felt anything like it. Like soft, warm, electrifying sunshine, her body against mine, her breasts kneading my chest, her moist lips moving against mine, my hands on the small of her back, feeling the top of her panties beneath the silkiness of the nightie and wanting to move down, then starting to . . .

She pulled back, her hands resting behind my neck, her body inches from mine from top to bottom, her eyes twinkling. "That was better, wasn't it?"

It was goddamn near lethal. I nodded.

"Don't you think that's a better going away kiss?"

"He won't go."

She laughed and stepped away. "I've got to get out there."

She turned her back, dropped the robe, pulled the nightie over her head and put on the flannel robe. She fixed her hair into a ponytail. "How do I look?"

She was a picture of self-assurance and good looks. "Elegant," I said. "Divine. Exquisite."

"Thanks. And thanks for helping me."

"Yeah."

She giggled, then left me there itching for more.

I watched the rest of the rehearsal. During the second scene, a coyote howling in the night signals the start of a "I'm scared spitless" discussion between soldiers sitting around a campfire. Mr. Hayes wanted the howl to come from directly behind the fort, in the middle of the stage. After the guy who'd been doing it, did it, Mr. Hayes asked me to try. I thought of Nancy and howled like an animal.

"Very good, David. I want it just like that tomorrow night, so the balcony rear can hear it. Position yourself before the scene starts and stay put till it finishes. And watch out for the braces and for the stockade. And be quiet."

The next night I slipped into my space feeling sorry for Mr. Hayes and everyone else taking the play seriously, because the audience wasn't. It was Tuesday night. Christmas vacation started Wednesday night, after an easy day at school ending with the annual Christmas present from the teachers—a feature-length movie they showed at Founders Hall with kindergarten through twelfth grade in attendance. A couple hours later and the guys whose guardians could pick them up at night left after supper. Everyone else left the next day for two weeks at home over Christmas and New Years.

So the mood started out festive, better suited for a comedy than a drama. It took the nearly five hundred students, intermediate as well as senior division, seated wherever they wanted and with a minimum of supervision because the officials hadn't expected such a large turnout, a full minute to settle down after the lights dimmed. I was off to the side and could see the guys sitting directly in front of the stage, most of them upperclassmen. Jim, Huey, and Brownie were among them.

Their eyes followed the sentry as he walked back and forth; they looked left when he stopped and stared to the right, some of them grinning because they had followed his gaze. "Sound the alarm! Someone's approaching!" The sentry ran toward the center of the stage, tripped and fell. His rifle slipped from his hands and slid out of sight. The guys chuckled. The rifle slid back into view and the fallen sentry dove to keep it from disappearing across the stage, which made the guys laugh out loud.

I walked to the back where Mr. Hayes told the guys to calm down, then sent them out. The sentry pointed, and the guy beside him ducked and the sentry's hand poked Timmy in the face, causing another round of laughter. Mr. Hayes moaned.

Another outburst occurred as I walked to the other side. Nancy was there. "Things aren't going well, are they?" she said.

"Not if you're not looking for laughs, they're not."

"Oh, well. That's how it goes sometimes." She was dressed in street clothes. "I got to get ready. Call me in ten minutes, okay?"

When I knocked on her dressing room door, she told me to come in and close it. She stood with the cloak open, the tied robe beneath, and grinning. I smiled. "You got something special under there?"

"You know I do." She opened the robe: sheer nightie, bare breasts, and red panties. Red? I pointed. "Your underwear. They're red."

She shrugged. "I forgot my blue ones. These will have to do."

"Timmy will never make it. He'll faint."

She stepped forward suddenly. "Let's do the going away scene again."

"I don't know, I . . . "

She put her hands around my neck and pressed against me. "Come on," she said, and swayed back and forth across my chest.

"Don't you, ahm . . . " My voice cracked, sounding weak, like my brain. "The play, it's . . . ahm, isn't . . . "

Someone rapped on the door. "Honey, you ready?" Mr. Hayes said.

Nancy kept her hands around my neck, preventing my escape. "Almost."

"Can I come in?"

"Just a minute." She pressed against me, her lips found mine. "Mmmm," she moaned, sending shivers through me. She stepped back, tied her robe, then tied the cloak. "Okay, Daddy. I'm ready."

Mr. Hayes opened the door and Nancy stepped outside. In the mirror, he saw me on the other side of the door. "What are you doing in here?"

"Nothing."

"I asked him to call me," Nancy said, moving off. "He helped me put on this stupid cloak. It's so bulky."

I stepped past Mr. Hayes, who eyed me as though that's all I had better been doing. They went one way, I the other. Thirty seconds before she was to go on, she slipped off her cloak and stood facing the stage between side curtains. All anyone behind her could see was her robe. She loosened the ties and held them. She saw me watching, smiled, then flashed the robe open.

"Wow!" a guy between the curtains beside me whispered.

Mr. Hayes came up behind her and said something. She nodded. He saw the robe, said something else, but it was too late; she moved forward opening the robe, revealing her legs, panties and breasts.

"Holy shit!" the guy next to me said. I hurried to the front of the stage. Timmy was facing the audience and his men. A startled hush fell over everything. Huey and the others sat up, eyes staring. The men gaped in amazement. Timmy turned around and his mouth fell open.

"What's the commotion, Dear?" Nancy said.

"Jesus Christ!" someone from the audience said.

"Yeah!" said another. Catcalls and whistles followed.

While Nancy fumbled at closing her robe, the men's heads shifted for position like chicks at feeding time. Timmy remained dazed.

The robe finally closed. "What's the commotion, Dear?" Nancy repeated. "Hmm?" She touched his arm. "Has a messenger arrived?"

Timmy nodded. "Yeah . . . yes . . . a messenger. He just arrived. He's come with bad news, I'm afraid. General Custer . . ."

At the end of the first scene, Mr. Hayes nearly beat the curtain to the center of the stage and scattered the guys lurking around Nancy. She stood with her hands deep in her robe pockets and listened to his tirade. "I was right and that's all there is to it," she said. "Besides, it's over." She spun on her heels, robe twirling, and left.

The audience buzzed with excitement and so did we as we set the stage for the second scene. The guys could hardly believe they'd saw her practically naked. They giggled and laughed and punched each other until Mr. Hayes snapped at everyone to keep quiet. "This is a play, a serious drama! Don't forget it!"

I got into position behind the stockade and sat on a small platform that had been used to hold bales of straw for a haystack affect. It was empty now, the bales piled on the floor beside it. They closed the black curtain behind me and lowered a night sky with a moon. It felt like I was in a cocoon; only four feet separated me from the stockade with the curtain pushing against both sides and against the back of the platform.

The lights dimmed, leaving me in near darkness. The main curtains opened and the actors began talking of their upcoming campaign. In five minutes my howl was due.

Something ruffled to my left. A fold of the curtain swayed gently back. A hand pressed it farther back and someone slid past it. Nancy! I stood up to meet her so she wouldn't walk into the platform. "Nancy," I whispered. "What are you doing?"

She inched forward until she touched my hand, grasped it, and stepped carefully beside me. "It's *dark* back here," she whispered.

My heart started pounding. "Kind of. Your eyes will adjust."

"Did you like my scene?"

"Yeah. Everybody did. Except your dad."

"He'll get over it. He knows I was right."

I listened to the guys talking. I still had a few minutes.

What was she up to? Not knowing made me nervous. "Don't you have a scene coming up?" I asked.

"Not for another fifteen minutes or so. I have plenty of time. . . . Where are you?"

I had moved a little away. She reached out, touched my arm, and stepped beside me. "You're not afraid of me, are you?"

"No," I lied. "Haven't you changed yet for your next scene?"

"No, see?" In the semi-darkness, she opened the cloak, untied the robe and spread it open. I squinted, but saw nothing clearly. "Not really, but I believe you. Maybe you should–"

"Here." She took my hand and touched it against her silk covered side, then slid it across both breasts, down her stomach, and released it after pressing my fingertips gently against her crotch.

BOING!

"See?"

I swallowed. "Yeah."

She wanted me to make a move, right? But what? A play was going on and we were practically in it.

"What are you wearing?" Her hands touched my chest, ran down my sides, over my buns, down and back up my thighs, and one hand zipped over my crotch, causing me to jerk backwards. She finished back on my chest. "You've got a nice body."

"Thanks."

Her left hand cupped my neck. "Let's do the goodbye scene again."

"I have to howl soon."

"I'll make you howl."

"But–"

She put her other hand around my neck and pressed against me. I stepped backwards and bumped the platform. "Come on," she urged, and leaned harder into me.

"But I . . . wait! Here comes my cue!"

"Just one kiss."

She pulled my head down until our lips met. "Mmmm." I heard the line before the line that preceded my howl. "Wait!" I said. "I've got to howl." I lifted my head, ready to howl, and she began nibbling at my neck with soft, moist kisses.

" . . . That's what I think," the guy said.

My howl sounded like the cry of a feeble, dying coyote.

One of the actors snorted, holding back laughter. "Louder," Nancy said. She shook my shoulders. "Come on, louder!"

I took a deep breath and howled a good one. I smiled with pride. "Nice," said Nancy, placing her lips back on my neck.

Okay, this was it, attack time. While she nibbled I brought my hands around and put them on her sides . . . she didn't notice or didn't care. She pulled my head down and we started kissing. I slid my hands lightly over her buns, then dropped my right hand farther until I felt her warm, bare leg. Slowly I slid my hand up to the firm roundness beneath her panties. Should I go under the waistband for my first ever feel of female ass? No; it might disturb her. Besides, there was easier prey to capture.

My hand crept up her side, . . . slowly . . . slowly, ready to jerk away at the first outcry. The smooth, heavy weight of her breast touched my fingertips; I paused. This was it . . . Iwo Jima. I inched my hand up and over her breast until her nipple nudged against my moist palm. Yeeoww! I'd made it! And not one protest. No "please don'ts" or . . .

She moaned, and I froze. Was something wrong? She tilted her head back, mouth open, then took my wrist and moved it so that my hand glided in circles over her breast, the nipple bending and twisting. "That feels so-oh good," she said. She let go and I continued, delighted for her direction and thrilled she liked it as much as I did.

I'd been breathing so as not to be heard; hers had been getting heavier and heavier and now started escaping in soft gasps, propelling mine into a quicker rhythm. "Come here," she said, and tugged me around so that she was against the platform, then sat down and pulled me over, laying back as I fell on her. I heard the voices of the guys on the other side of the stockade, only yards away. Could they hear us? Could the balcony hear us?

Her legs came up and wrapped around my waist. She squirmed; I squirmed. A rhythm developed. "Yes . . . yes . . . " she kept repeating, gasping each word as we rocked against each other. She pulled my head down and kissed me, turned my face to the side and her lips were at my ear, her breath hot. Her warm, moist tongue slipped into my ear, licking wildly. Sensations I'd never felt before spasmed over me. She moaned in pleasure. "Oh, yes, faster," she said.

I was a writhing, squirming, firebreathing mass of senses, attuned only to pleasure. Nothing penetrated my lustful quest but her urgent pleas, their meaning obliterated by the accelerating rhythm of her voice, carried to my ears by hot, darting breaths. Faster and faster we rocked. Nothing to stop us. This was it. Heaven!

Then, like a distant sound drifting harmlessly through the night until sudden recognition strikes fear and terror, my mind registered the words she was moaning, moaning so loudly the people in the parking lot could hear: "Fuck me! . . . Fuck me! . . . "

I'd be hanged!

I pulled up. She pulled me down. I yanked her arms from around my neck, then struggled to get free of her legs. As I twisted loose, she grabbed for me. I jumped back and her grasping fingers pushed against my chest, sending me stumbling backwards toward the stockade. I deliberately started to fall, hoping I'd hit the floor before the props. At the same time, I twisted around, thinking I might be able to catch myself by grabbing a wooden support.

I needed five steps but got only four. My arm and shoulder tore through the stockade at waist height; it started forward. I jerked my exposed hand up and shoved back with all my might. For a second I didn't think I could stop it. But then, slowly, it settled back into place. I withdrew my hand.

Nancy was gone. The audience roared with laughter. Through the hole I could see the guys around the campfire, laughing while rocking into each other or rolling on the floor. The broken section was still partially attached. I reached through and grabbed it. "It's alive!" Brownie yelled from the audience. I wedged the piece back into place, then sat down, head in hands.

In half a minute I'd gone from near orgasm to life-long humiliation.

5

The first Sunday after Christmas vacation I found Mike's cousin, Bobby Spangler, at the Boys Worship Service. He'd been sent to his seat early, along with the five other guys at his table, for laughing too much at breakfast, an indication that what I had heard about his unit was true. His was not going to be an easy life. Mr. Druggins, his housefather, was only in his third year at the Home and already had the reputation of one of the worst houseparents in the entire school. If they lost at sports, he made the guys work extra around the unit. He encouraged squealers and his favorite saying was, "Someday you'll thank me for this."

As I descended the balcony steps towards the section where Bobby was seated, I saw one guy whisper under his breath, then glance about to make sure he wasn't spotted. I reached them, explained who I was, and asked if they'd get in trouble if I talked to them. The oldest kid checked something over his right shoulder, then said, "Probably not. None of us will tell, and the only other houseparent that squeals isn't up here yet."

Bobby looked a lot like Mike: same wide eyes, small nose, and a quick, dimpled smile. I let him read the letter. When he handed it back, I said, "When Mike said you were a little scared about getting in here, he meant nervous like; but everybody's that way when they first come in. In a couple of weeks you'll know all the stupid rules and you'll see it's no big deal. All right?"

He nodded.

I talked with him for another couple minutes, asking about his classes and telling him what I knew of his teachers, many of whom I had had. By then guys were starting to come in, and I knew Mr. Druggins or the other housefather would be arriving soon. I told him I'd look for him in the lobby next week and we could talk more.

Mr. Druggins had been pointed out to me before I headed up to see Bobby. He was standing at the bottom of the right hand staircase, where he always stood to make sure his guys didn't go up before ten of–and they all had to go up that side. He was in his mid-forties, about six foot with a solid build, greased back black hair, and a small head. As I descended the stairs, he stood with one hand on the railing, one on his hip, and was glaring to the side. A kid hustled into view.

"You couldn't go to the bathroom before?" he said. "Get up there!" He swung his hand as though he would cuff the kid, who ducked.

I was near the bottom. Druggins' eyes flipped from the kid to me. Over my final three steps neither of us looked away nor blinked. "You got a problem, boy?" he said.

"Yeah," I answered, and walked around him toward the main doors. "I got a few of them."

"I'll bet you do."

The following week Bobby's unit arrived preceded by a short, pudgy man with a pleasant grin. Bobby spotted me and walked across the marble floor.

"Who's that, Bobby, you're second help?"

"Yeah. Mr. Wilcox. He's real nice."

"That's good. You guys deserve it. How's things going?"

"Okay, I guess."

"They give you a big brother?"

"Yeah. Matthew."

In the intermediates, new guys and incoming sixth graders were always assigned big brothers. Usually it was your roommate. They were supposed to inform you of the rules and show you how things were done. Often, if the new guy screwed up excessively, the big brother would receive half the blame and the same punishment.

"Which one is he?" I asked.

"He's the tall guy behind Mr. Wilcox, in the blue suit, laughing."

Matthew stood out not because of his height, but because of his laugh, a loud, annoying one.

"Is he an eighth grader?"

"Yeah. Mr. Druggins makes him jog around the cluster in the mornings a lot because he's always getting in trouble. He's kind of messy."

"Do a lot of guys have to jog around the cluster?"

"Sometimes. Once we all did. Whenever you mess up, he makes you jog. He even rides along on his bike or in his car sometimes."

Bobby scratched his left palm, his eyes apprehensive. I squeezed his shoulder. "Well, buddy, you just have to not get in trouble and you won't be jogging, right?"

"I guess."

Even as I said it, I knew the odds were against him. In the intermediates, getting into trouble was like breathing, how could you not? You didn't know your rights and were too frightened to go into Homelife to inquire or complain. The housefather, and oftentimes the housemother, could physical manhandle you. You were outsized, uniformed, and nearly defenseless. No wonder Bobby looked like someone walking a minefield. I had felt the same way.

"Are you Catholic or Protestant, Bobby? Anything like that?"

"My mom's Catholic. My dad was a Presbyterian but he didn't go to church much. My mom doesn't, either. Just Christmas and stuff. She works a lot."

"The reason I ask was because I go to the Catholic church. If you want, you can go, too. You'd get out of the unit more, and see less of Druggins."

"No one in my unit goes to the Catholic church. One guy goes to another one, though."

"You can still go," I said. "Afterwards they drive us back to the community center and you can catch your bus and meet the other guy in your unit."

"Can I go without asking Mr. Druggins?"

"Sure. Ask your second help. He'll tell you."

His second help put a hand on Bobby's shoulder as he listened to him. When Bobby pointed, I motioned with my hand. He turned back to Bobby, nodded, and said something. Bobby started back, skipping several steps on the way.

"He said I could go! Where should I meet you?"

"Down at the porte-cochere. There'll be three or four buses. If I'm not there, just wait for me. I'll stand outside. Okay?"

He nodded, smiling a big, joyful, dimpled grin. Mike's kind of grin.

The front left center seats in the Catholic church were reserved for Homeguys. I had liked sitting there when I was younger because there was always someone fooling around, especially among the older guys who sometimes had to be shushed or escorted out by one of several church monitors assigned to watch us. Not until I developed a social conscious did I realize what idiots we looked like, and then I hated sitting there. But we had no choice. One of the monitors always met the buses and directed us along the side and in the door nearest to our section, where another usher would herd us into our assigned seats. Occasionally I did spot a senior division guy standing alone or with a buddy amongst the townsfolk, and wondered how they managed it. By my junior year I was doing it myself. I'd either slip around the opposite side of the bus and go through the front door, or I'd follow the herd and step across the aisle and into the townsfolk side. It was only the older guys who did this and the monitors left us alone. I liked doing it for three reasons: I didn't have to sit with our guys and feel embarrassed, I showed the townsfolk we weren't all jerks, and the view of the girls was much better sitting amongst them than across the way.

I told Bobby about the seating arrangements, and he elected to stay with me, promising to be quiet. We took aisle seats in the back. Within two minutes the monitor we called String Bean was leaning over us. "I'm sorry, but you'll have to sit up front with the other Milton Hershey boys," he said.

"How come? I've sat over here before."

"I know you have. But he hasn't."

Bobby bent his head and began digging into his left palm. A girl, younger than Bobby, turned around in her seat in front of us. Her mother turned her frontward.

"Can't he stay here?" I asked. "He just got in the school. He's my cousin."

String Bean looked at Bobby, who snuck a peek at him before returning his gaze to his hands. "Okay. As long as he keeps quiet. And next week he sits with the others."

"All right. Thanks."

String Bean left and Bobby looked up, smiling that wide, dimpled grin. I elbowed him in the side. "Cousin."

6

Saturday, January 23, 1971

I had the best town privilege I ever had last night, Teach. The best. Why? Because I was with a pretty girl and we broke all kinds of rules. Milton Hershey rules, real world rules, and rules parents don't want their precious daughters ever breaking.

First rule I broke was getting into her car (her mother's station wagon actually), then we drove in it, crossed the Hershey line into Palmyra, went through Anville, past Cleona, all the way to Lebanon. And we broke real world rules, too. We sped most of the way, past on a double yellow line, went through three red lights that didn't change fast enough, and parked where it said no parking.

And you know what? It was fun. I liked it. Rebels is what we were. Rules, who needs them? Laws, they're for ball-less cowards.

(Which reminds me, we must never forget this diary is all fiction, and you can't nail me for fiction.)

HA! ha, ha, ha, ha, ha.

When Nancy had called a week earlier, she caught me completely by surprise. I'd thought of her a lot since the play, but always in the past tense and with humiliation, embarrassment, and regret over what I had done. While she made small talk about vacation and Christmas presents, my mind flip-flopped between why she was calling and how to apologize for being such an idiot. Then she abruptly focused my thoughts on one subject by saying, "I'm calling because I wanted to talk to you after the play but never got the chance. I want to apologize for what happened."

"You?" I said, incredulous. "You didn't do anything. I was the jerk who panicked and went flying through the stockade."

"But you wouldn't have done that if I hadn't of done what I did."

"No, no, you didn't do anything wrong. What you did was . . . I liked it; I just panicked. What you were saying–I wasn't paying attention until I started acting like a jerk because I thought everyone could hear us and they were going to come back and kill me. But I asked, and the guys said they didn't hear anything until I dove through the stockade like a moron."

"That was quite an entrance."

"Yeah . . . quite."

She chuckled a moment, then silence. Think of something! I told myself.

"So," she said, "you didn't mind what I did?"

"Mind? No. I liked it. I minded what I did."

"I'm glad, because I liked it too. You make me so . . . hot."

Yeow! "Well . . . , I was pretty excited, too."

"I could tell."

I laughed.

"So we're still friends?" she said.

"Sure. In fact," I said, "I was going to ask you out that night. See if you wanted to go to a movie or something."

"And now you're not?"

"No. I still want to."

"Want to what?"

"Ask you out."

Two seconds past. "Well . . . go on then," she said. "Ask."

"Do you want to go to a movie some time, Nancy?"

"That depends. With who?"

Nancy amazed me, and thrilled me. In just one date she showed me what it meant to live without fear, without timidness. From the first stomp on the accelerator that swept us from the curb on Chocolate Avenue into a hearty U-turn, my lesson began. I thought the U-turn amusing, entertaining, yet reckless, but that was before I understood her. She hadn't interfered with traffic, and when I asked if U-turns were legal she said, "I don't know. There aren't any cops around now anyway." On possibly getting caught in her other violations she said, "What are they going to do—give me a ticket? So what?"

As we ran lights, sped, and did all we could to make it to the movie on time, I marveled at her attitude and its simplicity. So what? Really, that was it. The consequences weren't that bad, and what were you're chances of getting caught? Why worry?

So when we sat in the balcony and she draped her legs over the chair in front of us, I first looked over at the only other couple up there, then threw my legs over too. What the hell. They didn't want us doing it, they'd tell us.

Halfway through the movie, Nancy shivered and sat up. "I'm cold," she said.

"You want your jacket?" I said, sitting up and reaching for it in the seat beside me.

"No."

"You don't?"

Her eyes stared into mine as she barely moved her head from side to side.

If she was cold why didn't she want her jacket? "You want my jacket? Or both of them?" I guessed happily.

She rolled her eyes then reached over, took my hand and drew it around her shoulders. "There, that's better."

"Oh," I said. "I see."

But quickly I realized I didn't. Was this it? Was this her way of resuming where we had left off, by giving me a jump-start into making out in a theater? Or was she really cold? But if she was, why didn't she just take her jacket? Because she'd rather snuggle close to keep warm? Or did she want to fool around?

I grinned at my confusion, then laughed out loud at a scene in the movie. Nancy snuggled closer and laid her left hand across my stomach. My smile dissolved.

Another move? Should I make a move? I inched closer to her hair and inhaled. Herbal. Fragrant. Nice. Going for seconds, I froze–her fingers had begun tracing tiny circles on my right side.

Whether she was making a move or not, I saw no harm in reciprocating, and began to caress her shoulder with an equally soft touch. Immediately her hand slid up to hug my chest and her lips began nibbling my neck.

Now *this* was a goddamn move.

It was also in a movie theater.

I moved into her, so that without losing suction I could turn and see if the other couple was watching. They didn't even know they were in public; it looked like soon they'd be naked and horizontal across the seats. Hell, if they could do it.

Nancy's tongue squirmed up my neck.

Yeow! Attack. Attack.

I slid my fingers off her shoulder and cupped her breast. Her hand dropped to my crotch. I shifted and aimed my right hand directly into the opening of her three-button top–I loved those button tops. Eureka and YEOW!–No bra, just a warm breast and an attentive nipple.

We began kissing opened mouthed. I moved my tongue wherever it seemed she wanted it, all the time concentrating on her tit. That's what I liked. And her handling of my crotch like play-doh.

The movie faded as our temperatures rose. Our hands groped, our tongues tangoed. Nothing else mattered until brilliant, blinding light burst upon us and we bolted upright looking like we had front row seats at a church meeting. It wasn't a mob of officials and state police and Nancy's father standing over us with flashlights, but a glorious sunrise blazing across the screen.

I exhaled and looked at Nancy. She rolled her eyes, we laughed, then she snuggled close, content to watch the movie.

Afterwards, we bought sodas in a nearby sub shop, then Nancy gave me a tour of Lebanon Valley's campus. She stopped in front of a three-story brick building. "This is where I'll be next year," she said. "And conveniently located on this side, is a boy's dorm." I looked. "Shit," she said.

"What's the matter?"

"Nothing."

She pulled from the curb. A tall, good-looking guy with long hair who had been walking from the dorm, stopped and watched us go. He wore a varsity jacket with a basketball sewn onto it.

"I think that guy back there wanted to talk to you, Nancy."

"He's an asshole. He can talk to himself."

Her old boyfriend. I wanted to make her forget him, to smile, laugh, and be herself. But how? Suddenly I recognized a building on our right and pointed to it. "Hey, that's where I got in trouble last month. I called two girls assholes, cowards, jerks, morons, and other unmentionables I won't say in front of you."

"Really?" She smiled, wonder and pride mixed together. "How come?"

I told her the story, and by the time we reached the golf course at quarter after ten, she had forgotten her boyfriend and was my date again. I had her pull into the service road on the seventeenth fairway. I'd been planning what to say and began as soon as she stopped. "Thanks for going out with me tonight, Nancy. I had fun."

"Me, too. Thanks for asking . . . finally."

I smiled. "Would you like to do it again sometime, maybe?"

"I guess so, maybe."

"What about a dance, then? We're having one in three weeks. It's Saturday, the thirteenth. It's our Valentines dance."

She raised one eyebrow. "Valentine's dance. Moving pretty fast, aren't we?"

"It can just be a dance, if you want. I don't care."

"You don't want me to be your valentine?"

"No, it's not that. It's . . . You can be anything you want if you come."

"What if I want to be late?"

"That too. If you come to the dance, I won't mind that, either."

"All right, then maybe I'll come late and maybe I'll be your valentine. Just let me check to make sure I'm free."

"Great. What about another Friday night date?" I said. "Like this coming Friday?"

"I'm going to a play in Harrisburg this Friday. I can the following one, though."

"Should I call to remind you or anything?"

"I better call you. My father doesn't know about tonight, and he might have a baby if he finds out it's you. He asked again about you being in the dressing room. Wanted to know what you were really doing."

"What did you tell him?"

"'Nothing.' Which is true. I'm the one who was doing things. I'm always the one doing things and starting them between us."

"I'm just not used to it," I said. "I like it, though."

"I can tell."

A second past before her hand popped off the seat. "Well . . . ? Do you want to give me a good night kiss or do I have to give you one?"

"No . . . Yeah . . . I'd like to."

"You going to do it from over there?"

I slid over, smiling and thinking how much fun she was. She was quick-witted, pretty, and horny. How had I gotten so lucky?

I kissed her softly, thought about stopping, she twirled the hair at the back of my neck, I cupped her breast with my hand, and the battle was joined. She ended it twenty seconds later when she pulled back and smiled. "Don't you have to get back soon?"

"Oh, shit. Oh . . . sorry." I scooted across the seat and jumped out. "Okay, you'll call me then, right?" She raised her eyebrows and I laughed. "Okay, you will."

7

That winter I decided to try something new: trapping. Eddie had trapped with Carl the year before, and in early November welcomed me enthusiastically to his one-man trapping line along the creek running through the golf course and woods behind our unit.

At first I liked trapping, especially for the freedom of being unsupervised and unwatched. I also enjoyed the cat and mouse games we played with the animals, the knowledge I learned, and for the link it gave me with trappers of the past. Some of the things we did, they must have done. Like boiling our traps in a large pot over an open fire, throwing in walnuts to cover our scent, and never touching them again unless wearing gloves; like walking upstream so silt didn't obscure our view as we probed the creek's edge with our boots searching for water entrances and looking for alternate entry and exit holes in the bank above; like putting contibear traps at underwater entrances and regular foot traps above ground—numbers two, four or six depending on the size of the paw print; like baiting spots with garbage, night after night, watching the food disappear and then setting traps and the following day's anticipation and the various results: finding the creature; its gnawed off foot; untouched garbage because they suspected something; or no garbage at all and a sprung trap, prompting a smile and a further resolve to outsmart the critter that outsmarted us. I was astonished at how easily they skinned: hang it, slice around each foot, then peel the hide from its muscle and bone, drawing it down like masking tape from the role as we scrapped off excess fat. Then we'd stretch the hide on wire, clean the underside, and let it dry. A few days later we had a soft, durable, second skin that could be fashioned into clothing, hats, gloves, containers, or whatever, just like trappers of old had done it.

For all those reasons I liked trapping. For other reasons, I didn't. It wasn't a necessity any longer. Was I an accessory to murder just for money? And the sleep deprivation. Though I had gotten better, I still didn't fall asleep until ten or eleven. Getting up at three forty-five deprived me of two hours sleep. Finally, I didn't like how we had to kill the animals that hadn't drowned in the contibear traps, weren't at the water's edge to easily step on and drown, or were too big to dare step on: we had to club them with baseball bats. Actually, Eddie did—I'd been used only as a diversion so he could take careful aim and whack them clean, crisp, knock-out blows to give us time to inject them with air from a hypodermic needle that the vet had discarded and which we used to rush air to the creature's heart, head, or lungs, killing them for sure if the blow hadn't already done it. Though it seemed as merciful as possible, it left me with a feelings of guilt and uncertainty.

Our first night back from vacation, Eddie and I placed and set the traps we had brought inside before leaving. As we made our rounds through the dark, cold, and breezeless night, I told Eddie I was thinking of quitting and why.

"Aww, don't quit man," he said. "I got something planned that'll be lots of fun. Wait till the fifth green and I'll show you."

Our farthest trap lay just beyond the fifth green, where the water rushed into the bank leaving a cave-like excavation beneath the roots of a large over-hanging tree. We set our trap where the animal would have to step into the water to get under the tree, then anchored the chain beside a hollowed-out log that lay on a small patch of dry creek bed. I helped Eddie remove the debris from inside the log, then sat down. "Now what's this big deal that's going to guarantee us so much fun?"

Eddie withdrew a small metal box from his duffel bag. Inside lay some-thing wrapped in cellophane. He lifted one end, and a sandwich bag half filled with something green and leafy unraveled. "Marijuana," Eddie said. "Wacky tobacky. Dope."

"Where'd you get it?"

"Over vacation. Some guy in our neighborhood sold it to me. Ten bucks. It's half an ounce. We'll be laughing our asses off."

"You do any yet?"

"Not yet. I was waiting to try it with you. Want to?"

I looked from Eddie's hopeful gaze to the bag. If you listened to health teachers and law officers, one whiff of marijuana and you were on to the harder stuff and filthy, germ-infested needles while you robbed, stole, and killed to support the habit you would undoubtedly fall victim to. On the other hand, I knew of guys who had tried it and hadn't turned into criminals or become addicted. In fact, they said it was harmless and a lot of fun. So who was I to believe?

A much more important consideration, however, was getting caught. If that happened, we'd get kicked out and lose the three-quarters scholarship the Home gave to any graduate who continued in school. I planned on going to college because I didn't know what else to do.

"Well?" Eddie said. "What do you think?"

"I think this falls under the category of 'quit being so ball-less, Purenut, and live a little.' But we can't get caught. Remember what happened to Artie."

"That's why I want to do it now, while we're trapping."

He reached into the bag and withdrew a pack of matches and a lumpy, twisted joint that he placed between his lips. He tore off a match, struck it, and put it to the joint. A second later he snorted three times and burst into a coughing fit.

"This is fun already," I said.

He grinned, still coughing and said, "Isn't it?" He handed me the joint.

I did no better than Eddie. Neither of us had ever smoked before. Five times we tried and five times we burst into coughing fits. We stopped from fear the effects might be slow in developing and we didn't want to find ourselves in the middle of snacks, embarking on a two-hour laughing spree that ultimately ended in expulsion.

After Eddie put the metal box inside the log, we stuffed each end with leaves and branches. "You feel anything?" I asked. "I don't."

"I think so. My eyes. They're kind of numb."

We finished resetting the traps and headed back to the unit. "Your eyes still tingling?" I asked, as we walked down the outside basement stairwell.

"Nah. I don't feel shit." We stepped inside. "Tomorrow," Eddie whispered with renewed hope. "Sometimes it takes longer. Tomorrow we'll feel something."

Sunday, January 31, 1970

You know why they say "playing possum," Teach? Did you ever see it in action–or inaction, actually? Boy, are they good. One whack to its head and Brownie was congratulating Eddie on hitting a first pitch grand slam World Series home run. The possum dropped like he'd never been alive. Then Eddie started swaggering the old "Yeah, well . . . , I do it all the time," swagger as they moved in to inject him with air when Peter Possum leapt up and latched onto Brownie's boot.

I sat on the bank and laughed and laughed. Their eyes popped way out of their heads and they both jumped about three feet in the air with Brownie shaking his leg and yelling "HEY! HEY! HEY!!" They were so pissed that when they finished beating him the possum looked dead enough for three critters. They unlatched him and BAM!–off he bolted like he was half-blind, couldn't steer and had sway back. They gave chase but couldn't catch him because they started laughing so much.

Boy, was that funny.

A new batch of marijuana is what made everything so funny. Eddie had gotten it Friday night during town privilege. He'd become impatient and suspicious of the original batch because we had tried it every day and felt nothing more than a slight numbness around our eyes. "This is Colombian," he told me. "It costs twice as much as Mexican and it's supposed to be like ten times as good. We'll be flying!"

Saturday morning, when we started out to check our traps after after-breakfast chores, Brownie was outside shooting basketball by himself. He asked to come along. Since he was our friend and could be trusted, we let him. Our planned surprise for him at the fifth green was reversed when he told us he had smoked marijuana with his brother over vacation. His experience proved immediately helpful.

"No, no" Brownie said, after Eddie had lit the joint, inhaled, and began coughing seconds later. "Take real little hits until you get used to it. That's what my brother taught me."

"Here." Eddie handed Brownie the joint.

Brownie inhaled easily and for a second, then withdrew the joint and inhaled a long draught of fresh air. He handed me the joint. "See?" he croaked, holding his breath. "The fresh air takes it down."

I tried it—a minor drag followed by cool air. I snorted, but held it down. Thirty seconds later a light trail of smoke left my mouth.

After Eddie successfully held down and released his smoke, he growled. "Oh man, Oh man, Oh man . . . !"

Buoyed by our success we eventually inhaled too much, which caused spasms of coughing and left our throats sensitive to even the tiniest of inhales. We stopped with half a joint left.

"Man, I'm feeling this!" Eddie said, hunched over the bag as he meticulously rolled it into its original shape.

We stayed out till just before lunch, then dunked our faces in the freezing creek to snap us back to reality. The next day, after I returned from second church, ate lunch, and did my dishes, we set out to "check our traps." Eddie brought a canteen of water and butterscotch candies to keep our throats cool and soothed. This allowed us to finish an entire joint with minimal coughing, which allowed for much more of the marijuana and its effects to take hold.

Everything, living or not, seemed to be glowing with an intensity of life, as though it had a soul and an awareness of its surroundings. Staring at a large, round, sun-washed rock, I'd ponder its uniqueness, its grainy texture and size, its positioning, how much sunlight it received, the multitude of beings and creatures it had seen over the years and how long it had been around to see them. Then I'd spot something else to stare at in wonder. The woods, golf course, and creek generated a quiet, enduring harmony that made me feel our presence was but a speck in time. I would drift into a zone of thought I had never been into, then be out of suddenly because of a noise or laugh, and I'd be unable to remember exactly what I was thinking but I was immensely aware of how lost I had been.

There was also the hilarity of things. Everything was funny. Mistakes or stupid things we did made us laugh, our laughs made us laugh, hearing a woodpecker's staccato hammering of a tree made us laugh–"Damn, that must hurt," Brownie said, then, in imitation, whacked his head much harder than intended against a tree.

"Damn that must hurt," I said.

"Damn that did hurt!" Brownie said.

Eddie thumped his head against a tree using his duffel bag as a cushion that didn't work well enough, and I put my palm against a tree and thumped the back of my hand.

We were laughing, hysterical, hammering tree trunks with our heads when Brownie spotted an elderly couple on the adjacent fairway watching through the trees. It was a moment of historical hysterics. Nothing was ever funnier. Bats in hand, we staggered up and over the hill to the next fairway, laughing and laughing.

That's when we met the possum. It was alternately chewing at its leg, then clawing at the ground to pull free, then gnashing at its leg again. As we ran down to it, it dashed in a tight circle around the anchor, trying to escape.

Although Brownie and Eddie were in a state of awe and good humor, for me, there was nothing funny about it–until the possum latched into Brownie's boot. In that instant, as it leapt to the attack, they knew as I did, this wasn't right, that something was terribly, terribly wrong, and maybe God or Nature was exacting revenge.

This possum was somebody's mother or father, or daughter or son, sister or brother, cousin, aunt or uncle. We didn't need its fur or flesh like it needed our baited garbage. Which is what I was trying to tell Eddie two days later as he reset a trap that had snagged yet another gnawed off leg. Our trapping just wasn't right. But I was being too analytical, too detailed to put it so simply, and that was the marijuana's doing. We hadn't tried it Monday morning because the memories of the previous day's adventures made us cautious. By Tuesday, however, we felt if we did just one or two puffs, we could enjoy the buzz and not fear getting caught. But the effects were slow in registering, and the two hits turned to three–long, steady intakes held down for half a minute each. By the time Eddie finished rolling his bag, we knew we had made a mistake. We were in hysterics over how funny it would be when we were caught. We dunked our faces in the creek and thought that was hilarious. We decided, when finished, we'd run back along our entire trap line to diminish the effects.

Minutes later we spotted the gnawed off leg. While Eddie reset the trap, I tried to explain why I was thinking of quitting. The marijuana ran my reasons together, leapfrogging my thoughts, confusing me. I stopped to start over.

What was the main reason to stop? The *real* reason? I concentrated hard, extremely hard, so hard that the feeling of concentration became my focus. I was concentrating on concentrating.

Eddie snickered and I realized I had zoned out. He stood up from resetting the trap and shook his head. I'd been saying something. But what? I grinned. "What was I talking about?"

Eddie thought a moment, then lifted his shoulders. "I don't know." We laughed. "You want a butterscotch?" he said. He reached into his bag. "You getting any nookie from Nancy? Any Nancy nookie?"

"Maybe."

"Man, I'll tell you. I love girls. Their tits, their asses, their legs–everything about them. And you got a college girl. You lucky bastard. You like her?"

"Yep."

"A lot?"

"I'm getting there. She's really funny. And smart. She makes me laugh a lot, you know? As much as any guy can. And she's got a neat personality; it's daring, or confident or something. Every time I see her, I like her more and more."

"That's probably because she shows you more and more."

"That doesn't hurt," I said.

When we reached our next trap we discovered the frozen carcass of the possum Brownie and Eddie had bludgeoned two days before. It was trapped by its foreleg, its skull crushed on one side, its spine misshapen, and the leg that had been snared the first time was barely attached.

Eddie threw it into the woods and reset the trap. On the way back, I told him I wouldn't be trapping anymore. I'd go out with him now and then, to get out of the unit or to smoke pot, but I wanted nothing more to do with trapping. I'd given it a shot and didn't like it.

8

As soon as I saw the long dark hair flowing over the back of the cheerleader jacket, I knew it was Lisa. I watched her sit down amongst the other varsity cheerleaders seated behind their team's bench, remove her jacket, toss her hair back, and join in on clapping and tapping her feet in time with the cheer in progress.

I was sitting in the balcony beside Nancy, in the bottom half of bleacher seats that stretched thirty rows to the ceiling. From our seats we could see the entire basketball court, the bleachers on either side of it, the candy booth at the other end, and the other balcony seats grouped in individual sections, five seats high and evenly distributed around the remaining three sides of the gym. Nancy had arrived during the first period and found me waiting and smiling right where she ordered.

"How'd you know about these seats?" I said, as she sat down. "You been here before, huh?" She gave me a look and I laughed. "I know, stupid question."

"My old boyfriend played for Palmyra and this is where I liked to sit."

Her old boyfriend? Just a week and a half ago he was an asshole outside the dorm at Lebanon Valley. What had changed?

"Was he any good?"

"He isn't as wonderful as he sometimes thinks he is. But he's good. He starts for Lebanon Valley as a sophomore. That's part of his problem—he lets it go to his head."

Why was she using the present tense? I liked it better when she used the past tense—as if he were dead tense.

"That won't happen to me," I said. "I'm not good enough in anything to do that."

"Maybe we can change that?"

Yeow!!

"Maybe," I said. "You want to go out to your car?"

She drew my arm around her shoulder, leaned us against the seats behind us, and patted my hand. "Not just yet, Romeo. Let's watch some of the game."

Because a majority of our senior division guys had chosen to attend the game, we outnumbered their spectators for the junior varsity game four to one. Nancy thought this unfair and began rooting for Hershey's team. We sat, my arm around her shoulders, cheering our respective teams and kidding each other over good and bad plays.

The game was decided by three points, and it was the most fun I'd ever had watching us lose. "You want any candy, Nancy?" I asked after the final buzzer.

"Definitely. Something chocolatey, like a Milky Way or a Hershey Bar. Nuts are fine, coconuts aren't."

She was opening her purse. "No, that's okay," I said. "I got it. You want to come along?"

"No, thank you. I'll just enjoy your efforts."

A crowd had gathered at the candy booth, a small room behind the far basket with barn-like doors, the bottom one closed, the top one opened, and two seniors working hurriedly inside. I glanced once at Nancy and saw her sitting with chin in hand, observing whatever. Then I concentrated on maneuvering to the front. I bought a Milky Way and a Hershey Bar and worked my way back through the crowd. As I broke free someone tapped my shoulder.

"Hi, Dave," Lisa said, smiling brightly.

"Hi, Lisa." My smile matched Lisa's, and both smiles seemed to intensify because of the other person's continued smile.

She looked around. "You here with your two buddies tonight?"

"No. Actually, I got a date."

Her face lit up. "Really? That's great. Where is she?"

"In the balcony." I turned to point Nancy out, but didn't spot her right off because she wasn't alone. A guy with long hair, wearing a varsity jacket, sat beside her. Her old boyfriend. The asshole.

"I don't see her right now," I said. "Maybe she went to the bathroom."

"Bring her by the drugstore some Friday night. I'd like to meet her."

"You would?"

"Yeah. It'd be fun."

"It would?"

She gave me a smack. "Stop."

Someone brushed by me and laid his arm around Lisa's shoulders. "Hey, Babe, got my candy?"

"Not yet."

"What are you waiting for? The games gonna start soon."

The guy was two inches taller than me, with blonde hair, blue eyes, and sharp, angular features.

Lisa said, "Dave, this is Ryan. Ryan . . . Dave. We met at the Hershey Park pool party."

"How'd you go there?" Ryan said.

"My roommate's girlfriend worked there. He and I snuck out."

"Ewwww. Past your bedtime, huh?"

"Yeah," I said. "It was." Dickhead.

"I'm glad he did," Lisa said. "Otherwise we'd never of met."

She smiled at me, and I couldn't help but smile back.

"Yeah, well," Ryan said, "let's get that candy before the game starts. See 'ya." He stepped between Lisa and me as he turned her around.

"Ryan," Lisa said. She looked over her shoulder and smiled. "I'll see you around, Dave. Bye."

"I hope they have Nestles here," Ryan said as they moved toward the booth.

Jerkface must have changed since meeting Lisa. No way would she have gone out with an asshole like that. And speaking of assholes . . .

In the balcony, Nancy's was standing. I hurried along the basketball court, up the stairs, and found Nancy alone. I held out my hands, palms open, a candy bar in each. "Eww!" Nancy said, and snatched the Milky Way. "Let's split them."

I unraveled the candy bar considering my options. Should I ask now or wait to see if she tells me? Maybe she didn't want me to know? Should I forget about it since it seemed like nothing had changed? But if I waited, it would be harder to ask later.

I leaned back against the seats. "Who was that you were talking to I saw on the way up here, Nancy? It looked like that guy we saw outside the guy's dorm at Lebanon Valley."

"You saw that, huh?" She took a bite of candy and nodded. "It was him."

"Is that the 'old boyfriend'?"

"Yeah . . . Eric."

Eric. The Norseman. The Invader. "Is he trying to get back together?"

"He's trying."

"Is it working?"

Nancy laid her hands in her lap, took a deep breath and exhaled. "He was my boyfriend for three years in high school and up until we broke up last October. I liked him a lot. But he was being such a jerk . . . " She shifted back beside me. "I don't know if it's working or not. I'm confused."

Great, just what I needed, confusion.

"He's always got girls coming on to him, and I don't think he discourages it. Either I'm your girlfriend and you act it, or I'm not your girlfriend. That's it. I could have guys sniffing around me, too, but I don't because I don't encourage it."

That made sense. If he wanted to play the field now that he was a big shot on campus, maybe I needn't worry?

I said, "I know you had hundreds of our guys pretty interested in you at the Christmas play."

She smiled. "Yes, I did, didn't I?"

"And he does have very good taste in girls, at least from the one I know."

"Yes, he does, doesn't he?" She drew my arm around her and shifted closer. "And right now he doesn't have me—you do."

She smiled, I smiled, and that's how he found us at half time of the varsity game. Nancy's moan alerted me to the problem. I followed her gaze and became instantly worried and confused and nearly moaned myself at the sight of Lisa and Ryan walking along the balcony railing. How did Nancy know who Lisa was and why was she moaning? It was my problem.

But then Eric scooted around them and darted up the seats at an angle. "Hey, how 'ya doing?" he said to me with a friendly, worry-free smile.

"Hi."

"Nanc, I forgot to tell you. That party starts at seven, not eight, next Friday. And it's at the boathouse."

"The boathouse? But I thought . . . "

I was watching Lisa, and what I saw, I liked. Ryan was obviously trying to make up for being a jerk. During the game he and two buddies sitting several seats behind the cheerleaders had been tossing something at them. Though the girls didn't like it they hadn't stopped until told to by one of their school officials. Now Ryan was trying to explain why it was so funny to Lisa, or why he had abruptly turned her from me, or some other asinine move that needed explanation. Lisa was annoyed and he knew it.

"It doesn't matter," Nancy was saying. "I'll get there whenever and leave whenever." She waved her hand in dismissal.

"Hi, Dave," Lisa said, spotting me and smiling that gorgeous smile of hers. She glanced at Nancy then back to me, her smile brighter.

"Hi, Lisa."

Lisa's greeting interrupted Ryan as though he wasn't there. He looked past Lisa, at me, Nancy, and Eric.

Nancy heard Lisa's greeting, saw her smile, and looked at me.

Lisa looked my way for a few more steps then wiggled her fingers. "Bye, Dave."

I nodded at Lisa, then laughed. Ryan was still looking over his shoulder, and Nancy's face hadn't turned a fraction from my direction.

Eric chuckled. "I'll see you around, Nanc. Next Friday, then, at least. Good luck," he said to me.

Nancy didn't respond. I said, "Nancy, he just said goodbye. He's leaving."

Her green eyes stared into mine. She didn't move nor blink.

"She's not a girlfriend, Nancy. I just know her. That guy she's with is her boyfriend." She kept staring. "It's true."

"You more than just know her," she said. "A girl doesn't smile like that at just anybody. She likes you. She likes you a lot for some reason."

"Well, I'm a nice guy, and I like her. She–"

"Do you date her?"

"No. I–"

"Did you ever date her?"

"No."

"Did you ever ask her out?"

"Yeah, last November, just about the time you stopped dating Eric.

Before I even met you. And she said no because she was already dating that jerk there."

"Why is he a jerk?"

I told her of the two reasons I knew of that happened that night. "And that's why her smile was so big. She was making him sweat and worry."

"That's not the only reason."

"Another's because she got to see you. When I was talking to her I told her I was on a date and I was going to point you out, but I couldn't because you were up here holding hands with Eric—"

She whacked me. "Don't lie."

" . . . And so she said to bring you by the drugstore—where she works—sometime because she'd like to meet you. She said it'd be fun. That's another reason she was smiling—she got to see you."

"That's not the only reason."

"You're right. And because she likes me. And we're friends."

"How did you meet?"

I retold every encounter I had had with Lisa, and how Mike's death prompted me to ask her out. It seemed to calm Nancy's suspicions.

"How come you didn't use this 'go for the gusto' vow with me? Wasn't I pretty enough?"

"You were way more than pretty enough. But all the guys were after you. I didn't think I had a chance."

"What about in the workroom when I helped you paint? I was dropping hints all over the place."

"I know. I'm shy, Nancy. I can't change over night, just like that."

"Shy's one thing, dense is another. A hint's a hint, and I gave you plenty of them."

"I know. I'm learning. I'm catching most of them now though, right?"

She didn't answer.

"Half of them? . . . Some of them?"

"A third maybe."

The next hint I caught was at the start of the fourth period. She asked me how I was enjoying the game. We were up fifteen points with their best guy in foul trouble. "Good," I said. "I like when we're winning big like this."

Her stare had a patient look to it that took several seconds to register. "But I don't have to see the whole game," I said. "There's other things I like to do."

We left for her car parked in the back portion of the back lot and started kissing and mauling. "Know what?" she said teasingly.

Was I getting laid right there and then? Was that it?! "What?"

"I can be your valentine."

The dance—she was coming. "Great!"

We resumed groping, eventually stretching out on the back seat. Her jacket opened, her shirt unbuttoned, her bra slipped up, and my lips found her nipples. YEOW!! Another first. If the game hadn't ended so soon, I think I might have gotten one more that night.

9

Carl dipped a plastic pitcher into the trash barrel filled with purple liquid and poured me half a cup. "Try this."

I took a sip, then another. "This tastes just like grape drink. Is there anything in it?"

"Grain alcohol," Carl said. "It's tasteless."

I took another sip, then a hardy swallow. "Wow, this is great. You mean I can get drunk from this?"

"You can get plastered from it." He raised his cup. "To getting plastered."

"To getting plastered." We touched cups, and with three gulps, I emptied mine. I plopped it down on the counter. "Hit me again, bartender."

"Now we're rolling," Carl said, and filled both cups.

I took a drink. "Shit, if this is drinking, I could do this all night."

It was Friday night and I was supposed to be in my hotel room in downtown Lancaster, getting a good night's sleep so I could attend the freshman orientation at Franklin & Marshall College the next day. The hotel was only eight blocks from the campus and Mr. Kennedy, our guidance counselor, had shown me how to get there, arranged for meals, then left me on my own, expecting I'd behave myself because I was a responsible person, headed for college, and it was to my benefit to attend the orientation.

As he drove off with Brownie, who was attending a similar conference at Delaware State the next day—which is why he couldn't stay and chaperone me—

he had no idea of the one kink in his otherwise reasonable plan. Carl. Carl attended Franklin & Marshall College. Carl, who had brought two bottles of wine to the senior's party at our unit and drank most of it himself. Carl, who had gotten drunk the night before he, Mike, and Beth were to come down and take me back to campus for a party, so drunk that the next day he felt it remedial to drink immediately upon awakening and had continued drinking until he past out. Carl, of the live now and forget about tomorrow mentality. Carl, my friend.

I didn't debate long about contacting him. I knew I'd have to be careful because Carl wouldn't be, but knowing that, I thought I could keep it under control.

The student union's information desk led me to Carl's dorm, his room-mate directed me to the four story frat house on College Avenue, and the guy who answered the door sent me down the basement steps to a dimly lit, wide-open room with a stereo system and speakers blaring music on one side and Carl behind the bar on the other, mixing "grape and grain" for the night's festivities. His delight upon seeing me doubled when he discovered I was on my own until seven p.m. Saturday.

With drinks in hand and carrying a pitcher, Carl gave me a tour of the house. He showed me the first, second, and third floors, the top two of which were mostly bedrooms, all similarly decorated with black lights, phosphores-cent and psychedelic posters, and Playboy bunny foldouts. In a third floor room four guys were sitting on the rug passing a joint around, all lights extin-guished except a black light and an illuminated glass cylinder with what looked like lava flowing within.

"Thumper!" one of them said, offering the joint.

"Later," Carl said, and closed the door.

"Where'd 'Thumper' come from?" I asked.

"From when I was pledging. I got in a fight and beat the guy. They said I 'thumped' the hell out of him. So they call me Thumper."

We went up one more flight of steps, steep ones, to the attic and two small rooms, one bed in each. "This is where I'll be living next year if I come back."

"What do you mean 'if'?"

Carl shrugged. "My grades suck. I dropped out of one class and had to repeat another. If I don't get my grades up to a "C" average, the Home won't pay three-fourths, and if they don't pay, I'm out of here."

"You think you'll do it?"

"I don't really care. I'm just doing this because they're paying. I don't know what I want to do."

"I know what you mean," I said. "I don't know what I want to do, either."

"Except party and chase women!" Carl said.

"I'll drink to that."

We each drained our cups then joined the circle of pot smokers on the third floor. Carl offered me the joint in silence, his eyes inquisitive. I took it, inhaled, sucked down fresh air and past the joint to my right. When I smiled at Carl, he shoved me over. "When the fuck you learn that?"

"Trapping. Me and Eddie."

"All right!" He shoved me over again.

The room had its own music, and people continually joined and left the group. There seemed to be at least one joint always circulating, once there were three. I only did small hits, and oftentimes faked it, but by the time we left, I couldn't stop grinning as I floated along, surrounded by an atmosphere of fun, excitement, and girls.

On the first floor the guy collecting money at the front door spotted Carl. "Thumper, take over for me, will 'ya? I need a break."

Carl set the pitcher on the floor and took the wad of money. "How much we charging?"

"Two bucks," said the other guy there, holding a rubber stamp to imprint a skull and crossbones on the back of each incoming person's hand.

"Two bucks!" Carl said to the three guys who entered the house. "Two bucks."

I sat on the steps behind Carl. The guy beside him had an enviable job. Every girl that came in, he got to stamp her hand; he could touch it if he wanted. I knew I would, or thought I would. I took a gulp of my drink and stood up. "Hey, I'll do that if you want."

"Thanks." He gave me the stamp and pad.

"Two dollars!" Carl said to the group of girls coming in. I put my left hand beneath their outstretched hands as though for support, and stamped them. All four girls thanked me and received an enormous grin in return.

Twenty minutes later Carl elbowed me and said, "One dollar, Ladies," to a group of girls entering. "A dollar discount for our sister sorority."

I stamped the first three girls' hands, then stopped and smiled at the fourth. "Hi, Beth."

It took her a second, but then she looked both surprised and pleased. "What are you doing here?"

I stamped her hand. "Stamping hands."

"He's my assistant," Carl said.

"You know what I mean." She stepped beside me to get out of the way of those behind her.

"He's here to have fun and chase woman," Carl said.

"Good for him," the sweet-faced, slightly overweight girl giving Carl her money said.

"Isn't it, though?" Carl said.

"Come on, what are you doing here?" Beth said.

I told her about the orientation and my unsupervised schedule. "So *we're* going to have fun," Carl said. "Right?"

"Right."

I'd stamped the last of Beth's group's hand. She stood beside me while her friends continued down the hallway. "Will you dance with me latter?" she asked.

I moaned. "I can't dance, Beth."

"Everybody can slow dance. And I haven't forgotten what I promised you."

I had. "What?"

"That I was going to introduce you to some of my sorority sisters." She elbowed me. "They'll like you, cutie. See 'ya later."

Carl and I stayed at the door for nearly an hour, stamping hands, collecting money, bullshitting, eyeing the girls, and finishing our pitcher of grape and grain. At ten thirty, relieved of our duties, we made our way downstairs and found the basement filled with people, dancing in the center and talking, laughing, and drinking along the perimeter. Carl stepped behind the bar to refill our pitcher. "Ready to dance?" Beth said, suddenly beside me.

A fast song was blaring from the speakers. "I can't fast dance, Beth. Honest. I look like a jerk."

"Come on. The floor's crowded. Nobody will see you."

There was a pleading in her voice; not for herself, but for me. To loosen up and enjoy myself. To give live a try. "All right," I said. "But no laughing."

Though I wasn't the worst dancer, and far from the best, I was glad when the song ended. The notes of Simon and Garfunkel's "Bridge Over Troubled Water" followed. "Here's our slow song," Beth said.

"This I don't mind."

Beth stepped closer than I expected and placed her head next to mine. We danced in shuffling half-steps, turning gradual circles while the lyrics told of friendship, and friends in need of friends. I thought of Mike. And Beth. I may have lost a best friend, but she could have lost her partner for life.

"Hey, Beth?"

"Mm?"

She didn't pull back, so I spoke into her ear. "I'm sorry about Mike. It stinks what happened." We moved in time with the music, . . . once . . . twice. "I wish there was something we could do, you know? But . . . he's gone. It sucks."

She nodded. Her hand released from behind my back and wiped at her eyes. A couple more turns and I laughed. "Did he ever tell you about the time he put Ben Gay in my jockstrap?" She shook her head. "It was just before a softball game. I was doing the floor and he knew I'd have to hurry and get dressed, and that's what happened. We were in the back seat of the wagon when I felt things heating up. I thought I was having a cancer attack or something. So kind of sneaky like, I pulled my gym trunks away from my stomach to get some air down there, and that's when Mike started laughing."

Beth pulled back, smiling, and wiped her eyes. "Did it keep getting hotter?"

"For a while. When we got to the other unit, I ran into their bathroom and wiped most of it out and lined my jockstrap with toilet paper. That helped, but, boy, did that burn."

Beth leaned back into me, a smile on her face. When the song ended, we walked over to Carl, who handed us each a cup of grape and grain. "To partying!" he said, raising his glass.

"To partying!" Beth and I repeated.

"Do you know where Mary Jo and the others are, Carl?" Beth asked.

"Nope."

"I'm going to go find them. You guys want to play a drinking game? Signs, or Prince of Wales?"

"Definitely," Carl said.

The game we played, sitting in a circle on the first floor TV room, required all seven of us to be constantly smacking our palms against our thighs while playing. It consisted of accusations, denials, and counter accusations, voiced at a rapid pace and requiring quick math because the accused were identified by the number of seats they sat from the speaker's left, which meant your number constantly changed according to whomever was speaking. If you failed to answer or answered out of turn, you drank.

At first I was one of the worst offenders, but after the others gained on me in relation to liquids consumed, I became one of the better players. I was especially adept at using a quick head snap and forceful "Two!" "Four!" "Three!" or whatever it took to get giggling, good-natured, sweet-faced and slightly chunky Mary Jo beside me to respond. The more I got her the more she poked me, shoved me, tickled me, and hung unto my shoulder while laughing at herself. "But I'm a psyche major," she said at one point. "That's why I can't play this game."

"That makes sense," I said.

"Doesn't it, though?" She looked up to see me silently laughing. She whacked me. Later, after I made a mistake, I mimicked her by whining, "But I'm right handed," and she whacked me again.

An hour after we started, we took a break. As I got up I teetered to my left and bumped into Mary Jo. "Drunk," I said.

She laughed. "Am not. You bumped into me."

"Crazy," Carl said, stepping beside me, Beth beside him. "Let's go upstairs."

"What for?" I said, not wanting to leave Mary Jo.

"You'll see. Come on, Mary Jo, you too."

"Okay," she said. Beth gave her a wink and a smile.

We headed up to the attic and into the small room on the right. Carl turned on the stereo, and sat at the desk. "Where's Pete tonight?" Beth asked.

"He went home for the weekend. So'd Blue. I'm sleeping in here tonight."

"Then Crazy can use Blue's room if he wants, right?"

"Yeah, I didn't think of that. Sure. He can sleep here."

Beth had sat down on one end of the bed and I on the other. I was watching Mary Jo wiggling her butt into a beanbag when the conversation reminded me why I was in Lancaster. "Shit, what time is it?"

"Calm down, Crazy," Carl said. "It's only about eleven thirty, twelve."

I started to get up. "I got to get going."

"No, you don't," Carl said, and pushed me back onto the bed, where Beth held me by the shoulders and Mary Jo grabbed my legs.

"But I–"

"What time's the thing start?"

"Nine thirty."

"Hell, that's plenty of time. You can shower here in the morning. Get up at eight thirty and you're there. No problem."

With Beth holding my shoulders and Mary Jo cuddling my legs against her breasts, it made sense. "Okay. If I have to, I can stay here."

"You *will* stay here," Carl said. He turned from the desk where he'd been working at something. He held a blue, foot-high urn with a large opening on top and a small opening on the side. "Now for the bong."

Drawing the marijuana's smoke through the bong's water made it easier to intake and allowed me to fill my lungs to capacity. Each time I held my breath as long as possible. When I realized the effect this was having, it was too late– I'd already done three or four hits that hadn't yet registered. My chances of remaining in control had vanished.

We stayed in the room playing drinking games until we'd finished the pitcher we brought with us, then went downstairs for more. Mary Jo asked me to dance and I accepted immediately. I now had no inhibitions and rhythm enough for three people. And Mary Jo, she kept getting sweeter and sweeter looking. What had I been thinking about earlier when I thought she was a little chunky? Every part of her looked so enticing. I wanted to grab her and be engulfed by her arms and breasts and legs and ass, and her sweeter than sweet face.

Later, I felt like I was floating. I didn't know if it was the marijuana still progressing in its effects, or the grape and grain I was downing by the cupfuls. My head was numb, I slurred my words, and I bumped into people while dancing. I danced with Mary Jo, a slow dance, the two of us pressed together, the feel of her so inviting. She sang with the music, her voice astoundingly clear and pretty. Carl and I had a race drinking a cup of grape and grain. Mary Jo cheered me on. I had a serious talk with Beth about something; she took my cup of grape and grain. I let her, saying, "Okay,

Mom, I won't drink anymore." I think I made out with Mary Jo outside somewhere. I smashed my knee on something. Vaguely I remember wolfing down some stale cookies with Carl. I fell off the back porch and laughed about it for half a day. The last part of the night I'll never remember.

10

"Hi, Bobby. What's the matter?"

He stepped past me and sat down with a thud, slamming his back into the bus seat. "I hate this place."

"How come?"

"Because it stinks."

"It stinks for everybody."

"It stinks more for me."

"That's because you're not used to it yet. Kind of like when you take a really smelly poop and you're still on the toilet when someone else comes in—they almost faint, but you think, 'This ain't so bad.'"

He smiled Mike's smile. "What happened?" I said.

"My stupid roommate left his window open this week and Mr. Druggins found it. Now I can't go to the Ice Capades tonight."

"What's your roommate's window got to do with you?"

"It's 'our' room," Bobby said mockingly, "and I'm partly responsible. Stupid jerk. I'm the new guy, and he makes all the mistakes. Now I can't go to the Ice Capades."

The Ice Capades were playing at the Hershey Ice Arena, home of the minor league Hershey Bears hockey team, two events that the Home bought us tickets to once a year.

"The Ice Capades are no big deal," I said. "I'm not going tonight, either."

"But you probably already seen them. I haven't. I wanted to see them."

"So you'll see them next year."

"Not in this stupid unit, I won't. I hate this place."

"It'll get better," I said.

"When? Never."

His anger made me chuckle; I knew he'd get over it. "You're right," I said. "I might as well just kill you right now and end it." I grabbed him around the neck and shook him back and forth. "Die, you dog. Die." Once he started giggling, I released him. "Stupid place," I said.

"It is."

I tickled him. "Really stupid place."

He pushed my hand away. "It is. *Really* stupid."

"I know. It is."

"It is," he insisted.

"I know."

He turned his gaze to the window.

"Look, Bobby, I know it sucks, especially in the intermediates, but it sucks for everybody. What can you do?"

"It doesn't suck as bad for my friend Melvin."

"Who's Melvin?"

"He's in my class. His housefather's okay."

"Well, Melvin's lucky. You're not—just like everybody else in your unit. That's the way it is."

"It ain't fair."

"Neither is our parents' dying. But that's how it goes. It *sucks!*" I poked him in the side, diverting his gaze from the window.

He grabbed my hand and kept me from tickling him as we continued to talk. "He knows you."

"Who? Melvin? He does not."

"He does too. He's on the J.V. swim team."

The junior varsity swim team finished their practice just before we started ours. I knew some of the eighth graders who had come along on away varsity meets, but not many of the other junior varsity members.

I said, "Is he the guy with the pointy head and webbed feet that looks like a dolphin and they call him Flipper?"

Bobby grinned. "No."

"Is he any good?"

"He says he is."

"Can you swim?"

"Yeah."

"You want to join the team?" I stopped trying to tickle him—our hands remained pressed together in mid air. "Well . . . , do you?"

"I'm probably not that fast."

I resumed my tickle attack. "So? That's why they have practice—to get faster. And you'll get out of the unit every night. Less time with Druggins the jerk."

"He is a jerk."

"He's a *stupid* jerk."

"A *really* stupid jerk," Bobby said.

I grabbed him in a headlock. "So, should I ask the coach to sign you up so I can do this to you every night?"

"Okay."

"This place sucks," I said, releasing him.

"It does," he said, and smiled.

"I hate it."

"Me, too."

On Thursday, Bobby's name appeared in the bulletin as a member of the swim team. On Friday, I dunked him and his pal, Melvin, three times each.

11

Saturday, February 13, 1971

You should have seen my one and only, Teach. Wow! sums it up nicely. First, she's pretty, and she had her hair pulled back into a loose ponytail with a white shell clasp that matched her pearl earrings and necklace. Very cute. Second, she had on an emerald green dress that barely gripped her shoulders, hugged the rest of her curves like a second skin, and ended wonderfully short on her sexy legs. But most eye-catching of all, was the way her dress scooped down in front. Even from my sitting position I knew I was seeing a lot more than the Home or her father would like. Then I stood up and pushed in her chair and as she (and her dress) scooted forward I almost fainted from what I saw below me. Holy Moses, Teach.

And she was my date, for the Valentine's dance! This gorgeous girl with the "look-what-I've-got" dress on. Not only that, she's smart, and witty, and lots of fun. Know what she did when Mr. Stevens interrupted our slow dancing to ask me to move back a little, to the stupid six-inches-between-us rule? She looked down at the chasm between us, then at him and said, "What fun is this?"

He didn't know what to say at first, then he said, "Well, you don't want to get our guys too excited."

Know what she said? She said, "Why not? I like 'em excited."

And she meant it, too! YEOW! A minute later she was right back in there, chest to chest, and asking if I wanted to take a walk later. And she meant more than just walking. Unfortunately, in Founders Hall there's no where to hide and play "spin the bottle" or "here, feel this." The stupid chaperones check the cars continually and it was freezing out anyway, all the offices are locked, so is the auditorium, so that just leaves the dance floor, lounge areas, and hallways. I told her there was no where to go and she said, "Well, we'll see," kind of sneaky like.

Half an hour later I found out what she meant. At first I thought she was crazy. Brownie and Jim were in the middle of their infamous, "I want the last piece of cake" wrestling match, deep under our table, and the chaperones were trying to break it up when Nancy whispered, "Come on," into my ear.

Was she nuts? Didn't she want to see what happened? I looked at her, and she nodded this urgent kind of nod with twinkling eyes that said something illegal and exciting was going to happen and I'd miss it unless I left right then.

WHOOSH!!–I was gone. Who cared what happened to those guys? It was fooling around time!

Did we find a spot to play doctor amidst all the commotion? I'll never tell.

At the far edge of the lounge area we looked back at the crowd gathered around our table. Nancy smiled at me, took my hand and began strolling down the long incline toward the porte-cochere.

My first hand-in-hand walk with a girl, a girl I liked a lot. Most enjoyable–yet sullied by my drunken groping of Mary Jo the Friday before. All week I had told myself it didn't matter. We were drunk, it hadn't been planned, I barely remembered it, and most importantly, I wouldn't do it again. But that didn't stop the thoughts from surfacing throughout the week, reminding me how I was keeping it from Nancy despite knowing how important being each other's 'one and only' was to her.

All through the dance I thought of it. At quiet moments, when we were laughing, when she smiled. Now, walking hand-in-hand, it felt like each step was widening a divide I wouldn't be able to overcome if it expanded much further.

Halfway down the corridor, Nancy tugged on a door handle to the auditorium. The dead bolt clanked against the wood. "I think they're all locked," I said.

"Hm-mm," she said, and grinned, knowing something I didn't.

Her unsuspecting innocence wrenched the gap wider than I could stand it. I stopped. "Nancy, this weekend, when I got drunk with Carl, there was something that I barely remember. I don't even know how long it lasted or what happened exactly, and I don't think it was much, but I still have to tell you."

"What?"

"My buddy who died, his girlfriend goes there, and her and her sorority sisters know Carl and we ended up playing some drinking games."

"You didn't play strip porker, did you?" she said, and smiled.

"No. At least I don't think so. Anyway, one of the girls, sometime during the night . . . " I shook my head. " . . . I remember—but just barely, making out with her outside on a swing or something. I don't even know how long it lasted, but I don't think it was long. It might have even been just a kiss or two. I can't remember. I can't even remember how it started or anything hardly."

I'd been looking at the carpet. I now looked at Nancy; her green eyes stared into mine. "I'm really sorry, Nancy. I wouldn't have done it if I'd been thinking or if I hadn't been drunk. I just . . . I don't know, it just happened, and I don't know why. I swear I won't do it again. If I could, I'd take it back. I just wasn't thinking. I'm sorry. Really sorry."

After a moment, Nancy turned and continued walking us, hand-in-hand, slowly down the corridor. "Was she drunk, too?"

"Yeah. We all were. The whole place was, I think."

"Do you like her?"

"She was a nice person, and funny in her own way, but it's not like I'd choose her over you. You're funnier, and prettier, and sexier. It doesn't matter who it was, though, because I wouldn't do it again. I know how important it is to you. I was just drunk and wasn't thinking, that's all. I'm sorry."

We took a few more steps. "You were both definitely drunk?"

"Definitely. Way beyond drunk. Blitzed. Gone."

Nancy nodded a slight nod. "Okay," she said. "I've been there. You're forgiven."

I blew out a long breath. "Thanks, Nancy."

She yanked my hand down and spun us face to face, nose to nose. "But it better not happen again." Her eyes stared hard into mine. I shook my head. "It won't. I swear."

"Good. Now . . . " She looked toward the lobby.

We had reached the end of the corridor. Two couples stood laughing at a portrait at the other end.

"Come on," she said, and stepped quickly toward the port-cochere, taking us out of the corridor. She nodded at the glass doors leading outside. "Anybody out there?"

She opened her purse as I walked to the doors. "No one right now," I said and turned—she was slipping a key into the door leading backstage. "What are you doing?"

Nancy opened the door. "Come on!" I hurried over and stepped inside. She locked it. "They're my father's keys," she whispered. "He has a set because of the plays. I hid my mom's so he'd have to give me his."

"Smart thinking," I said.

"Of course."

Nancy took my hand and led me around to the stage where we removed our shoes. I took a running slide across the hardwood floor. Standing center stage, I looked out into the cavernous space of row upon row of empty seats, the tiny night lights glowing softly along every aisle, and into the balcony, clear to the rafters.

Nancy glided across the stage, spinning and turning in ballet steps. Her dress restricted her legs, yet she twirled gracefully. She made a circular loop and stopped directly in front of me, then curtsied. "Ta-daaa."

I applauded lightly. "Bravo," I whispered. "Bravo."

She bowed three times. "Race 'ya," she said, and hopped off the stage to dart up the center aisle.

I caught her just as she reached the double doors. She peered through the crack. Even through this restricted view, the rotunda's size and opulence was apparent. And amidst it all, over one hundred properly dressed Homeguys and their dates, trying to have a good time.

After half a minute, Nancy said, "Let's dance."

"Here? Dance?"

"Why not?" Though a fast song was playing, she chose a slow one. The six inch rule was out; our bodies made full contact almost to our knees. It was nice, not just erotic. I was thrilled I'd unburdened myself, and even happier she forgave me. I really liked her. And she me, I think.

She giggled, said, "Come on," and walked me down to the stage. "Stay there." She hopped up. "Do you know the stripper song? Tah-da-da-daaa . . . Dah-da-da-daaa . . . ?"

"Yeah."

"Do it."

"What?" I said.

"Do it!"

A striptease. My first. YEOW!

I started whispering the stripper song, and she began swaying, eyes closed. Her shoulders and hips undulated from side to side as her arms rose above her head. Her right hand floated down and began inching her dress off her left shoulder. . . .

It was hard watching all the doors and backstage while whispering the stripper song to a girl who was actually stripping. Beneath her dress was a white, satiny slip. I was relieved to see it—it might make the punishment less severe if we were caught—yet I was also disappointed—I wanted to see her breasts and panties and scantily-clad body.

The dress crumpled to the floor. She stepped out of it and slid it to the side. I stopped humming and applauded.

"Keep going," she said.

YEOW! YEOW!

The palms of her hands slid slowly up her sides, bringing the slip with them. Lacy white panties showed briefly before she let go and trailed her hands up to her slip straps. She hitched each shoulder close to her face then slid the straps off. The slip dangled precariously while she strutted to my humming, her hips shaking from side to side. Finally, she inched it down: over her breasts–covered by the skimpiest of bras, past her belly button, her hips, and by her equally skimpy panties. The slip dropped to the floor. "Ta-daaa!" she said, hands upraised, one knee bent.

I clapped and whistled softly. "More, more," I called as she took her bows.

"*Now* come up here," she said, hands on bare hips.

"But . . . " I looked over my shoulder. Was this it?! How far would she go? Would we get caught? Would we do it here? I was too excited to crawl up there; I'd be embarrassed. I didn't even know what the hell to do.

"I know," she said. "Come on."

She ran off to the right. I jumped up, grabbed her clothes and hurried after her. I heard a soft thumping sound. "Where are you?"

"Up here."

She was nearing the top of the steps to the control room.

"Aren't you cold?"

She giggled. "Yeah. Bring up my clothes."

The floor was carpeted and clean. The dimly lit control panels beneath the three walls of glass gave the room a space-age feel.

"Neat, huh?" she said, slithering toward me.

"Yeah. Here's your clothes."

She tossed them to the side. "I don't need them. I'm hot."

She cupped the back of my neck with her right hand and pressed her lips hard against mine. Her tongue darted inside my mouth. "Take off your coat," she said, tugging at the shoulders.

"Nancy, this is, this is like . . . I'm getting excited and–"

"So am I." She threw my coat on the floor and grabbed my tie.

"Yeah, but if we go too far, you might . . . I mean, I don't know, but–"

"Don't worry about it." She undid my top button and moistened half my neck with one hungry lick. The shiver wiggled my toes.

"Yeah, but . . . You never know. You might–"

"I'm on the pill. Now shut up. Here." She grabbed my hand and placed it on her ass. Firm, warm, smooth, round. I'd found my pot of gold.

By the time my shirt was off, so was her bra. Her nipples felt like rubber bullets. When my pants dropped and she grabbed me, I was gone, possessed by lust. Hallelujah.

We spent a hot, frantic hour up there. The only time I made a noise was whenever her groans and cries reminded me I could be shot if caught. "Shhhh!" I'd whisper. "Fuck you," she'd respond and giggle. Then I'd laugh, and she'd quiet down until my next request.

We came down when we realized we'd been gone for some time but uncertain of how long. "You don't think it's over do you?" I asked, as we hurried down the stairs. "I'm dead if everyone's gone. Jesus Christ. What can I tell them? I'll miss the bus. I'll–"

"Shhh, listen."

I stopped on stage. The music and hubbub of the dance reached our ears.

"Good. Jeez."

"How about right here?" she said. "Center stage? We'll hear them if they stop."

I looked around. She grinned. "Okay," I said

What a night.

12

As I entered Founder's Hall Sunday morning no one in the world could have been happier. It was impossible. I had a girlfriend I liked more and more every time I met her, talked to her, or even thought about. And for some delightfully, amazing, unfathomable reason she liked me, and had been the one to initiate our courtship, pursued it, and happily guided me along the path I would never have found without her help and encouragement, and her wonderful sense of humor. When we finished on stage the previous night, she kissed me, wrapped her arms around my neck and asked where my unit sat. She looked to the spot I indicated, waved and said, "Hi, Dave!" She kissed me again and said, "Tomorrow, and every time you're ever in here, you're going to look at this spot and think of us. And of the best Valentine's dance you ever had."

I kissed her back and smiled. "You're right."

"Damn right, I'm right."

I laughed, and laughed and smiled even more in the lobby next day as I took more ribbing from Jim, Brownie, and the other guys who had been told Nancy and I had disappeared for more than an hour and came back grinning without equals. I didn't say, but my constant smile spoke for itself. I was a lucky guy and life was a wonderful thing.

Then I saw Bobby.

Head down, face red (was he crying?), he went straight to the stairs and up them. Druggins hitched up his pants, grinned that jackass sneer, and took his stance beside the stairs.

I started for the balcony. "Where're you going, Dave?" Suds asked.

"The balcony. I want to see Bobby, Mike's cousin."

Suds looked at his watch. "It's eight of. By the time you get there it'll be time to go in."

He was right, I hadn't enough time.

During service, my emotions and thoughts flip-flopped between watching 'our' spot and thinking of Nancy, and remembering Bobby's face and rush upstairs. What had happened?

Bobby didn't attend second church. Afterwards, in the community center parking lot, I searched for but didn't find the other the guy in his unit who attended another church. I waited until after super to call. When Druggins answered I asked to speak to Bobby. "Who's calling?" he said.

What business was it of his? "Dave Purenut," I said. "I was his cousin's roommate last year."

A short silence followed, then he said, as though having considered not allowing it, "Just a minute. You have five minutes."

"Thanks." You moron.

"Hello?" Bobby said.

His voice was apprehensive, which meant Druggins hadn't told him it was me.

"Bobby, it's me, Crazy. How 'ya doing, buddy?"

"Hi, Crazy" he said, his voice flat. "I'm okay."

"I saw you in church today. Boy, you went up those steps faster than I'd ever seen it done. I'll have to start calling you Speedy Gonzales."

"I had to go in. I was in trouble."

"For what?"

"I was laughing in the kitchen this morning."

"Laughing? What's wrong with that?"

"I was the only one."

"So? I laugh all the time by myself. You can't get punished for that."

"He didn't believe me when I said I was laughing at nothing."

"Why didn't you just tell him? What were you laughing at?"

Bobby hesitated. "Nothing," he said. "I was just laughing."

"How come you didn't go to second church, then? He didn't stop you from that, did he?"

"No. But I had to do the Sunday dishes, and–"

"What?!" I said. "You had to do the dishes for laughing?"

"Yeah, and–"

"What a jerk."

" . . . And he said if the guys had to clear off the tables and put away the food and stuff because I was at second church, then he'd find other stuff for me to do to make up for it, and I'd be working all afternoon maybe. So I didn't go."

"You're housefather's a fucking asshole, Bobby," I said. "You know that? He's the biggest dickhead in the school. They ought to take him outside and shoot his worthless, ugly head off."

As soon as I called Druggins an asshole, Bobby tried stopping me. "Crazy, don't! You can't say that. You'll–" Now he said, "Crazy, don't say that stuff. They . . . Sometimes they listen."

"What!? Well that makes him an even bigger asshole–*you hear me, asshole*?! That's unconstitutional. You know what that means, shit for brains? Huh! You . . . *jerk*!"

Bobby was nearly breathless. "Crazy, you got to be careful. You'll get in trouble. You can't–"

I heard a noise and a man's voice say, "Give me that!" Then Druggins barked into the phone, "What's your name again, foulmouth? Purenut, is that it?"

"What's yours, eavesdropper? Bucket Ears?"

"I want to talk to your housefather, right now."

"Yeah? Well then call him right now. I'm in Brookfields." I hung up.

I stared at the phone, then snatched it off the hook. Not only would it piss him off, it would give me time to think. Should I tell Suds before or after he called? And what about Bobby? Did Druggins hear him say they listen in? If he did, he'd get in more trouble and it was going to be bad enough already.

Son of a bitch, bastard.

Monday, February 15, 1971

Bucket Ears Druggins illegally listens in on my phone conversation and who gets in trouble? Me. That's fair, huh, Teach?

Besides never saying anything bad about someone or writing it down, Old Man Hatch told me I should also never say anything over the phone about someone because that someone may just be, at that very moment, picking up the extension and they'll hear you.

"That's not what happened," I said. "He was listening in. If he wasn't, why did Bobby warn me that he was? Say, 'Crazy, don't! They . . . they listen in.' He wouldn't just make that up. He listens in on all the guys, and they know it."

"That's not true. They just think he's listening in, when he's only picking up to tell them their time is up. It's happened at other units , too."

What a bunch of crap, huh, Teach? The typical Homelife give-the-boys-the-shaft job. I got three stupid weeks of detentions and thirty hours to work off. Luckily my housefather agrees with me and said Bucket Ears shouldn't have been spying on us and therefore I can consider the thirty hours worked off already. HA!

I'm sure going to miss, Nancy, though. Really miss her.

13

Twenty-six days. From the time Nancy helped fulfill my life's dream, to the very next time I could possibly try it again, twenty-six days had past. Three weeks of detentions and five more days until the Thursday night wrestling match. Twenty-six days of thinking about her, about what we had done, about what we would do. Twenty-six days of waiting to do again what before I'd waited seventeen years to do, and the twenty-six days seemed more agonizing than the seventeen years.

I hadn't talked to her since the night after the Valentine's dance–the night Bucket Ears eavesdropped on me. She'd phoned just after snacks, calling me lover boy when I answered. I called her cutie-pie and smiled the entire five minutes on the phone. Before we hung up she told me not to call her just yet because her father wasn't pleased about her dating me–a Milton Hershey guy, a guy one year younger than her, a guy who'd been alone with her in her dressing room, and the guy responsible for the biggest embarrassment of his directorial career.

"So then you call me next week," I said.

"Why?"

"Because. I like talking to you, that's why."

"And because you miss me," she said.

"That's right. I do."

"Do what?"

"Miss you."

"And you like being with me."

"And I like being with you."

"Of course you do."

I laughed.

Then three weeks of detentions with its "no calls allowed" rule set in.

"A girl named Nancy just called you," Suds told me as I entered the kitchen for snacks the first Wednesday of my detentions. "I told her you weren't allowed to take any calls."

"Did you tell her why?"

"Yep. And for how long." Suds set the can of cookies on the counter then lowered his bottom lip in a pout. "She said, 'Tell Honey Buns I'll miss him.'"

The guys laughed. "Did you tell her I'd miss her?"

"Sure did."

"What did she say?"

"'You bet he will.'"

For three weeks I couldn't talk to her, hold her, feel her, fondle her, hug her, squeeze her, smile at her, revel in her presence. One night I thought of hooking out but it started raining, and I wouldn't have known where I was going or if she would have been at home. When she didn't call by the Tuesday after my detentions ended, I chanced calling her and got her mother, who agreed to ask Nancy to meet me at the wrestling match, in the balcony section, if her schedule permitted.

Thursday night I hurried everyone going so we got to the high school early. Maybe Nancy would bring her mother's station wagon and we could have our own little wrestling match in there? That'd be great—another first, and a long time to have waited for seconds. But just seeing her and being with her would be enough. For a while.

I waited in "our" seat in the balcony. And waited. And waited. I was still there after the junior varsity match ended and the varsity match began. Why hadn't she come? Or contacted me beforehand? Something had to have happened to her. On the way there, an accident? That day? I hoped not, but if not, why hadn't she come?

But then, suddenly, there she was walking along the railing. I waved. She spotted me and barely smiled back.

"What's wrong?" I asked when she sat down.

"Nothing."

"You sure? You don't look so happy."

"I'm okay."

"You sick?"

She shook her head.

Why wouldn't she tell me; maybe I could help? Was it a girl thing? "Well, at least take off your coat so you don't sweat to death."

She undid the zipper but left the coat on. "I can't stay, Dave. I . . . " She tucked her hands into her pockets and looked down at the floor.

"What's the matter, Nancy?"

"I've got something to tell you and you're not going to like it. I don't like it."

"What is it?"

She looked at me, her beautiful green eyes filled with sadness. "We can't go out anymore."

It felt like someone had told me I'd never leave Milton, or I'd never see my family again.

"Why? Your father? He already knows, doesn't he? It doesn't matter to me if he doesn't. We can–"

"It's not just him. It's Eric. We're seeing each other again."

"But he's a jerk, isn't he? An 'asshole'?"

"He was. He's promised not to be anymore. And we're going steady. Just him and me."

"But what about us? I thought we were going steady?"

"We were. It's just . . . " She sighed. "Eric was my boyfriend for four years, Dave. You and I are just starting. And I like to cuddle, and be around my boyfriend, and do other things. I can only see you Friday nights mostly. It's been almost four weeks since last time."

"But that wasn't my fault. That was other things, jerky housefathers and stuff."

"Still, our time's limited, no matter what. Right?"

I didn't say anything. She leaned forward to catch my eye. "Right?"

"Is this because of what happened at Franklin and Marshall? I said I was sorry."

"No, it's not that. It's Eric, and the past we have together. That's all." She stared at me a few seconds, then put her hand on my arm. "Tell me you understand, Dave. Please?"

I did, but I didn't. How could this be happening? "Maybe," I said. "It's just. . . . We were having so much fun. You're the first girlfriend I ever had and–"

"You're going to have more," she said. "Lots more. What about that girl in the drugstore? She likes you."

"She has a boyfriend. Like you."

"You'll find others."

How did she know? It only took me seventeen years to find her. No one could know when I would find another.

I stared at the wrestlers grappling below us–their wrestler with parents and cheerleaders rooting for him, a school with girls in it, a home to go to; and our guy with nothing. In the same weight class but far from equals.

After half a minute of silence, Nancy said, "I've got to go, Dave. I have–"

"Going to meet 'What's-his-name?'" I said, without looking up. "Mr. Lucky?"

"I'm sorry if I've hurt you, Dave. I didn't mean to. I . . . ," She stood up. "Bye, Dave."

I watched her hurry across the bleacher seats, head down, and my heart twisted. I caught her in the stairwell. "Nancy, I'm sorry," I said, and tugged her to a stop. "That didn't come out right. I'm just bummed out. I know it's not your fault."

"I didn't plan this," she said. "It just happened."

"I know."

"You know I like you, Dave. A lot. I just . . . it's just how things worked out."

"I know. Come on, I'll walk with you to the door."

It was the longest walk I ever had. Somehow I wanted it to stop, to turn back time, to make her mine again.

At the door she hugged me, and said, "I'll miss you."

"Not like I'll miss you. Not even close."

She smiled. "You'll find another girlfriend."

"I hope so."

She kissed me on the cheek. "Bye, Dave."

So then I went back up and sat in the balcony. But that was no good because it reminded me of her, as did the other couples up there acting stupid and having fun. So I headed for the candy booth to drown my sorrows in chocolate, only Lisa showed up because we were wrestling Hershey and she was smiling that gorgeous smile of hers, which reminded me of more shit I lost out on, and even though she looked like she wanted to talk and I didn't see her asshole boyfriend around, I couldn't, I just said I had to go and then I slammed open the door leading upstairs and some asshole housefather caught me and said if I broke the door I'd be paying for it. I ignored him and went upstairs and stood off to the side at a railing and thought about how much this place sucks until I heard the crowd and saw our guy, Bill Hoffa, almost getting pinned, which pissed me off even more so I started yelling, and then their guy went too far and just like that Bill flipped him and it was his turn to try for the pin. Only this guy had one of those bull necks that he kept arching to keep his shoulders off the mat, and since Bill needed a pin to win because their guy was way ahead on points and there were only twenty seconds left, I started yelling the only sure-fire way I knew Bill could win. "Break his neck! Snap it! Cripple him! Rip his head off. Sever his spine!!!"

*I knew Bill would win if he could do that. Only he couldn't, and he lost,
and a minute later Brubaker was looking down his nose at me saying he heard
what I was saying and unless I wanted to discuss my inappropriate behavior
with Homelife, I'd be reporting to his office every day for the next week after
lunch for work detail to teach me civil behavior and sportsmanship.*

Thus endeth maybe the worse night of my whole life.

14

Losing Nancy compounded the affects of losing Mike, expanding my awareness of how fickle life was. I could do everything within my power and still not
control the outcome. Why bother, if that's what could happen? Why should I
even care? I did my chores, homework, workouts, just enough to get by. Whatever noontime assignment Brubaker gave me I did in an even, methodical pace,
not worried about finishing on time nor what would happen if I didn't.

On Thursday, a warm, March day with nearly everyone outside after lunch
enjoying the promise of spring, I stood on a chair in Brubaker's office, removing books, knickknacks, and pictures from his shelves. The shouts of guys
playing outside, and people as they past by, drifted in through the open windows.

I heard the distinctive chuckle of Mr. Asp, our history teacher. I bent
down, dipped my rag, and saw him walking with Brubaker toward the science
wing.

He chuckled again, and in his high to low intonations the hint of superi-
ority or disdain he often used with us was absent. For three years I had heard
that chuckle and it always irritated me. He was one of those teachers that
demanded his way be the only way, no matter how asinine you proved it to be.
Though we never had a confrontation of any significance, we shared a mutual
annoyance that began the first week we met.

I wiped the top shelf. Asp was also the faculty advisor to the National
Honor Society, and the person I suspected of keeping me off its membership
rolls. I'd been eligible as many times as possible–each marking period after the
second one of my junior year, and I'd never made it. Why? Was it Asp? Besides

making the honor roll each period, I'd also made the effort and conduct honor roll, which meant I'd achieved at least a "B" average from all my teachers in effort and conduct. Occasionally Asp gave me a "C" in conduct, but usually I'd gotten a better mark. So if I'd done "above average" in his class, why hadn't I made it onto the National Honor Society?

I replaced the books and moved the chair to the next row of shelves. Behind Brubaker's desk stood three wooden file cabinets of four sections each. I walked over and examined them. The first was arranged by class, 1971 through 1974, each class with its own row. The next was alphabetized. The last contained files from years past.

I leaned out the window; Brubaker and Asp were barely in sight. I checked the main office; one secretary sat typing at the front desk. I pulled the shade to the window closest to the cabinets then eased open the third drawer of the second file.

There wasn't a file on the National Honor Society. Asp probably had it. I shut the drawer, checked the secretary again, then found my folder in the Class of 1971's drawer. Report cards first–freshman, sophomore, then, starting with the second marking period of my junior year, a piece of paper followed each report card–an evaluation form for the National Honor Society, with my name, boxes to check if approved or disapproved, and a comment line. "Needs to improve his attitude," was printed in neat, rounded print on the first form, signed by Asp. Each subsequent form mentioned attitude and had the same signature. Only the fall report card of my senior year had an additional form, which made me grin–my snap on One-eighty had given Suds a reason not to approve me.

I left the drawer open and checked the secretary. Still typing. I looked behind the report cards and found a picture of when I first entered the school. My father had his arm around my shoulders. He was smiling obligingly, but I wasn't, the sun shining into our eyes and making us squint. What had I been thinking? Was I scared? Did I feel like I was being abandoned though I'm sure my father had told me why I was being enrolled? Did I understand?

So much had happened since then to make me what I was. Was it all just fate? Could I have been Mike, and Mike Eddie, and Eddie Gary, and so on and so on? Why hadn't my father been born into wealth? Who decided that? Why'd my mother die, leaving my father with three young children? Why did

Milton Hershey establish a school for boys only, so that my sisters couldn't be with me? Who decided how the chips fell, good or bad? Or was it happenstance and no one was to blame?

I heard Brubaker greet his secretary. When he entered the office, his file was closed and I was stepping onto the chair.

"Disgustingly filthy shelves, Dave?"

"A little." I removed a handful of books to the counter.

"Tell you what," Brubaker said. "Why not replace those books and finish up tomorrow? Get outside and enjoy this weather."

"I don't care. I can finish."

"I do. Now here . . . " he handed the books up to me. "There's no reason to punish yourself if I'm not willing to do it."

I climbed off the chair and carried it into the outer office. When I returned for the bucket, Brubaker said, "Smile, Dave. Life can't be treating you that badly."

"Maybe. Maybe not."

"Well, whatever it is, enjoy today the best you can. You'll not have it to do over."

While at my locker getting books for the afternoon classes, Brownie arrived. Five minutes later he was being lookout while I checked Asp's files. Two juniors sat in the room. One I knew, the other I recognized, and neither cared what I was doing.

The National Honor Society's folder opened to a master list of current members, with a sheet for each detailing their grades since obtaining membership. Behind that, separated by tabs, were the previous marking periods, last one first, containing a list of eligible candidates with a line drawn through those not accepted. The evaluation form that excluded the candidates followed. Four out of the last five marking periods, I was the only guy listed not to make it. No other teacher but Asp had rejected me.

How could one teacher overrule all the others? I was president of my unit, co-captain of the swim team, liked well enough by the guys, had qualified every time, and because of one teacher, I wouldn't make the National Honor Society. How was that fair? Who was he to affect my life so? And not once had he ever told me that he was responsible or what I had to do to be accepted. Was I supposed to figure that out? Or did he not care? I wasn't worth it, maybe–he'd already decided my presence was undesirable for his precious society and though I might earn a "B" in conduct in his classroom, it was only an aberration not worth overlooking in the long run.

I closed the cabinet. "Did you find out why?" one of the guys asked.

"Yeah. Asp, every time."

"He's an asshole," the kid said. The other kid nodded. "He is, especially if he's the only one who kept you off."

I walked with Brownie to our next class. If I could do all that was necessary and still not make the National Honor Society because of a guy like Asp, why bother to do it? Why bother doing any of it or even worry about things? Why be scared, cautious, quiet, obedient, or anything else if the outcome was so indeterminate? If fate could work against me when I was doing the right things, why couldn't it work for me when I wasn't?

It could. So what the hell.

FIVE

1

Monday, March 8, 1971

*H*ad track tryouts tonight. You know how water bugs glide over water? That wasn't me in the hurdles. Maybe I had raw, unhindered speed? Tried the 100, got a slow start and lost ground from there. Long jump, maybe? Barely made it into the pit. Huey assessed my discuss and javelin abilities. Wasn't much to assess.

Finally I gave distance a try. Brownie and the boys were doing a steady pace around the track, and I kept up. Then we went on a five mile run around the intermediates and near the end everybody started racing. I ended up eighth out of twelve guys. Mr. Stevens said I did pretty good for someone who missed the first two weeks of practice and never ran more than three miles in his life. Says maybe I'm a natural. I think maybe having swum all winter helped me keep up. But you know what? It's too much like swimming. Run, run, run, that's all we do. What fun is that? I'd better be pretty damn good, pretty damn fast, or I'm going to be pretty damn gone.

On a night we were scheduled to run only distance—no interval or sprint training, Mr. Stevens let me run on my own at the high school so I could use the saved travel time to and from Catherine Hall, where the team practiced, to help Mr. Hart with material for the year book, something I had been interested in and had promised to do when swimming ended. Mr. Hart had me proofread the short blurbs that accompanied the photos of the football and cross country teams, double-check their scores listed for the season, then take the blurbs and scores to Mr. Castle in the printing shop.

"If they're doing anything interesting, can I stay and watch?"

"Sure. Just be back by six thirty."

My footsteps had a hollow snap as I walked through the empty hallways, past empty rooms. The academic section of the school was one long, straight corridor, divided into four sections, with stairs at each end and between each section. I could see the length of the building, and only a janitor, hunched over his mop at the opposite end–the science wing, was in sight.

Parallel to the academic section was the equally long shop corridor, the two areas connected by the auditorium and the hallways on either side of it. I turned down the first hallway and heard music coming from the music class-room, which was opposite the auditorium doors closest to the stage. A melody ended as I past the door. "Let's try the ending once more," someone said, "then we'll do the whole thing and take a break."

In the printing shop classroom I gave the blurbs to Mr. Castle, then wandered out into the shop area. It smelled of ink and oil and reminded me of a newspaper office, with machines of upside down print and large rollers. From the back came a methodical, heavy thumping, where I found Rich sitting in front of a guillotine-like machine that sliced through foot-long pieces of white printed cardboard. Rich had skipped swimming practice, which continued to the end of the year for conditioning purposes, to stay late and do a rush order of invitations that a sophomore had misprinted. He said he'd probably be staying late now and then to help with any year-end rush jobs.

"What's that machine doing?" I asked, referring to the one he was working.

"Cutting invitations in half; there's two invitations on each sheet."

"Do you have to fold them?"

"A machine does. That one over there. Soon as this is done, I'll show you."

I spent the next half-hour, first, running the machine that folded the invitations, and then listening to Rich as he explained the others. I left the printing shop at ten after six. I stopped and listened to the orchestra for a moment, then, on impulse, opened the huge auditorium door opposite the music room and stepped inside. Instead of the up-sloping room filled with students and teachers, there was a vast emptiness. I walked on stage and over to the lectern. I tapped the microphone. "One, two . . . testing, one, two," I said, and imagined my voice reverberating throughout the room. I sat in one of the four wooden chairs behind the lectern and surveyed the room, my imaginary subjects as respectively silent as Brubaker would have wanted. I gave them the finger.

I left through the door opposite from where I came in. What would I say if someone caught me and asked why I was in that corridor and not the other, seeing as how Mr. Hart's classroom and the printing shop were both on that side?

So what? I was taking the scenic route.

The hallway ended outside the reception area and offices of Brubaker and the vice-principal. Lights were on inside. Were they left on, was a janitor cleaning, or was someone still working? With a right, I would pass through the lobby and back toward Mr. Hart's classroom. I took a left.

Each step took me farther from where I should have been going. What excuse could I use now? There wasn't one.

I reached the section between corridors, with the bathroom and stairwell. Though it was safer to go up—no one could come out of Brubaker's office and see me walking down the hallway—I continued straight ahead, ignoring the urge to slink along the wall, and straddling the centerline of the linoleum.

When I reached the end, I turned and gave the entire academic section, from science to English, the finger. Then I scooted up the stairs.

No one was in sight on the second floor. I began to feel safer as I headed for the opposite end. I past the first stairwell and continued toward the center lobby. Once there I would be on the right side of the building and could say—

A door opened on the left, twenty feet ahead, and I jumped into the nearest classroom. What door was it? It wasn't a classroom because they had glass on top—thankfully, or I would have been spotted. But who was it and would they pass this way?

I looked into the glass of my door reflecting in the direction I had been going. Someone was easing the door shut, both hands on the doorknob. Lionel McNecker, a member of the orchestra, and he was sneaking out of the barber shop located inside one of the school's third story towers. He glanced left, then turned right and hustled quietly the other way, disappearing down the lobby steps.

What was he doing in there? I crept to the door and tried the knob: unlocked. I eased it open and listened. Ten seconds of silence past before I started up the narrow, steep stairwell.

The room was eerily quiet. Two barber chairs stood sentinel-like facing a bench and two chairs with a coffee table piled with magazines. Behind the barber chairs, on the counter, were various utensils. I searched the cabinets and found nothing of interest; same with the four drawers. Why would anyone sneak up here? There wasn't the smell of cigarette smoke, so that wasn't it. The view from the window, overlooking Hershey, was nice but not worth detentions. The trash barrel was empty. I felt the clippers for heat and examined the combs; they didn't look recently used, and why would anyone come up to cut their hair? If anything, they'd. . . .

I looked at the appointment book, the book that contained every homeroom in the high school with every boy listed in alphabetical order; the book the barber cut his way through page by relentless page, only to begin again once he finished.

I flipped it open to the marked page. Section 12-4. Some of the guys had their names checked under the date, but most didn't. I ran my finger down the list. McNecker, Lionel, was in the middle. Across to the right, and there it was, a check mark under the date. Son of a bitch.

Some guys, just a few—maybe ten at the most, and McNecker was one of them—always seemed to have longer hair than the rest of us. It was never as long as you'd see at other schools, but it was longer than the style they embarrassed us with. Whenever I questioned them on it, I received sly smiles and evasive answers and simply thought they somehow got lucky or the barber liked them.

Now I knew. Your classroom had to start haircuts one day and not finish until the next, you had to arrange to stay after school for some reason (or could you do it at lunch?), and finally, you had to sneak upstairs and check off your name without being caught.

Son of a bitch.

2

Sunday, March 21, 1971

My buddy, Bobby, didn't show up for second church again today. He went straight up to his seat at the Hootenanny with his roommate. I tried calling him tonight, disguising my voice and saying I was a platoon mate of his brother's who just got discharged from Nam and had promised to call. But his housefather wouldn't let me talk. Said I'd have to wait until Bobby learned to behave himself.

Imagine that? A guy from Vietnam and he won't let the call through? There's too many jerks with too much power around here, don't you think?

Once a month on a Sunday night the presidents of each senior division unit gathered in the music classroom of Senior Hall for the Senior Senate Meeting, one hour of voting on things that hardly mattered, or listening to directives and new rules we had no control over. The meeting was chaired jointly by the senior class president, Al Rose, and the student body president, who, for the first time ever, was the same person. "Advisors" to the meeting were representatives of the school, usually Brubaker and/or a Homelife official. Al would open the meeting, the minutes to the last meeting were read, old business rehashed, new business revealed, then adjournment.

The democratic process was in effect as long as it was a matter of no importance. We could vote on any triviality and the Board of Directors let pass whichever way the majority ruled. On matters of significance, however, nothing we did mattered. A unanimous vote would return during the next meeting as old business, rejected by the Board.

That Sunday, after I finished talking with Druggins, the wagon arrived to take me to the meeting. Thirty minutes later Al was wrapping up his end of new business. Mr. Kramer sat to his right. Brubaker sat to Kramer's right.

When Al asked if anyone had any matter they'd like to bring up, Bill Hoffa, sitting in the back, raised his hand.

"It's about haircuts. When's the barber going to start cutting them like he's supposed to? Seniors are supposed to be allowed a square cut in the back. Does this look like a square cut?" He twisted around so everyone could see. 'Square cut' meant the back was to be cut straight across the bottom, the hair all the same length. Bill's, like most everybody's, appeared nearly shaved at the bottom, then gradually lengthened to a point preferred by marines. "I told him I wanted a square cut and he did this. If he does it again, I'm going to punch him."

"You'll do no such thing," Kramer said. "If you have a problem like that, you come to Homelife."

"I did. Last time. To Mr. Hatch. And I still got the same lousy haircut."

"I think your hair looks fine, Bill," Brubaker said.

"That's your opinion. Not mine. And anyway, he's supposed to be cutting our hair a certain way and he's not."

I raised my hand for the first time all year. "Bill's right. If we break the rules you always make sure we get punished and that we don't do it again. Why not him?"

Another guy said, "We've had this 'square-cut-for-seniors' rule for about two months now, and he's still not doing it all the time, just whenever he feels like it."

Murmurs of dissent filled the room.

Kramer stood. "Now look, if you guys are having problems with your haircuts, you come into Homelife and tell us. I know we haven't received this many complaints."

"That's because we know it won't do any good," Bill said.

"That's not fair," Kramer said. "You know if you guys have a legitimate complaint, we take care of it."

"Then why hasn't anything been done? We're still getting hacked to death."

"We'll do something," Kramer said. "Tomorrow one of us will speak to him again and remind him what the rules are and ask him to follow them."

"And what if he doesn't?" I said.

"We'll cross that bridge when we get to it. Fair enough?"

"But we've already crossed it."

Kramer put a hand up. "We'll take care of it. I promise."

He sat down and Rich raised his hand. "I move that we ask the Board to allow everybody's hair to be longer, and longer than this 'square-back' stuff. They've had the same rules since who knows when. It's time we changed."

"I second the motion," Huey said above the din of approval.

Several guys called for a vote.

Al looked to Kramer and Brubaker. "Shouldn't there be a discussion first," Brubaker said, "on how much longer? Give the Board a reasonable length and they're more likely to accept it."

Ten minutes later we voted unanimously to request two inches over the collar and ears, leaving the front to just touching the eyebrows. That seemed more than reasonable.

"Anything else?" Al said.

Bill Hoffa said, "While we're at it, and because Homelife will be talking to him, I don't think we should have to say thank you to the barber after he cuts our hair. The old barber never made us do it."

"Come on, now," Kramer said. "That's only common courtesy."

"There's nothing wrong with being taught manners," Brubaker said. "Being polite and saying thank you after you've been given something is the gentlemanly thing to do. Now isn't it?"

He said it as though it was fact, that there was no other alternative and the discussion was over. With the same unquestioned authority Druggins had asked me who was calling, then decided not to let me talk to Bobby. With the same dismissive manner Kramer had ended the previous discussion—as though we were slaves and had no other option.

By the time I spoke up, most everyone had accepted Brubaker's verdict. "I don't agree with that," I said. "If it's something we like or need, sure, say it. But if it's not, then I don't see why we should say thank you."

"You'll say it," Brubaker said, "because you are a student in this institution supposedly learning proper manners."

"That still doesn't make it the 'gentlemanly' thing to do. I think we should tell him what we think, and say thanks only if we like it. Would you thank a tailor who's cut your pants six inches above your ankles, even if it was for free? I wouldn't."

A few guys chuckled, but most sat quietly as Brubaker stared. "This meeting is over for you, Mr. Purenut. You may leave now."

"Why? I didn't do anything. You asked a question, I answered it. I'm allowed my opinions, aren't I? Isn't this supposed to be a discussion?"

He leaned forward. "You have a flippant, disrespectful attitude that is not appreciated. It hinders rather than helps these proceedings. These other students are serious, trying to accomplish something. You're not. Now leave."

"I am too being serious," I said. "No one in my unit likes saying thank you for getting butchered."

"You will leave this room immediately, or you will find yourself on detentions until the day you graduate. If you graduate."

For a moment I returned his stare, then I stood, sidestepped to the left, started forward, and stopped. "Mr. Kramer. You said if we come to you with a legitimate complaint you'll deal with it. Tomorrow will be too late. All I did was answer a question. I should be allowed to stay without being thrown on detentions. I was doing just what the guys in my unit elected me to do."

Kramer hesitated for half a second, then said, "I think it's best if you leave, Dave. We can talk about this another time."

"When it doesn't matter anymore. Right?"

3

"Come on, Bobby, tell me what's wrong. Maybe I can help."

"You can't."

We had ridden the entire trip from Founder's Hall with Bobby staring out the window. When my attempts at humor had failed to elicit a response, I quieted, figuring he would eventually tell me. Now that he had sniffled, I thought I would try again. "How do you know I can't? Maybe I can."

He wiped at his eyes. "I miss my dad," he said.

"I know, Bobby," I said. "It sucks. It'll get better."

"Not for me." His head dropped and tears ran down his cheeks. "I hate this place."

We were pulling in front of the Catholic church. I rubbed the back of his neck. "Bobby, it always gets better. Now listen, instead of going right in, we'll sneak off and talk some. Just follow my lead."

String Bean stood outside the bus directing guys toward the church. When we stepped off last, he noticed Bobby. "What's wrong with him?"

"It's his housefather. He's a jerk. He'll be all right. Look, my father, his uncle, is taking us out today. He said to meet him out here. If he doesn't show up by five of, we'll come in, okay?"

"Fine. And you cheer up," he said to Bobby.

We crossed the street and slipped behind the long, one-story school building, walked past the playground and field to the nearby nuns' residence and sat on some large rocks on the far side of their garage, in the warmth of bright sunshine.

"Bobby, listen," I said, "everybody hates it here at first. You got an even bigger reason with you're asshole housefather. You just got to hang in there. It'll get better. I promise."

He held a pebble in his fingers and was tracing along the seam in his shoe, his head resting against his knee. "Not for me," he said. "It's getting worse."

"How?"

A tear splattered onto his shoe and he slid his finger through it.

"How's it getting worse, Bobby?"

"I have to get up and run now in the mornings."

"How come?"

"Because he caught us talking after the lights were out."

"Why were you talking?"

"I *have* to. If I don't answer him, my roommate gets mad."

"Yeah? Well you tell you're roommate . . . No, never mind, I'll tell him. But don't worry about him, he won't bother you anymore with that. What else? Running's not so bad. You can do that easy. Why else is it getting worse?"

"I have to do the snack dishes all by myself for the next two weeks. We were throwing pretzels around and he caught me. Other guys were doing it but he didn't see them. He just saw me."

"You got caught, Bobby, that's all. If someone else got caught they'd be doing them. That's the chance you take."

"I know," he said, the tears beginning to trickle. "It's just that . . . " His hand turned upwards, then dropped. His shoulders sagged.

"It's just what, Bobby?"

He sobbed twice then started crying. "He was banging my head against the wall. He said if I didn't straighten out, things were going to get worse and worse."

"What? What do you mean, banging? Smashing it? Did you get cut?"

"No, he wasn't smashing it, just pushing it. Bouncing it. It didn't hurt much but . . . " He broke off, crying in sobs.

I stood up. "What an asshole! What a freaking son of a bitching, bastard. He's a . . . Man, what a jerk."

"I don't like it here, Crazy," Bobby said, his face contorted and turned up, eyes streaming tears. "I want to get out."

I sat down and put my arm around his shoulders. "It'll get better, Bobby. You'll see. It'll be all right."

"Why'd my dad have to die?" he sobbed. "I didn't do nothing."

"I know."

I let him cry, giving myself time to think. Once it felt like he'd cried himself out, I said, "Bobby, I got a plan. Here, get up. You got a hankie?"

As he wiped his eyes, I said, "Look, you can get transferred to another unit. It's not easy, especially in the intermediates, but it's possible. You have to go into Homelife and ask for it and they'll–"

"Go into Homelife?"

Instantly I knew I had to change plans. I'd forgotten that in the intermediates, Homelife was where you were sent to be punished, not to have a good deed done. "Yeah, usually that's how it's done. But in the intermediates, maybe it's different. In fact, I know it is. You don't go in, actually."

"Good," he said.

I couldn't help myself, I laughed. He smiled in return.

"No, I think we'll have to get your mother involved. When will you see her again?"

Bobby had looked hopeful, now he visibly sagged. "She took me out yesterday. I asked her to get out, but she won't let me. She said she doesn't have time to take care of me."

"Bobby, she probably doesn't have time to take care of you."

"But I'll take care of myself!"

"All right. Calm down. It's more than that I'll bet. She has to work full time now, and she might not have enough money. She probably doesn't make as much as your dad did, and she's got to pay the rent, and the bills, and buy food and clothes. They give you all that stuff here, free, so that's less she has to make, and maybe she doesn't have to work as hard."

He had resumed tracing along his shoe seam and didn't respond.

"You know, it's not easy for her, either, to leave you here. She lost your dad, just like you, and now she doesn't have you around. In fact, it's probably harder for her. You're around fifteen other guys all the time; she doesn't have anybody. She's the one that put you here. You can always blame her when you're feeling bad, but who can she blame? Nobody. She probably feels guilty about it, and she's only doing it because she thinks it's best for you. You don't think she misses you and feels bad sometimes?"

"Yeah."

"Okay, then. Don't blame her. It just happened. That's why most of us are in here. Nobody likes it, but our parents can't help it. Okay?"

He nodded.

"And she loves 'ya, right?"

He nodded more positively.

"Okay. Now, does she know what a jerk Druggins is? Have you told her about the stuff he does, about his banging your head off the wall?"

"Some of it, but not stuff like that. She might ask him about it and then I'd really get it."

"You're right. At least you're learning. What about the things you do tell her? What's she say?"

"She either doesn't believe me—thinks I'm exaggerating, or she says I have to learn the rules and obey them. Everybody else does, so so can I."

"Yeah, they always get us with that one. We'll have to—"

A kid shouted in the distance, and I realized where we were supposed to be. I stood up. "Let's get in to church first. I'll think about it there."

When the church came into view around the school building, I stopped, causing Bobby to bump me. "Get back! String Bean's coming this way. Let's go around. I told him we'd be in by now."

We hustled around the far corner so fast we must have looked guilty to the other church monitor halfway along the back of the school. "What are you guys doing back here? How come you're not in church?"

No way was I taking a chance on getting Bobby in more trouble. "Let's go, Bobby," I said, and ducked back behind the building.

"Hey! Come here!"

We ran across the street, started down it and took the first right.

"You two, stop. Come back here!" The man was looking to cross the street just as String Bean came around the other side of the building. He didn't see us before we past the first house and out of sight.

"Let's go, Bobby, run! Run like the wind!" We ran down the hill for a block, took a right, ran another block, took a left, ran two blocks, then took a right into an alley and didn't stop running until we crested the slight hill. "Can you believe it, Bobby? Here we are, trying to get into church, and they're chasing us from it."

"Will we get in trouble?"

"No. 'Cause they won't catch us. Come on!" Three more blocks and I was certain the chase was over. We took another corner and slowed to a walk. Halfway down the block, my heart felt a tug. In front of us stood Lisa's father's funeral home.

I led Bobby to the enclosed parking lot and we sat on their back porch. "I think we can get you transferred, Bobby. All we need is for your mother to insist on one. But you got to convince her how crummy it is first."

"That's impossible," he said. "She doesn't believe me, or I can't tell her because then Druggins will find out."

"What about your brother in Vietnam, would she listen to him?"

"Maybe."

"Good. I'll write him a letter, tell him about Druggins, and get him to get your mom to call me. I got two guys in my unit who were in your cluster and know all about Druggins. It'll be easy to prove you're not lying. Then I can show her how you'd be better off somewhere else and tell her how to get you transferred without letting Druggins in on it."

"You think that would work?"

"Sure. There's always openings in other units. If a parent really insists, there's no reason not to transfer a guy."

"What if it's a worse unit?"

"Bobby, have you heard of any housefather worse than yours? Melvin said the whole intermediate division knows Dipshit Druggins. If there was somebody worse, you'd of heard of him. Chances are you're going to get somebody no worse, and most likely, a lot better. Okay?" He nodded. "Good, now tell me more of the stupid things Dipshit's done that I can tell your brother."

Bobby spoke non-stop until a car pulled around the funeral home. "Relax, Bobby," I said. "We're not doing anything."

Two people sat in the car. The driver, a man about fifty, who didn't look angry but wasn't smiling as he parked the car in front of us. And Lisa.

The man opened his door. "What are you boys doing back here?"

"Just talking."

"I'd appreciate it if you weren't back here. This is private property."

Lisa's door opened. "It's okay, Daddy. I know him. Hi, Dave."

"Hi, Lisa."

"Were you waiting for Lisa?" her father asked.

"No. We were just sitting here talking."

"He's the Milton Hershey boy who walked me home from work one night, remember? I showed him back here." He gave her a look and she laughed. "The stars were out and we came back here to see them better."

"Oh." He shut his door. "Well, you shouldn't be back here even if you are only talking. Just in case."

"I know. I'm sorry. We just needed a place to talk. We'll leave."

"Thank you."

As he opened the door to the funeral home, Lisa said, "I'll wait out here." She stepped from the car, her jacket covering her uniform. "Going to work?" I said.

"In a little bit. It's such a nice day, I wanted to get out." She smiled at Bobby. "Who's this?"

"This is Bobby. He's the cousin of my roommate last year."

"Hi, Bobby," she said.

"Hi."

"How come you guys are back here? Playing hooky?"

"Sort of," I said, and told her what happened without revealing Bobby's difficulties. "So now we got to go back and make sure we're not caught sneaking into the parking lot."

"Do you want a ride? Would that help?

"It might. You could park near the buses and we could sneak out."

"I'll get the keys."

After she backed up and put the car in gear, Lisa glanced at me. "How come I haven't seen you in the drugstore lately?"

"I haven't been going. Are you working Fridays again?"

"Most of them. I'm done with cheerleading for the year. I want to keep my grades up for college."

I felt awkward because of the last time we met–the night Nancy dumped me, when I left Lisa at the candy counter with barely a greeting. "I'm sorry about not talking to you at the wrestling match. I wasn't feeling so good."

"I thought something was wrong. Are you okay now?"

"Yeah."

"Good." She smiled, I smiled, I elbowed Bobby for smiling, and the world was a better place.

Once Lisa pulled into the parking lot we had no problem slipping unnoticed out of the car. I thanked her for her help. "You're welcome. Promise you'll stop in and see me?"

"Sure."

She smiled her smile of angels. "Bye, Bobby. Nice meeting you."

As she drove down the street, she looked over and waved to us before disappearing from view. "Is she your girlfriend?" Bobby asked.

"I wish."

"She's pretty. You ought to go out with her."

"Okay, Dad, I'll try. And make sure you bring your brother's address to school tomorrow. We'll see what we can do."

4

I checked off my name, closed the barber's journal, and hustled down the steps. Instead of heading toward the central lobby, I turned right. I had less chance of getting caught by any of the small group of teachers I had seen meeting in the health class minutes before. Though I had dashed up the central lobby steps, going down them now was unwise. Especially with Brubaker around. He had been standing on the hill overlooking the old track and baseball field after I finished my workout. I hadn't noticed him until I started up the path, too late to change directions.

"Having yourself quite a workout, Mr. Purenut," Brubaker said. He was ten feet away. Moments before we had made eye contact and nodded.

"I guess so. I said I'd work hard."

"I should think you'd rather do that with your teammates at Catherine Hall. After all, misery loves company."

"I'm going to help Mr. Hart with *The Spartan*, so I asked the coach if I could workout up here tonight."

"Mr. Bower or Mr. Stevens?"

"Mr. Stevens."

He nodded. "I'll inform him of your commendable efforts."

I left him there, looking over our practice fields and Hershey, and went to homeroom where Mr. Hart had an editorial I could drop off while down that way in the locker room. The editorial would be my excuse to be in other parts of the building. When I saw the meeting in progress, I decided to check my name off then, before the meeting ended and before Brubaker got back inside. Which is why I turned right out of the barbershop–I'd be farther from the meeting and Brubaker.

I smiled as I headed toward the science wing, from where I would cut across the parking lot to the shop corridor entrance and down to the locker room. Tomorrow the barber would finish our section and start on the next, and I'd be sitting in class with plans of finding a barber some Friday night who would cut my hair how I wanted. Now maybe my senior picture would look halfway decent, and I might look normal for the prom and graduation, too–if I could manage another name cross-off.

Entering the passageway between corridors, I heard footsteps starting up the stairs and I backtracked to the first room on the right. The footsteps faded once on the second floor. I looked and saw Popeye, our wiry old janitor, headed for his closet beside the bathroom. He opened the door, filled a bucket with water, then rolled it into the hallway. When he turned my way, I ducked into the classroom.

All the student desks were tabletops only, leaving nothing to hide behind or under, just four rows of three tables each, two chairs per table. I ran to the front of the room and squatted behind the teacher's wide, paneled desk.

"Hi, Popeye. Working hard?" Mr. McFadden, the science department head, said from a slight distance.

"Hardly working," Popeye said, outside my door.

"That's the best kind of work," barked a voice that made my heart jump. Horrible! What was he doing around?

"You bet'cha," Popeye said. The lights came on in the room.

I moved to the side of the teacher's desk and peered under the tabletops at Popeye's legs. He pulled a sponge from the bucket, squeezed it, turned toward the side chalkboard, and began whistling as he walked toward the front of the room. He reached the corner, returned along the side wall, dipped his sponge, and started back up. On his return trip, I crawled to the far edge of the first row and squatted, hidden by the chairs and desktops. Only if he was looking for me would he see me. Next up and back and I moved to the second row. Then the third. He rolled the bucket to the front of the room and I slipped beside the fourth row. As he sponged along the front chalkboard, I edged around behind the table. It would be easy getting to the door now—which appeared in such shockingly plain view that any large-limbed, short-fused gorilla walking by would spot me.

Popeye went right, and I went with him two tables. Soon as he past my point going left, I hurried right again, looking up at the bright, gaping doorway, and the editorial I held in my left hand crinkled against the chair leg.

Popeye stopped. He took a step forward. "Hey? Is somebody there?" He stepped to his right, then again. "Who is that?" He started toward the corner and I exited on all fours, pulling on the door as I left.

"Hey, stop!" he said, just before the door slammed shut.

I started running. A movement reflected in Mr. McFadden's door in the next corridor. I turned down the steps and took them two at a time.

"What's the matter, Popeye?" Horrible said from down the hall.

"Some student was just in here! He's run down the steps."

"Yeah?!" Horrible's footsteps started pounding down the hallway above me.

I checked the corridors, jumped to the exit door, slammed the bar to open it, and darted back past the bathroom and into the first classroom on the left. Horrible charged down the steps, slammed open the door, and sprinted off. I headed for the windows.

"Mr. Brubaker," Popeye said, now in the hallway, "a student was just up in one of the classrooms. Mr. Hatch is after him."

"Did you see him?"

"No. I was—"

I dropped out the window. Fifteen seconds later I entered the shop corridor that led past the auditorium hallways and to the locker room via the gym. Halfway down it I heard the distant thunder of running feet. I retreated to the electricity shop doorway before Horrible ran into the corridor and directly into the gym. Which meant he was going to the locker room because Brubaker had fingered me as a suspect.

Out the door and around the outside, past the electricity shop, carpentry shop, and into the outcropping that housed the printing shop. I tried the hallway door. Locked. Shit!

Now what? If Brubaker did finger me, then he might be checking homeroom, or even calling Mr. Hart, and once Horrible dashed through the locker room he'd probably head for the printing shop. I'd have to say I kept practicing. I decided to workout more—forgot something I was going to do. Hopefully the baseball team wouldn't notice that I came back or how long I'd been there when Horrible showed up.

I started for the practice field. Behind me a window slid open. "Hey, asshole. What are you doing?"

It was Rich.

"Is there anybody in there with you? Mr. Castle or Horrible?"

"Just another guy. Why?"

I pushed through the bushes. "Help me up." Rich reached down and grasped my upraised hand. Seconds later I was hauling myself inside. "Is Mr. Castle around?"

"He's in his office."

"Has he been out here lately?"

Rich looked at the other kid. "I haven't seen him," the kid said.

"Me, neither," Rich said. "Not for about twenty minutes anyway."

"Good. Now listen, I've been here for *ten* minutes, okay? At least. If anyone comes here, that's how long I been here. Okay?"

"Sure," Rich said. The other kid nodded and offered me some paper towels. "You want to clean that up?" he said, indicating the floor behind me.

My dirty shoes had left tracks. "Thanks." I took the towels and dropped to the floor.

"What's going on?" Rich said.

"Not now, later. Just remember, you've been showing me these machines. I brought you that editorial for *The Spartan* from Mr. Hart." I stood up and wiped the bottom of my shoes. "How's this machine work again?"

"You put the original in here, face down, pull this down till it clicks, press this, and wait until you get your twenty-five copies. When it stops, unclick it, and repeat with the next original."

"Okay. Whew!"

"You're sweating like a pig. What happened?"

"I was up in the math area, just walking around for the hell of it when Popeye—"

"Pssssst!" The kid, at another machine, nodded toward the office.

"Oh shit." I looked for a trash barrel for the paper towels. Rich grabbed them and stuffed them inside a drawer.

"They went into Mr. Castle's office," the kid said. "Horrible and Brubaker." He jerked forward, suddenly concentrating on his machine. "Here they come."

I pointed at the button to start the machine. "Do you have to push that again if you want two sets of copies?"

"You can," Rich said, "or you can just set the number to fifty. Duh!"

We laughed. With peripheral vision I saw Brubaker spot me. They started toward us.

"And if you want three times as many," Rich said, "you can set it to seventy-five. Imagine that?"

. . . I now know what people felt like who got interrogated by the Spanish Inquisition, those nice folks whose motto was, "innocent until we make you confess." Horrible could have been one of their best employees.

"You were just up in the math wing, weren't you," was his first statement— not a question. When I said no, he said, "You ran down here from outside, admit it!"

"No, I didn't."

"Then why are you sweating?"

"Because I was just at track practice, and it's hot in here."

He charged over to the sophomore nearby, so fast I thought for sure the kid would scream, "Yes, yes, whatever you say," even before Horrible asked his question. "How long has he been down here?"

"About ten minutes."

Horrible looked at him like he'd better be telling the truth, then he turned back to me, but Brubaker and Mr. Castle had already started asking reasonable questions, like, "Why didn't you give the editorial to Mr. Castle?"–Cause he looked busy and I figured Rich knew what to do with it. And, "What have you been doing for ten minutes?"–Just talking and seeing how these machines work. "Is that what Mr. Hart needs you to do?"–No, but that's the deal we made.

Meanwhile, Horrible was pacing back and forth. He started in with more accusation/questions. He even made me show him how to run the machine Rich had "supposedly" been showing me for ten minutes. I did.

Eventually, Brubaker told me to report to Mr. Castle and to you, whenever I return from somewhere. Then he gave me twenty-five minutes to shower and get back to homeroom.

As I was leaving, Horrible looked like he was inches away from applying punishment by death–to which he'd plead insanity and probably get off.

Anyway, why would I be in Mr. Trotsky's room? I never had him for anything.

On my way out, I nodded to the kid I didn't know and said, "See 'ya." But it was more than just a parting. He'd saved my butt without knowing me, without knowing what I had done, and by facing down Horrible with a believable lie that could have gotten him in trouble if ever discovered. I'd probably never be able to repay him.

He acknowledged my nod with his own. "See 'ya," he said.

5

Saturday, April 9, 1971

. . . Do you think that's why she told me to still come in to see her, because she wants to talk to me when the jerk's not around? Could be. Maybe she's getting tired of him and I should ask her to the prom? Imagine if she said yes?

With that wonderful thought on my mind, is it any wonder I did what I did as I crossed the stadium parking lot headed for the concert when someone honked and yelled "Hey, Cow!" at me? It was a long-haired commie inside some kind of delivery van, throwing me the finger as he sped by. I returned the favor with a friendly wave of my own, nice and high and just like his.

Next thing I hear is a squeal of wheels and this nutcase is almost flipping over turning into the parking lot, using the exit lane marked off with cones and ignoring the attendants yelling at him. Then he floored it, and I heard him scream as he headed right for me from two hundred yards away.

Luckily I was in the middle of the parking lot with no other cars around. Half my brain, both testicles, and my sphincter muscle were all screaming the same thing, "RUN, you dumb bastard! RUN!" But the dumb bastard, Joe Cool part of my brain was saying, "Now wait a minute. We don't want to look like some chicken-shit, scaredy-cat, afraid of Charley Manson in his truck for no reason. So we'll just keep walking toward the stadium. Maybe Charley is cutting across the parking lot to save time?"

So I took about six steps, looked, and Charley had adjusted the wheel to keep me in his sights. I started to trot—casual like, and the wheel adjusted some more. I took two more steps, then I made a move that would drop the jock of any professional linebacker, and I took off toward the Hershey Park Pool corner of the parking lot, zigging and zagging like the biggest chicken-shit, scaredy-cat, dumb bastard that ever lived, with Charley behind me honking and hollering and squealing his wheels with every zig and zag.

I ended up halfway between the exits, leaping over the chain link fence, sprinting across the road and up the steps to the Hockey Rink. Charley stopped at the fence and got out. He raised his hand to speak but couldn't because he was laughing so hard. So he waved, like, "You were so-o-o-o funny."

"You're a f-ing asshole!" I yelled. He was big, but I was so pissed I would have gotten a rock and smashed his head in if he came after me—and could still catch me.

He kept laughing, sat on his fender, and said, "Crazy, it's me. Carl. Oh, man, Crazy." Then he started laughing again.

It was a guy who was a senior in our unit last year. He's supposed to be at Franklin and Marshall College, not scaring the crap out of me. The asshole.

Carl had dropped out of college the week before and was working for his stepfather's printing shop. Done with deliveries, he was racing home to Palmyra when he saw me. He suggested Eddie and I hook out that night, and though I had track practice the next morning, I accepted.

The joint Eddie rolled was unnecessary because Carl brought along two six packs, four joints, and a bottle of whiskey that he insisted we partake of as soon as we jumped in the car. An hour later, with a portion of each vice consumed while parked in front of the high school, Carl put the car in reverse and sped backwards for two hundred yards before sweeping onto the main road. He hollered, slammed the car into drive and stomped on the accelerator. "Know what we're going to do now, fellas?" he said, a smile spreading across his face as we raced down the hill. "Fish'in! . . . Carp fish'in!"

There was only one place to do that: Hershey Park, where the carp swarmed beneath the center bridge, thriving on popcorn, peanuts, candy and whatever else the hordes of people tossed to them while visiting the park, which was scheduled to open soon for weekends only. All we had to do was avoid any rent-a-cops cruising the outside streets while sneaking in.

Beneath the roller coaster, in a wooded area where the fence pulled up from the ground, we rolled under and in. Lights thirty feet high and fifty yards apart lit the park. We skirted their exposures and arrived at the bridge without having seen anyone.

This was the center and lowest point of the park. Two thoroughfares met on both sides of the bridge, and above us was a large walkway running from the kiddie section of the park on the west hill to the penny arcade and concession stands on the east hill. The closest lights hung from the turnpike ride, thirty yards away and under renovation. We stood in the center of the bridge, cloaked in darkness, the only sound that of running water.

Eddie leaned over the railing. "Think any of those suckers are down there?"

"Hell, yeah," Carl said, and ripped open the loaf of bread he'd brought along for bait. "Me, Mike, and Bonzei were in here graduation night. What a blast."

I said, "Is that why Mike never dumped the soap into the fish sculpture graduation night? He told me he was going to."

"He wanted to, but I had other plans, and I was driving. I wish I had now."

Mike had talked about his soapsuds caper for weeks before graduation. He'd even mentioned it the first time we ever saw the sculpture–large bronzed fish leaping amidst cascading water in front of Founders Hall. We were headed in for the inaugural Sunday Worship Service, me a freshman, him a sophomore. He said, "Man, I'll bet that'd look neat with suds shooting out all their mouths." He remembered his words his senior year and vowed to do it. I'd forgotten to ask him why he hadn't the two times I could have. I was glad I knew.

"Maybe I'll do it when I graduate," I said.

"You should," Carl said. "Now give me a beer."

I removed a beer for each of us, then took a swig of the whiskey Carl handed me. "I think I'm getting drunk," I said.

"I know I am," Carl said.

"Me, too," Eddie said. "To getting drunk."

"To getting drunk," Carl and I repeated.

"To Mike," I said.

"To Mike."

The fish weren't under the bridge, nor were they anywhere along the creek's edge as we wandered along it. Eventually, we sat on the bank and began playing drinking games, shrouded in the shadows cast by the umbrella ride behind us. We continued occasionally tossing bread into the water, which took it swiftly downstream and into the curve near the runoff of the jungle safari ride. Following one "team drink" Eddie jerked forward. "What's that?"

"What?" I said.

"That noise. Listen." Eddie tossed another morsel at the creek. Second's later we heard a splashing sound. "Hear it?"

We staggered up and over to where the creek curved left. "Look," Eddie said. The water shimmered with movement as a mass of slick, dark bodies swarmed over and against each other trying to position themselves for the morsels we had been tossing in.

We rushed to unstring and bait the hand-size pieces of rectangular wood with line wrapped around their centers that Carl had brought as our fishing poles. When ready, we threw in more bread, followed quickly by our lines. Immediately our arms jerked forward.

"Let the line out," Carl said. "It's fun to fight them."

We let the pieces of wood twirl inside our cupped hands. Thirty seconds later, Carl said, "Last one to land theirs, chugs."

I flipped the wood over and over, battling the constant, strong tugging motion at the other end. Eddie started walking backwards. When he reached the embankment below the ride, he still hadn't landed his fish. "Shit."

I twirled in more line, then hurried backwards just after Carl. When the resistance stopped, I could see a fish flopping on the ground. "I got mine."

"Me, too," Carl said.

We ran forward and pinned them to the ground. Both were over a foot long. Eddie landed his a moment later. "You drink," Carl said. We joined him.

"Ain't this a blast?" Carl said, as we unhooked the fish.

We had contests of who could land the longest fish, the shortest, the ugliest, the smelliest, with team drinks following each. During the fight for the heaviest fish, I stumbled and fell on my side. "I think I got Moby Dick," I said. "I'll need a crane."

The bank around my head lit up, the stones glittering in the light. I thought the moon had suddenly come out or perhaps a light from the ride behind us had come on from a faulty connection. I rolled back to look and the upside down view made me wish I hadn't. The light was directly in my eyes and much too low.

"You boys having fun?" someone said.

I rolled to my side and sat up, my head spinning.

"What are you doing here?" another voice said.

"Fishing," Carl said.

Four men stood on top of the embankment, each carrying a flashlight and nightstick. On their left shoulder was a white triangular patch. All of them looked a little older and bigger than me, with one bigger than Carl. That one shown his light on Carl's face. "Fishing, huh?"

"Looks like you're trespassing to me, asshole," the guy on the right said. "And drinking." He played his light on the beer cans and whiskey.

"Where're you from?" the big guy said.

"Palmyra," Carl said.

"All of you?" He shown his light on my face, then Eddie's. We both nodded.

"Those two look like cows," the one on the right said.

"You got any proof?" the big guy asked.

"I don't," I said.

"Me neither."

"I got some," Carl said.

"Who asked 'ya?" the guy on the right said. He jumped off the embankment and strode up to Carl while smacking his leg with the nightstick. "When we want to know something from you, we'll ask. Got it?"

Carl didn't answer.

The guy chuckled. "I guess you do, huh?" He stepped past Carl and snatched the remaining beers out of the water. "Hey, four left. Just enough. And a little Old Granddad to boot."

"Okay, grab those empties and get up here," the big guy said.

"Where're we going?" Carl said.

The guy below turned around. "What do you care? Just do what he says."

Carl looked from the guy below to the guy above, who nodded. "That's right. You're trespassing, and drinking under age maybe. You'll go where we tell you."

"So grab your shit and get up there," the guy said, pushing Carl with his nightstick. Carl smacked it away, and the guy raised it. "You want a whack tough guy? Huh? Is that it?"

"Billy," the big guy said.

"What? I'll only crack him if he wants me to. Right, tough guy?"

"Just get your shit and get up here," the big guy said.

I still held the fishing pole in my hand, the carp tugging at the other end. "You want us to reel these in and pull out the hooks, or just drop them with the hooks in?"

"Reel them in. But hurry it up."

I began flipping my piece of wood, the line drawing in inch by inch.

Their patches read "Sentinel Security." Were they Park or some kind of construction security? We weren't doing anything destructive or stealing, maybe they'd let us go? But the big guy seemed too official–a by-the-book-type.

I could make a run for it, but what good would that do if Eddie and Carl didn't? Besides, I was too drunk and high. Just reeling in the fish was difficult. But if I–

"Hurry up!" Billy snapped, suddenly beside me.

I dropped the line, then fell to one knee hurrying to pick it up. He laughed. "You think we got all night? Come on!"

I quickened the end over end moves.

On my left, Carl tossed his carp into the creek and moved to help Eddie.

"Billy, cut those other two with your knife," the big guy said.

Shit, what was I going to do? If they called in the cops, I was dead. Detentions till I graduated, at least. Would they not pay three-quarters of college? Worse—would they kick me out before I got my diploma? Shit. And less than two fucking months left.

"You almost got it?" Carl said, coming up to me.

"I think so. Maybe."

He took my line. "Get ready to run," he whispered.

"Huh?"

Billy was cutting Eddie's line, the other three remained atop the bank.

"We'll meet at the car. If it's not there, you're on your own."

"But what if . . . "

Billy headed our way. I glanced up the creek toward the bridge. It was a clear shot, but could I outrun the guys behind me? Maybe. Maybe not. Probably not.

"Hold it out, asshole," Billy said.

Carl faced him, right hand holding the wood, left hand extending the line.

I looked at Eddie. Where would he go? He was in worse shape then me—drunker and farther to run. He was at the water's edge, inching toward us.

Billy sliced through the line. "Now get your ass—"

Carl slammed his knee into Billy's groin. "Fuck head!" he said, and pushed his crumbling body backwards.

I took two steps to my right and heard splashing. Carl and Eddie were charging through the water. I dashed in. Over my left shoulder I spotted the big guy bending over Billy and one guy standing beside him. Where was the other?

I yanked my feet out of the water in giant steps until I reached knee level, then I thrust forward with my legs. Carl and Eddie past halfway, angling away from me. I angled toward them and looked back. Nobody but Billy's curled form. I looked right. I saw the big guy and another one running toward the bridge. Then I saw the fourth guy, in the water, five yards behind me.

I pushed harder, faster.

Knee-deep, calf-deep, ankles. Eddie was throwing up, blocking the one path up the bank. Carl struggled around him, cursing. Several feet to their right, an outcropping looked easy to climb over. Once near it, I jumped, got my hands on it and muscled my way up. Suddenly my right ankle was seized. I twisted around and pulled back. The guy slammed his nightstick into my thigh, nicking my knee. I hollered. He raised the stick again and I smashed the heel of my Weinberg into his hand. He let go, fell forward, and caught himself on the bank. He grasped at my ankle again and a boot flashed by my head and slammed into his face. He cried out and slid out of sight.

Carl yanked me up. "Come on!"

We jumped over the railing and turnstiles, ran into the thoroughfare, and turned left. A large area occupied that end of the park, the rides arranged in a sweeping semicircle with a concession stand in the center. We darted to the right. In the distance, two flashlights pumped in motion with running arms.

"I don't think they saw us," Carl said, as we hurried into the woods behind the first ride. We made our way up the side of the hill and stopped when we heard footsteps below.

"You check that end," the big guy said.

The backside of the roller coaster where we snuck in was to our left. We made our way toward it as footsteps ran off and others came in, not as fast.

"Jesus, what happened?" the big guy said.

"That long-haired bastard kicked me in the face. We're going to kill you, you fuckers!"

"Shut up and listen."

We stood motionless for half a minute, then angled quietly up the embankment to the fence. Eddie crawled under first, then Carl, then me. The roll under the fence turned my stomach. Once through, I got to my knees and threw up.

"Listen."

"Up here, fuck heads!" Carl shouted, directing my head so the vomit landed where we had just crawled through.

"Carl," Eddie said.

"Come on you stupid bastards! I'll fuck you all up!"

Eddie scrambled toward the road as Carl helped me up. Below, footsteps rushed toward us. I hopped over the guardrail and started for the car. Carl stopped. "This way dick heads, blowhards, pussies!"

"Carl, let's go!"

We could hear the rushed voices, hurrying to find the opening. Then, "Shit! Oh, man, fucking puke."

Carl roared with laughter. "Suckers!"

Once in the car, Carl pulled across the road and rolled down his window. "You fucking asshole prick dumb mother-fucking, rent-a-cop, security dickheads! Eat my shit!" Then he laughed and peeled away as the big guy's head came into view hurrying up the embankment.

Carl sped down the road, his left arm out the window, his middle finger up, honking the horn with his right forearm. He darted into the underpass laughing at the two security guys standing far behind us.

He was in the middle of the tunnel. The road on the other side curved quickly left, so anybody could . . . "Carl!"

The car coming around the bend swerved right, as did we, our backside spinning off the road. A blue and white car with lights. Carl took the quick right as the other car backed up, then nearly hit a second car coming toward it.

"That's the police," Eddie said. "He's coming after us."

"He's a fucking rent-a-cop," Carl said, and stomped on the gas, sending us through Chocolate Town USA at seventy miles an hour.

Carl veered right off of Chocolate avenue toward the quarry and the back road to our unit. I turned around from watching behind us. "Okay, he didn't see us." Carl continued speeding down the road and under the railroad bridge. "Carl he didn't see us!"

I grabbed the dashboard. We flew into the turn, then fishtailed past the quarry, guarded only by a "no trespassing" sign and a flimsy, wire fence.

"Carl, slow down!"

"I'm going to throw up," Eddie said.

"Can't stop now," Carl said.

We sped around the curves, past the sewage plant, up the hill and Carl pulled over. I jumped out. Eddie leaned over and threw up. My throat quivered; I emptied my stomach. Carl laughed. "Come on, get out before he comes this way."

Eddie crawled out and sat on the side of the road. "You're crazy, Carl," I said. "Slow down."

He grinned. "See 'ya." He raced up the road, blaring his horn. A minute later we scrambled off the road and behind a tree as the cop car sped by.

In the basement, in the dark, we peeled off our barn clothes, then made our way to the sinks to clean up, dry off, and brush our teeth. Upstairs, I cracked the windows in case our breaths stunk of alcohol. As I crawled into bed, I felt a tightening just above my knee and remembered I had track practice the following morning.

6

Next morning, when Suds saw I could barely bend my leg, he had me switch jobs with the silage guy. The fully loaded silage cart weighed over two hundred pounds, and whether I pulled or pushed, the going was slow and painful. Each shovelful of silage I scooped out of the deep cart then had to lift over the railing in front of the cows, was equally painful.

I was fifteen minutes behind when I finished with the silage, which included filling the feed bins outside. Next I had to throw down bales of hay and straw and distribute them. I wasn't looking forward to climbing the ladder to the second floor, crawling through the hatch door, scaling to the tops of the hay and straw piles to throw down the bales, then climbing back down and tossing those same bales down to the first floor.

When I lifted the hatch to the second floor, a bale of straw hit atop a pile in the middle of the floor and tumbled toward me. "Watch it!"

I came through and got to my feet. Suds, finished with the straw, was climbing the hay pile. "Mr. Sawyer, you don't have to do that. I can get them."

"And then we can wait all day for you to finish before eating breakfast, right?

I grunted as I hauled myself onto the first row of stacked hay. "Stay down there, Dave. Toss those ones down. I'll get these."

I groaned in protest. Suds heaved a bale past me. "You should have just gone back in like I told you."

"I thought doing silage stuff wouldn't bother me."

"Why don't you go in now? I'll finish up."

"No, I can do it." I leaned over and yelled through the hatch, "Bales coming down!"

I'd always enjoyed trying to slide the bales across the wooden floor, length-wise, so they'd reach the hatch opening and fall through. Eventually they'd bunch up and I'd have to go over and knock them through individually. This time I dragged them over one by one.

Suds finished and moved to the pile in the center of the room; I stood at the hatch. "Stay there," he said. He slid the bales across the floor, and those that didn't drop through, I helped along. When we finished, Suds motioned for me to go down first. "Nah, you go, Mr. Sawyer. I'll take too long."

"Get going. You got work to do."

Coming up, I had used a nearby bale to pull myself up. Now the floor was bare. I tried bending down twice, but the pain stopped me.

"Here, use this." Suds bent to lift the hatch door.

"No, I got it." I fell forward and caught myself in a push-up position, rolled onto my back, then shifted toward the hole. "See?" I said.

"You plan on going to track practice today?"

"I doubt it." I sat up, swiveled my legs, and lowered myself onto the ladder. Suds said, "I saw you didn't make the National Honor Society again?"

"Yeah, well . . . It's no big deal."

"You know, every time that form came around I signed it but once."

I smiled, remembering my snap on One-Eighty. "Can't blame you, Mr. Sawyer. I'd probably have done the same thing. Besides, it's not you. I've been up for that thing six times and have never made it. Somebody has it in for me." I reached the first floor and Suds followed. I said, "I just wanted it because I figured it would help me get into college. I already got accepted so it doesn't matter."

"Where're you going?"

"I'm not sure. Franklin and Marshall accepted me, but I was only going there because Carl was. Shippensburg might be pretty good. They have a communications department which I might like for TV. They also have business. I applied to two others, too."

He wiped his forehead and mouth with his bandanna. "I never went to college. It's good you do. Especially if the school pays for it. Take advantage."

"I plan to. I don't know what else to do, and seeing as how I probably don't have to worry about the draft anymore, I might as well."

"And don't blow it like Carl. That diploma gets you one step ahead of everyone else." He looked at the bales scattered around us. "You want help with these?"

"No, I got them. Thanks for helping me."

He waved his hand.

Normally I'd carry six bales in the wheelbarrow at a time. I got four steps and the pain stopped me. I took two bales off, then another. It hurt, but I made it to the center aisle. On my way back, Suds intercepted me at the doorway between the barn and the calf pen area. He took the handles. "You stack 'em and divide up the hay; I'll bring the rest out. You'll take forever."

"Thanks, Mr. Sawyer."

. . . I couldn't even bowl today with my father and sisters when they took me out. They always take me out on the weekend closest to my birthday. (Turning 18 on Monday, Teach. Legal drinking age. Ya-hoo!)

We always put three candles on the cake. One for me, one for my father–whose birthday was last week, and one for my mother–whose birthday was two days after mine. I still remember our last birthday together, when I was five, her and I blew out the candles across from each other and she kept blowing and blowing, right in my face, and I kept laughing and laughing. My sisters do it with me now, one for my mom, one for my father. Kind of a tradition.

We had the cake in their motel room. My father said, "Eleven years. Boy, did they go by fast."

"Fast? I think they took forever."

Imagine that, though? I've been in here for 11 years and now I have 51 days left. Amazing.

7

Wednesday, April 21, 1971

You know, Teach, for three weeks I've been being invisible, avoiding all contact with authority while my hair grows to a reasonable length, and in one moment of stupidity I forget, and "BAM!" just like that, I'm chasing Brownie and Jim past Homelife when their door opens and Horrible catches me in mid sprint.

Of course he remembered me from the night he thought I was the one he was chasing all over the school but couldn't prove. "Having track practice inside now?" he said. Then he started lecturing me about how seniors aren't above getting punished, how we can be made to stay the summer, how we can even be kicked out without our diplomas.

And then he noticed my hair—the hair I was going to get cut this Friday on town privilege. Being Horrible, he didn't smile, but his eyes did kind of widen with the thrill of the kill. "When did you get your hair cut last?" he said.

"I don't know. We're scheduled to go again next week, though."

"You'll be getting yours cut earlier than that. Right this minute, in fact."

And that's how it all started.

I stepped onto the floor. Sunlight cut warmly into the room. Around the barber chair lay a multi-colored cushion of hair. One kid occupied the barber's chair, another sat on the bench. Both looked like sophomores.

"Lookey here," the barber said. "How'd your hair get so long?"

"It must grow faster the closer you get to graduation."

"I'll cut it extra short so you'll have nothing to worry about."

"That's okay. You don't have to do me any favors."

"No, but I want to."

I smiled along with his joke, then sat down and picked up a magazine.

After the first kid left and the barber started on the second, the door below opened and footsteps trudged up the stairs. The scissors stopped when the kid reached the top.

"Well, well, well. If it isn't Mr. Smartmouth. Waited till last, huh? It doesn't matter. I get you sooner or later."

The kid, tall and skinny, flopped onto the bench. His sandy blonde hair already met the school's standards. "You always get us," he said.

"That's right. And I'm going to get you again. I always get the smartmouths."

"That's because you can't cut normal haircuts."

"I don't need to. Everybody likes my haircuts now."

"Yeah, right."

"You like my haircuts, right?" the barber asked the kid in his chair.

"Oh, yeah. A whole lot."

"See? He likes them."

"Then he's the only one."

"You like them, too, right?" the barber said.

I thought of not answering, just focusing on my magazine until they ignored me. But that could backfire. "I like it the way it is now," I said.

"See? And I cut it."

"But he won't like it after you cut it."

"Yes, he will. Right?"

The barber wanted an affirmation, however jocular or sarcastic, to sustain his position. The kid wanted what he had never gotten and figured he never would–someone else to tell the barber the truth.

All I wanted was not to be there.

"Right?" the barber repeated.

"If you leave it kind of long I will."

"But he won't," the kid said.

"That's right. You'll get what everyone else gets." He snipped his scissors a few more times. "Well . . . ?"

"Then . . . I probably won't."

The kid sat up and grinned. "See?"

"Is that so?" the barber said.

"I like my hair longer, like you see in other high schools."

"Like normal people get," the kid said. "Ha!"

"'I like my hair longer,'" the barber mimicked. "You'll like it no matter how short I cut it, and you'll thank me for it, too."

"Well . . . " I said, hoping the conversation would stop.

"No, 'Wells' about it. You will like it, and you will thank me for it."

"If I like it, I'll thank you for it," I said agreeably.

"You won't, though," the kid said.

"Will you shut up?" I said to the kid.

The barber stood motionless, staring at me. "I remember you," he said. "You're that smartmouth who walked away from me and didn't say thank you last summer. You got that Bogart kid in your unit."

"There's no Bogart in my unit."

"You're still the punk who didn't say thank you." He resumed clipping. "Thought you got away, huh?"

"I don't know what you're talking about."

"Yes, you do. Not so tough now. You guys think you can do what you want, say what you want. You're going to find out you can't. You're in my chair, and I'm cutting the hair. I do the talking around here.

"Go ahead, read your magazine. It don't change nothing. You guys think . . . "

No amount of nodding or innocuous, one-syllable responses could stem his continued harping. Gradually, the kid beside me resumed hurling comments back and forth with the barber. I didn't stop him because my sentence had already been decided.

"All right, Smartmouth, you're next," the barber said.

When I reached his chair, I met his gaze. "I'm a senior. I want a square back."

"You'll get what I give you. Now sit down."

He draped the apron across my front and tied it behind my neck. "You guys think you can tell me how to cut your hair. That'll be the day."

He snipped a cut of hair above my left temple, then continued around my head. The hair tumbled into my lap in large, long chunks. How was I going to talk to Lisa now? My senior pictures were next week, what would they look like?

It would have been all so perfect.

When the barber combed my front hair straight down and hacked it off halfway between eyebrows and hairline, the kid said, "He's really going to like that haircut."

"You just keep quiet," the barber said, and set down the scissors and comb.

"I'm allowed to talk. Just cause you're always talking doesn't mean we can't."

The electric clippers snapped on. I said, "Remember, I want a square back. That's supposed to be longer back there."

"See why I'm always talking? I got kids telling me how to do my job."

"Just reminding you."

"Sure you are." He bent forward. "Square back, right?"

"Right."

I stayed rock-still, staring at the blurry form of the kid in front of me, who was staring back. My head inched forward, the clippers droned, and I knew he had screwed me.

"Hey, what are you doing?"

"Sit back. I'm not done."

The square back was to be squared just above the collar. I could feel the swatch he'd cut intersecting my ears at midpoint, the hair hanging down a full inch on either side. I stood up. "You've cut it too high up."

"I cut it the way I'm told. Seniors get square backs. That's a square back."

"It is not. It's a hack job!"

"Don't start yelling at me. You don't like it, go tell Homelife."

I turned to the kid. "How bad's this?"

"Really bad, man. It's way up there. He hacked you."

"You shut up," the barber said.

"He can talk."

"Yeah. He asked me a question."

"I'm not taking this from you punks. Either sit down or get out."

I'd been feeling the scalp mark. Why me? Why now? No matter what, I'd have to let him finish because it would look worse if I didn't. Damn.

"I'm sitting down, but I'm going to Homelife soon as you're done butchering me."

"Won't do you any good. I followed the rules."

He leveled off both sides. "There. Nice and square back."

"It may be a square back, but it ain't nice," I said.

"You guys don't know what nice is."

After he finished with the back, he began combing the hair on top of my head opposite the direction I wore it. I jerked my head away. "I don't comb it that way. Cut it where it is."

He resumed cross-combing. "I'm the barber. I'll cut it–"

I stood up. "You're not combing it to that side to cut it."

"I'll cut it any way I want. Now sit down or I'm calling Homelife."

"Go ahead, call," I said, and untied my apron. "Tell them I'm coming."

I grabbed my glasses and looked in the mirror. My hair stood up in the middle while the sides were shorter than I'd ever seen them. "What a hack job! There's no way they won't think you're finished when they see this crap."

"Go on, run to Homelife," the barber said. "I'll still have to finish it."

I started down the stairs. Above me, the barber said, "Okay, Smartmouth, get over here."

8

Saturday, April 24, 1971

Yesterday I had my talk with Dr. Davis, who talked with Bobby on Thursday. No luck. Even though he agrees Bobby's having problems and might be happier somewhere else, he didn't think a transfer was necessary or wise. He said that would be like learning to run from your problems. "Bobby's a good kid, he'll adjust. All he needs is more time."

He needs distance, not time. Question is, what unit should he go to? Just saying "this unit" or "that unit" because they're good ones won't flush in Homelife. We have to have a reason to get him there. But where? And why?

"Did they say why?" someone asked.

Al picked up a piece of paper. "It says, 'The traditional dress and grooming codes in force adequately reflect the high standards of Milton Hershey School. With the exception of the new cut allowed for seniors, we feel these codes should remain as is for the time being.'"

"What a bunch of bull," someone whispered behind me.

"I'd like to discuss what's being done to get the barber to cut hair the way he's supposed to," Bill Hoffa said. "He's not doing it all the time, and I think it's time *we* did something about it, if nobody else will."

My response was lost among all the others.

"You boys won't do nothing," Old Man Hatch said, silencing us, " . . . except *get* the haircuts."

No one responded to his jest and he ran his hand through his white hair. "Listen, fellas. When the barber was hired, he was told 'this' was how you cut the hair, and he agreed. Now, after a year on the job, we suddenly ask him to cut it another way, but only for certain boys, and only if they want. It takes time for anyone to adjust to something new, the barber included. We talked to him since the last meeting and I think he's finally getting it right."

"What about Crazy then?" someone said.

"Who's that?"

Guys called for me to stand, those nearest prodded and pushed. I stood. "Show him the back," someone said. I turned. "That's no square back," Bill said.

"Did you ask for a square back, Dave?" Brubaker said.

"Yep. Just before I sat down, and once while I was in the chair."

"His was a special case," Old Man Hatch said. "His hair was extra long and he hadn't said thank you last time it was cut."

After my butcher job, I'd gone directly to Homelife, saw Kramer at his desk and nearly shouted, "Do you call this a square back? Is this what your talking to the barber gets us?" Kramer said he'd look into it, called me back two classes later and informed me that my not saying thank you was the reason for the cut, and though the barber was wrong for doing it, there was nothing that could make my hair longer and it was best forgotten. As I was leaving, Old Man Hatch walked in, whistled, and said, "What happened to you?"

"It's the new square back you guys have been making sure the barber gives us. Nice, ain't it?"

I looked at Old Man Hatch now. "It wasn't for not saying thank you after my last haircut. It was for not saying thank you last summer. And my hair being long just before it was cut should have nothing to do with it. I was a senior asking for a square back. If he has a problem with my not saying thank you, he should go see you guys and then you punish me, he shouldn't butcher me. If I have a problem with him, should I do what I can, like punch his face in, or should I come see you? Which is it?"

"Anger's not going to help the situation, Dave," Brubaker said.

"That's right," Old Man Hatch said. "And it can get you in trouble."

"Whatever the reason," someone said, "Crazy's a senior and he should have gotten a square back and didn't. You guys keep telling us something will be done, and we keep getting butchered."

Old Man Hatch said, "Look, most of you are seniors. You'll probably get one more haircut, then you can go the rest of your lives without one. Why not accept it and enjoy your last few weeks here?"

"Because we don't want to look like jerks at our prom and graduation," someone said.

"What about the juniors?" one of the few juniors there said. "What are we supposed to do–get butchered until we graduate?"

"The haircuts are getting better, and they'll continue to get better. It just takes time."

"That's what you always tell us."

" . . . And it never happens."

" . . . It's time *we* did something about it."

Bill Hoffa said, "I move we continue this meeting without any officials present." Several guys seconded it.

Old Man Hatch conferred with Brubaker, then said, "Okay, we'll leave, but let me say this: You guys know how the school operates. Don't do anything stupid. I'd hate to see any of you get this close and not graduate. Whatever you decide, make sure it's something constructive, within the rules, and something the Board will accept. Remember, a little is better than nothing."

. . . This time we asked for one measly, lousy, stinking inch over the ears and collar, then extending it to two inches come October. That's reasonable, right?

But what if they say no again? Well, I'd like to tell you what we decided, but everyone said they wouldn't tell anyone so that it would remain a secret until the day it happens–if it's necessary–so I can't tell you. But as soon as it does happen, you'll know. He-he-he-he.

9

Sherlock pulled into the community center parking lot and stopped. "Got a big date tonight, Dave?"

"No, I'm trying to get one. To our prom. That's why I asked for the late– in case the drugstore's crowded, I'll ask her after everyone leaves."

Lisa had been busy the Friday before. First with Ryan, who looked as though he was begging forgiveness, and then, an hour later with Huey and some other guys. I never went in.

Now, as usual for the start of town privilege, the counter was full. I sat on the stone wall behind the community center and waited until only two guys remained. When I entered the store, Lisa dazzled me with her smile. I sat in the same seat I sat in the previous fall. "Here I am, like I promised."

"It's about time," she said. "Want some ice cream with nuts on it? My treat, a graduation present."

"Sure. Vanilla, please."

If only I lived around Hershey, after graduation I could stop in occasionally and maybe become her boyfriend. Elmira was two hundred miles away, though–not exactly dropping by distance.

"I got you the wet nuts," Lisa said, walking toward me, dish in hand. "That's the kind you like, right?"

"No, I like the . . . "

The ice cream, two scoops, was covered with dry nuts. "Got 'cha," she said, and sat down in the stool on her side.

I took a bite. "So what's new?" I said. "How's Mr. Lucky been treating you?"

"We broke up."

I stared at her. She smoothed back her hair and raised and lowered her eyebrows. "Really?" I said.

"Yep. I like him but . . . " She shrugged. "He always acts different around his friends, and he never wants me talking to other guys. This job was giving him fits. He just, I don't know, it just didn't work out."

"Wow, that's too bad."

"I can tell you're really broken up about it."

"Well I don't care about him, but you I do. You'll get over it, though. And it's not like you'll never have another date. I know about five hundred Homeguys that would go out with you. In fact–"

"Except for you," she said.

"Ha! That'd be the day. I'd have to be dead, not to."

"What about your girlfriend?" she said, and stood up to head for a customer waiting at the register. "What would she say?"

The last time we spoke, just for a minute outside the drugstore while Ryan had continued inside to get seats, Nancy had come up. Too embarrassed to tell Lisa I had been dumped, I told her Nancy wasn't with me because she was busy.

Now, as Lisa drew a soda for the customer, I pictured her in a beautiful gown, hair spilling over bare shoulders, the front modestly revealing, causing constant looks and envy of her lucky date–me. Maybe it would be my last weekend in Hershey, but who cared? We could write, right? And phone. What about carrier pigeons? Telegrams? Monumental thought waves? YAAAHOOOOOOOOO!

I suppressed my grin when she returned. "Well?" she said. "What would she say? She wouldn't be too happy."

"Yes, she would. Even though we broke up, she still likes me." I smiled for both our futures.

Lisa didn't. She looked more shocked than surprised. "When did you break up?"

"Beginning of March."

"But I asked you about her not too long ago, right outside, and you said she was doing something, or busy."

"I was guessing. I didn't want to go into it then."

She shook her head. "Why didn't you tell me you had broken up?"

"What's it matter? You had a boyfriend. You would have just felt sorry for me."

"Do you know why I made you promise to come in?"

"I guess because you wanted to see me."

"Right. Because I knew I was probably going to break up, and I wanted to tell you. Remember I promised I would?"

"And you did. So what? I wanted to know so I could ask you out. Now I can. Want to go out? Want to go to our prom?"

How could she not smile now? I was all a-twitter.

She said, "I can't. Somebody's already asked me, and I accepted."

"To our prom?"

She nodded.

Not again. How could she be free of the jerk and not be going with me? Why did she say yes? Didn't she know I was dying to go out with her?

Lisa said, "I wanted to tell you because I said I would and because I thought, maybe . . . But then you said your girlfriend was fine, so I figured there was no way. Then, last Friday, Huey asked me to go."

Figured. The lucky bastard. The persistent, good-looking, charming, lucky bastard. Got my girl for the prom. With my luck, he'd probably end up marrying her and I'd be tortured for the rest of my life at every Homecoming. There they'd be, Huey and my wife, his wife, at every event. Why even go?

"You know how he is," she said. "He's funny, and polite. He treated Carey fine at your dance. So I thought, why not, it's just a date. He is a nice guy, right?"

"Yeah. Definitely," I said. "He's also lucky. The bastard."

"I'm sorry, Dave," she said, and touched my hand.

Her fingernails shone a pretty blue that matched her eyes. Probably the same color she'd wear at the prom, where we would have walked hand in hand, danced close, laughed.

"It's not your fault," I said. "It's God's. He's punishing me for some stupid, stinking reason."

"Stop," she said. "Don't say that."

A group of Homeguys burst into the store. While Lisa and her partner served them, the boldest guys tried to impress the girls with small talk, one jokingly asking Lisa out. Why hadn't I done that? I'd talked with her alone for half an hour, got her to laugh, and still I didn't ask her—until it was too late.

When Lisa returned to her seat she drew my empty dish across the counter. "So will you be going to the prom?" she asked.

"I don't know. Maybe. Maybe not. I don't know."

"Do you think we could have a dance together?"

"A slow one?" I said.

She nodded, the corners of her mouth turning up.

"Sure," I said. "That'd be nice."

"It will," she said and smiled.

What a goddamn, glorious, beautiful smile. Why hadn't I—

"Hey, what if we go out next Friday night? And the one after that, and the—"

"I can't," she said. "Huey's already asked me and I said no because I'll either be visiting colleges, going back home to visit, or working for someone so I can have that Saturday off."

I nodded–blocked out for life. I got up. "Well, I guess I'll see you at the prom, then."

"You won't be coming in any more?"

"I don't know. You might be working, you might not."

"So come in when I am. All right?"

"I will if I'm over here."

Outside, as I past the last window, Lisa stood before an elderly couple. She glanced at me. We gave each other small hand waves, she added a slight smile.

And that was that.

. . . The girl of my dreams, gone, just like that. One last shot I had, and I shoot too late. I can't believe it.

I do have some good news. While walking to the park, I almost got run over by Carl, he of the maniac disposition and sound barrier driving speeds. When I told him why I had such a long face, he suggested I ask Mary Jo to the prom, the bubbly blonde at Franklin and Marshall I dallied with on the back porch.

"Yeah, she was fun," I said.

"Fun?" Carl said. "She said you were an animal."

Did you hear that, Teach? An animal. And I don't even remember what we did.

Carl's going to get me her number, and I'll ask her. Otherwise, it's blind date city, and with my luck, it's scary to think what I might get.

Can you believe it, though? Man, I hope I've finally learned my lesson.

10

I took the phone from Jonathan. Joe had already spoken. "What do you think now, Mrs. Spangler?"

"I just can't believe it. The Drugginses seem like such nice people."

"They only have to be like that for five minutes while the parents are there.

Then they can go back to being Hitlers."

"All houseparents aren't like that, are they?"

"No," I said, "that's why I want to get Bobby transferred. Most are okay. I mean, we know they can't be nice all the time–they got us to deal with–but you don't have to be jerks all the time, either. Druggins is. That's why Bobby should transfer."

"What about all the other poor boys there?"

"I don't know. All I can do is help Bobby for now."

"They shouldn't even be houseparents, if they're like that," Mrs. Spangler said.

"I know."

"This makes me mad," she said. "I'm going up there tomorrow and–"

"No, no, no, Mrs. Spangler. Don't do that. That'll just make things worse, especially for Bobby."

"But how? After they see the things they do, they'll have to do something about it, to stop it."

"Yeah, like call the Drugginses in to ask them about it. And they'll have an excuse for everything. 'Why do they get up so early?'–because they can't get their chores done right getting up later. 'Why do they have to run around the cluster?'–because they didn't do this or that right, and besides, it's good exercise. 'Why'd Bobby and his roommate have to paint the fence by themselves?'–because they were walking on it and dirtied it. 'Why do they encourage them to squeal on each other?'–they're only informing the houseparents of something wrong the other guy has done, and shouldn't misbehavior be punished?

"They'll come up with a reason for everything, and then, when they go back, watch out. And if you go in, they'll find out and Bobby will be the one that really gets it. There's all kinds of ways they can make life miserable for him and do it legally. And they will."

"But it's not fair all those boys having to suffer through that."

"I know. If you want to try and save them all, do it after Bobby's out of there and in another unit. Then he'll be safe."

"But how can I get him out of there, if you don't want me to go in?"

"I want you to go in, but not like a maniac." I laughed. "You know what I mean. Don't even mention the Drugginses and things Bobby told you that are wrong or happened. Just go in and ask to talk to someone about Bobby. Tell them you think he's unhappy, he's not acting normal, he's depressed, he's not the same. Of course you expected him to have some problems at first, but he's been in four months and he's getting worse, not better. They'll probably say it takes some guys longer to adjust than others and that you should give it more time, but—"

"I don't want to give it more time. I want him transferred now."

"That's the spirit, Mrs. Spangler. But don't say it so it sounds like you know something you're not telling them, they might ask what it is."

"I'll tell them, if I have to."

"No, Mrs. Spangler. Don't do that. You'll just make it worse for Bobby."

"What if they want to give him more time there?"

"Be persistent. Look, tell them you were talking to another mother whose son got a transfer and it worked for him. Out here in the senior division all we have to do is go in and ask for a transfer because we don't like it, and we usually get one. In the intermediates, you don't know about it or you're too scared so you're stuck where you're at. But there's no reason they can't give him one. And because we'll be graduating soon, all the eighth graders will be moving up to the senior division and that means every intermediate division unit will have openings. Bobby could go to any one of them, and I have the perfect one to ask for. Has he ever mentioned his friend, Melvin, on the swim team?"

"Yes."

"Melvin says his houseparents are pretty good, and if a guy says that, then they must be. Which means they'll be light years ahead of the Drugginses. So, since they're friends, maybe Bobby could transfer there? Melvin could help Bobby 'adjust.' Say you're positive he'd do better with a friend's help."

"That's an idea."

"They might say they don't do that, that that's giving special treatment to one boy and it's not fair, but—"

"Who cares?" she said. "Nobody will know he's getting special treatment. He's having a difficult time, why not try to make it easier for him? He's only a child, for Pete's sake."

"That's right. There really isn't any reason they can't transfer him. There's some reasons they may not want to, but none they can't. And if you really insist, I think they'll do it. Why not, you know? What's it matter to them where he goes?"

"It doesn't," she said.

Suds knocked on the door. "Let's go, Dave. Bedtime."

I nodded. "I got to go, Mrs. Spangler. It's bedtime."

"All right. Well, thank you so much, David, for helping me and being Bobby's friend. Will we ever meet, you and I?"

"Maybe. Do you plan on taking Bobby out for the weekend any time soon?"

"In three weeks. The fifth and sixth, I believe."

"If you go to our church service or the Catholic church on Sunday, we can."

"Then I will," she said.

"Okay. That's our graduation weekend. Tell Bobby to find me and we'll meet."

"Wonderful. I'll be looking forward to it. And thanks again."

"You're welcome. Good luck. Remember, be persistent."

"I will. Believe me."

11

Sunday, May 16, 1971

Twenty-three days and counting. Got a date for the prom last night with Mary Jo. She remembered me right off and accepted just as fast. Maybe I truly was an animal and she liked it, huh? Yeow!

She has a cousin in Palmyra who she can stay with that night and asked me to get her a date. I asked for a description. "Tall, good-looking, college freshman cheerleader, Miss Dauphin County two years ago."

"Can I take her?"

I didn't say that, but sounds like Brownie's got himself quite a date. Lucky for him we talked last night and not this afternoon. I told Bobby at church about talking to his mom and to keep his fingers crossed, then he asked me about the secret plan we all vowed in the senior senate to keep to ourselves until next Thursday night.

Can you believe it? The plan I wouldn't mention in here, is already in the intermediates. And that's because of blabbermouths like Brownie. Who he got it from, I don't know, but if it doesn't happen, I'll bet it's the blabbermouths who do the loudest complaining.

Twenty-five minutes less time here and counting!

I shifted in my seat beside Huey. All week I had debated about telling him about asking Lisa to the prom. Did he already know? Wouldn't he have said something during track practice? Would he care? It wasn't like we were the only guys interested in her. Hundreds of others might have asked her out, too.

Still, it didn't feel right keeping it secret.

"Huey," I said. "I stopped in to see Lisa last Friday night, to ask her to the prom. But you beat me to it, you dog."

He smiled. "Early bird catches the worm, bro."

"Yeah, well . . . I did promise her a slow dance."

"You promised her?"

"Yeah."

"She asked you?"

I nodded. "That's okay with you, right?"

"Sure. Long as I can dance with your date when you're dancing with mine."

"Long as she lets you."

He spread out his arms. "Come onnnn!"

"May I have your attention please?" Al Rose said.

On the platform to Al's right, sat Brubaker and Horrible. When the room quieted, Al said, "We might as well start the meeting with the hair proposal. It's been rejected. Basically, they said the same thing as last time, adding that if the new square back for seniors works out, then sometime in the future, they might consider making additional changes for the rest of the student body."

"What's 'sometime in the future' mean?" Bill Hoffa said. "Two months? Two years? Two centuries?"

"Any of those will do," Horrible said.

"It doesn't say how long we'd have to wait," Al said.

Brubaker said, "Perhaps this fall you can resubmit the proposal. After demonstrating the new hair style hasn't changed the behavior of two senior classes, the Board might look more favorably upon reviewing the standards for the entire student body."

"What if they say no again?" one of the juniors present said.

"Then nothing changes," Horrible said.

Bill Hoffa raised his hand; Al acknowledged him. "I'd like to continue this meeting without the officials present."

"Why?" Horrible said.

"Because we'd like to discuss something without officials being here."

"Why?"

"Because we would."

"We did last time," I said.

"That was last time," Horrible said. "This is this time. My job is to monitor this meeting, and that's what I'm going to do." He flicked his hand. "Next item."

"He knows," Rich said. "They all must."

"Probably," I said. "All the intermediate guys know. Now what?"

"I say we still have it," Huey said. "Tell everyone this Thursday night just like we planned, and tomorrow make sure the other presidents are doing the same thing."

From the front of the wagon, Suds said, "What are you guys whispering about? Something top secret?"

It had been Suds' turn to pick up the presidents of each unit in our cluster. Instead of spreading out into all the wagon seats like we had going to the meeting, the eight of us occupied the last three seats, leaving the front two empty because we wanted to discuss our strategy—something Horrible had prevented us from doing by walking among us as we returned to the wagons after the meeting.

"A little top secret, Mr. Sawyer," I said.

"You mean secret like your sit-in this Friday?"

"Jeez, does everybody know?" Rich said.

"All the houseparents do. Nothing like broadcasting your moves ahead of time."

"They didn't pass our proposal for longer hair," I said.

"One inch, is all we asked for," Rich said.

"So now you're going to have this sit-in?"

"Yep," said Huey. "Friday as planned."

Suds shook his head. "Good luck."

"You don't think it'll happen?" I asked.

"Nope. Surprise attacks only work when they're a surprise. This isn't."

12

Friday, shortly after homeroom began, the loudspeaker clicked on. "May I have your attention, please," Brubaker said. "There will be a meeting of the senior senate in the music room at the start of first period. That is all."

Brubaker and both Hatches sat up front. When the bell rang, Brubaker stood. "We've called this meeting because of the illegal demonstration you have planned for after lunch. We expect it not to happen. If there are any disturbances, the senior senate members will be held responsible and the consequences will be severe. Those of you who are juniors, will be placed on detentions for six months, you will receive one hundred hours to work off, and you will not be allowed to take your summer vacations. The seniors will be expelled immediately. You will not receive your diplomas, and those of you who planned on continuing your education will do so without three quarters being paid by this institution, and only after you've earned your general equivalency degree or completed another year of schooling. Those are our terms and there will be no exceptions."

He sat down and Old Man Hatch stood. "I'm really disappointed with you fellas. Mr. Brubaker and I left this room in good faith, believing you would come up with a genuine proposal, and instead, you stab us in the back with this underhanded scheme. We thought–"

"The proposal was for real," Bill Hoffa said. "Only if–"

"You want to talk," Horrible said, "you raise your hand. And don't anyone else interrupt."

"It may have been real," Old Man Hatch said, "but this sit-in was planned right from the start."

Hoffa raised his hand. "That was just in case they didn't pass it. Had it past, we wouldn't have done it."

"What did you expect?" Old Man Hatch said. "The Board doesn't change the rules just because you guys want them changed. You don't run the school. You should be thankful to be in it and for everything you're given. Now it looks as though they were right in waiting; you can't handle the responsibility. They let you have longer hair and look what happens—you demand more. The guys left behind, the guys you're supposed to be representing, will have to wait longer now."

A junior raised his hand. "We had an indefinite wait anyway," he said.

"And now it'll be even longer," Horrible said.

Al raised his hand. "What if we try and can't stop this from happening? Most of us are seniors; the guys in our units are all over the place."

"Everyone's aware of this meeting and its purpose," Brubaker said. "They'll be anxious to discover the outcome. Three hours will be more than adequate to inform them."

"Any more questions?" Old Man Hatch said. No one answered. "Get back to class, then. And for your sakes, nothing better happen."

. . . You should have seen Bigmouth, Teach. He was just as loud at the student assembly as he was in class, yelling revolt and not shutting up when asked to. And when Al told us that the school vowed to extend the same punishments to anyone sitting-in, Brownie yelled, "Bullshit! They won't do it to all of us."

Al tried reasoning with them, but the Bigmouths kept up the, "We don't care, let's do it," attitude and kept chanting "sit-in, sit-in." So Al asked all those willing to lead the sit-in to stand. About thirty guys jumped up, including "I've got balls" Brownie. "Okay, see all these guys?" Al said. "They're your new leaders. Remember their names for when Homelife asks. These guys are willing to get kicked out, lose their diplomas and tuition, and spend the next six months working off hours and on detentions with no vacation just so you can have longer hair. Ain't that great?"

Everybody clapped and cheered. Most of the Bigmouths sat down and chicken squawks filled the room. "No one has to lead," Brownie said. "We'll do it together. They won't kick us all out and put us all on detentions. Come on!"

No one said anything.

"I advise everyone not to do it," Al said. "Meeting adjourned. And Brownie? Nice knowing you."

Like I predicted, Brownie was the biggest moaner of all. And pretty fast to haul his big balls out of harm's way as soon as Horrible showed up outside the science wing with five minutes left to go in lunch period. Of course, the rest of us weren't exactly languishing behind. At the bell, it almost turned into a stampede.

Too bad, too, cause it could have worked had it been kept a secret.

And now for a real dilemma. Huey talked to Lisa last night, found out she did ask me to dance a dance at the prom, talked to her about the other times her and I met, and today told me I could take her to the prom if I wanted. He says he likes her but not like I already like her and how he thinks she likes me. So he'll say some girl he already asked who couldn't go, can, and then I can ask her.

Which would be great except for one thing–Mary Jo and her cousin, and Blabbermouth.

Now what?

And finally, seventeen days from this very moment, I'll be on stage with maybe half an hour left in the Home. You'll have a tear in your eye and I'll be smiling from here to Kingdom Come.

Amazing, ain't it, Teach?

13

I stood near the bus door, watching a pretty girl walk with her brother toward the parking lot and thinking of Lisa. And Mary Jo. Lisa was my dream girl, my dream date. How could I not take her to the prom given this chance and after all the chances I missed?

But how could I not take Mary Jo? She was fun, had accepted when I needed a date, and was getting Brownie a date. It wasn't fair to dump her just because Lisa was prettier. That was like girls not talking to us because we were in Milton Hershey; it wasn't our fault, and it wasn't Mary Jo's.

But it was more than Lisa being prettier. From the first time I saw her smile, I was in love. This was heads over heels stuff–infatuation bolstered by acquaintance, rocketed by friendship. How could I not take her?

But how could I not take Mary Jo? She accepted first.

Maybe I could tell her about Lisa and then ask her not to go? She might understand. But could I make such a call, and was it right? And what about Brownie and his date?

"Crazy, quick, get on the bus," Bobby said, and tugged on my suit coat. "Hurry." He glanced over his shoulder and dashed up the steps.

We hadn't seen each other before church service because my unit had been late. I looked for Druggins or someone else coming through the crowd after him.

"What's the matter?" I said, when I reached the top step.

He looked through the windows, then stuck his face inches from mine. "I got it!" he whispered. "I got it! I'm getting transferred!"

"All right, Bobby. Congratulations."

He spun around, grabbed the seat backs on both sides of the aisle and kicked his feet into the air, expelling a quiet, exuberant yelp. Three times he did it, then swung into two empty seats. "And you know what else?" he said.

I sat down. "What?"

"I'm going to Melvin's unit!" He grasped the seat in front of us and bounced up and down. "It worked. It worked. It worked."

"Cheer up, will 'ya?" I said. He laughed. "When do you go?"

"The day after the eighth graders move out."

I elbowed him. "Less than three weeks, buddy, and you'll be away from Dipshit Druggins. Forever."

He pushed back into his seat. "I know; I can't wait. I can't believe it." An enormous grin captured his face—Mike's kind of grin.

"When did you find out?"

"My mom called me Wednesday. She said I was getting transferred but not to say anything until Druggins told me about it."

"Lucky thing he wasn't listening," I said.

"I know. My Mom didn't know when I'd go, so I was kind of nervous. But then Druggins told me and—"

"When? Where were you? What'd he say?"

"Friday morning. I was cleaning the basement with Neil. We were in the bathroom. I thought we did something wrong. But then he said, 'I suppose you know you're getting transferred.' I played stupid; I said—"

"That wasn't hard for you."

He smiled. "I said, 'I am?' He said, 'Yeah, your Mom says you're not happy here so they're transferring you.' Then he said, 'A little momma's boy.' Just like that."

"Screw him. Who cares what he says. At least you're out of there."

"I know. So then I asked him where I was going and he said Liberty. He told me when I would be leaving, then left. Boy, I was jumping up and down and running back and forth. Man, I can't believe it. I'm getting out of there!"

"Congratulations, pal," I said, and wrapped an arm around his neck.

"Thanks. And thanks for talking to my Mom and writing my brother."

"No problem, buddy." I pulled his head down and gave him a head burn with my knuckles. "This is all I want."

I let him go and for the first time noticed his hair as he combed it back in place. "Nice haircut," I said. "That's almost as bad as mine was."

"I know."

"Yeah?!" I grabbed him and ruffled his hair again.

"I don't care," he said, "mess it all up. I'm getting transferred!"

. . . Besides that good news, I tried what the guy who gave the sermon dared us to do today. To make a long story short, a guy saved his life in Korea, then died before he could thank him. It bugged him, he went and saw a psychologist, and the psychologist suggested he do a favor for someone, even a stranger, and not tell them and dedicate it to his friend. So he did, liked it, and still does it. He calls them "Frannie's" for the guy that saved his life. Shovels out people's cars, rakes their leaves, cleans their desks at work. He never tells them, figuring not knowing might cause them to do a favor for someone else, and you could get a domino effect going.

I don't tell for the laughs. Tonight I milked Gary's cow when he was on the other side of the barn milking. When he got to her, he must have checked her tag number and utter three or four times. Sherlock did the same thing when Gary told him about it. Confused them to death. When I was late getting done, Sherlock asked if maybe I milked the wrong cow. I told him, but not NoChest.

And when the silage guy dropped off his first load of hay in the center aisle, me and Jonathan ran around and distributed them before he got back with the next load.

I like doing these "Frannie" things. I'm going to be doing more, so watch out.

And, finally, I decided not to take Huey up on his offer. When I called Mary Jo, she was so psyched about going–was never here and always wanted to check it out, said she and her cousin had a surprise for us–that I couldn't ask her not to go.

Even if I did take Lisa, what would be my chances of something happening in the long run? She'll be here all summer, I'll be two hundred miles away in Elmira, then I'll be at Shippensburg this fall and she'll be who knows where, probably at some rich school with rich guys hanging all over her. So what are the chances? It'd been nice to have her as my date, but having just a taste of honey might be worse than having none at all.

I'm just going to use this as my incentive to never, ever not try something I think of that's a good idea.

Hopefully, anyway.

No, I will. I will. I swear.

14

Tuesday, May 25, 1971

Thirteen days till liberation. Can hardly stand it.

How many "Frannies" you do or have done today, Teach? It wasn't me who washed your blackboards. And it wasn't, "I've done them all" Brownie, either. Today I did one and had two done to me. Everybody's doing them. It's like an epidemic. Starting to turn into practical jokes, too, but that's okay.

I've been trying to think of one grand slam, end-all, beat-all one to top everybody, but I can't. Know any?

Fifteen minutes less time left here than when I started. Yaba-daba-doo!

"What do you say?" the barber said.

I looked at my hair in the mirror. Not as hacked as last time, but still much too short. "This is the last lousy haircut I'll ever get from you. I'm thankful for that."

"And I'm thankful I don't have to cut it no more."

"Maybe someday you'll learn how to cut normal haircuts."

"Only if they make me. Next."

Outside the door, the ultimate Frannie popped into my head with such clarity and unquestionable appeal, it felt like divine intervention had provided it. And if I kept it to myself, no one would know.

I hurried to class and as soon as it ended I asked Mr. Hart if he would be staying late. He had finished with school publications for the year, but he could have other reasons to stay.

"I might," he said. "I've got some papers to grade."

"Can I stay, then leave when you do? Please? I don't want to go to track practice. This is the last really hard one we'll have before states this weekend, and I'm sick of them."

"Mr. Stevens still making you work hard for team spirit and all that?"

"Yeah. And I've done it enough. None of my times have improved since I got hurt. The team won't miss me this one last time."

"All right. But I'm not staying past five thirty."

Getting Mr. Stevens to let me skip practice under the pretense of helping Mr. Hart proved just as easy, and I spent my remaining free time working on the wording of my Frannie. By last class, I had it the way I wanted, and printed it on tablet paper in a broad, circular style much different than my own. Across the top I wrote TOP SECRET, then evenly spaced the following four lines:

Haircut sit-in, Friday, May 27
From 1 to 1:20, Science wing soccer field
Everyone sit, shut-up, and don't move
At 1:20, go to assembly. . . . Thanks, Frannie

I could make and fold the copies in the printing shop, hide them in my locker, hook out Thursday night, run the two miles to the high school, sneak in a homeroom window I'd leave unlocked, slip the papers through the air slates in every locker, then run back. A lot of work, but I could do it. And why not? It could make up for all the things I chickened out on through the years. And if I never told anyone, I'd never get caught.

Using the excuse to stay in shape, and with the folded message between my sock and shoe, I jogged for thirty minutes then climbed the hill to the high school. I swung my arms as though warming down and watched the windows as I walked past the English wing. I continued down the road and drifted back into the printing shop area. The corridor door was open. I stepped inside and moved to the printing shop. Lights out and locked.

Back outside, I pushed through the bushes beneath the lowest window, leapt up, grabbed the windowsill, muscled my forearms onto it, then pushed on the window. It wouldn't open. The next window was a bit higher and also unopenable. The remaining three were unreachable.

In the shower, I considered my options. Without the help of a printing shop guy, which was out of the question because Homelife would interrogate them first and somehow, someway trick them into talking, my next best option was to hook out Wednesday night to make the papers and Thursday to distribute them. But what about the window? I'd have to break it if it wasn't open, or crack it open myself at lunch time and hope nobody connected my presence there with the sit-in on Friday.

Other considerations arose as I returned to homeroom, pretended to study, then rode with Mr. Hart back to my unit. Was there a master power switch to all the machines that were turned off at night? Was there any prepping involved with the machines I would use? Hooking out two nights in a row was doubling the chances of getting caught. Should I risk it?

When Mr. Hart turned left off the highway, I noticed the field. Newly planted? Would it be faster to cut across it or follow the highway? Would the nearly full moon be blocked by clouds, or shining brightly?

After I said goodbye, I subtracted the mileage I'd read off Mr. Hart's odometer. Two point three miles—a little longer than I thought, with the last mile up a steep hill. Thirty minutes maybe? Coming back would be faster. So an hour for the trip and—

A horn blared. Mr. Hart slammed on his brakes, and a van sped by in front of him. He shook his head, waved to me, then drove off.

I waved back, my mind still on the speeding van and the wondrous idea it had given me: Carl could make the papers for me.

"Eddie?" I whispered. "You awake?" He didn't respond, and I slipped out of bed.

It was midnight, Thursday. I was to meet Carl at the golf course service road at twelve thirty. He had liked my idea so much he offered to drive me to and from the unit and help distribute the papers. Wednesday night he called to verify our rendezvous time. "You ought to see the papers, Crazy. They're great. You'll love 'em."

"Nobody saw you, right?"

"No. Don't worry about it; I told you I'd keep it secret."

"I know. It's just . . . I am worried about it. I want to go to college, and I won't if they find out."

I tiptoed down the front steps and stopped in the dining room doorway. The kitchen light was on. I waited for more than a minute, didn't hear anything, then retraced my steps and continued past my bedroom and down the back stairs to the basement.

I put on my barn clothes, grabbed my duffel bag with my track road-shoes inside and headed for the door. The kitchen light was out. I listened briefly, then continued on through. It had probably been Big M getting a late night snack.

Outside, I sat on the bottom stairwell step to put on my track shoes. Leaves swirled around my feet, tossed by the wind and illuminated by bright moonlight. I'd have to hug the edges of the unit and barn, and Carl and I would have to be extra careful not to be seen approaching, crawling in and out the windows, or leaving.

I placed the folded duffel bag in the corner, covered it with leaves, turned, took the first step and gasped—someone stood atop the steps.

A flashlight flicked on, blinding me. "Where do you think you're going?" Sherlock said.

Damn. Damn, damn, damn.

"Huh?" Sherlock said.

"Well . . . I thought I was going to hook out."

"Where?"

"In town."

"Why?"

"No reason."

"You better have a reason, or you'll be in Homelife tomorrow."

Damn.

"You going to meet some buddies?" Sherlock said. "Have a little fun before you graduate?"

"No. I was going to meet a girl."

"The one you asked to the prom?"

"I was hoping to."

"Doesn't she have school, parents to watch her?"

"They're into finals; she doesn't have to be in till after lunch. And it's easy for her to sneak out."

"Not like here."

I nodded. "Right."

Sherlock shut off the light. "Get back inside. I'll have extra work for you after supper starting tomorrow."

"Can I start this weekend and do extra then? I got track practice tomorrow. Our last one."

"All right. But don't try getting back outside tonight. I'll catch you and then I will report you to Homelife."

At ten of one, I got up from my desk overlooking the basketball court and got into bed. Only one car, with three people inside, had past down our road.

15

"Hi, Fathead," I said.

Jim stood at his locker, studying papers. He grunted.

I opened my locker and saw the same color green sheet of paper in Jim's hand sitting atop my books, folded in half. I opened it. "SSSHHHHH!!!" was printed across the top, between profiles of two guys facing each other with forefingers to their lips. The next line read: "Haircut sit-in, Friday, May 27th."

Carl had done it! He'd put them out himself. I scanned the rest of the paper—saw two guys shushing each other at the bottom—and looked at Jim. "Ehn! Huh, Jim?"

"Ehn." He pinched me. I pinched him. We shoved each other.

"What's this?" Brownie said.

"Keep it to yourself, bigmouth," I said.

Brownie read the paper, looked around, and whispered, "Who did this?"

"How should we know?" I said.

"You doing it?" he asked.

"Maybe. Why not? Are you?"

"You kidding me? Yeah! Jim?"

"I don't know."

Brownie stepped closer. "Come on. They can't get you for this. The senior senate didn't start it."

I said, "Just show up and see what happens, Jim."

"I probably will," he said, tearing the paper in half, then again and again. Brownie and I did likewise.

All morning, smiles lit everyone's faces as we walked the halls and attended class. In lowered voices guys asked each other about going. Affirmations or "why not?" responses fueled the possibilities. The soup, tuna fish, macaroni salad, and Jell-O couldn't pass fast enough. The first guys leaving seemed to leave earlier than usual. I left at twenty-five after, and two-thirds of the guys had already gone.

"Hey, Crazy," Joe said, catching me on top of the stairs. "You doing it?"

"Why not?"

"This is neat."

"The rest of your homeroom doing it?" I said.

"Yep. And nobody's talking."

"Good. Don't go too early. We don't want them catching on."

Jim and I were the only ones in homeroom at five of when we left for the science wing. Guys were everywhere–playing half court games of basketball on the four backboards along the left, far side of the parking lot; playing softball on the near side of it; playing touch football in the soccer/softball field beyond; but mostly watching, a continuous mass of bodies along the perimeters of all these games, watching and waiting. Above and beyond the basketball games, on the long, gentle, tree-covered hill that served as a natural border for right and center fields for softball, more guys watched and waited.

Several younger teachers stood near third base, scouting the softball game in preparation for the upcoming, last day of school, students versus teachers softball game. When the bell sounded, they started inside. Several guys past them going the other way. One teacher stopped and turned, then said something to the others.

"Hey, Josh, what's going on?" one of them asked a kid walking toward the softball field.

Josh shrugged and continued by. The teachers smiled at each other and went inside.

"Let's go up on the hill so we can watch," I said to Jim.

By the time we reached our spot, the guys who had been watching along the perimeters and those involved in the various games, had moved back to the soccer/softball field to join those already there. Commands and whispers of "Sit down," spread through the crowd, and once done, our stance was impressive. Forty to fifty yards across, seventy yards deep, and the hill, covered with guys, sitting, waiting, and watching.

One minute past in silence. Then another. The buzzer sounded the start of assembly. When it finished ringing, a murmur rippled through the crowd, bodies shifted, heads turned. Another minute past. Guys started to laugh and joke. Suddenly the science wing door swung open, and everyone quieted.

Brubaker stepped out followed by the vice-principal, holding one of the papers. They gazed across the large, empty parking lot for several seconds. Brubaker said something and the vice principal left and returned fifteen seconds later as Brubaker's secretary announced over the intercom: "Al Rose, report to Mr. Brubaker immediately. Al Rose, report to Mr. Brubaker immediately."

When Al failed to stand, heads turned, looking for him. Ten seconds past. Twenty. The vice-principal stepped back inside.

"Al Rose . . . report immediately to Mr. Brubaker. Al Rose . . . report imme–" Seconds past, then: "He'll be right there, Mr. Brubaker. He's coming from the office."

"The chicken-shit didn't show," someone said. An underclassman, four yards away.

I said, "I wouldn't have either, if I was him, jerk. He's the first one they'd blame."

"Yeah, asshole," somebody else said.

"Dirt!" someone said, and tossed a stone at him. Others followed, and the kid covered up. "Okay, okay, I'm sorry." The pelting stopped.

Al came out the door. Brubaker said something as the vice-principal waved the paper in front of him. Al shrugged. Brubaker and Al spoke briefly, then Al headed toward us.

The only sound was that of a car swishing along the nearby road as Al crossed the vacant lot. He stopped at the front and began talking. I strained to hear but couldn't. He spoke for twenty seconds. Guys looked at each other. Al's hands rose pleadingly. One guy stood. When no one else followed, the kid sat back down.

Al threaded his way through the crowd. As he spotted guys he knew, he spoke to them. Nobody moved. Al stopped, looked around, then walked to within ten yards of the center and bottom of the hill, where a fifth of the guys sat before and above him. "Listen," he said, raising his voice, "they said if everybody goes in right now, nobody will get in trouble. But we got to do it now."

"What if we don't?" somebody asked.

"I don't know. But we've already proved our point. They know we don't like the haircuts, so why not go in? Nobody gets in trouble."

"What are they going to do? Punish us all? Kick all the seniors out?"

Al shrugged. "All I know is–"

"Oh, shit," somebody said, "here comes Horrible."

Face jutting forward, arms stiff, Horrible steamed across the parking lot.

"Man, I'm glad I'm not down there," someone said.

Horrible pounced into the front lines and grabbed two guys unable to avoid him, lifted them to their feet and shoved them toward the school. He grabbed two more scrambling to escape, lifted and shoved. Around his entry point, guys stood and began backing away.

"Look over there," Jim said.

A car had stopped near the backstop, and a thin guy in bell bottoms with long, brown hair beneath a baseball cap worn backward was moving forward taking pictures. Other guys noticed and started shouting. "Take pictures of that! Get him beating us!"

The uproar reached Horrible, ten yards deep into a semicircle of removed bodies. He turned, saw the photographer, and froze. The camera clicked.

"That's it, get him beating us!" somebody yelled. Someone raised their clenched fist, others followed, and immediately all hands rose in a sea of defiance.

Click. Click. Click.

Horrible started for the photographer. "Down in front!" somebody yelled. Those scattered by Horrible's presence sat and raised their fists. More pictures.

The photographer backed up, adjusting his camera as he went and taking photos, oblivious to Horrible's approach.

"He's going to kill him," somebody said.

"Run!" someone shouted.

The photographer took another picture, glanced at Horrible thirty feet away, said something, then returned to his viewfinder.

"Run!!" several guys shouted.

. . . Obviously he thought he was dealing with a rational, democracy loving, live free or die, human being. Then he saw Horrible's face and the wisdom of retreat surfaced, accelerating his backward walk into a trot, then a sprint for his life as Horrible turned into a cheetah going for the kill. "Get this guy away from me!" he yelled, running behind the backstop.

Horrible could use the corner posts to whip himself forward but the photographer couldn't because he had the camera in his inside hand. Which meant DEATH AND DESTRUCTION closed in on him with nightmarish speed.

"This is my job!" he yelled, and dashed for his car after only one time around. He didn't make it. Horrible trapped him against the door, ripped the camera from his hand, yanked out the film, lifted it high in the air, then stomped all over it.

By this time Brubaker had gotten to them. The guy was pissed, but couldn't do much. Brubaker talked to him, probably telling him he was trespassing or something. Then the guy got in his car, slammed the door, drove around the backstop, real wide, so he was away from Brubaker and Horrible and kind of close to us, stopped, raised a camera from the seat, we raised our fists, he took a picture, and another, then took off before Horrible could get to him. He beeped his horn and gave the finger as he drove onto the main road.

We cheered for a couple of seconds, then got quiet. It was kind of a neat silence, Teach. There we sat, all smiles, relishing our unity and what had just happened. And there they stood, staring back, not as happy.

Then Horrible started forward and the pleasant, fulfilled feelings we had vanished. The guys in front got up out of the way. Those behind, now enjoying an unhindered view of Godzilla's advance, did the same. It was like a giant game of tag and Horrible was "it," splitting our ranks like Moses at the Red Sea. He couldn't get near enough to grab anyone, guys were running so fast. From atop the hill, it was kind of funny—until he made a dash toward where all the laughter was coming from.

Then I ran like the dog I am. We all did.

Brubaker walked on stage from behind the curtain and stood at the podium. Before complete silence occurred, he said, "That's okay, I can wait."

The room erupted in chatter.

"Silence!" The microphone wrenched with backfeed. "Immediately!"

We quieted, grins everywhere.

"This is not a laughing matter," Brubaker said. "What you boys did out there was irresponsible, against the rules, and childish. It accomplished nothing. In fact, it will work to your detriment. This institution is governed not by you, but adults. Adults willing to listen to reason, not intimidation. Adults willing to work in a spirit of cooperation and understanding with young men capable of cooperation and understanding. You demonstrated today your inability to do that. Now you will suffer the consequences. Especially those not graduating. You will have to go a long way in proving you're not the immature, irresponsible, witless children you acted like today."

He paused and gazed about the auditorium. "And those responsible for today's outrage? . . . I assure you, you will be caught, and you will suffer the consequences. You have made a terrible mistake."

16

I'd finally done it. I thought of something I should do, was scared to do, but did it anyway. Granted, Carl was involved and did more than planned, but it was my idea. If I could have I would have done more, and to me that was the same as doing it. It gave me a feeling of confidence, hope, enthusiasm. Not just for the moment, but for the future. The next hurdle wouldn't be as high nor as hard, and I had this experience to remind me of what taking a swing could feel like and accomplish.

All afternoon I smiled at the commotion and excitement around me. Between classes, rumors as to who was responsible raced through the hallways. The printing shop guys tallied the most suspicions, followed by those in plumbing and carpentry–the shops closest to printing. Homelife seemed to confirm these suspicions when they began grilling printing shop guys first period after assembly.

During last class–English–someone theorized that maybe a guy working on the yearbook or *The Spartan* might have done it. Brownie immediately plopped his hands on the desk, stood up, and turned his widened eyes and raised eyebrows toward me. "Well, well, well. . . . ?" he said.

"Yeah, right," I said. "I wish."

The suspicion past quickly, but not my worries. If the finger could be pointed my way within two hours by guys simply guessing, what could Homelife do with relentless investigation?

I vowed not to tell anyone, anything, and hoped Carl would be as secretive. Saturday afternoon he called. "So how'd it go, Crazy?"

"It went great, Carl. You haven't told anyone, have you?"

"I said I wouldn't, didn't I?"

"Yeah, it's just . . . They're really looking for the guys–they already talked to all the printing shop guys. They're talking about sending whoever did it to jail for trespassing, stealing, stuff like that."

"Crazy, how are they going to catch us? You tell anyone you did it?"

"No. And I'm not going to."

"Neither am I. It's bullshit. They're fishing."

"I hope so. They told one of the printing guys they're checking all the printing shops and newspapers and businesses like that."

"So?"

"So I just thought maybe it'd help to know if they came around."

"It will. I'll say 'Hi, dickheads,' and go on my way. They can't prove nothing. I got the original at home for a souvenir, and the paper I used is paper every shop carries for Saint Patrick's Day. The Home even has it. They're not going to catch us. Jesus Christ, who do you think they got looking into it, Sherlock Holmes?"

"I guess not."

"You're talking about a stupid little sit-in at a stupid little school. Just deny everything, if they ask. Don't be going belly up on me; they can send me to jail, I'm nineteen."

"Me, too, I'm eighteen. I ain't saying nothing."

"Good. Now what happened? Did anyone from the paper show up? I gave them a call Friday morning, but I haven't seen anything yet. And why didn't you show? It took me two hours to . . . "

. . . *It's all anyone was talking about at church today. Homelife's been out to some units, questioning guys. The guys in the printing shop are really getting grilled, several times, like it's a conspiracy or something.*

Isn't it great? I told you it could work if the guy or guys just kept their mouths shut.

Want to know how he did it? Whoops! Or they did it? Well, they . . . Ahh, I can't tell you. That'll be like going against what I claimed would get the guy caught, you know? Who knows who you would tell.

What's that? You won't tell? Promise? Okay, I'll tell you. It's not that hard to figure out anyway. We've discussed it and the biggest vote getter is this: the guy made the copies ahead of time, hid them at the high school, hooked out Thursday night, distributed them, and ever since has kept his mouth shut. Until now. He-he-hee.

Only kidding, Teach. I don't know who did it, but that's how I would have done it, and I'll bet that's how they did it. How else could they have done it?

Anyway, as long as they don't talk, how will they ever catch them? It's not like they got Sherlock Holmes on the job. It's more like the Three Stooges. But it's fun to watch, isn't it?

Monday morning, Mr. Hart called me to his desk during homeroom and handed me a piece of paper. "I want you to see this, Dave. I'll have to put your name on it."

It was a memo from Homelife addressed to all faculty and staff. "Please list below those students, who for whatever reasons, were absent from class or the unit this past week while the other students were in attendance. This includes, but is not limited to, those going to class early, staying after school, or attending practice for a sport or activity. It also includes doctor, dental, and eye visits, clothing fitting, and any time a student was by himself and unsupervised. When in doubt, include the student's name and the reason for his absence."

When I finished reading, Mr. Hart said, "I'll tell them you were with me most of the time and I gave you a ride home, but I still have to tell them."

"Okay."

"I'll also have to tell them you went running."

"That's all right, Mr. Hart. That's what I did. They can't kill me for that."

17

Tuesday afternoon, first period after lunch, they called me in. Horrible sat hunched over his desk. Behind him, Old Man Hatch stood near the window. "Sit down, Dave," Old Man Hatch said.

Horrible reached over and started a tape recorder sitting on my side of his desk. He leaned back and crossed his arms. I looked at him, then at Old Man Hatch. "We're waiting," Horrible said.

"For what?"

"Don't give us that. You know why you're here, and we know you were involved. Just tell us why."

"I'm here because of the sit-in thing, probably, because Mr. Hart put my name down. But I didn't do it."

"Dave," Old Man Hatch said, "you tell us now, that you did it, and we'll let you graduate. If not, if you make us prove it, your father will be down here tomorrow to pick you up–without your diploma."

They were bluffing. They used the same tactic with some of the printing shop guys. "I'm not going to confess to something I didn't do. Why should I?"

"You're going to sit there and tell us you're not responsible for what happened?" Horrible said.

"That's right."

"And you had nothing to do with it? Nothing at all?"

"Tell us now, Dave," Old Man Hatch said. "It's your last chance."

Even if they let me graduate, they wouldn't give me the scholarship, and that's what mattered. Carl said he wouldn't talk, neither would I. "I had nothing to do with it," I said.

Horrible said, "Where were you last Tuesday night?"

"When?"

He slammed his palm into the desk and sprang up. "Don't give me that. You need me to come round there and jog your memory?"

"No. I don't know what you mean. When Tuesday night? After school, after supper, after bed? I don't know what you mean."

"Jerry, sit down," Old Man Hatch said.

Horrible hesitated, then sat. "These damn kids think they're so smart. Every one of them, 'What do you mean? When?' I'd like to give them smart."

Old Man Hatch said, "After school, Dave, what did you do?"

"I stayed late with Mr. Hart. I jogged for about fifty minutes, then studied until Mr. Hart left. He drove me back."

"Why didn't you go to track practice?"

"Because it was going to be hard, and I didn't want to do it."

"That's what you told Mr. Hart," Horrible said. "What did you tell Mr. Stevens about not going?"

"I said I was going to help Mr. Hart with some *Acropolis* stuff."

"But you didn't, did you?"

"No."

"So you lied to him. That's one." He marked a paper on his desk. "And didn't you tell Mr. Stevens that Mr. Hart *asked* you to stay and help?"

"I might of said it that way."

"But he didn't ask you, did he?"

"No."

"That's two." Another mark. "Why did you lie to him?"

"Because I didn't want to go to practice."

"Wasn't it because you wanted to be up here alone when you thought nobody else would be around?"

"No."

"You sure?"

"Yes."

"Is that a lie?" Horrible said. "Number three? Number four? How do we know when you're telling the truth?" He turned his palms upward, not expecting an answer, and I dropped my gaze to the tape recorder. Jerk.

Old Man Hatch moved to the seat on my left. "So what did you do after school ended, Dave?"

"I went for a run. I—"

"Funny thing for someone to do who didn't want to go to track practice," Horrible said. "Isn't it?"

"I didn't want to go because we were doing suicides. I don't mind jogging."

"Ahhhh," he said, and nodded.

"Where did you go for your jog?" Old Man Hatch said.

"Down on the track."

"Anyone see you?"

"I don't know. I didn't see anyone."

"For how long?"

"About fifty minutes."

"Then what?"

"Then I showered, went to–"

"You went straight from the track to the locker room?" Horrible asked.

"Yeah."

"How did you go?"

After checking the printing shop windows, I'd gone back into the shop hallway to get to the locker room. Someone must have seen me walking along the road, past the English wing, because I knew no one saw me once inside the building. "I went down along the road, around the shop areas, and in near the electricity shop."

"Why did you go that way?"

"Because I was cooling down outside, and it was shorter than going back through the English wing."

Old Man Hatch said, "Dave, Mr. Tyler saw you outside the printing shop that night. He identified you this afternoon at lunch."

"Imagine that?" Horrible said.

Mr. Tyler was head of the carpentry shop, which was parallel to the printing shop. Had he been in his shop area he could easily have seen me.

"Now you want to tell us about it?" Old Man Hatch said.

I shook my head. "Okay, look, I did go that way. But it was only because it was a shortcut to the gym. It is the fastest way if that's where you happen to be."

"And you just happened to be there," Horrible said.

"Yeah. I was cooling down."

"Then why didn't you tell us you went that way, instead of waiting till we caught you in another lie?"

"Because why should I mention I went by the printing shop, when I know you're looking for that kind of stuff, and I didn't do anything? It just makes you more suspicious."

"All this lying, makes us more suspicious."

"Did you go into the printing shop, Dave?" Old Man Hatch said.

"No."

"Did you try?" Horrible said.

"I jumped up and looked in the windows, to scare guys if they were in there. But I didn't go in."

"Why did you try opening them?"

I shrugged. "Just to see if they were open."

"Why?"

"No reason."

"I think you had a very good reason," Horrible said. "You were sneaking in to make the pamphlets."

"No I wasn't."

"Let's cut the crap," Horrible said. "It wouldn't take you long to make them, because you know how—I seen you. You lied so you could stay after school when no one else would be around. You were caught trying to climb in their windows. Your unit's close by, so you could run up and back easily enough Thursday night. And you had the motive—you didn't like the last haircut the barber gave you because you cried to Mr. Kramer about it. Why don't you just admit it instead of being a coward?"

"Because I didn't do it. How could I get in if the windows and doors were locked? Were any of them broken? How could I do it if I couldn't get in?"

Horrible looked at Old Man Hatch, then at me. "How do you know they keep the doors locked?"

"Because I wiggled the knob as I went by. I wiggled all the shop door-knobs. They're all locked at night."

"So you did it in the afternoon then, during lunch period. Or Wednesday night—left a window open. Or Thursday night before you past them around."

"No, I didn't."

Old Man Hatch said, "Did you have help, Dave? A printing shop guy?"

"No."

"You did it alone, then," Horrible said.

"No."

Old Man Hatch said, "You tell us now what you know, and you'll still graduate with your three-quarters scholarship. Otherwise, you'll lose it. Then what'll you do? Think about it."

"And think about this," Horrible said. "You had the motive, the time, the know-how, you were caught trying to sneak in, and you lied to us. You're our prime suspect. Don't admit it and you're life will be crap for a long time. The police call it trespassing, breaking and entering. And we'll make it stick. You're eighteen—how do you think it's going to look on your permanent record?

Forget college. Do you think you'll get a job after you get out of jail? Doing what? Milking cows, cleaning toilets?"

"Tell us now, Dave," Old Man Hatch said. "It's your last chance."

"I didn't do it, so I'm not going to confess to it."

"Fine," Horrible said. "When no one else suspicious turns up, you'll be our man." He grinned. "See you soon, liar."

18

I pushed Brownie. "Asshole." I turned, took a step toward Dana, who tossed my diary to Jim. I put out my hand. "Come on, Fathead, give it to me."

"Ehn." Just before I reached him, he tossed it to Brownie, the person who had pulled it from beneath my arm as we left first period study class, where Mr. Hart said if others had written as diligently as I had, their grades might have been better.

"Go ahead, keep it," I said. "I don't care."

I opened my locker as Brownie started down the hall. "Let's see what Junior wrote about us this week. 'Tuesday, June first, nineteen seventy-one. It was like a scene out of a movie, Daddy. Good cop, bad cop, and I was the innocent criminal sweating his volleyballs off.'"

"Isn't that funny?" Brownie said.

He continued reading aloud while leading our section to math class. I grabbed my books and followed, gradually getting close enough to sprint and pin Brownie against the wall. He held my diary above his head. I yanked his arm down just as he flicked his wrist. Dana picked the diary off the floor a second before I got to it. We tugged on either end. Brownie wrapped his arms around me.

"Hey! Knock it off." Horrible strode through the guys nearby. "Give me that." He saw me, then looked at Brownie and Dana. "Whose is this?"

"It's mine," I said.

"What do you guys want it for?"

"Nothing," Brownie said. "We were just fooling around."

Horrible glanced at the diary—a standard issue notebook, then dangled it upside down by the binder. "There's not a stolen final in here, is there?"

"No. It's just my English notebook."

He opened it, read some, then began flipping through the pages. "This doesn't look like a notebook."

"It's a daily journal for English. It's made up." I held out my hand.

He turned to the back, read for ten seconds, then closed the diary. "I think I'll keep this awhile."

"But it's mine. It's personal."

"Your teacher's reading it, isn't he?"

"That's different. Besides, I need it for class."

"You'll get it back."

He stepped by me and headed down the hall.

"Dave, don't worry about it," Mr. Hart said. "It's a fictional account."

"But they think I did it. You haven't seen Monday's entry yet. I said, 'This is how he did it.' They'll take it as proof that I did."

"Didn't you also say, 'It's all lies?'"

"They won't care. And what about the other stuff? Guys can get in trouble. Big trouble."

We stood outside homeroom; inside a class of sophomores waited. Mr. Hart said, "You're getting worried over nothing, Dave. Just go to class. I've got this test to give. When we're done, I'll go get it from Mr. Hatch."

"It'll be too late, then. He'll already have read it."

"It doesn't matter. All you say is, 'It's fictional. I made it up—all of it.'"

"But I called him 'Horrible,' and swore, and stuff like that."

"*You* didn't—Danny Numbnuts did. It's a fictional account by a fictional character. An assignment I gave you. Believe me, you can't get in trouble for that."

"Yes, I can."

"Dave, I've got to give this test. Just go to your class, and I'll talk to you at lunch. It'll be all right." He stepped into homeroom and shut the door.

Before the period ended, Horrible strode into math class holding a stack of notebooks under his arm. He took any journal that hadn't been in our lockers.

"We're in deep ca-cas now," Brownie said, once Horrible had gone.

When class ended, besides telling section twelve-two what happened—too late because their journals had already been confiscated—every guy in my unit I saw, every friend, teammate or acquaintance I thought might be in my diary, I warned them of what could happen, to be prepared to deny accusations from as far back as June, and to spread the word. Everyone else in my section whose journal had possibly incriminated others, did likewise. Same thing following the next class. I was glad to see Jonathan stop and listen when he saw me talking to someone about it.

"They got my diary from English class, Jonathan. If Homelife calls you in, deny everything. No matter what they say, just—"

"They already talked to me," he said. "Last class."

"Already? Did you say anything? Who did you talk to?"

"Horrible. I told him some stuff—whenever he said you said I did something, and I did, then I said I did. Other stuff, when I didn't, even if I knew you did, I said I didn't know. He said it'd be better if I told him right then, than to be found out later; said the punishment would be less. I wouldn't of said nothing if you told me earlier, Crazy."

"I know, Jonathan; don't worry about it. Was anyone else in there?"

"They called in Joe just after me. I think I heard Gary in another office."

Half an hour later, two and one half hours after Horrible took my journal, Homelife called me in.

19

All three of them were there—Horrible, Kramer, and Old Man Hatch. They sat on one side of the desk, my diary, with numerous pages marked with slips of paper, lay on top of it, the tape recorder lay nearer to me.

Old Man Hatch indicated the diary. "It's all here, Dave. How you did it . . . when you did it. You might as well tell us about it."

"That's all lies," I said. "Nothing in there says I did it. How can I get in trouble for a fictitious diary?"

"Because it isn't fictitious. We talked to guys in your unit. They've admitted to doing things you wrote about. If some of it's true, we have to assume it's all true."

"But it isn't all true. Besides, I never said I did it. I just guessed at how it was done."

He put on his glasses and turned to the back of the diary. "'Want to know how he did it? . . . The guy made the copies ahead of time, hid them at the high school, hooked out Thursday night, distributed them, and ever since has kept his mouth shut. Until now. He-he-he.'"

"But you're reading around what I wrote. I wrote other stuff, like 'just kidding,' and 'I didn't do it.'"

"That's the lying parts," Old Man Hatch said. "Covering your tracks."

"No way. If I had done it, I wouldn't of put it in there."

"Why not? You wrote about last Thursday night when you hooked out to run up to the high school to distribute the papers, didn't you?"

"No I didn't. I wrote about seeing Mr. Muncie outside after lights out."

"While trying to hook out."

"Trying to. I didn't, though."

"Who's to say you didn't go later? At two in the morning, or three? Mr. Muncie was in bed then."

"Who's to say I did?"

"You are." He tapped the diary. "We have it all right here. You wrote you'd make them ahead of time–you got caught trying to sneak in the printing shop to do it. You wrote you'd hook out Thursday night–you got caught hooking out Thursday night. You had a slip of the tongue and wrote 'He's just kept it to himself. Until now. He-he-he.'" He waved his hand. "You did it, Dave."

"But none of that's actual proof. It's the way I figured whoever did it, did it. That's all. I didn't do it."

Old Man Hatch shook his head. "There's just too much evidence against you, Dave. You might as well admit it. You can still graduate if you tell us now. If not, it'll be up to Headmaster Seals to decide. To make it easier on you, all the things mentioned in the dairy won't be used against any of the other students if you confess. If not, not only will you be the one held responsible for the sit-in, everyone mentioned will be punished for anything they've done. If the seniors have to stay the summer and work off hours, so be it. It's your decision. We'll give you some time to think about it."

He stood and headed around the desk, followed by Kramer. Horrible, circling the other way, reached over and grabbed my diary. "Not bad for the Three Stooges, huh?"

How many guys would get in trouble, and for what? Would they use all the diaries or just mine?

And what about me? Was my scholarship gone? Was graduating the only option left to salvage?

I could say I did it just like I wrote about it. They wouldn't bother to verify it. They only wanted someone to hang.

But why blame myself? I didn't do it.

I thought of it, though.

"Well?" Old Man Hatch said, after fifteen minutes of leaving me alone. "What's it going to be?"

I decided to do what I would want any of my friends to do in the same situation. I said, "All I know is . . . I didn't do it, and I don't know who did."

He wagged his head. "That's a shame, Dave. Go ahead, Jerry."

Horrible snapped on the tape recorder and lifted a pad of paper to read from. "Did you hook out last Thursday night?"

"I tried to, but I got caught."

"Ten hours for hooking out." Kramer marked something on a sheet of paper. "Why were you hooking out?" Horrible said.

"I was going to see a girl I know."

"What's her name?"

"She didn't know I was coming. I was going to surprise her."

"What's her name?"

"She can't help you; I never hooked out. If you called her parents, she could get yelled at for something she knew nothing about, so I'm not going to say her name."

Horrible glared for several seconds. "That's real noble of you," he said, "while you're stabbing your friends in the back. Ten more."

Kramer marked it down.

"Did you work the thirty hours you were supposed to work for calling Mr. Druggins names?"

If I said no, Suds could get in trouble for not making me do the work. If I said yes, and Suds did the same, nothing would happen.

"Yes."

"I called your housefather. You didn't. You get ten hours for lying to me, the original thirty added back, and ten more for not doing them. How many's that so far, Mr. Kramer?"

" . . . Seventy."

"Did you trespass into the gravel company's storage shed to play football?"

"No."

"Others say you did. Ten for lying, ten more for trespassing. Did you skip second church with Bobby Spangler last month?"

Damn.

"That was my fault. I told Bobby we'd take a walk, then I—"

"Ten more. Did you and your friends corner his roommate at Sunday service and threaten him?"

"Yeah—we told him to quit making Bobby talk after lights out, and being a jerk and getting Bobby in trouble, and to speak up if he's the one responsible for something and not letting Bobby take the blame."

Horrible scoffed. "You should talk. Ten more. Did you . . . "

On and on he went, backtracking through the year. Every possible infraction received five hours, confirmed violations ten or more, cuss words or name-calling five more. Whenever I said I didn't and one of the guys said I did, ten more were added.

He asked about things I'd forgotten about, things I joked about, things I didn't think I mentioned. Who stole ice cream from the cafeteria, who scratched Brubaker's car, who dropped the eggs on Kramer, did I walk back from the unit after swim practice, did I stop in the drugstore, was I involved in the fight in the parking lot after the Cumberland Valley football game?

When Horrible finished, Old Man Hatch said, "If you want your diploma, you'll be working the hours no matter how long it takes. Whether you get it will be up to Headmaster Seals. Your three-quarters scholarship, you might as well forget about. The only thing that can help you now is your confession. You'll help yourself, and the others won't suffer because of something you've done. The sooner the better, though."

I stood up. "The only reason you want me to admit it is because you still don't have the proof. None of what's in my diary proves I did it, and you know it."

Old Man Hatch shook his head. "Dave, not one other student in this entire school was caught doing anything wrong, or suspicious, or telling more than a harmless lie about this. You're the only one. There's no one else with a better reason to do it, the know-how, the opportunity, and you were caught trying to sneak in, caught sneaking out, caught telling lies. It all points to you, Dave. If this was a trial by jury, we'd win our case."

The problem was–he was right. Even now, years later, I know I looked guilty and there was nothing I could do about it.

20

In the cafeteria, lunch had already started. When I reached our table, Mr. Hart stood. "I went to his office, Dave, but he refused to give me the journal. He will, though, don't worry–all of them. What happened? Did you do as I said?"

"Yeah. I ended up with four hundred and eighty hours of work to work off before I can graduate–if I graduate. Headmaster Seals will decide that. And my three-quarters scholarship is gone."

"I don't believe this. That's insane. All because of your journal?"

"That started it. They called guys in, told them I said we did whatever and they'd go easy on them if they confessed, they did, and now they say since some of it's true, it's all true. The 'this is all lies,' part was just cover up. And now they got me."

"There's no way they can do this, Dave, believe me."

"Yeah? Well look at that."

Halfway down the cafeteria, in the middle of the juniors' section, Eddie was sidestepping toward the front where Kramer waited for him. They exited away from us.

"That's Eddie, my roommate. Where do you think he's going? At least I got to him before Homelife did. The other guys I didn't. They say if I "confess," they'll not punish anyone else. If not, everyone, including seniors, gets punished and will have to work off the hours before they can graduate."

"This is just too much," Mr. Hart said. "You sit down and have lunch. Believe me, this is far from over. Those journals are class assignments, not easy pickings for the Gestapo." He strode off as I headed for my seat.

I told the guys what happened, and we spent all of lunch time and between classes, spreading the word. As news filtered back to me throughout the afternoon, my mood rose and fell depending on how much Homelife had squeezed out of someone. Once it became apparent our strategy was to deny everything and claim whoever said what was mistaken, Homelife no longer pressed for confessions. They simply distributed punishment based on "suspicion."

After school, when the last guy got in the wagon, Suds turned in his seat. "A lot happened today, huh, fellas? Looks like I got a bunch of delinquents in my unit. Everyone's on detentions with lots of hours to work off."

"We're all just criminals," Gary said. "Plain and simple."

"Don't I know it. That's why I'm putting you to work right now." He looked at his watch. "Four o'clock. By bedtime you'll all have five hours worked off."

"What are we going to do?" Jonathan said.

"You're doing it." He pulled out following the other wagons. "This is my unit. I know what's going on. I want to stop something, I will. I want to punish someone, I'll do it. I don't, I won't. Homelife doesn't run this ship. I do."

Eddie said, "All our hours going to be this hard, Mr. Sawyer?"

"That's right. So keep it to yourselves."

In the barnyard, while scrapping the lot, Suds and Sherlock approached me. "Did you tell Hatch I didn't make you work off those thirty hours?" Suds asked.

I said I didn't and told them about the diary. Sherlock said, "That's how he knew about your trying to sneak out, huh?" I nodded.

"No matter how we do it," Suds said, "those hours are going to take you a long time. You're not graduating with the others?"

"I might not even graduate. Headmaster Seals has to decide that. My homeroom teacher's meeting with him tomorrow morning to see what he can do."

"Would it help if I put in a good word for you?" Suds asked.

"Me too?" Sherlock said.

"I don't know. Can't hurt."

Next day, Mr. Stevens caught me coming out of math class after second period. "How'd Mr. Hart's meeting go with Headmaster Seals, Dave?"

"They're meeting this period."

"Right now?"

"Maybe. Some time before it ends, anyway."

"I think I'll drop by," Mr. Stevens said. "Maybe I can be a character witness."

"Really?"

"I'm your class advisor, aren't I? You're one of my charges. Besides, you busted your butt for me and the team and didn't quit when you wanted to. I can do the same for you." He smiled, smacked my shoulder, and headed down the hall.

Maybe I did have a chance of getting out of this?

At lunch, Mr. Hart told me he had brought to Headmaster Seals' office a letter signed by every member of the English department, denouncing Homelife's confiscation, reading, and exploitation of the diaries. He also brought copies of my report cards from sixth grade on. Not only had I made the honor roll or distinguished honor roll every marking period, but more importantly, I made the effort and conduct honor rolls as well—a six year record of continuous good behavior and effort verified by my teachers.

Mr. Stevens, Suds, and Sherlock gave glowing character references and sparked an idea for Mr. Hart. "I want you to make a list of all the teachers, coaches, and houseparents that you got along with. Mr. Stevens and I will call them to see if they'll put in a good word for you with Headmaster Seals."

"You're having another meeting?"

"After assembly. Headmaster Seals is reading your diary to determine just how incriminating it is, and then he, someone from Homelife, and I are going to sit down and go over each accusation, one by one."

After assembly, we had gym, then back to homeroom for English. Mr. Hart asked me to step outside and handed me my diary. "Did you actually try hooking out Thursday night?"

I nodded.

"And Mr. Tyler saw you trying to get in the printing shop windows?"

"Yep."

"Why, Dave? What were you doing?"

"Does it matter? I didn't get in."

"They say no one else looks anywhere near suspicious; only you. Did you do it?"

I raised my right hand. "I swear on the bible I didn't do it, Mr. Hart–may my whole family die. I didn't make them, I didn't distribute them."

"Do you know who did?"

"Yeah, but I'm not telling them."

"You've got to," he said. "Losing a college scholarship is more important than not being seen as a squealer. This person can't be much of a friend if he's willing to let you lose all that."

"There's more to it than that."

"No, there isn't. I'll tell them myself, if I have to."

"And then what?" I said. "They'll want to know who it is, and if I don't tell them, I'll still lose the scholarship."

"Then you'll tell them."

"No I won't."

"Why, Dave? Why?"

Mr. Hart was doing all he could to help me and deserved an explanation. It didn't matter now anyway.

"Because . . . if I do, then I'll have to tell them I was the one who thought of it. That's right. I thought of it, planned it, tried to make them–got caught and couldn't, tried to distribute them–got caught and couldn't. Someone else made them and put them out, but it won't matter. They'll still take my scholarship for what I did."

"Why did you do it, Dave?" Mr. Hart said. "You were so close to graduation."

"Because I thought it was a good idea, the ultimate Frannie. Because I was tired of being a chicken about doing stuff, thinking of something I should do, then not doing it and regretting it, like football and Lisa. Because it wouldn't hurt anyone. Because our haircuts suck and there's no reason for it. Because I got butchered. Because I didn't think I'd get caught. All kinds of reasons. Because I'm stupid."

He looked at the floor, wagged his head, then gazed up the hallway. "Did Homelife tell you what's going to happen?"

"Not yet."

"Because of all the teachers and houseparents who spoke on your behalf, and because the infractions weren't that bad, you'll only have a hundred hours to work off. You can still go to the prom and graduation, but you'll have to stay here and work those hours to get your diploma."

"What about the scholarship?"

"I'm afraid that's gone. I'm trying to get a meeting with one of the Board members I've golfed with, but I'm not optimistic."

21

That weekend I spent a lot of time thinking, about my future, about my past. Had I stayed with my innocuous, cautious habits, I would have been graduating on Monday, enjoying my first full summer of freedom in eleven years, then starting at Shippensburg State in the fall surrounded by girls, taking classes I wanted and looking forward to my future.

Instead, I'd be attending a state school in New York to save on tuition, or, more likely, joining the Navy or Air Force so my father wouldn't feel obligated to try to help out with tuition like he was doing with my sisters, already in college. It was my fault, why should it make their lives harder?

To have spent eleven years looking forward to one moment, then having that moment ruined–by myself, was hard to accept. Was this fate slugging me for being stupid? Or me simply being stupid?

What did it matter? It was over.

Would I join the Air Force or Navy? Probably the Air Force–couldn't get seasick on land. They had bases all over the world and I always wanted to travel. They also had some kind of college savings plan I could take advantage of–let them pay my three-fourths. And being in boot camp and saying yes sir and no sir to someone who didn't necessarily deserve it couldn't be worse than being in the Home.

Girls lived all over the world, too. Girls who might find short hair and uniforms attractive. In four years I would also have a better idea of a career choice. Right then I wasn't certain. I was good in math, writing, liked several subjects, but I didn't know how that translated into a life's work. Four years would give me time to grow and consider. Maybe I'd find something in the Air Force that I'd like doing when I got out? It might not be all that bad.

The prom proved more enjoyable than I thought it would. With Brownie's promise not to reveal my difficulties, and our dates determined to have a good time, we began the evening by sitting in their car in the Community Center parking lot, waiting for the buses to leave and sneaking drinks from the small bottle of champagne they'd brought along as our graduation present.

The alcohol eased the worries I'd been having over the school-wide interrogations and distribution of punishment caused by my diary. I was prepared for my fellow seniors to be cold-shouldered, even angry. None were. Years of conditioning had ingrained in all of us to confess only minor infractions, squeal on no one, plead memory loss when pressed, and deny, deny, deny. The freshmen, excusably, had revealed the most, but instinctively, like Jonathan, had withheld information whenever possible. What I feared might be weeks of extended stay and work for my classmates, had been only hours. And many of the guys, like me, had been given no chores, easy chores, or an accounting system that sometimes quadrupled the actual hours worked, by houseparents who knew we had served our time and didn't deserve this last minute aggravation.

Guys had heard about my plight, showed commiseration and concern, and some offered ideas on how to rectify things. Another sit-in on Monday, perhaps, with me alone attending assembly? Several of those who had written journals said they could point to segments that insinuated they had done it, possibly allowing me to wiggle free. "Hell," Brownie said, "I came right out and said I did it."

So their humor, goodwill, and concern made the evening much more fun than I'd expected. Then I danced with Lisa.

She looked as gorgeous as I had pictured she would. Lustrous hair; long, satiny blue gown wrapped around her slim figure; and that beautiful smile lighting the night. Huey started our dance by grabbing Mary Jo and telling her I had to dance with his date so he could have the pleasure of dancing with mine.

It was a slow dance: "Crystal Blue Persuasion," a song I often daydreamed of dancing to with Lisa. And here we were, for the first and last time, inches apart, her hand in mine, my arm around her waist, just where I always wanted to be.

I couldn't believe this beautiful, kind, intelligent, cheerful girl following my lead could have been my girlfriend for the past nine months had I only asked her out when I had my chance. Why hadn't I? What might have developed between us, now never would.

"Huey told me what happened," Lisa said, after we'd been dancing for half a minute. "I'm sorry."

"It wasn't your fault. It just happened."

"I know, it's just . . . not right." We stepped once, twice, and she smiled. "But now that you'll be here, maybe you could stop by on Friday nights? I'll give you free treats? Maybe get Carrie to work for me a night or two, and we can do something?"

"I doubt they'll let me. I'll be on detentions. I'd sneak out, but if I get caught, then I won't get my diploma."

"Then you'd better not."

After a few turns, she said, "What will you do next year? Go to college still? Work?"

"I'll probably join the Air Force. If I was getting the scholarship, I'd be going to Shippensburg, but . . . , that's over. I'll have to wait, I guess."

Lisa caught her breath. "Oh, Dave," she said.

"What?"

"I'm going to Shippensburg."

22

Graduation Sunday I stood in Founder's Hall, dressed in cap and gown, surrounded by seniors and classmates, and looking for Bobby. The afternoon before, I had called his mother concerned that Horrible might cancel Bobby's transfer because of what he had read in my journal. She assured me no one would stop Bobby's transfer. It didn't matter who had tried to help him, his unhappiness was real and the reasons to transfer him legitimate. He was transferring, and that was that.

When Bobby found me, his mother was at his side. Short, stylishly dressed, she had large, brown eyes like Bobby's, that turned from thoughtful to jubilant when she smiled, which she did now. "I'm so glad we could finally meet. I just want to thank you again for your help and for being Bobby's friend."

"You're welcome." I ruffled Bobby's hair. "He's a good kid, that's why I did it."

"I also want you to know that once Bobby's transferred I will be going in to Homelife to see what I can do about the Drugginses. People like that shouldn't be in charge of kids."

"Okay," I said, "but wait a couple of months, until Bobby shows his new houseparents he's a good kid and he's getting along. That way you'll have proof it wasn't Bobby's fault, and if the Drugginses talk to his new houseparents afterwards they won't be influenced by what they say because they'll already know Bobby."

She clicked her tongue. "I can't believe you have to go through all this rigmarole when you know you're right."

"That's the way it is," I said. "Luckily, there's only a couple of houseparents as jerky as they are."

"If I have anything to do with it, they won't be houseparents for long."

"That won't be too bad, huh, Bobby?" I said.

"No way."

Organ music began playing. "We won't keep you any longer," Mrs. Spangler said. She looked at Bobby. "To show our appreciation for all you've done, Bobby and I got you a little something for graduation." Bobby held out a small, gift-wrapped package he'd been hiding behind his back.

"You didn't have to do that. I did it because I like Bobby."

"And he likes you. That's why we wanted to get you something."

Bobby stood grinning at me. I shoved his shoulder and took the gift. Inside was a pen and pencil set atop black marble. Inscribed on the silver plate were the words, "To our friend, Dave. Thanks." Beneath that, the names, "Bobby, Martha, and Mike."

"This is really nice, Mrs. Spangler. I . . . Jeez."

"You like it?" Bobby said.

"Yeah. A lot. It's nice. Thanks."

"Bobby said you were headed for college. We thought you could use it."

"Well . . . , eventually I will be. This'll probably help me get better grades."

"Maybe I should get Bobby one then?" Mrs. Spangler said. "His grades could use some improvement."

I raised my eyebrows at Bobby; he grinned Mike's grin.

Mrs. Spangler shook my hand and wished me luck, then I shook Bobby's hand. "Thanks for the gift, buddy. If you want, zip by tomorrow night." I looked directly above us. "I'll be right here."

Bobby fixed the spot. "Okay. I will."

I watched as they made their way across the floor, then past Druggins standing guard at the stairs. Mrs. Spangler nodded. Druggins barely responded.

The bastard. He'd be getting his. At least that was one thing I had done right.

That afternoon I volunteered to mow the lawn. It was a nice day, I didn't mind the task, the other guys wouldn't have to do it, and it would be something Suds and I could honestly name as one of the chores I'd done to work off hours.

While I mowed, the guys played softball in the field behind our unit. I was nearly finished with the front when Carl pulled into the driveway. He walked over to where I had stopped under a tree.

"I heard they're really fucking you over, Crazy, huh?"

"Yep."

"Those bastards. You didn't even do it."

He gazed across the road, toward the large field the guys had walked across the year before after our 'Bogart' haircuts. In the distance, atop the hill, loomed the high school, overlooking all of Hershey and beyond.

"I'll tell them if you want," Carl said. "I don't care. They won't do shit, anyway."

"It won't do any good, Carl. My diary 'proves' I did it. They'll say you're making it up or just helped me do it."

"Not if I tell them exactly how I did it. Where I parked, the car I saw with a flat tire, where I snuck in, shit like that."

"But then you could get in real trouble, go to jail maybe. I won't."

"Maybe not," Carl said. "What did I do? Didn't break anything, steal anything. What harm was there? I might just get my wrists slapped."

"And you might go to jail, which would end up on your permanent record."

"I doubt it. I'm going to check with the cops. See what they say I could get."

"Carl, they know about it. They might get you somehow, and if it is bad, then you're screwed."

"I know," he said, "I'll call the paper and ask them about it. I'll also ask them why I didn't see a story or picture, the ball-less cowards. You said a guy was there and got some pictures, right?"

"One or two. Horrible ripped up his others."

"I'll talk to him, have him do a big story on it. If he doesn't, I'll rent a billboard and put on it, 'Milton Hershey Screws Orphan Out of College Scholarship. Boycott Hershey Candy.' That'll get the bastards."

"I doubt they'd print it."

"I know."

We talked a few more minutes, then Carl went around back to watch the game. When he left, I was mowing that side. "I'm still checking with the paper," Carl said. "If I can't get in trouble, I'm squealing on myself."

"Don't, if you can. I'm screwed anyway. Thanks for offering, though."

"Hey, we're cows for life, man. We got to stick together."

When I finished mowing I went inside, asked to use the phone, and called the police. I told them I was the guy the Home was blaming the sit-in on, and was wondering what I could have gotten if I was just some teenager from another school.

"How old?" the cop said.

"Nineteen."

"It wouldn't be good. Breaking and entering, trespassing, causing a riot—"

"A riot? It was a stupid sit-in."

"Doesn't matter, that's what they'd name it. . . . Disturbing the peace. We had a list of things, and because it was Milton Hershey, you'd probably get the maximum on each. I'd say, with the right judge, you could have served a year or two."

"Really?"

"Yep," he said. "They own this area. You're lucky you're in the place."

Sunday, June 6, 1971

This would have been my last night here. After eleven years, I'd have less than twenty-four hours.

It sucks that it happened this way. I wish if I was paying for it, I at least had done it.

If I had to do over . . . I think I still would. It was a good idea. I just got caught not doing it.

Still, it may not be too bad. Suds will go easy on me. Then it's, "off we go into the wild blue yonder."

Not looking forward to telling Dad tomorrow night. When do I tell him? How?

This sucks.

23

Next day, graduation Monday, the seniors spent the morning signing year-books for underclassmen and each other. In class, teachers wished us luck. The mood was jubilant. I knew my classmates' expectant joy, had felt it for years, but couldn't participate.

Minutes before lunch, Homelife called me in. Jim grunted. "What more can they get you for?"

I knew it wasn't the meeting Mr. Hart had planned with the Board mem-ber, because it never happened; the Board member wouldn't see him. Maybe it was one last chance to confess? Or worse, no diploma?

Old Man Hatch sat behind his desk. Across from him sat a guy around thirty, thin, with long hair, wearing a corduroy jacket, tie, and jeans. He was chewing gum, and sized me up as I sat down in the chair beside him.

Old Man Hatch took a deep breath and held my gaze for several seconds. "This is it, Dave. Your last chance. I want you to be completely honest. Did you have anything to do with the sit-in? Anything at all? Making them, distributing them, forming the idea, planning it? It's very important you be honest. Your future depends on it."

What was going on? One last chance for what? If I told the truth would I get less of a punishment somehow, maybe my scholarship back? He seemed to be saying no matter what I said, if it was the truth, I'd be better off telling it.

But would I? If I told them I thought it up, was going to do it, and never squealed on the guy who did, they'd let me off? I doubt it. Maybe if I told just part of the truth, or a little something extra? Say I had heard it was going to happen but couldn't remember who said it? What if I simply admitted to it, would they let me off for whatever reason?

Had Mr. Hart told them what I said? Part of it? Was this a final chance to be honest, otherwise the diploma was gone?

Had Carl got caught, or admitted to it? He wouldn't have mentioned me if he did. And I couldn't mention him.

And who was this stranger and what did he have to do with anything?

"Well . . . ?" Old Man Hatch said. The guy stopped chewing his gum.

"I already told you," I said, returning Old Man Hatch's stare. "I had nothing to do with it. Nothing."

The guy resumed chewing and a grin spread across his face. He looked at Old Man Hatch. "Satisfied?" he said. "What did I tell you?"

"This is Mr. Starks," Old Man Hatch said. "He works at the *Patriot News*. He's come in today because he says he has proof you didn't do it."

"I *have* proved it," Starks said. "And with more evidence than you guys framed this poor bastard with."

"Cussing isn't necessary, Mr. Starks."

"Oh, yeah . . . , sorry."

Old Man Hatch looked at me. "He brought in the master copy of the pamphlet used for the sit-in and told us some things that shows he's spoken to the guy who did it. Thirty minutes ago he dialed a number and had me speak with someone who claims to be that person. Not that that proves he is, or that you weren't involved."

"I wasn't, though."

"See?" Starks said.

Old Man Hatch waved his hand. "Regardless. The school has decided this new information, right or wrong, casts enough doubt on the matter to alter our ruling. You'll still have to work the hundred hours, but you'll be getting your scholarship to college, provided we never find proof you were involved. If we do, you lose it."

"And this," Starks said, writing on a business card, "is the name of the guy to contact at the paper who will always know where I am." He handed me the card. "If they ever back out on the agreement, contact him, he'll contact me, and we'll have a story the big papers won't be afraid of. All right?"

"Sure. Thanks."

He clicked his tongue and winked.

"That's all," Old Man Hatch said.

Outside the office, I executed my version of Bobby's "I'm free!" dance. I leaped, pumped my arms, leaped some more, screamed as silently as possible, danced, started to–

"Hey, kid . . . !"

It was Starks. He trotted down the hall and handed me a manila envelope. "Here's a souvenir for you. Your buddy Carl says 'hi.'"

"Tell him 'hi' back and thanks. And you, too. Thanks a lot."

"No problem. I couldn't believe my paper wouldn't publish the story or at least the picture. The big boys will, though, so if they ever double-cross you let me know. Take care."

He went out the side door and I continued back to class. The envelope contained a large, black and white photograph of the sit-in, taken from inside the car. A sea of raised fists and smiling faces, stretched from side to side and top to bottom. I could see where I was sitting, but just barely.

It didn't matter; the essence of the picture was the important thing, a feeling I experienced again shortly after lunch, during assembly, when Brubaker called my name as one of those who would be receiving a scholarship to attend college. I had kept what happened a secret, and as I walked toward the stage everyone was looking around as though a mistake had been made. But when they saw my grin and realized it was legitimate, the guys started clapping and didn't stop until I stood with everyone else.

I framed the photograph and kept it with me all through college. Beneath the picture I wrote, "One For All, And All For One."

I still have it.

24

I walked through the woods until I could see the front of Founder's Hall, then sat down, the only sound that of the water sculpture, with its bronzed fish and marble backdrop lit by floodlights.

It was Wednesday, midnight. By putting in ten hours a day of "work," I'd finished my punishment in just over a week. Carl's mother, with my father's written permission, had taken me out the day I finished, and Carl would be driving me home Thursday afternoon. I'd already said my good-byes and had visited Lisa in the drugstore. Her parting smile, kiss on the cheek, and promise to do something together as soon as we got to school, would make it a long, exciting summer.

After five minutes I opened the two large boxes of laundry detergent, walked from the woods, and moved along the front of the sculpture, spilling their contents into the pool.

The water cascaded from the fish's mouths, gradually building a froth. Bubbles appeared, purples and blues and yellows and greens, floating atop the growing mass as it widened and blanketed the surface. Waterfalls of foam spewed from the fish, spilling into the pool to form thick, white, bulbous mounds of suds. In ten minutes, the bronzed sculptures leaped above and swam amidst a sea of clouds, sparkling with a million, tiny rainbows.

I looked into the clear night sky. "That's for you, buddy. It does look neat, huh?"

I watched a bit longer, then headed into the woods. The moonlight lit my path through the trees as my footsteps touched the soft, dry ground. I began to jog. Gradually I picked up speed, moving swiftly through the warm night air.

I'd finally made it. I was on my way.